TO FALL FOR
MR. DARCY

a Pride & Prejudice Variation

Renata McMann
&
Summer Hanford

ACKNOWLEDGEMENT

With special thanks to Doris Studer and Leah Pruett.

Dear Reader,
After enjoying our story, consider signing up for our mailing list, where you will have the opportunity for free gifts, information about new releases and in person events, and more. Join us by visiting
www.renatamcmann.com/news/

By Renata McMann and Summer Hanford

Mr. Collins' Will
More Than He Seems
After Anne
Their Secret Love
A Duel in Meryton*
Love, Letters and Lies
The Long Road to Longbourn
Hypothetically Married*
The Forgiving Season
The Widow Elizabeth
Foiled Elopement
Believing in Darcy
Her Final Wish
Miss Bingley's Christmas
Epiphany with Tea
Courting Elizabeth
The Fire at Netherfield Park
From Ashes to Heiresses*
Entanglements of Honor
Lady Catherine Regrets
A Death at Rosings
Mary Younge
Poor Mr. Darcy
Mr. Collins' Deception
The Scandalous Stepmother
Caroline and the Footman
Elizabeth's Plight (The Wickham Coin Book II)
Georgiana's Folly (The Wickham Coin Book I)
The Second Mrs. Darcy

*available as an audio book

Collections:

A Dollop of Pride and a Dash of Prejudice.
Includes from above: *Their Secret Love, Miss Bingley's Christmas, Epiphany with Tea* and *From Ashes to Heiresses.*

Pride and Prejudice Villains Revisited – Redeemed – Reimagined A Collection of Six Short Stories.
Includes from above: *Lady Catherine Regrets, Mary Younge, Mr. Collins' Deception* and *Caroline and the Footman,* along with two the additional flash fiction pieces, *Mrs. Bennet's Triumph* and *Wickham's Journal.*

Georgiana's Folly & Elizabeth's Plight: Wickham Coin Series, Volumes I & II
Includes from above: *Elizabeth's Plight* and *Georgiana's Folly.*

Other Pride and Prejudice variations by Renata McMann
Why Wed?
Is Esteem Enough?
Heiress to Longbourn
Pemberley Weddings
The Inconsistency of Caroline Bingley
Three Daughters Married
Anne de Bourgh Manages
The above five works are collected in the book:
Five Pride and Prejudice Variations

Historical Romance by Summer Hanford

His Yuletide Kiss

The Duke's Bequest Series:
Grace's Story
Sleigh Bells & Slander
Wildflowers & Wiles
Heartache & Holly
Meadows & Mischief

Crown and Dagger Historical Romance:
Kestrel
Red Fox
Forest Hart

Epic Fantasy by Summer Hanford

Rise of the Summer God Series:
Daughters of Awen
The Battle of Greypass
Wyvern's Call
Shroud of Fate
Aestias Unbound
A Destiny of Truth

TO FALL FOR
MR. DARCY

Chapter One

George Wickham lounged in a chair in the little parlor in the Darcys' rented house in Ramsgate, about to go mad with boredom. Georgiana sat at the pianoforte, brow wrinkled in concentration as she played the long, difficult piece he'd selected. The sort of lofty twaddle enjoyed by the accomplished set. It would be endearing how hard she worked to perform it properly for him if he didn't have to endure listening to it.

The pianoforte had been moved and reorientated at Wickham's insistence, ostensibly so that morning light would fall on the pages for Georgiana to better read them. This left it woefully out of tune, which mattered not at all. The difference between discordant sounds and boring music meant little. The tuning of a pianoforte was, in Wickham's mind, an unnecessary expense, but Mrs. Younge had it tuned anyway citing Georgiana's worry that her performance wouldn't please him. The only pleasing thing about her performance was that he didn't need to do anything except appear to be enjoying her music.

She reached a particularly tricky section and redoubled her efforts, haunching over the keys in a way that emphasized her gangly form. Heaven help him, once they were married he'd ensure she never played for him again, not wishing to see or hear her do so. In fact, he wouldn't even permit an instrument in their home. A pianoforte was an absurd waste of funds better used for actual entertainment.

While Georgiana concentrated, her governess, Mrs. Younge, rose. She gave Wickham a nod and slipped from the room, her ability to do so unobserved by her ward the real reason for his insistence on moving the instrument. Stealthy as a cat, she disappeared down the hall to pry in Georgiana's room.

Mrs. Younge returned to the parlor a short time later, entering as quietly as she'd left. She retook her place and picked up her knitting, appearing for all the world as if she hadn't left. Once she'd ordered herself, she turned to him, a look he met with raised eyebrows. With a slight smile, Mrs. Younge gave a tiny shake of her head.

Good. That meant Georgiana hadn't mentioned his presence in Ramsgate in her latest letter to her brother. Nor had she since Wickham's arrival some weeks ago. Her omission indicated that she had some inkling that he and Darcy had fallen out. Her tacit compliance in keeping his presence a secret suggested his suit was working. Soon, she would be ready to elope with him.

Wickham settled back, pleased with the progress of his plan and with his fellow conspirator. Mrs. Younge was proving worth every penny of the hundred pound advance he'd given her to help him implement his plan. And when she never saw the nine hundred he'd promised after that plan came to fruition, well, that was on her for believing him. He suppressed a chuckle at the recollection of how she'd had him pen and sign the offer, as if a scrap of paper could actually force him to turn over nine hundred pounds. Really, to whom did she think she could take such a letter and hope for justice?

Wickham studied the plaster ceiling, daydreamed about what he could buy with Georgiana's dowry, and tried to ignore the ongoing playing. Askance, he noted that Mrs. Younge knitted quite fast. Did she think Georgiana observant enough to notice if she hadn't produced a certain quantity? He highly doubted she was.

Finally, to his relief, Georgiana's hands stilled. She sat taller and swiveled on the bench to look at him, expression eager.

"That was beautiful," he said. "As are you."

Georgiana smiled, preening under his praise, another sign of his ongoing success with her. When he'd arrived, even the slightest compliment had rendered her face an ugly red and made her study the floor. Now she sought the affirmation he provided, which made her marginally more attractive, at least.

Mrs. Younge ceased her stitching to smile at Georgiana. "Have you any further thoughts you wish to put in your letter to your brother?"

Georgiana swiveled all the way around on the bench, to see behind her on the other side. She shook her head, making her middling brown curls dance. Any intelligent young woman would brighten them to blonde, but Georgiana didn't. "No. I already made mention of the Milfords." She smirked. "Do you know, I believe their son has become engaged to marry?" She darted a look at Wickham as she spoke.

Mrs. Younge chuckled in what Wickham read as feigned amusement, which experience told him Georgiana wouldn't see through, and said, "That is for the best. You wouldn't want your brother to worry you've grown attached to young Mr. Milford."

The Milfords were a fictional family supposedly introduced to Georgiana by a distant connection of Darcy's. In concern that his sister wasn't socializing enough, Darcy had written to Mrs. Younge suggesting that Georgiana go out more. As Georgiana mingling in society directly hindered Wickham's plan to seduce her, Mrs. Younge had playfully invented the Milfords and convinced Georgiana that the harmless deception of writing to her brother about them would give him solace and permit her to do as she pleased. The duplicity played into Wickham's hands well, encouraging Georgiana to see herself as a young woman ready to make her own decisions and Darcy as an overprotective older brother.

Georgiana nodded. "I thought so, too. I feared that after I wrote that I was stranded there overnight when that last storm came through, he might begin to worry." She rolled her eyes. "He does so worry. As if I'm a child."

"Which you are certainly not," Mrs. Younge agreed. "But you are a young woman who'd best sign and seal her letter. I'm sending a footman over with the post soon."

Georgiana stood and smoothed her skirts. She turned to give Wickham another smile. At least her teeth were good. "I won't be long."

As soon as Georgiana's footfalls faded down the hall, her clomping tread nowhere near as light as Mrs. Younge's delicate steps, Wickham said, "Dance lessons in town today?"

"Yes. An important lesson, during which I will take tea on the corner."

The usual time and place of their meetings, then, but Wickham frowned. Why had she added 'important?' Had something come up to jeopardize their plan? He gave her a searching look, but she shook her head. He tipped his to the side and heard it too. Footfalls in the hall as one of the servants passed. Moments later, before he deemed speech safe once more, Georgiana returned, steps quick in her hurry to be with him.

Wickham endured the remainder of the morning in Georgiana's presence, then took his leave, feigning regret that her dance lesson would keep them apart. He vowed that, to balance out those excruciating hours of pretending to be enamored with a brat of fifteen, he would make a late night of it. That plan in mind, he returned to his rented room for a nap, to pass the time until he must meet Mrs. Younge in the teashop.

He woke a bit later than he'd hoped and went to find his fellow conspirator. Entering the shop, Wickham waved off the proprietor as he made to come over and went to the back. He dropped into the seat opposite Mrs. Younge, hoping she was worrying about nothing.

She took a sip of tea. "Do you want to order anything?"

How like her. She wanted him to spend money on something that wasn't worth it, simply to please someone who didn't matter. "Are you buying?" She could afford it, after all. He'd given her a hundred pounds.

She sighed, waved the proprietor over, and ordered coffee for Wickham. It pleased him that she remembered he preferred coffee to tea.

They waited in silence until the coffee was brought. Once the shopkeeper retreated again, Mrs. Younge lowered her voice and said, "We have a problem. Mr. Darcy wrote to me to make certain that Miss Darcy will be available the day after tomorrow. He wishes to surprise her with a visit."

"So, tell him she will not be available."

"I already wrote back to him expressing as much and claiming an engagement with the Milfords but it seems he has somewhat pressing business with a holding in Scotland and this is his only opportunity for some time to visit his sister. He insists she be available."

Wickham cursed. Precisely like Darcy to change his words from request to command when the request failed. He liked to appear amiable but wouldn't let appearance interfere with his will being carried out. "Too many people have seen me. Even if Georgiana can last a whole visit without mention of me, someone else may." Darcy would never condescend to speak with the cottage's staff but his valet, Stevens, would, as would any other servants he dragged along. "And what if he asks to meet the Milfords?" A scowl pulled down Wickham's mouth. "Foolish idea, that, on your part."

"You've made no complaint before now. The Milfords have been very helpful in keeping him away. They've admirably filled her schedule."

"That they have, but you should have arranged some way for them to be more difficult for her to beg off from."

"Such as?" Mrs. Younge asked tartly.

He opened his mouth to reply that figuring out a reasonable 'such as' was her concern, not his, but closed it again as the proprietor returned to ask if they required anything further.

"You could ask her tomorrow," Mrs. Younge said once the man departed with their assurance that they required nothing more.

Wickham shook his head. "It's too soon. She won't agree to elope with me yet. I need more time."

"We don't have more time. Mr. Darcy will be here the day after tomorrow. He's already in Kent."

"Is he?" An idea sparked in Wickham. They'd traveled in Kent together, as boys. Visited Darcy's aunt and then gone on to Ramsgate, but with one all-important delay. An ill coachman had combined with a broken wheel to keep them betwixt the two destinations for days. While Mr. Darcy the senior had dealt with that, a young Wickham and Darcy had explored the region quite thoroughly. "At Rosings Park?"

"Yes." Mrs. Younge's expression became speculative. "Why?"

"I can delay him." Wickham reached to pour more coffee, confidence restored. "I know the route he'll take." Or rather, he had an idea of how to ensure that Darcy went the way he wished.

Would Darcy remember their trek off the two main roadways between Rosings and the coast? The winding dirt road, wide enough for only one carriage, a sheer drop to a river running along one side and a steep slope upward along the other? The bridge over the ravine, water glinting far below, where they'd played at being highwaymen? Wickham nodded to himself. Darcy would remember. He never forgot, or forgave, anything.

Mrs. Younge studied Wickham with raised eyebrows. "How can you be certain? There are two main roadways between here and there, and who knows how many smaller ones."

"You forget how well I know Darcy." And Wickham had barely enough time to make certain that Darcy couldn't go either of the well-traveled ways.

Mrs. Younge shook her head. "Assuming you truly do know him well enough to predict the route he'll take, you will delay him how? By chopping down a tree to fall across the road? Mr. Darcy has the resources to easily overcome any such obstacle. A few hours delay won't be enough."

"If I fail, a few hours is all we'll have so you'd better make it enough."

"I'll do my best to have her ready," Mrs. Younge said dubiously. "But the longer the delay the greater our chance of success."

Wickham hoisted his coffee, grinning over the rim of the cup. "Don't worry. If all goes well, he'll be delayed for days." In fact, if Wickham had his way, Darcy would take ages to reach Ramsgate, if he ever made it at all.

Chapter Two

Elizabeth's Uncle Gardiner returned to the inn a bit grim faced and retook his place at the table she shared with her Aunt Gardiner in the somewhat crowded common room.

"It's as rumored," he announced. "Both bridges are out, though there's strong hope the least damaged will be traversable by tomorrow."

"Both?" Aunt Gardiner frowned. "How is that possible?"

Uncle Gardiner reached for a roll. "Like as not, some sort of Luddite nonsense spilled out across the country."

"Edward," Aunt Gardiner said, tone full of reprimand, and cast Elizabeth a look askance.

Elizabeth tried not to smile. "Never fear, Aunt. Papa lets me read the papers. I know all about Luddites."

"Still, it's not a fit subject for conversation," Aunt Gardiner said with a continued frown at her husband. "Not for young women or common rooms."

"Whoever did it, they'll have cause to hide," Uncle Gardiner continued as he reached for the butter. "When the northern bridge went down, it took a team and wagon with it. Team and driver died."

"Edward," Aunt Gardiner gasped. "Honestly, consider who you're with."

Uncle Gardiner shrugged and slathered butter on the roll. "So, as we must perforce spend at least one more day here, how will we carry on?"

"Can we not take another road?" Elizabeth asked, for the village was quite small and they'd thoroughly explored it the previous afternoon when they arrived.

Uncle Gardiner lowered the roll he was about to bite to say, "There are local roadways but the nearest is reputed to be hardly wide enough for one carriage, let alone passing, and along a steep ravine at that. If one bridge wasn't expected to be working by tomorrow, I would chance it but as it is, the risk of having to back half a mile down a winding roadway along a ravine seems hardly worth a day's travel." He bit into his roll.

Aunt Gardiner nodded. "We can take a turn about the village."

The village, a term Elizabeth felt too liberally applied, consisted of the posting inn in which they stayed, two shops and a small cluster of homes. They'd walked the length of the single street four times the afternoon before. Fortunately, Elizabeth had spotted a winding trek into the forest as they'd gamboled.

"Might we explore the forest road?" she asked, hopeful yet doubting her aunt would wish to.

Aunt Gardiner, not one for much walking, shook her head, but smiled. "You may if you can scrounge up a chaperone. I will be content with town."

"The innkeeper has a daughter. Perhaps once the morning crowd thins, she'll agree to accompany me."

Elizabeth's supposition proved true and, after being extolled by the innkeeper to return his daughter, Lucy, in time to help with luncheon, the girl was permitted to accompany Elizabeth. Leaving the inn, Elizabeth set a quick pace through town, pleased that Lucy didn't seem to have trouble keeping up. In short order, they crossed from the bright sunlight of a summer morning into the cool shadows of the forest and Elizabeth took a deep breath, the air already less hot and dust choked.

"Do you always help with breakfast and luncheon?" she asked to make conversation as they strode deeper into the woods.

"Since I was six."

"How old are you now?"

"Eleven, Miss."

Elizabeth cast Lucy a quick look, decided she was tall for her age, and wondered if she'd been tall at six, too. That seemed to delve too far beyond light conversation, so rather than pursue it, she asked, "Where does this roadway go?"

"Over the ravine, Miss."

So this was the nearby route that her uncle deemed too precarious to attempt? "Is it safe for us to walk here?"

Lucy cast her a surprised look. "Oh, aye, Miss." She brought up both hands, palms held near together. "It gets narrow is all, for a cart and horses, along the ravine."

Reassured, Elizabeth walked on. A short time later, a tromp and a creak alerted her, and she turned to see a buggy and one coming up from behind. She and Lucy moved off to the side among the trees' gnarled roots and the buggy clattered by, the driver offering a passing nod of greeting. Elizabeth imagined it would take skilled handling to get anything much wider down the road.

A short time later, the trees to their left thinned, then disappeared altogether to reveal clear sky as a ravine cut through the forest. To their right, the slope grew ever steeper. Elizabeth soon realized she wouldn't wish to have a buggy pass now, let alone a carriage. Should one, she and Lucy would need to either climb the slope into the trees or swim, and the gurgling little river at the bottom of the ravine was a long way down.

"Are we nearly to the bridge?" Elizabeth asked. She'd like to see it before they turned back but not if that meant too much longer on this road.

Lucy raised her hand in a squiggling gesture. "Yes. Two more bends."

Lucy seemed unconcerned and Elizabeth imagined there was little traffic on the road and that the girl wouldn't mind clambering into the tree trunks on the steep hillside. Elizabeth had a touch more dignity however, or possibly just more care for her boots and gown. Dust and mud she could endure but if she tore her skirt, she'd be forced to do mending, an activity she'd prefer to avoid.

Not that there would be much else to do in the little town come evening.

Resolved to see the bridge even at the expense of her hem, she decided they should continue. The view up and down the gully would be lovely from the bridge, she'd no doubt. Worth any incidental sewing.

They rounded the next curve, then the following, and the bridge came into view, spanning the ravine farther up the roadway. Elizabeth lengthened her stride eagerly, then sighted a man and halted. She caught Lucy's arm, stopping the girl as well.

He stood among the trees to the right, broad shoulders to them as he faced the bridge. He had an old, floppy hat like a farmer might wear when the sun was too bright, but it was cloudy, and a scarf hung about his neck. One of his arms wrapped about a low limb to keep him on the ravine wall. The other he held low to his side and in it…a pistol. One didn't hunt with a pistol.

Elizabeth let out a gasp, the hand that held Lucy's arm squeezing. Very quietly, she said, "That man is armed."

Lucy gave her a wide-eyed look. "We should go, Miss," she whispered.

Elizabeth squeezed her lips tight, thinking. They should go. That was clear. Lucy was a chaperone to Elizabeth's virtue, not a guard against armed men.

Yet…he obviously waited for someone to cross the bridge. His position, likely selected with care, made him all but invisible from the far side of the ravine and allotted him a stout trunk to duck behind should anyone come from the village. Were Lucy and Elizabeth any less light of tread, he may well have heard them and taken cover.

With that thought, Elizabeth backed them up around the previous bend, then released Lucy's arm and turned to her. "He's waiting for someone."

"We don't have anything to do with that, Miss."

Elizabeth nodded. They certainly didn't, but the man had a pistol. He meant to shoot someone. "Maybe if I shout, I can alert whomever it is before he can," she murmured, mostly to herself.

"You can't shout." Fear filled Lucy's eyes. "He could shoot you." She swallowed.

Elizabeth could read Lucy's next thought in the girl's eyes: 'He might shoot me.'

Lucy edged away from her, angling back down the roadway in the direction of the town. "I have to get back. I need to help with luncheon."

"Lucy," Elizabeth hissed, reading flight in the girl's eyes.

Lucy shook her head, turned, and ran.

Elizabeth stared after her disappearing form, irresolute. She'd no way to know who the man meant to shoot. It could be someone terrible. After all, what sort of person would someone want to shoot?

A person who couldn't possibly be any worse than a man waiting to do the shooting, which meant they might be better. She turned to look up the roadway, then back down in the direction Lucy had run, already out of sight on the twisting lane. Hands balled at her sides, Elizabeth wracked mind and heart, trying to decide what to do.

Finally, she turned and marched back to the bend that hid the bridge from view. She peeked around the curve to see the man still waited, pistol in hand. Elizabeth set to studying the remainder of the scene, in case more men hid ahead. She saw none but realized the posts that held up the rails that lined each side of the bridge appeared askew. In fact, they were sawn nearly through.

That settled things. Tampering with the bridge put more people than the one he awaited in danger and may even speak to a larger plan involving the other sabotaged bridges…which would make him a murderer already. If there was anything Elizabeth could do to thwart him, she was duty bound to try.

Should she go back and seek help? She had no way to know when the man might act. Perhaps long before she returned to the village and managed to summon anyone. Did his presence mean his prey drew nigh? How early did one arrive for an ambush? She wished Lucy hadn't fled. Elizabeth would have sent the girl back to seek help. Now, she had no way to know if Lucy would tell anyone about the waiting gunman.

Elizabeth's best course must be the assumption that the masked man's victim could arrive at any moment and that no help would come. Were anyone to be saved, she must do the saving. She drew in a fortifying breath and then, keeping to the right along the steep upward slope, darted around the curve and behind the nearest tree.

She stuck her head out to find the man still faced away from her, watching the bridge. Mustering her courage and hoping that Lucy would send help, she ran to the next tree, then the next. As carefully and quietly as she could, she worked her way closer. Each time she left the shelter of a tree trunk, she prayed that the man with the gun wouldn't turn around.

Chapter Three

Upon learning that both major bridges were out, one incident resulting in a fatality, Darcy made discreet inquiries, discovered the landholder of the area was rather impoverished, and took the liberty of settling a small sum on the dead man's widow, for her and their children. He then went to find his driver, Daniels, who was in the process of unhitching the carriage with the assistance of Darcy's tiger, a lad of twelve or so years.

"We'll still be leaving," Darcy informed them.

"But the one bridge will be out for weeks and the other won't be repaired until tomorrow," Daniels protested, then grimaced. "Nasty bit of business all round, I say."

Darcy nodded. One bridge giving out and dropping a wagon driver and his team to their deaths wouldn't have been suspicious on its own but coupled with the removal of the planks that formed the roadway of the other bridge, what would have been seen as a horrific accident smacked of murder.

"A tragic business indeed but no concern of ours," Darcy noted. The only tie he had to the area was that it happened to stand between his aunt's estate in western Kent and the house he rented for Georgiana in Ramsgate. "And not one that will slow us overly. I know of a third route."

"To Ramsgate from here?" Daniels asked.

Hardly to or from anywhere else, as here was where they were and Ramsgate where they were going, but all Darcy said aloud was, "Yes, but the roadway is very narrow. I'll ride up top with you to assist. I've a good memory of it." Darcy supposed his valet, Stevens, might enjoy the unaccustomed solitude of riding alone inside.

"You'll get dusty," Daniels protested.

Darcy's tiger looked between them with wide eyes, tack draped over his arms.

"We'll be going slowly." And a little dust was worth not taking a turn too quickly and ending up at the bottom of a gully.

Daniels shrugged his acquiescence and directed the tiger to start re-hitching the team.

Later, as they went down a roadway which was wide enough for two coaches to pass but which would become quite narrow after they crossed the bridge that lay ahead, Darcy couldn't help but remember days spent exploring the area with his childhood friend, George Wickham.

After a few days of detailed exploration, still delayed in the town ahead which was small and, to two boys, very boring, they'd come up with a game of French invasion. Pretending the French were coming, they'd scouted the roadway for places from which to ambush them.

Darcy's mind ranged back over their boyhood discussion, which they'd taken very seriously. He'd said, 'The first thing for us to do would be to take out the bridge, so the French can't bring anything with wheels across the ravine, even if they can climb down and back out on foot. That might buy time to mass English forces.'

Wickham had nodded, pushed too-long blond hair from his eyes and said, 'Not only take it out. Take it out with filthy Frenchmen on it.'

Darcy recalled that he'd thought that through, weighing the morality. He'd finally decided that if the French were invading England, it was acceptable to drop them into a ravine, and rejoindered, 'If they came with horse drawn cannons, a shot to scare the horses might make them run right off the bridge.'

It had seemed unfair to the horses, but French cannons were notoriously destructive. Better French horses than English lives. They were talking about war, after all. Darcy had heard many stories about how much death there was in war. He'd hoped to fight the French himself someday, like his older cousin Richard had planned to do.

Wickham had shaken his head. 'The rails might keep the horses in. We'd have to weaken them. And best to shoot one. They're horses that go to war. They probably won't be scared unless they feel a ball hit. Then they'd run like mad and end up in the ravine.'

'You'd have to make certain not to shoot the horse dead. Even if there are two, a dead one would make it so the other couldn't run.'

They'd gone on in this way, discussing with great seriousness how they could save good English lives, until they'd grown bored of speculating about the bridge and found a new ambush location. Hidden in the trees on the slope across the bridge, they'd studied passing conveyances and speculated on how to ambush each. Wickham's talk had turned from stopping the French to simple highway robbery and what he could hope to loot.

Darcy sighed. He should have known, even then, what sort of man George Wickham would grow up to be, but he had pleasant memories of their years growing up together regardless. He regretted that his childhood friend had not become someone he wanted to know now that they were grown.

And then the bridge over the ravine was before them and Darcy pulled his thoughts thoroughly into the present, for the way would become treacherous soon. Once they crossed the ravine, they'd enter a stretch of road with a cliff rising to one side and a drop on the other. The roadway ahead snaked along, following the lip of the gully.

At least, he thought he'd put his memories from his mind but there, ahead, jumping free of the bank to stand in the middle of the road on the other side of the bridge, was Wickham. Or, rather, a man of Wickham's height wearing a large hat that partially hid his face and with a scarf pulled up over the lower half, like a highwayman seeking loot. Darcy stared, stunned, wondering if the man before him was a hallucination, brought on by his memories.

But he would hardly hallucinate that Wickham, hat pulled low, and scarf pulled up, pointed a pistol at him.

No. He wasn't the target, but rather the horses.

Suddenly, Darcy knew what Wickham meant to do. He reached over to grab the reins from his driver, who gaped at Wickham with surprise that echoed Darcy's. Darcy hauled on the strips of leather that connected them to the horses, trying to halt his team before they reached the center of the bridge, with only a thin railing between them and the bottom of the gorge.

Wickham brought his other hand up to join the first, aiming the pistol. His eyes narrowed.

A yowling woman leaped down the slope, arms out, and shoved Wickham. Her momentum took them across the roadway. Wickham braced his feet, sliding to a halt near the lip of the gully. A pistol report rang through the forest. The horses whinnied and tossed their heads, backing up.

Wickham unleashed a howl of rage at the woman and shoved her. She tumbled backward over the lip of the gully. Wickham whirled and ran.

A second shot sounded, right beside Darcy, making him jump and startling the horses. He bit back a curse, ears ringing, as he fought to control the team before the horses did the work Wickham had clearly meant them to do and landed his carriage in the ravine.

Wickham kept running. Daniels dropped the spent weapon and fumbled under his seat for another. Wickham disappeared around the bend ahead, shielded by the slope.

"Don't shoot," Darcy ordered, struggling to gain enough control over the team to back them up, rather than permit them to dart farther onto a bridge he no longer trusted. The moment the horses were calm enough, he pressed the reins on Daniels. "Back them up. Don't cross that bridge. See if you can turn but first get around the corner, in case he comes back."

Darcy jumped down. Framed in the carriage window, he noted his valet's startled face, but he didn't slow. He raced down the slope, only taking enough care not to topple head over heels, readily sighting the still form beside the stream at the bottom.

He splashed through the river, fortuitously shallow in summer, and dropped to kneel beside her. She sprawled on her stomach, unmoving. As gently as he could, he turned her over. Mud obscured much of her face. Her eyes didn't open. He lifted her with great care and climbed back up the slope.

His carriage was gone now, and he darted a look along the roadway, apprehensive Wickham would return to finish the evil he'd set out to do. Worry prickled along Darcy's spine as he strode up the road, his back to where Wickham had disappeared from sight. Darcy could only hope that Wickham had run, not moved around the bend to reload for a second shot.

Stevens came barreling around the corner, Daniels' second pistol in hand. He skidded to a halt when he spotted Darcy and the unconscious woman, then jogged forward to meet them. Darcy's long legs took them away from the bridge and the threat of Wickham.

"I'll get inside the carriage with her," Darcy said to Stevens when he reached him. "I want everyone else to be on the lookout. You take the boot seat, with the gun."

Stevens nodded. "I'll put the boy up top with Daniels." He let Darcy pass him then followed, backing around the bend to where the carriage waited.

The moment they were out of sight from the bridge, Stevens turned full around and jogged ahead to open the carriage door for Darcy. He stood back, eyes bright with interest, while Darcy lifted the woman in. "Who is she?"

Darcy shook his head. "I've no idea." Mud coated as she was, he felt he should still recognize her if he knew her, which he didn't. By her garb, though, she was a gentlewoman. Her finger bore no ring, but that custom was hardly absolute. "She saved me, though. She pushed Wickham out of the way."

"That was George Wickham?" Stevens asked, voice low.

Darcy nodded. "He wore a hat and a mask, but I'd know Wickham anywhere."

"Fancy him so desperate as to raise a gun to you."

Darcy grimaced, well able to imagine Wickham that desperate. He'd become a desperate sort of fellow. "Let's get back to town. If I recall correctly, there's some sort of doctor there."

"Not down the road after Wickham?" Stevens looked in that direction now, eyes narrowed in anger.

"The next village is very small. They would need to send for the same doctor, and I don't trust that bridge. When we arrive at the inn, there must be someone to alert to the prospective damage done. Find them."

"You think Wickham had something to do with the other two bridges as well?" Stevens asked.

"I wouldn't put it past him," Darcy said, voice as grim as the idea made him feel.

"A man was killed."

"Yes." With that, Darcy climbed in.

Stevens closed the door behind him. Darcy listened to the clatter of his valet and tiger clambering into position. Daniels began the arduous task of turning the carriage and Darcy could only be glad they hadn't crossed the bridge into the narrower section of the road. There, the maneuver would have proved impossible. Not that they were likely to have made it over with Wickham tampering with the bridges in the area.

Darcy sat beside the woman he'd propped in the corner of the seat, bracing her with one arm so she wouldn't fall as they started moving. Examination showed that blood oozed from a lump on her forehead and several cuts on her face. Scratches marred her arms. A tear rent her skirt up to her knee, exposing a shapely calf he endeavored to ignore.

He longed to use his handkerchief to clean the mud from the stream off her face so he could look upon her visage, but that would be inappropriate. Through the mud, she appeared young. She had a slender, pleasing form. An elegantly long neck. Thick dark hair.

He prayed she was married.

When they reached the town from whence they'd set out that morning, Darcy had no choice but to carry her into the inn, for all to see. She remained unconscious, hardly seeming to breathe, and his worry for her increased. He stood in the entrance hall with the woman in his arms and people gawking at them while Stevens arranged a room, despairing to hear the innkeeper inform them that there was but one available, yet aware they were fortunate to have even that.

Stevens accepted the key and Darcy stepped forward to address the innkeeper. "Send for the doctor immediately."

The man nodded. Face alive with curiosity, he asked, "Who is she, sir? What happened?"

He may as well reply now, in front of everyone. Rumor would abound regardless. "We tried the gully road. The bridge stands, though I question if it has been tampered with. A man waited on the far side, masked and brandishing a pistol. He made to fire, but this woman rushed from the forest and pushed him, sending his shot wide. He then threw her down the gully and fled."

That set the crowd to murmuring. Before any more questions could emerge, Darcy started for the staircase that led up to the inn rooms. Stevens hurried to catch up, then passed him once they reached the top of the stairs. He went down the hall to the end and applied the key. Darcy followed, carrying the woman into a much smaller room than the one he'd taken the night before. He placed her atop the bed, the only furnishing aside from a very small table and a wooden stool.

"What do we do now, sir?" Stevens asked as he set the room's key on a small shelf mounted inside the door.

"Go down and ask that the doctor be sent up upon his arrival, then see about getting someone out to inspect that bridge, then get me clean clothes."

"Should I search for her family?"

"I daresay that scene downstairs will bring them if they're in town," Darcy observed wryly. "But yes, put out word." He glanced again at her muddy face. "We don't have much of a description yet. See if there is a maid who can come up with towels and warm water to clean the mud from her, and a room where I may wash up and change."

"Yes, sir, and should I have inquiries made in the next town over, in case she came from there?"

"You'll have to find someone who can go on foot and climb down into the valley and out again. No one's to ride across the bridge until it's found to be safe." Darcy glanced at the window, surprised how far gone the day was. "If her family isn't in this town, I can't imagine we'll be able to find them before tomorrow."

"I agree, sir, but I'll do my best."

"Thank you, Stevens. I'll stay here and await the maid."

Expression neutral, Stevens nodded and stepped from the room.

Darcy stood near the door, waiting for the maid and the doctor, and studied the woman atop the coverlet. Who was she, this stranger who'd risked her life for his? This woman who, were she unmarried and a lady, was now hopelessly compromised as thanks for saving him?

This woman he may very well have to marry.

He scrubbed his hands over his face, then stopped as he realized mud spattered his palms. Not the day he'd set out to have. What had Wickham been about? Had he truly sabotaged the other bridges to bring Darcy to that long ago one from their childhood? Why attack Darcy now, with so much at risk if he failed, as he had, and absolutely nothing to gain?

No. Wickham had something to gain. He must. He wouldn't do what he had otherwise. The man would hardly get out of bed in the morning if he didn't view the day with hope of some sort of profit.

But what? What could he possibly—

Georgiana. Darcy was on his way to Georgiana. That must be why. For some reason, some gain to him, Wickham didn't want Darcy to reach his sister. Didn't want him to so much, Wickham had been willing to kill.

Darcy pulled out his watch. There was still daylight left. He could ride to the bridge with his tiger, send the horses back, cross on his own, walk to the next town and...and nothing because the town was too small for him to be certain he could secure a mount there and it would be dark by the time he arrived, rendering the task doubly difficult.

Not to mention the woman on the bed. There would be questions, and expenses, and words to exchange with her family.

He shoved his watch away. He'd give it until tomorrow. One day. No, a morning. He'd remain until noon tomorrow but then, even if he had to depart and leave her in the care of Stevens, even if not a single bridge were passable, Darcy would resume his journey to Ramsgate, posthaste.

A maid arrived and began cleaning the woman's face, already discolored and swelling, providing no real view of her. She had a fine nose and small ears, but beyond that he couldn't be certain. A large bump distorted her forehead. Her lips appeared full but could simply be swollen. The bottom one was cut, split on a rock or possibly her own tooth. When the girl lifted a hand to clean it the woman's whole body jerked, though she didn't wake, and Darcy realized her left arm twisted at an odd angle. The maid carried on cleaning with more care for the limb.

A manservant, sent by Stevens, arrived with Darcy's clothes and a towel, and permission to wash in the scullery if he made haste. Darcy left the unknown woman with the maid and went down to clean up. He made it back to the room as the maid, dirty towels and basin in hand, departed.

The doctor arrived next, turning out to be a surgeon, a fussy young man named Evans. After introducing himself to Darcy he turned to the woman. "What is her name?"

"I don't know."

Evans turned a startled look on him. Once again, Darcy offered a quick recounting of the incident at the bridge, leaving out the name Wickham as he had while standing below in the inn's entrance hall.

"Saved you, did she?" Mr. Evans said and turned back to the woman. "Very well. I find using the names of my patients helps them respond better. Since she is unconscious, I suppose it doesn't matter."

He examined her injuries, confirming Darcy's suspicion that her left arm was broken, and electing not to bind her head. He did set her arm and peeled back her eyelids to look into unresponsive eyes. Darcy thought they might be brown.

Finally, he stood and turned to Darcy. "I cannot assess the extent of damage done by the blow to her head nor find all her injuries until she is conscious. I can, however, return in the morning."

That suited Darcy's need to leave by midday. "Yes. Come first thing in the morning."

"If she wakes up, she should be given something to drink. Broth would be best. Try to keep her from choking."

"If?"

30

"Yes, well, she appears young and fit. She'll probably wake." Mr. Evans began returning his instruments, salves and wrappings to his medical bag, while continuing, "She appears to be unmarried. Judging by her clothing, she isn't poor. If she does recover, you saved her life, but you've also ruined her reputation." He closed his bag and turned to Darcy.

Darcy nodded, grim.

Evans dipped his head once and left.

Darcy studied the woman again, finding little to tell him more about her. Should he ask the maid to return and undress her? Perhaps seek a borrowed nightgown? He didn't feel as if he should give such instructions, but who else could?

A husband could. She could be some man's wife and simply not wear a ring.

What if she was no man's wife and he must marry her?

An edge of panic crept in as he watched her breathe by the last pink rays of the lowering sun. She might prove vile. He might hate her. Must he truly be bound to this unknown creature?

She appeared by her smooth hands and garb to be the daughter of a gentleman or at least someone of wealth, but were she not, he could offer compensation of a different order. He could give her a generous dowry which should satisfy both her and her family. If she was a farmer's daughter, which seemed likely with her being in the woods alone, money would make them happy. She may have saved his life, but he would not marry an uneducated nobody. Much depended upon her class and her situation.

In a desperate bid to undo what couldn't be undone, Darcy sought the innkeeper, asking, "Have you a female relation who could stay in the room to protect the reputation of the woman I brought in?"

The man, serving drinks now in the inn's common room, shook his head. "No sir. Wife's dead and we never had any daughters."

"What about the maid from earlier? She'll do."

Another head shake. "She's gone home. Only comes in to help the cook with the peeling and chopping."

Darcy frowned. Had he known, he would have paid her to remain. "Is the cook still here? I require broth, in case the woman wakes."

"Aye. I'll ask what can be done, sir."

"Thank you."

Darcy pivoted and went back to the room. Some time later, a knock sounded. Darcy looked up from the flickering glow of the candle he'd lit. He rose from the hard seat of the stool and went to open the door, startled to find Stevens rather than the innkeeper. Stevens handed him a bowl and spoon.

"The proprietor said I may as well bring this up, as I was on my way."

Leaving the door open, Darcy went to put the broth on the little table. "Any luck?"

"I'm afraid not, sir. No one knows her. I sent word to the next town over. They've declared that bridge safe, except for the railings. Should I head over and search more tonight?"

And wake people from their beds to ask if they knew a woman he couldn't even accurately describe? "No. If you already sent someone, I'm sure they'll get word out."

"Is there anything else I can do for you, sir? Should I bring up a meal?"

"That would be appreciated. I could also use some blankets and a pillow."

Stevens looked past him to the woman on the bed. "We're sleeping in the carriage, sir, if you'd rather join us? The inside seats are comfortable enough to get a good night's sleep."

"No. Someone should be here if she wakes." Darcy supposed that was his responsibility now, unless he learned something to make it otherwise.

"Very well, sir. And, ah, sir, you should know that I asked Daniels if he thought that man was Wickham and he said he'd no right idea who the man was. Course, he didn't know Mr. Wickham well."

Darcy nodded, absorbing that. Was he certain the man was Wickham? He'd left out any name in his recounting to the innkeeper and Evans. Why? Because he knew he couldn't prove the man with the gun was George Wickham or because his guess as to the assailant's identity hinged on the memories in which he'd stewed?

"Sir?"

Darcy shook his head. "I'm certain it was Wickham." He knew George too well not to recognize him in an instant, even with part of his face obscured. "But let us keep that between us until we can find proof. Without proof, my certainty means little and if he has any inkling he was identified, finding proof will be that much harder." Wickham would take any steps he could to thwart them.

Stevens nodded. "I'll tell Daniels as much. I'll return shortly with your dinner and the blankets."

He did and, after dismissing him, Darcy lay out a bed as best he could on the hard plank floor then sat to a meager dinner. As he ate, he studied the woman once more, her worsening bruises appearing quite dark by the light of the single candle on the little table. She showed no sign of waking.

When he finished his meal, he went to the end of the bed and unlaced each boot, not wishing her to sleep in them. With great care, he clasped her left calf and raised her foot to tug the boot free. He repeated the process with the other, trying not to note how well turned her ankles were. He placed her footwear, fine enough to belong to the daughter of a gentleman, at the foot of the bed. Finally, he carefully inched the coverlet out from under her so he could drape it over her to keep her warm.

Her comfort seen to insomuch as he was able, he settled into his makeshift bed. The floorboards were hard against his back. The bed and stool seemed to loom on either side of him. He felt cold, despite the summer heat. He wished he could at least have darkness to aid his slumber, but he didn't want to blow out the candle in case she woke. He could only imagine how frightened she would be alone in an unknown place in the dark, covered with bruises. With that blow to her head, she may not even remember what had happened to bring her here.

Sure he'd never find sleep on the hard floor, he closed his eyes and settled into slow, deep breaths.

Chapter Four

Darcy blinked his eyes open, sleep clouding his mind. He took in the looming bed and stool and realized he lay on a floor. He'd fallen asleep on a floor?

"Hello?" a sweet female voice said, ragged at the edges and touched with worry. "Is someone here?"

The day flooded back to him. He sat up.

"Oh," the woman gasped, eyes wide. "Ah…hello?"

Definitely brown, he thought, though one of her eyes was partially swollen closed. A warm honey brown by candlelight and, though wary, holding a commendable lack of panic. With no idea what to say, he mimicked her. "Hello."

"Where am I? What happened?" She made to raise her broken left arm and winced, looking down to take in the splint. With her other hand, she gingerly touched her head. She then glanced about the little room before focusing on him once more. "And I apologize for my rudeness, but who are you?"

"Do you remember being on the roadway, at the bridge?"

She nodded, then grimaced and touched her head again. "Yes. I recognize you. A man was about to shoot you, and I tried to stop him. You and another man were driving a carriage."

It relieved him that she'd suffered no loss to her memory. "You did stop him. At least, you kept him from hitting anything important."

A frown of thought turned down her bruised lips, then her good eye went wide. "He pushed me down the hill," she gasped. "He tried to kill me."

"Yes. He seems to have been bent on murder."

"Who was he?"

"I have a suspicion, but I wouldn't wish to slander anyone without proof."

"So, he was at the bridge waiting for you, Mr.…." She trailed off expectantly.

"Mr. Darcy. Fitzwilliam Darcy of Pemberley." He may as well give his Christian name, as her cultured tones and intelligence were additional evidence that he was going to have to offer for her.

She studied him with a lack of recognition, not that he expected everyone to know his name. In London, important people would know that Mr. Fitzwilliam Darcy of Pemberley possessed sought after wealth, connections, and holdings, but they weren't in London. Sitting on the floor beside a battered woman he didn't know, who was obviously not part of the ton, Darcy suddenly longed for the opportunity to parley his assets into choosing a wife, an obligation that had only inconvenienced him afore. Now, he doubted he'd ever be able to. Fate had chosen for him.

"Well Mr. Darcy of Pemberley, I would very much like to understand why I'm in what appears to be an inn room with you, and to ask if whoever doctored my arm realized that some of my ribs may be broken."

"He did not, as you were unconscious and could not tell him what hurt, but he'll be back come morning."

"He?"

"Mr. Evans."

She nodded and he had the impression of a keen mind filing away the information. "And why am I here with you and not with my aunt and uncle?"

Her calm, reasonable attitude steadied him. There could be worse things than a woman with a pleasing figure and a quick mind. A brave woman, he amended. One who did what was right in the moment action was needed.

Or a madwoman with no sense of propriety or consequence.

With no way to know which, he could only answer plainly, though he preferred to believe he would regardless. "You are here because your injuries seem dire. We couldn't leave you. We couldn't cross the bridge to search for those who know you." Not with Wickham around the corner with a gun and the trusses possibly sabotaged. "We had no choice but to bring you here to the local surgeon, and with the bridges out, this is the only room."

"Where is the other man?"

"My coachman, valet and tiger are sleeping in the carriage."

"But you were driving."

She thought him a coachman? She'd saved him without even realizing he was a gentleman? No. She wasn't saving the life of one man but of everyone in the carriage. Wryly, he realized that her goal may even have been to save the horses, or his tiger, a mere boy. He couldn't know her motivation.

Darcy blinked in the candlelight, taken aback by his own thought. Should social standing factor into saving a life? His gut said no and yet, would he risk his life to save, say, a murderer about to hang? But that was more an issue of moral standing than societal.

Many people thought the two equated.

"So, you aren't a coachman?" the woman prompted. She looked him up and down. "I suppose not. Your clothes are not the clothes of a coachman."

Darcy shook his head, more to clear it than in answer. It had been a long, stressful day and he hadn't slept well on the hard floor. "I am not. I was assisting my driver in navigating a difficult roadway as I'd traveled it before, years ago."

She nodded, digesting that information.

Absurdly, Darcy hoped it reflected favorably upon him. "May I have your name?" he asked.

She made to raise her left arm again, glanced at the bandage, and used her right hand to push thick dark tresses behind her ears. He realized her hair had fallen out of its proper arrangement and no one had thought to do anything about it. "I'm Elizabeth Bennet. Miss Elizabeth Bennet."

He couldn't help noting the emphasis she placed on 'miss.' He struggled against a sinking feeling. His fate was sealed, then. A decision he'd long been loath to pursue had been made for him, by this woman and George Wickham.

He looked away from her as a terrible thought came to him. They couldn't have planned it, could they?

"Mr. Darcy?"

He turned back to her, taking in anew her swollen face, flecked with cuts. No. Even his wealth wasn't worth being pushed down a hill, not that he'd put it past Wickham to charm a woman into such a scheme without telling her that he planned to shove her. He'd no way to know if she would survive, though. Too uncertain a plan even for Wickham. He must be up to something else.

Georgiana. Darcy had to get to Ramsgate. He needed to ensure that whatever Wickham plotted didn't involve his sister.

"May I impose on you to alert my relations to my whereabouts?" she was asking. "The Gardiners." She named the inn Darcy remembered from his childhood adventure, in the next town over.

"Yes, certainly," he agreed. "They may already know. I sent a man to ask about missing persons, but armed with their name, I will send another."

"Thank you, sir. That is very kind. I really cannot thank you enough for your help."

"You saved my life. It is I who should thank you."

Her split and puffy lip would only allow half a smile. "Perhaps we are even, then," she murmured, settling deeper into the pillow. "I am sorry, Mr. Darcy, but I am so very tired."

Should he tell her that he must leave as early as possible in the morning? Her eyes already drifted closed. If she could find sleep with the pain she must be in, he should let her have it.

He noted the broth on the table. He'd forgotten to offer her any.

Not 'her.' Elizabeth. Miss Elizabeth Bennet. He sought through his connection in the vain hope he might know a Bennet or a Gardiner. He did not, which meant they likely weren't worth knowing, by London standards or even local ones, as he was moderately familiar with Kent. Of course, if they were in an inn, they were traveling and could be from anywhere.

An inexpensive inn, as he recalled. Did they stay there because it was the only place to stay in a small town, or because they couldn't afford to come one village over to have better, this aunt and uncle?

And why aunt and uncle, not parents? Were they dead, then?

So much more he should have asked her.

But she was already asleep. As she would no longer wake in a strange room alone with no way to know what had happened, Darcy rose as quietly as he could and slipped out, locking the door behind him and pocketing the key. In the hall, lighted by two opposing sconces, he pulled out his watch to find they were in the small hours of the morning. Still, he could hear the murmur of late night drinkers below. Perhaps he could find someone reliable enough to hire to go find the Gardiners.

Stevens' head appeared, followed by the remainder of him, as he crested the staircase. Surprise, echoed in Darcy, flashed across Stevens' face before he organized his features and hurried down the hall. Voice low in consideration of the closed doors around them, he said, "Sir, I was coming to tell you, a Mr. and Mrs. Gardiner are below, seeming quite distressed. The man we sent found them."

"How did they get here?" He couldn't imagine anyone taking the gorge road in the dark.

"The north bridge has been repaired. Traffic resumed about an hour ago."

It appeared Darcy's desire to leave as early as possible would be met. "The horses are rested?"

"Yes, sir."

"I know it's an imposition, but I have an unsettled feeling about all this. I'm afraid I must ask you to rouse the others. We'll resume our journey to Ramsgate the moment I finish my business with Mr. Gardiner."

"Yes, sir. I had them put in the private dining room downstairs, at the back."

"Good thinking. If you can, see that food and drink are brought. Anything available will do."

"I already asked, sir."

Darcy nodded. Stevens knew he would wish to be welcoming to the Gardiners. He was a good man.

Leaving Stevens to go ready the carriage, Darcy went to the indicated room at the back of the inn, finding his valet correct about its suitability. Noise from the common room would reach them but only as a dull murmur. They would be able to discuss Miss Bennet's fate without being overheard.

He went in to find two well-dressed individuals, her handsome if a touch matronly. He looked like a gentleman and had keen intelligent eyes that reminded Darcy of Elizabeth's. Rather, Elizabeth's one eye, Darcy thought with grim humor. The other was too swollen to use as a comparison. Sandwiches and ale waited on the table but neither sat, Mrs. Gardiner twisting her gloved hands in a tight, torturous manner.

Darcy halted inside the doorway and offered a nod. "Mr. Fitzwilliam Darcy. May I assume you are Miss Bennet's relations?"

Unclutching her hands, Mrs. Gardiner hurried forward. "Mr. Darcy, I'm Mrs. Gardiner. Where is Elizabeth? What has happened? All anyone has told us is that there was an accident on the roadway, and she is injured."

Deciding Mrs. Gardiner wouldn't be able to sit in her state of anxiety, Darcy made no move to. Instead, he recounted yet again the story of the incident on the bridge.

"So she is here?" Mrs. Gardiner asked when he finished. "In this inn?"

Darcy fished the room's key from his pocket. "It is the final door on the left. She was asleep when I left her. There is broth on the table if she wakes and is thirsty. The local surgeon, Evans, is already commissioned to return first thing in the morning and should be made aware that Miss Bennet believes some of her ribs to be broken."

Fear flashed in Mrs. Gardiner's eyes at that, but she exerted a commendable calm as she took the key, impressing Darcy. At least he'd stumbled on a pair of reasonable females. A laudable trait in a wife and her relations.

"If you'll excuse me?" Mrs. Gardiner said. "I will be with Elizabeth."

After the door closed behind her, Mr. Gardiner gestured to the laden table. "Shall we?"

Darcy nodded and took a seat.

Mr. Gardiner poured two glasses of ale, handing one to Darcy, then said, "If you do not mind the observation, something in your demeanor when you spoke of the man who attempted to waylay you leads me to feel that you know him."

Darcy grimaced. "I cannot be certain. A hat and scarf obscured most of his face and we weren't that close. But yes, I fear I do, which is why I will be leaving here rather shortly."

"Leaving?" Mr. Gardiner asked sharply.

Darcy supposed he must trust this man, at least somewhat. "If I am correct about who the man is, my sister may be in danger. What sort of danger, I cannot be certain, but I am on my way to her, and I cannot count it as a random act that he has delayed me."

"If that is the case, you perforce implicate this acquaintance in the damage done to the other two bridges. A man died."

Mr. Gardiner's words stoked a deep anger that Darcy had sought to master for years at the sheer recklessness, the selfishness that marred George Wickham. "I am aware."

"You must go to the authorities."

"And say that he was wearing a hat and mask so that I only saw part of his face from a distance, but I think he was familiar and so, possibly, was his voice, even though he only employed it to issue an inarticulate curse?" As he shoved their niece down a hill. "That would only delay me further in reaching my sister."

"Still, if you believe you know—"

Darcy interrupted with, "You don't know this man. He is charming and cunning. He will have an alibi ready. Someone to swear he wasn't within a hundred miles of that bridge or any other." And Darcy knew from many painful incidents in the past that even though he was an honest man, at first meeting people would always choose to believe George Wickham's word over his. He would hire runners to search for proof that Wickham had sabotaged the bridges but without any, all Darcy would accomplish by leveling the accusation would be to get sued for slander. He shook his head. "No, accusations will do no good at this juncture."

Mr. Gardiner didn't appear convinced, but he nodded. "About Elizabeth. Your story suggests that she spent considerable time alone with you. First in your carriage and then here at this inn. More than that, a goodly number of people witnessed you carry her in and then up to a room."

Darcy nodded. "I saw no alternative. I couldn't leave her injured by the road. She was unconscious and in very obvious need of a doctor."

"And you could not cross the bridge knowing the other two had been tampered with."

Darcy spread his hands. "And, somewhat familiar with the area, I know there isn't a doctor in the town in which you were staying."

Mr. Gardiner nodded, seeming to find no flaw in Darcy's reasoning. "Thank you for taking such care with Elizabeth. It was very good of you."

"She did save my life," Darcy said dryly.

"She's fortunate you're a decent man." Mr. Gardiner cleared his throat, expression pained, and continued, "Are you also a wedded man, sir?"

Darcy shook his head. "I am not." Before Mr. Gardiner could move to the next most obvious question, Darcy posed one that had been troubling him. "Why was your niece in the forest alone?"

"She was not. A local girl, from the inn, had accompanied her. We knew of nothing wrong until the day waned, for Elizabeth enjoyed rather long sojourns into the countryside. Finally, when our worry grew to great, we made inquiries of the innkeeper. He grew concerned as well, having assumed his daughter with Elizabeth." Mr. Gardiner frowned. "It turned out the girl ran the moment they sighted the man with the pistol and then hid, afraid she would be in trouble for abandoning Elizabeth, which I gather from her father she is. Needless to say, we were frantic, searching and rallying others to search, when the man you sent found us." He paused to study Darcy and then added, "And here we are."

Darcy nodded.

Mr. Gardiner appeared glum. "Even if she makes a complete recovery, she is hopelessly compromised."

"I saw no alternative." Darcy wouldn't apologize for not abandoning her at the bottom of a gully.

"I understand," Mr. Gardiner replied. "You acted in what you considered to be her best interests. Indeed, it is possible that if you delayed, she would have died. Because the alternative to you compromising her might have been her death, I don't think it is appropriate for her family to press for any form of compensation from you."

"Compensation?" Darcy reiterated, angered.

Mr. Gardiner held up a staying hand. "Her mother will want you to marry her, even if you are destitute."

So, she had a mother. "Are Miss Bennet's circumstances that bad?"

"They are not, but someday will be. Her father's estate is entailed to a cousin, they haven't saved, and she has four unmarried sisters as her only siblings."

"Then her father is a gentleman." He'd deduced as much but it still stung to have that last thread of hope cut.

"Yes, but her mother, my sister, comes from trade. I am in trade."

That surprised Darcy. Mr. Gardiner had the garb and bearing of a gentleman. He'd rather thought the man similar to his acquaintance, Mr. Hurst. From a good family but fallen on hard times. Maybe that's what he'd wanted to see.

Mr. Gardiner continued, "My sister is…. I don't want to speak ill of family, but she did not receive much of an education." He gave a rueful smile. "I'm trying to do better with my daughters."

Darcy respected Mr. Gardiner's careful phrasing. His words were vague enough to make it possible that Mrs. Bennet was only a little ignorant or possibly much worse. It didn't really matter. Miss Bennet was the daughter of a gentleman and Darcy had ruined her, and he might possibly owe her his life, and that of his valet, coachman and tiger, as well as four horses. He would marry her if she had a hundred uneducated relations who didn't save.

He might as well make that known. "It seems there is nothing for it, then. I will marry her."

Chapter Five

The mirror showed two black eyes, various small cuts on her face and a huge bump. Not to mention a swollen, cut lip. Her head hurt, her ribs hurt, and her arm hurt. If she thought about it, there were numerous other things that hurt, but not nearly as much. She tried not to think about it.

Aunt Gardiner brought in more candles and a basin and towels. They'd brought Elizabeth's things with them, on the chance that she couldn't be moved. She was glad they had done so, since the thought of bouncing about in a carriage for even a short journey made her cringe. Or would have, if cringing didn't hurt so much.

Her aunt helped her wash and dress in a nightgown. Aunt Gardiner tried to be cheerful but sweat stood out on Elizabeth's forehead by the time she settled back into the bed, from struggling against dizziness, tiredness, and pain. Properly ensconced in the sheets this time, she let her aunt help her to sit up against a pile of pillows. Aunt Gardiner dragged the table away, replacing it with the stool, and took up the cold broth. Elizabeth endured being fed, knowing she couldn't manage even that simple task on her own.

"It will all come out right," Aunt Gardiner murmured as she proffered another spoonful, but the shadows in her eyes had far more to do with worry than candlelight.

Elizabeth nodded, then grimaced as the motion made her head throb and spin.

"You said that the gentleman who brought you here, Mr. Darcy, claims the surgeon will return in the morning?" her aunt asked.

"Yes." It hurt far less to force the syllable past her abraded lips than to nod, at least.

"When he arrives, I'll request some laudanum for you, dear."

Stifling the inclination to shake her head, Elizabeth instead uttered, "No. Thank you."

Aunt Gardiner lightly touched her arm. "But you're obviously in considerable pain."

"No," Elizabeth repeated. Her father had always warned her to avoid laudanum.

Aunt Gardiner pursed her lips and offered more broth.

Elizabeth ate her fill, which wasn't much. Her aunt returned the remainder to the table. Elizabeth's eyes drifted closed.

"Elizabeth, dear, I know you're tired but please, tell me your side of what happened."

Elizabeth blinked her eyes back open to her aunt's worried face. "I walked with the girl...Lucy, was it not?"

Aunt Gardiner nodded.

"We walked down the woodland road." Elizabeth worked to conjure the sight in her mind. "It grew narrow, a cliff up on one side and a cliff down on the other. I wanted to see the bridge before turning back, so we went on. A man lurked near the bridge with a pistol. Lucy ran away but I couldn't..." Her throat constricted, the import of what she'd done pushing to the forefront of her mind. Ruined, to save this stranger and his servants. Who would ever have her now? Tears leaked from her eyes. "I'm sorry, I truly am. I couldn't permit him to shoot at unsuspecting people."

"Shh. Everything is perfectly well, dear." Aunt Gardiner smoothed Elizabeth's hair back from her forehead with a gentle touch. "I'm sorry. I shouldn't have asked. And please don't worry so. Your uncle is downstairs right now, speaking with the gentleman."

"Is he?"

"Yes. I left them to it."

"No. I mean, is he a gentleman?" He seemed one to Elizabeth, this Mr. Darcy, by manners, conduct, clothing, and staff, but she couldn't know for certain.

"I believe so, dear."

Elizabeth swallowed against the ball of pain and tears in her throat. "Is he...married?" Were he, she had no hope. She'd ruined her future and likely hampered her sisters'. Were he not, that didn't mean he would do the right thing and offer for her. If he did, must she accept? Accept a man she knew very little of? One she might even despise once she came to know him, for what sort of man had someone with a gun waiting for him?

No. No, she could not despise him, could she? Not when he seemed noble enough to care for her despite the obligation under which it placed him. Or not, were he married. If another woman already claimed the role of Mrs. Darcy, he risked little, and she'd risked all.

And this Mr. Darcy may not have been specifically targeted, and so may not be the sort of man another would wish to shoot at. The man with the gun could have been waiting for any passerby.

"I cannot say if he is wed," Aunt Gardiner was saying. "I pray he is not and that he is a good, honest gentleman."

Elizabeth prayed for that, too. "I'm sorry," she repeated.

"You had no choice, as you said."

But she had. She could have retreated and sent the authorities, though they would have arrived too late. She could have shouted alone, rather than run at the man to try to stop him. She could have, maybe, done something to prevent him from flinging her down a hill, though she knew not what for he'd been far stronger than she. Realizing hot tears made tracks down her cheeks, she lifted her usable hand and wiped them away.

A light knock sounded. Her aunt went to the door to exchange a murmured greeting with a voice Elizabeth recognized as her Uncle Gardiner. Aunt Gardiner turned slightly to say, "Your uncle and Mr. Darcy would like to come in."

Elizabeth nodded. The two entered and she took in for the first time that Mr. Darcy stood half a head taller than her uncle, with broader shoulders and, even aggrieved and by candlelight, a handsome face. Heat rose in her cheeks as he looked down at her, abed, though she knew he'd already seen her thus. Somehow with her wearing a nightgown and fully awake, his presence seemed far more scandalous.

But of course, the time to be scandalized had long since passed. That knowledge added to the throbbing spin in her head.

Uncle Gardiner came to stand at the head of the bed, looking down at her with a face lined by concern. "How are you?"

"Pleased that nothing more than my arm, and I suspect my ribs, broke."

Uncle Gardiner nodded. "As are we." He gestured to the tall gentleman who lingered near the door. "Mr. Darcy tells me that your intervention likely saved four lives. You are to be commended."

"Thank you."

"An unfortunate consequence is that you were compromised," Uncle Gardiner continued. "Mr. Darcy has a solution."

"A solution?" she asked, daring to hope.

47

Mr. Darcy stepped forward, to the foot of the bed. "Miss Bennet, will you do me the honor of becoming my wife?"

It was the best for which she could hope, but to bind her future to a man about whom she knew so very little... "We don't know each other."

"That is irrelevant," Uncle Gardiner said. "Mr. Darcy assures me that he can support a wife and everything I see of him suggests that to be true."

Mr. Darcy raised an eyebrow at that but remained silent.

"I would like to give you time to get to know each other," Uncle Gardiner continued, "but that doesn't seem to be possible."

Elizabeth frowned. "Why is it not? I believe I will not be able to travel for some days." She met Mr. Darcy's gaze, speaking directly to him rather than to her uncle. "Sir, would you not prefer a brief chance at acquainting yourself with me before making this very important decision? I know I would." If Elizabeth could think of anything worse than being ruined, it was being wedded to a man she loathed, bound to him, obliged to give her body to him, for the remainder of her days.

Mr. Darcy shook his head. "I cannot remain. I have an exceedingly important matter to which I must attend."

"More important than coming to know your wife?"

"I am afraid so. In fact, important enough that my carriage is being readied as we speak."

He would leave now? At what she guessed to be the third hour of the morning? The matter must be important indeed. "You could return. We could—"

"Elizabeth," Uncle Gardiner said firmly. "Time will not change what must be done. I will write to your father to get his consent, of course, but there is no alternative. You and Mr. Darcy must marry."

"T-the banns," Elizabeth stammered weakly. Once her parents knew, she would have no way out of the union. Her mother would insist on it. Her head spun, pounding in a discordant rhythm. She couldn't help but think that if she were able to stand, to make her mind work clearly through the pain that clouded it, she could find a way to halt her fate. Instead, the room only swirled faster with each exchange.

"There is no need for banns," Mr. Darcy said. "I will procure a special license and return with it as speedily as I can."

A special license? A man with clout, then, accustomed to being obeyed. Elizabeth wasn't certain that would suit her, or that she would please such a man. "Why isn't it possible for us to get to know each other?"

"I am the guardian of my sister, and she needs me. I plan to leave within the hour. I doubt you will be able to travel for at least a week. Will you marry me?"

"Elizabeth, you have no choice," Uncle Gardiner said sternly.

"Elizabeth, dearest, please," Aunt Gardiner urged.

Temples throbbing with each harsh beat of her heart, Elizabeth murmured, "Yes."

"Thank you," Mr. Darcy said and quit the room.

Chapter Six

Darcy pushed his servants and his team hard, shortening the journey to Ramsgate as much as possible. When they finally turned down the street which held the house he'd rented for Georgiana, Stevens, who rode in the carriage with Darcy, stuck his head out the window in a most undignified manner, caught up in Darcy's worry.

He ducked back in. "There's a carriage out front with bags being loaded."

"Tell Daniels to block it," Darcy said grimly.

Stevens stuck his head out the window to call to the coachman. Darcy worried he would look like a madman or a fool with his staff hanging out windows. His carriage maneuvered to block the other and he couldn't help but add that to the tally of inappropriate behavior. It could be a neighbor, after all, parked before Georgiana's residence for unknown reasons. Loading cases…

In his gut Darcy knew the carriage didn't belong to a neighbor, and better to appear foolish for a moment than lose his sister forever. Over the course of the journey to Ramsgate, he'd concluded that was the stake in Wickham's game. Only marriage to Georgiana, taking possession of both her and her dowry and, were Darcy actually killed, the entirety of the Darcy fortune, would make Wickham do something so criminal and rash as he had on the bridge.

The carriage halted, the jerk of movement punctuated by the squeal of distressed horses. Darcy imagined the other team didn't appreciate coming face to face with his Cleveland Bays. He flung open his door and jumped out, aware of Stevens doing likewise on the other side. They had to act quickly, before the driver realized he could back up a few feet and then easily go around Darcy's carriage. Georgiana's head poked out from the window of the other carriage. Upon sighting him, her eyes flew wide.

"Georgiana," he called, rushing forward.

She moved as if to open the door but then jerked back. Yanked? Darcy's jaw clenched. Inside the carriage, his sister shrieked. He broke into a run, passing the agitated face to face teams. Reaching the door of the other carriage, he jerked it open.

Georgiana tumbled into his arms as if shoved. Darcy caught her before she could come to harm. Over her head, he saw Wickham jump out the other side, satchel in hand, and bolt.

"Stevens," Darcy bellowed, making his sobbing sister start.

"Sir?"

Darcy looked to see Stevens had come around to their side. "He's getting away." Darcy nodded with his chin, arms full of his sister. "Catch him."

"Sir," Stevens acknowledged enthusiastically. Yelling for their tiger to join the chase, he broke into a run. He disappeared around Georgiana's carriage as the tiger slithered down from Darcy's.

"I'm sorry," Georgiana babbled against Darcy's chest. "I'm so sorry."

"What the devil is going on here?" the driver of Georgiana's coach demanded.

"What is going on," Darcy snapped, "is that man was about to kidnap my sister and you were aiding him."

The driver flinched back from Darcy's tone but, expression stubborn, pressed, "Madam, were you going willingly?"

She shook her head, face pressed to Darcy's chest, and sobbed, "No. Not anymore."

The driver grimaced. "My apologies, sir. I didn't know."

Darcy nodded, not much caring one way or the other. The important thing was that he'd arrived in time. Dread unclenched in his chest. He gentled his voice to say, "Come now, Georgiana, let's go inside. I'll have a maid bring tea. Come."

Where the devil was her governess, Mrs. Younge? Had Wickham harmed the woman?

Darcy unwrapped Georgiana's arms from about him, unable to help a flicker of comparison between his sister's hysteria and Miss Bennet's calm. He addressed the driver again as he offered Georgiana his arm, saying, "I'll send some footmen to remove the cases so you may depart."

"Thank you, sir. Again, Sir, Miss, I apologize for misunderstanding the circumstances under which I was employed."

Darcy nodded and turned away, bringing his sobbing sister around to face the cottage. Aware of Wickham's knack for subterfuge, he had no intention of seeking retribution against the carriage driver. He escorted Georgiana up the walk, tears flowing down her cheeks and her steps wavering.

In the entrance hall he found a cluster of servants, who'd like as not been watching out the front window. Unfamiliar with the staff, he addressed them as a group, assuming those best suited to each task would act, saying, "Retrieve my sister's luggage. Have tea brought..." He looked around and pointed to the nearest room. "There. Someone stay with Georgiana and someone please tell me where Mrs. Younge is."

Georgiana sobbed harder at the mention of her governess. The footmen rushed off to bring in her luggage and someone, possibly the cook, hurried away as well, presumably to see to the tea. A maid came forward, looked between Darcy and his sister for a worried moment, then moved to Georgiana's other side to take her arm.

"Mrs. Younge went out the back with her case, sir," the maid said before turning to Georgiana to murmur, "You come with me, Miss, to the parlor. We'll get you some tea." With continued coaxing, she led Georgiana into a cozy room that was visible from where they stood.

Darcy looked back out front to see his carriage backing up and Georgiana's cases coming down from the other, but no sign of Stevens yet. Certain his valet would come find him the moment he returned, Darcy went through the house and out the kitchen door, to the stables. He looked up and down the narrow alley, unsurprised to find no sign of Mrs. Younge. He went up to her room and searched but she'd left nothing behind.

He came back down to find Stevens coming in, disheveled. "He got away from us, sir."

Darcy bit back a curse. No Wickham. No Mrs. Younge. Only one person remained who could tell him what had happened, and he didn't even know if she'd stopped crying yet.

Unless that family she'd befriended could. The Milfords.

Best to start with Georgiana and see how far that got him. But first, he turned to Stevens. "The team is tired?"

"Very," Stevens said with feeling.

Darcy imagined his valet spoke for himself, Daniels and the tiger as well. "There is no housekeeper." Mrs. Younge had filled that role while they were in Ramsgate. "You'll have to arrange with one of the maids for meals and accommodations for us all. We won't depart until tomorrow morning."

"Yes, sir." Stevens nodded and strode off.

Darcy removed his coat and hat, somewhat surprised to realize he still wore them. He hung them near the door, not troubling to summon a servant, then went into the front parlor. Georgiana sat on the sofa before a sparse tea service, face blotchy from crying and a crumpled handkerchief in hand. The maid he'd left her with sat off to the side against the wall, staring down at her hands, but she looked up when he entered.

Darcy met her gaze. "If you will excuse us?"

The maid got up, cast Georgiana a worried look, curtsied and left.

Darcy crossed to take the chair nearest his sister, wondering why the pianoforte was turned the wrong way around, so listeners would be staring at the back of the player's head. "Tell me what happened."

She looked up at him, eyes watery, and whispered, "George asked me to elope."

"And you were going to do so?"

She nodded. "Until I saw you. You looked so worried, almost afraid really, and desperate, and I realized how much what I was about to do would hurt you. So, I tried to get out and George wouldn't let me, and he grabbed my arm so hard, and his face was so...so...so mean and..." She hiccupped and burst into tears.

Darcy inched to the edge of the armchair, not reaching for his sisters' hands but ready to do so if he deemed she needed the comfort. "Georgiana, I know this is very awkward to tell your brother, but I must know. Did he...are you..." Darcy grimaced, drew in a breath and asked, "Exactly how compromised are you?" Heaven help George Wickham if she gave Darcy the wrong answer.

His sister's eyes went wide, her face scarlet. "Not that compromised," she blurted. "We were waiting until we married. In Scotland." Darcy suspected Wickham would not have waited. Their first night in an inn may not have suited Georgiana, but it would have bound her to Wickham.

Scotland. Darcy cursed inwardly. He was supposed to be in Scotland in a few days' time. He had a rather fine holding there that he rarely had cause to visit. His steward had died, and the man's assistant had kept up writing to Darcy for months, pretending to be taking his usual dictations from the steward, while robbing the holding of all he could. Darcy would never have known if a disgruntled staff member hadn't written with his resignation over the new shoddy management.

Darcy was to meet the local constabulary. The old steward's assistant, who hopefully did not know Darcy was coming, was to be arrested. Darcy must give testimony. Must find a new steward and, while he searched for someone competent and reliable, put the holding back in order as best he could before the entire staff quit.

But first he had to procure a special license and marry Miss Bennet.

"I swear, Fitz, George didn't compromise me," Georgiana said, breaking into Darcy's runaway thoughts.

"I believe you."

"Then why do you look so dreadful?"

Darcy sat back. Georgiana was distraught. Did he truly wish to tell her about Miss Bennet now?

He must. He would be hard pressed to get a special license and marry Miss Bennet before leaving for Scotland, but he would. He intended to be there for too long to delay their nuptials until his return. He couldn't leave her in that sort of purgatory, wondering if he truly meant to marry her. Perhaps if she could recover enough to join him there…but no. He'd said he would come back with a special license, and he would. He'd already begun their union by leaving within hours of proposing. He wouldn't add to that a failure to keep his word.

Which meant he must tell Georgiana now, or she would learn of the marriage from someone else, or the paper. "I have to marry."

Georgiana's mouth hinged open. She closed it, licked her lips and asked, "Anne?"

Darcy winced. He'd forgotten his supposed engagement to their cousin. A union he'd never proposed or agreed to but one to which his Aunt Catherine and Cousin Anne clung with increasing veracity as Anne grew older, while each passing year failing to meet a suitable gentleman. "Not Anne."

Georgiana let out a breath. "That's a relief."

"It is?" Did Georgiana not care for their cousin?

She shrugged. "Anne is not right for you, nor you for her."

A bark of laughter left him before he could call it back. "I'm afraid I have no idea if that is true of the woman I will marry, too."

A line of worry creased Georgiana's brow. "I don't understand."

"There was an accident." He paused to choose his words with care, not wishing to alarm her or bring up Wickham. "Rather, there was nearly an accident, involving my carriage and a bridge. A woman, Miss Bennet, jumped out to stop the calamity. She succeeded in doing so but became injured in the process."

"Oh," Georgiana gasped, a hand coming up to cover her mouth.

"Miss Bennet was rendered unconscious. Unable to leave her and not knowing from whence she came, I was forced to take her with me to get treatment. I'm afraid we were unchaperoned together for some time. In consequence, I have offered to marry her and she has accepted."

Georgiana dropped her hand, eyes shimmering with fresh tears. "So, she saved you, and then you saved her, and now you will marry?"

That summed it up well, so he nodded. "Yes."

"Oh," she repeated, but on a breath this time. "How romantic."

He supposed it would seem so to a girl of fifteen. "Yes, well, we can only hope we will suit."

"How can you not when you both behaved so nobly?"

She made a fair point. One he hoped was correct.

"Is she pretty?"

Darcy shook his head. "I have no way to know. Her face sustained considerable bruising when she fell down the gully."

"Fell down the gully?" Georgiana gasped.

Darcy hadn't meant to impart that. "Her form seemed pleasing enough. I'm certain her appearance is perfectly reasonable." Not that the details of her face mattered when it came to his duties.

Georgiana's eyes looked far away. "I'm certain she's beautiful." She refocused on Darcy. "When can I meet her?"

Not anytime soon. He needed to come to know Miss Bennet before exposing his obviously impressionable sister to her.

And were she not a suitable companion for Georgiana? What then? He fought down a surge of panic at that fear, pointless as his commitment had been made the moment he put her into his carriage. He girded for his sister's dismay as he said, "Not yet. For now, you must go stay with Aunt Catherine."

"Fitz, no," Georgiana cried. "Please, I swear I won't ever again do anything so foolish as I nearly did today. Only, don't make me stay with Anne and Aunt Catherine."

So, she did dislike their cousin Anne. "You must. I have no time to hire another companion, or to take you to Uncle Matlock." Not when he had to race to London, procure a special license, return to marry Miss Bennet, and reach Scotland in time.

"Can I not stay with Richard?" Georgiana asked in reference to her co-guardian.

"Richard has military duties to which he must attend and no household proper to a young woman's needs."

Georgiana's face twisted. "But isn't there anywhere other than with Aunt Catherine?"

"No."

She heaved a sigh, then brightened. "What about with your Miss Bennet?"

"She needs care, not someone to care for. She was abed when I left her."

Wide eyed again, his sister asked, "Will she be well? She won't...die, will she?"

He didn't believe so, though she'd taken quite the blow to her head and that often had mysterious consequences. She'd seemed lucid enough. Cogent in her arguments even if ultimately unable to avoid their union. It had hurt a bit, how much she'd tried. Most women would jump off a cliff on purpose for the prospect of being Mrs. Darcy and now he must wed one with no appreciation of his worth.

"Fitz?" Georgiana sounded very worried now. "She won't die, will she? That would be terribly tragic of her."

He shook his head, aware recent lack of sleep was making him distractible, and said, "She seemed well enough when I left her. If she lives long enough for me to return with a special license and marry her, I will assume she means to survive."

Georgiana's worry vanished into a smile. "You're in a hurry to marry her. Very well. I will agree to remain with Aunt Catherine while you rush to your new bride."

Darcy let that stand. "Good. We leave early tomorrow." He didn't tell her to make ready. Her cases were already packed. "If you'll excuse me, I'll send for a maid to sit with you. I must make arrangements."

She nodded, her abstract expression revealing that she didn't fully attend him. No doubt she dwelled on foolish romantic imaginings of Miss Bennet saving his carriage, even though he'd provided almost no detail. Darcy rang for the maid, asked her to remain with his sister, and called for Stevens.

The more Darcy thought on Miss Bennet and her relations, the more he realized he'd almost certainly left them in a very anxious state. They clearly did not know him and so did not know the value of his word. They would be wondering at his quick capitulation and subsequent speedy departure. He would send Stevens back to make arrangements for Miss Bennet and to assure her that his business in Ramsgate was concluded, and that he would arrive with the special license in short order.

He gave Stevens several letters and considerable funds, with instructions that he was to employ Mr. Gardiner's aid in selecting a residence to rent for Miss Bennet. Darcy wouldn't leave his soon-to-be wife in a cramped inn room. He hoped Stevens would find someplace close, since he doubted she was up to a long trip.

And, with Stevens and Mr. Gardiner trusted to take care of the matter of renting a house, Darcy wouldn't need to risk stopping on his way to Rosings and exposing Georgiana to Miss Bennet and her relations in trade. That thought made him cringe, giving as it did his kindness to his intended an ulterior motive, but offered not a fraction of the distress conjured by the idea of introducing a battered and unknown woman to his sister.

Chapter Seven

Wickham pushed open the door to the tea house near where Georgiana met with her dance instructor. Relief filled him to see Mrs. Younge waiting at her usual table in the back, sipping tea, despite nearly every table being full of better paying customers. The proprietor turned a knowing smile on him, and Wickham realized the man thought their meetings were of a romantic nature. He gave the proprietor a wink as he passed. It was always better to encourage misinformation than to correct it. One never knew which subterfuges would prove useful.

Wickham slipped into the chair across from her and dropped his bag to the floor. Mrs. Younge had a case as well, and a satchel. The proprietor probably thought they were about to run off together. If Wickham had his way, they would. At least until he found a means by which to get back his hundred pounds.

The owner appeared at Wickham's elbow. "Coffee, sir?"

"He's not taking coffee today," Mrs. Younge said.

The man raised his eyebrows, dipped his head, and backed away.

"I'm not?" Wickham asked.

"Not unless you're paying for it. My source of income has been taken away from me." She tapped the side of the little pot. "I only ordered this so I could stay a bit, in case you came."

Wickham wouldn't waste his coin on coffee so he merely shrugged.

She took another sip of tea, as if to taunt him. "Do you have anywhere to go?"

As if he'd tell her if he did…which he didn't. "Why do you ask?"

"I will pay your fare to London if you escort me there."

He didn't need to ask her why. Travel wasn't terribly safe for anyone but for a woman alone, it was especially risky. She might be carrying something valuable. He certainly hoped so.

He used his charming smile, the one that didn't show all his teeth, and said, "I should be pleased to."

"Thank you."

Another party entered, filling the final empty table. Wickham could feel the proprietor's gaze on him. Because it would be easier to remain until the stage left than wander the streets, especially if Darcy's men still sought him, Wickham ordered a coffee.

He preferred his coffee black but since he'd been forced to pay, he endeavored to use every bit of the small servings of milk and sweetener offered with Mrs. Younge's tea, dumping them into his coffee. Mrs. Younge watched with a sardonic expression but said nothing.

Wickham took a sip and grimaced. It was disgusting. He would drink it regardless. "This is all Darcy's fault," he muttered, including the awful coffee. "Damn him and his fancy carriage and his changes of horses. Another ten minutes and I'd be riding north right now, teaching Georgiana what it means to be a woman."

Mrs. Younge's sardonic look twisted into distaste. "Yes, well, you are not."

He studied her, swirling the day through his thoughts. "You got out quite quickly." His gaze dropped to her case, obviously packed in advance. Had she betrayed him to Darcy?

"I planned to depart the moment you did. You believe I would remain for the consequences? How do you think I found a place for two on the stage? I was planning to convince one of the maids to accompany me, but I was in too much of a hurry to do that." One of her eyebrows winged upward. "I may have staffed the house with young, illiterate servants, but one of that lot would have stumbled onto the idea of contacting Mr. Darcy and eventually figured out how to do so."

Wickham nodded, relatively certain she told the truth. "Ten more minutes," he reiterated with a sigh. He took another sip of his cream and sugar concoction and grimaced again.

Mrs. Younge shrugged. "We took the risk. We didn't succeed. On to other things."

On to other things? There were no other things. Darcy's father had promised to support him, which meant Darcy owed him. Wickham would never stop trying to collect. "I'll find a way."

"You may try, but you'll never have an opportunity with Miss Darcy again," Mrs. Younge predicted.

He didn't mean a way to marry Georgiana, although that had always seemed the best way to get what was owed to him and to torment Darcy, in one fell swoop. The only drawback to the plan was being saddled with Georgiana, a childish, pampered brat. Although, with the money she would bring him, he could certainly afford to stick her somewhere out of the way and ignore her.

Not that he would need to waste Georgiana's dowry on her. Darcy would be happy to pay for her comfort. And wherever she was comfortable and well fed, Wickham could be also, whenever he required a bit of pampering.

And if he got a son on her and Darcy could be kept from ever marrying or made to marry that sickly cousin of his who obviously wouldn't bear, then, someday, everything would be Wickham's. He opened his mouth to refute Mrs. Younge's certainty, but a glance showed her head cocked to the side, eyes unfocused as she listened.

Did she hear something on the street? Darcy's damn valet come looking for him? Wickham cast about, trying to discover what held her attention.

At a nearby table, the two bridges and the dead man with the wagon were being discussed. Was that what held her focus? He didn't need anyone speaking of that and he definitely didn't need her hearing it, so he adopted an easy expression, took a sip of sickening sweet milk touched by coffee and asked, "Will we be taking the stage the entire way to London?"

Her gaze sharpened to focus on him. "We'll be taking the mail part of the way."

Wickham frowned. That was bound to be far less comfortable. "If you insist."

"As I am paying, I do."

They finished their drinks shortly thereafter and left to catch the coach. Wickham offered to carry her satchel along with his bag, but she refused. He thought he might be able to search it at some point on their journey, but she never let go of the thing and didn't even nap on the coach which, while cramped, did turn out to be the more comfortable leg of their journey and the only conveyance they took on which she might have done so.

After an arduous day of travel, they reached London with night closing in. Wickham climbed from the final carriage with a string of invectives aimed at Darcy running through his thoughts. He'd had such great hopes for that day and every day thereafter, and Darcy had ruined everything.

After they disembarked in the lantern lit square Mrs. Younge turned to him, her bag held close against her side. "You can earn a meal and a place to sleep for the night if you help with a small task."

Both sounded appealing but not if he had to do much. He had coin, after all, and although he felt worn by their journey, a pint or two and a comely barmaid would put him right again. He needn't lower himself to working for food. "What would I have to do?"

"Escort me home. It's a lodging house and the woman who runs it is cheating me. I'll be kicking her out. I believe I will be more successful if you stand with me, appearing stern."

He bet he could get the meal and bed simply for walking her, it being London at night, but he supposed a moment of looking stern wouldn't cost him anything. Who knew when it would come in handy to know someone with a lodging house and have them owe him a favor?

He slung his bag over his shoulder. "I can do that." He made no offer to carry her case. Let her lug it and the satchel. Being her porter hadn't been part of her offer.

They set out, their course taking them into an only slightly undesirable neighborhood. As they walked, Wickham asked, "If she's cheating you, why have you kept her on?"

"Because she's cheating me less than the previous landlady."

He snorted. "Fair enough. What do you expect to happen?"

Mrs. Younge cast him a quick look askance, likely aware he wouldn't help if he felt he had to do much. "I'll look things over, exclaim at how she's cheating me. She'll protest, then beg for another night's stay. I'll let her stay until morning. She'll take her possessions and leave."

"So I won't get her room."

"No. Nor will she. I will. There's a common room with a sofa that you can have for tonight."

They arrived at a fairly well-kept house on a decent street. Ascending the front steps, Wickham wondered why Mrs. Younge didn't simply sell it and save the hassle of being a landlord. It would go for a fair sum and be far less work. They halted on the stoop and, as she had the key, she let them in, then called for the landlady.

The exchange went as Mrs. Younge had predicted. The nature of the cheating turned out to be renting a small room that was supposed to be for a couple to a family of five and pocketing the difference in rent. The landlady was given until luncheon the next day to leave, the family a week. All Wickham had to do was stand slightly behind Mrs. Younge and scowl. He pretended he was looking at Darcy.

Her house in better order thanks to him, Mrs. Younge took Wickham to the kitchen to see what she could scrounge for their supper. Part of the deal with the landlady was that the food in the kitchen belonged to Mrs. Younge and the landlady would sleep in the attic tonight. He flopped into one of the two chairs at the little table while she started opening cupboards. His gaze settled on a keg he could see through the larder doorway.

As she pulled out a heel of bread she said, "Thank you. I appreciate your assistance."

He grinned. "I'm a useful fellow to have around."

She cast him one of her sharp looks. "Yes, and in acknowledgement of your usefulness tonight, I'll give you breakfast tomorrow in addition to feeding you now. Then we part company."

He propped his elbows on the table, mind working. She would have a free room in a week. "I'd be happy to stick around for a time, until everything is settled. You gave that family a week, after all. I can look menacing for a week, if required."

"Certainly." She pulled a long knife from a drawer and started on the bread. "If you agree to post banns this Sunday and that we will marry as soon as it's legal to do so, I'd be pleased to have you stay."

"Marry?" he choked out.

She stopped slicing to look at him. "I'm not keeping you if we aren't man and wife."

Wickham shook his head. "If we marry, we both give up the possibility of advantageous matches." He'd never have Georgiana's money then. "Why bother?"

"Because you would leave me without a backward glance if we weren't married."

He would leave her without a backward glance if they were married, but she needn't know that. She set a paltry plate of sliced bread on the table and went into the larder. Wickham took a slice of bread, tore off a bite with his teeth, and looked about the kitchen.

A nice enough kitchen, in a nice enough house on a nice enough street. If he married her, he'd own this place. He could sell it, take the money, move to another part of England, pick a new name, and fund another attempt at getting more of Darcy's money.

He brought his roving attention back around to find that Mrs. Younge stood in the larder doorway, several wax-wrapped parcels in hand, studying him. Expression unreadable, she returned to the counter and her knife. Her back to him as she unwrapped a partial wheel of cheese, she said, "Tempting as it is to fool you, I don't want to live with your enmity if we marry. The house can't be sold."

Chagrin shot through him. She knew him too well. They'd been much in one another's company while he courted Georgiana. "Oh?"

"It goes to my nephew." She carved off a thick slice of cheese. "I own it, so he can't take it from me, but there are many conditions that, if I violate them, make the house go straight to him. Such as attempting to sell it. Or, for example, I'm not permitted to lease the house to anyone who can't be kicked out in a month. I can't board up the windows."

"Board up the windows," Wickham interrupted. Windows were boarded up to avoid the window tax. Doing so would decrease the home's value. Maybe even that of every home on the street. "I thought that was only for slum neighborhoods."

"The neighbors might complain, but day laborers would prefer to live here than in a slum. It's safer, for one thing. If it weren't for my nephew, I would have boarded them up as soon as my husband died."

"It's too bad you can't sell the place. We could have lived on the proceeds."

"For how long?"

He answered that with a shrug, the real answer being, long enough to get money out of Darcy.

Mrs. Younge brought over the plate of cheese and set it beside the bread, frowning at Wickham. "Perhaps it's better that we don't marry. You never look to the future." She returned to open the second wax-wrapped bundle.

He reached for a piece of cheese, gaze narrow as he studied her back while she sliced cold meat. He thought of the future right now, and it would be better if he could get more from Mrs. Younge. Not free lodgings or a house to sell, apparently. She must have taken something to ease her way, though. She'd left Darcy's employ in disgrace. No reason not to rob him as well.

"Did you have time to take the silver?" he tried, looking for clues as to what he, in turn, might steal from her. "That would set you up nicely. Too bad Georgiana had her jewelry with her. Her pearls alone would—"

"Send me to New South Wales," she interrupted. "Darcy's not going to track me down for nearly letting you ruin his sister or for cheating him in little ways. Retribution for either isn't worth his personal time or the embarrassment of hiring someone to do it, for then they would know that he'd been foolish enough to be taken advantage of. That's in addition to the risk any such admission would be to Miss Darcy's reputation. Outright theft, however, would demand action."

She'd said, 'cheating him in little ways.' Did that mean she had managed to get something from Darcy? Something Wickham could, in turn, take? "You cheated Darcy?"

She gave him another of her sardonic looks, over her shoulder, then returned to chopping. "Why do you think I agreed to so little? One thousand pounds with only a hundred of it in advance? That's not even a year's worth of the income you would have obtained by marrying Miss Darcy."

Income? He didn't trust banks enough for that. Once he had Darcy's money, he would keep it all locked away somewhere far safer. He cleared his throat to ask, "That hundred pounds—"

"Is mine," she cut in. "Absolutely mine. I met the terms of our agreement. And I have in writing your willingness to pay me nine hundred pounds upon your marriage to Georgiana Darcy."

He frowned slightly, wondering why she bothered to bring up a contract he couldn't honor, until her meaning dawned. Without the marriage, his signature on that page could be used as a threat, or for blackmail. He cursed himself for signing. He'd thought nothing of it at the time as he'd had no intention of making good on it and she wouldn't be able to undo his triumph once he and Georgiana married.

He mustered a casual tone and asked, "Where is that contract, anyhow? I'm not going to marry her, so you may as well return it to me."

A bark of laughter left Mrs. Younge, her shoulders shaking so much she nearly dropped some of the sliced meat she was transferring to a plate. "Don't be ridiculous."

Heat ran up his neck. He clenched his teeth tight together. She would laugh at him, would she? Treat him without the respect he deserved. Like Darcy. He stood, all menace. She wouldn't be laughing once he got the truth from her.

"Where is it?" he growled.

She turned with the plate of meat. Rather than appear intimidated, she came to the table and sat, putting the plate down near the one with cheese. "Do you want your dinner? I'm afraid this is all that's in the larder that's quick."

He leaned over the table, bringing his face near hers. "Where?"

She met his ire with complete calm. "I mailed it to someone I trust shortly after you signed. After all, I wouldn't want Darcy to have found it when you were on your way to Scotland with his sister." She reached for a slice of bread. "And I put the hundred pounds in a bank, so do sit and eat your dinner. You did earn it, after all."

Wickham plunked back down in his chair. He shouldn't have made such a fuss before discovering if she had the contract with her. He tried for a casual air and stated, "Since I didn't manage to marry Georgiana, that contract is worthless anyhow. I hope your friend enjoys using it for tinder."

"Oh, I think my friend will hang onto it for a short while longer. Until I write to them to assure them that you and I are through." She added cheese and meat to her bread, then took another slice.

If she meant for their dinner to be eaten in the form of sandwiches, she could at least have assembled them. "How about some of that ale?"

"No," she said firmly. "You may eat your dinner, sleep on the sofa, and expect breakfast and departure come morning."

Later, while he lay on the lumpy sofa, he considered that he could have handled Mrs. Younge better. He'd let his temper keep him from her good graces and possibly her bed. More than that, she had a boarding house. It was good to know people who would give him lodgings and food on occasion.

Come morning, he packed back up the few items he'd removed from his bag and went to the kitchen to find her. To his disappointment, breakfast consisted of gruel and milk. How was a man supposed to get through the day if it started with gruel? Well, it could be worse. He could start his day with an empty stomach. Rather than take the bowl she gave him to the main room with the others, he ate in the kitchen with her. He made the meal take as long as possible, employing his good manners and conviviality in full.

Finally, she stood to clear the table. He rose with her, as a gentleman would. After carrying the bowls into the scullery, she turned back around, and he was waiting for her. He took her into his arms and kissed her. It pleased him that, after a moment's hesitation, her lips moved against his. If he couldn't intimidate her, capturing her heart was the next best way to control her.

When he finally raised his head, she let out a little sigh, eyes closed, her fingers splayed over his chest. "Do you know," she murmured, "I believe I've been a little bit in love with you."

He grinned.

She opened her eyes. Not much in the way of love glowed in them. "But not anymore. You shouldn't have sabotaged the bridges. That was going too far."

His arms, still about her, spasmed before he could suppress the motion, but a lie sprang readily as ever to his lips. "Bridges?" He frowned, feigning confusion. "I didn't sabotage any bridges."

"I doubt you meant for the wagon to go over," she continued, voice still soft. "That wouldn't really suit you. You must have planned to take the bridge down and that poor man everyone was speaking of in the tea house arrived at precisely the wrong time. Too early to see that he shouldn't cross. Too late for you to finish the job before he had his team on the bridge."

Wickham gazed down at her with what he hoped was enough adoration to thaw her. "I have no notion what you're going on about. When I left, it was to sabotage Darcy's carriage, but I couldn't get to him. As that meant he couldn't get to us, I came straight back."

"Is that your story?" she asked, studying his face.

"It is." He gave her another, lighter kiss. This time, she didn't respond. "Furthermore, if anyone ever says I did sabotage those bridges, I'll tell them I was with you, and if you deny that, I won't have any reason to keep quiet about your role in everything that we did."

She let out another sigh, this one of resignation, and stepped free of his arms. "I suppose we understand one another, then, and the time has come for you to go."

He let his arms fall to his sides. "I suppose so." He put on his most charming smile. "I hope I may call again sometime."

"I very much wish you wouldn't."

He shrugged. He'd got through to her. He knew it. She'd responded to his first kiss. He could have more anytime he wished to apply himself to taking it. He donned his hat, took up his bag, gave her a jaunty smile, and turned to the kitchen door.

"Mr. Wickham," she said. "George, listen to me."

He didn't turn back, his cheerfulness departing at her tone.

"We lost. Darcy won. Let it go. Chasing after Darcy, any Darcy, will be the ruin of you."

Wickham didn't even shrug. He pulled open the door and stepped through, then set off down the alley. He didn't need Mrs. Younge and her sanctimonious lecture. If her home didn't present such a potentially useful tool, he'd have turned around and let her know what he thought of her warning.

She didn't understand. No one ever did. Darcy's very existence was the cause of all Wickham's problems. If Darcy hadn't been born, old Mr. Darcy would have treated Wickham even more like a son. Not that he would have expected to inherit Pemberley, but he should have had at least the thirty thousand pounds Georgiana did. He was old Mr. Darcy's godson and had been treated like a second son. It was Darcy who didn't respect that.

Mrs. Younge was right about one thing, though. Wickham had lost. But only for now.

Chapter Eight

In an armchair pulled up to the table in the front parlor of the delightful little house that her future husband had leased for her, Elizabeth sat across from her Aunt Gardiner, staring down at the cards in her hand. Cribbage. They were playing cribbage. Now, if Elizabeth could only recall how. Trying to made the still quite prominent bulge on her forehead throb.

"Elizabeth, dear? Are you well? It's your turn."

Rather than admit that the rules to the game they'd been playing for hours had suddenly flown from her mind, she lowered her cards to address another trouble. "I cannot believe we're sitting in this room."

Aunt Gardiner frowned her lack of understanding. "You would prefer the back parlor? Or to be abed?"

Elizabeth caught back a shake of her head. Experience told her that would make her infinitely more dizzy. "In this house, rather. It's nearly as fine as Longbourn in its way and rented for me by a gentleman who should appear any day now for me to marry. It's...It is so strange." To her shame, her voice caught.

Aunt Gardiner put her cards down as well and stood. She came around the table to wrap an arm about Elizabeth's shawl swaddled shoulders. "That he thought to rent it for you shows he is considerate."

"Or that he is too proud to have the future Mrs. Darcy in an inn." He'd seemed overly proud to her, on their brief meeting, and the bearing of his valet on the man's arrival to rent the house had added to that impression.

"And," Aunt Gardiner pressed on over her, "renting you this house shows that he has sufficient funds."

"Or is a terrible spendthrift," Elizabeth countered.

"Well, your uncle has written to London to find out. We should know soon."

They should...but Elizabeth must marry Mr. Darcy either way.

A maid appeared in the doorway, for Stevens, Mr. Darcy's valet, had insisted his master required Elizabeth to have a full staff, which he seemed to feel meant nearly as many servants as Elizabeth's mother employed at Longbourn where there were both of Elizabeth's parents and her and her four sisters to look after.

"You have visitors," the maid began but got no further before Mrs. Bennet burst past her into the parlor.

"Elizabeth," her mother cried. "You look horrible. I shouldn't even recognize you. How did you manage to convince a man to offer for you in the state you're in?"

"Mama." Elizabeth's eyes welled with tears despite the quite typical insensitivity of the greeting. She knew her uncle had written to her father, but she hadn't expected anyone to respond in person. "It's so good to see you."

"Certainly, it is. I came as quickly as I could, to ensure you marry. I know how contrary you can be, and we have to think of your sisters. I brought Mary. I doubted anyone in a small town such as this would be worthy of your pretty sisters, so I left them home. You and Mary will do for the gentlemen here."

Happy as Elizabeth was to see her mother, the rambling words set her head spinning.

Mary stepped around Mrs. Bennet. "Elizabeth. Aunt Gardiner. It is good to see you. Lizzy, I have letters for you from Jane and Papa." Mary darted a look at their mother. "Jane says she very much wishes she could come to you, but she has a cold."

Elizabeth gave her sister a weak smile to show she understood. Mrs. Bennet had undoubtedly dug in her heels. "I am happy you could come, Mary."

A smallish gentleman entered behind her sister, his face familiar and cherished and yet, his name would not come to Elizabeth's mind. Staring at him, panic began to fill her.

"And your uncle is here as well," Mrs. Bennet continued. "I told Mr. Bennet that I will not be reduced to traveling without a gentleman."

"Uncle Phillips," Elizabeth said, filled with relief as her mother's inadvertent clue brought the name to the surface of her mind. "Thank you."

He nodded, greeted her with, "Elizabeth," then turned to hand his hat and coat to the waiting maid.

"I should send for tea," Aunt Gardiner said. "Or should I first show you the house? I'll ask the staff for haste, but they will require a moment to ready rooms for you."

"You?" Mrs. Bennet frowned, jowls drooping. "Is that not Elizabeth's duty?"

"Elizabeth has been ordered to rest and is not yet able to walk far," Aunt Gardiner explained.

And it would also take forever to untangle her from the pile of blankets that wedged her into the chair. Even would it not, Elizabeth agreed with her aunt. She wished to save her strength for important tasks like managing the staircase later, not wandering a house she hadn't even seen much of with her mother, who was like to be little satisfied.

Mary came over to look down at her. "Are you truly that bad? They said you can't ride in a carriage and that you broke your ribs and, well, not to sound like Mama, but you do look horrible."

Elizabeth fought back a chuckle at that, knowing how much laughing would hurt. "I do look horrible, I know." More of her face seemed purple than not. Her lip was healing, which was a boon as the cut made it difficult to eat or even to drink broth. She felt very fortunate for her strong teeth, which remained fully in place. Her arms and legs were bruised and scratched. Her ribs, not that she'd permitted anyone but her new maid and Aunt Gardiner to see them, were a disgusting molten mix of purple, green and yellow that seemed to cover most of her torso.

And soon it would be her wedding day.

All inclination to levity squelched by that thought, she closed her eyes as Mary took the chair nearest her. The sofa creaked, indicating that her mother settled there. Elizabeth couldn't hear where her Uncle Phillips sat.

"Please bring tea," Aunt Gardiner said, presumably to the maid. "And see that three more rooms are made up."

"Three more?" Mrs. Bennet asked. "How many are there?"

"Six," Aunt Gardiner replied calmly. "Three on each side of the hall."

"I told you it looked like a big house, Mama," Mary said.

"Why would Elizabeth need such a large house?"

"There weren't many options," Aunt Gardiner said, retaking her seat on the other side of the small table from Elizabeth. "As you pointed out, this is not a large village."

Mrs. Bennet huffed. "Like as not, you're putting this Mr. Darcy into debt before even marrying him. Really, Elizabeth, you should consider before you act. I read my brother's letter. You attacked someone and that's how you fell down a hill."

Elizabeth forced her eyes back open. "Someone who was about to shoot another person and I didn't fall down a hill. I was pushed into a gully."

"You should look before you leap and bear in mind the consequences of your actions," Mary offered.

"I considered the consequences if I had not acted," Elizabeth snapped, her temper less under control than usual. "Someone might have died."

"A stranger. No one we care about," Mrs. Bennet said.

"My future husband," Elizabeth rejoindered.

"Yes, well, at least he offered for you. That is a fortunate thing."

"Even if I've already consigned him to debtors' prison?"

"Don't take that tone with me, Miss," her mother replied with a sniff.

"Cursed is anyone who dishonors their father or mother," Mary added.

Elizabeth certainly felt cursed.

"At least he is wealthy enough to drive a carriage." Mrs. Bennet said into the silence that followed Mary's statement. "Does it have two horses or four?"

Mrs. Gardiner answered, and Elizabeth let her, closing her eyes again. She didn't realize she'd fallen asleep, and slept right through the others having tea, until she woke late in the afternoon. Her Aunt Gardiner sat nearby reading. Had the arrival of Elizabeth's mother, sister and uncle all been a dream? Elizabeth sighted two letters on the table, her name in Jane's hand on the top one, and realized it had not.

"Aunt Gardiner?"

She looked up from her book with a smile. "Elizabeth. I sent your mother and sister to walk the village. Mr. Phillips is with Mr. Gardiner, working on your marriage contract. Not that they can finalize the details until Mr. Darcy returns, of course.

"I would like to go back to my room if I may? My mother was…" She paused, not wanting to speak ill.

"Exhausting?" Aunt Gardiner supplied with a wry smile. "Yes, dear, I know." She sighed. "I am sorry to say this but with her here, your uncle and I truly must return to London."

72

Elizabeth nodded, tears prickling in her eyes. "Of course." She'd been selfish not to suggest they go. Uncle Gardiner had a business that couldn't be run forever by correspondence and Aunt Gardiner had a household and four children she must miss dearly. "Thank you for staying with me until Mama arrived."

Aunt Gardiner looked down. "I'm so sorry about this, Elizabeth. We wanted to take you on a nice trip, let you see some of Kent, and—"

"You aren't at fault," Elizabeth cut in. "I am the one who went walking in the woods. I'm the one who didn't run away with…" The girl's name wouldn't come to her now. "I could have gone back and sent help."

"If you had, would it have arrived in time?"

"I do not believe so."

"Then it is good that you stayed." Aunt Gardiner smiled gently. "Your actions were right and laudable. I am sorry you suffer for them."

"I'll heal," Elizabeth said firmly.

Aunt Gardiner nodded. Neither of them said what they both must be thinking, that if Mr. Darcy proved a disagreeable man, Elizabeth would suffer for years without recourse. That unspoken thought hung between them as Aunt Gardiner helped her from the chair and up the stairs.

Elizabeth's aunt and both of her uncles left the following day, as Mr. Phillips likewise had a business to which he must return. He'd only come to escort her mother and Mary and to help Uncle Gardiner draft the marriage contract.

Before leaving, Uncle Gardiner gave her a letter from his agent in London, saying, "I think you'll be pleased with what my man found about your Mr. Darcy." He'd then bid Elizabeth farewell, echoing his wife's sorrow at leaving her.

Elizabeth also had the letters from her father and Jane. She didn't read any of them. Attempting to made her head hurt too excruciatingly. Instead she put them on the dressing table in her room, unable to decide if she should admit her need for help to her mother or Mary, or if she wished them to know the contents of the letters. Maybe, once the swelling went down enough that she could open her right eye all the way, she'd be able to read them on her own. When another letter arrived, her maid added it to the pile.

Elizabeth began to sleep more and more which, when she was awake, worried her, but when Mr. Evans returned, he said she was healing nicely, and that rest was essential. She'd worried that her mother's care would be an imposition and her company unpleasant. Instead, she found that her mother and sister were content to spend their days exploring the village and leaving her alone. Elizabeth didn't blame them. She'd snapped at both repeatedly. Her throbbing head put her in a bad temper, and everything was difficult with only one hand, her dizzy spells, and the need to be careful of her ribs.

Several mornings after her aunt and uncles' departure, she lay in bed wondering if she possessed the strength to dress and go down to the parlor. She hadn't since the day her mother and Mary arrived. She didn't wish to at all, but it seemed like the correct course. She should make the effort. Her maid would help her. A soft knock sounded at her door.

"Enter," Elizabeth called, her voice cracking with lack of use.

Her maid stepped in. A shock of worry making her dizzy, Elizabeth wondered if she'd rang for the girl already and then subsequently forgotten. She pressed icy fingers to her forehead.

The girl closed the door and hurried across the room. "Miss, Mr. Darcy is in the parlor. He has the special license. He says he's here to marry you and must depart before noon. He says he wrote." Eyes wide, she added, "He didn't appear happy that none of us had any notion he was coming."

Elizabeth's gaze went to the stack of letters. How many had there been before? There were certainly more now.

She levered herself up, the room spiraling and tilting. "Send someone to tell Mr. Darcy that I will be down shortly and then for the minister." She held out her good hand. "Help me up and help me dress, please. If we've the staff—" Was there more than one footman? She couldn't recall. "Uh, if we've the staff, send someone else to find my mother and sister."

Where had her uncles left the contract? They'd told her, Elizabeth felt certain, but she simply could not remember.

Her maid sped off, but quickly returned to help her to dress. Moving as fast as she could, Elizabeth did her best to balance hurry and pain. Still, the process took far longer than it should have. Only pinning up her hair didn't take an inordinate amount of time. With Elizabeth's face still a molten mix of lumps, half healed scratches, green, yellow, and purple skin, and an eye that didn't fully open, there seemed little use in doing much with her dark locks.

When they were done the maid, who surely deserved some sort of largesse, helped her down the stairs. Leaning on her, Elizabeth hobbled into the parlor to the sight of a tall, broad, darkly clad gentleman, back to her as he stood very rigid, gaze trained out the front window.

"Mr. Darcy?" she said tentatively.

He whirled, the annoyance on his face instantly turning to concern. He crossed and took her arm from the maid with murmured thanks to the girl, then helped her to a chair. "My apologies, Miss Bennet, for demanding your presence."

"Insofar as I know, sir, you have the right."

A commotion in the entrance hall cut off whatever he would have replied and, all at once, everyone spilled in. Her mother. Mary. A soberly dressed man carrying a bible.

"You are Mr. Darcy?" Mrs. Bennet gasped, a hand going to her heart. "Heavens."

Mr. Darcy looked to Elizabeth in query.

"Mr. Darcy, may I introduce my mother, Mrs. Bennet, and my sister, Miss Mary. Mama, Mary, this is Mr. Darcy."

They both gaped at him in a rather uncouth manner. Elizabeth's cheeks heated. Sardonically, she supposed that red was the only shade missing from the collage of colors that was her face.

Mr. Darcy bowed with careful precision. "Mrs. Bennet. Miss Mary."

"Mr. Darcy is here to marry me," Elizabeth added, in case it needed saying.

The man with the bible stepped forward. "Ah, yes, I believe that is why I was asked to come. Mr. Darcy, sir, may I see the license?"

The two examined the paperwork while Mrs. Bennet fussed with Elizabeth's hair. Then, Elizabeth seated and Mr. Darcy standing beside her with one hand on the back of her chair, they were married. After the priest declared them wed, Mr. Darcy stepped away to sign some papers. Mary and Mrs. Bennet signed as well, to bear witness. The pages were brought to Elizabeth on a tray. She awkwardly scrawled her name with her right hand, wishing she'd listened to her Mama all those years ago and learned to write right-handed, rather than with her left hand like her father. She blushed again, aware of Mr. Darcy beside her, taking in her floundering attempts to write her own name. Belatedly, she once more recalled the marriage contract her uncles had worked on. She hoped she hadn't just made a terrible mistake.

The papers were removed, and Mr. Darcy went into the hall with the priest. When he returned, alone, he crossed back to Elizabeth. He lifted her good hand, gave a gentle squeeze, and said, "And now, I am afraid, I must depart once more."

"Depart?" Elizabeth echoed, then remembered that the maid had said he couldn't remain for long.

"You're leaving, Mr. Darcy?" Elizabeth's mother cried.

He glanced at her but turned back to Elizabeth. Frowning slightly, he said, "Yes. You have it in my letter but in case it...went awry...you should know that I have pressing matters at a holding in Scotland. I made the arrangements before, ah, any of this occurred, and I must keep them."

He released Elizabeth's hand. He hadn't even kissed it, or any part of her. She didn't know that she wanted him to. She didn't know him at all.

He looked about at the three women in the parlor with him. "I believe Mrs. Gardiner had begun a ledger of household expenditures." Sounding doubtful he asked, "Could I impose on one of you to locate and order them, and maintain them? I've decided to send down a man to be your steward while you reside here."

"I can," Mary said brightly. "If anyone is not willing to work, let him not eat."

Mr. Darcy's brows drew together but he nodded. Elizabeth's head pounded. She pressed light fingers to her temple, on the side away from the bump. A steward? Because she hadn't read his letter?

Everything was happening too quickly. She was in a house somewhere in Kent. Mistress there. And married. Heaven above, she was now Elizabeth Darcy.

"I will return once my business in Scotland is concluded," Mr. Darcy said. "I'll send my address there." He gave Elizabeth a polite nod and left the parlor.

Mrs. Bennet raced to the window and yanked the curtain back. "Oh, that stunning carriage out front is his. I can see why you'd save a man in a carriage like that, Elizabeth."

Elizabeth stared at her mother, too befuddled to form a reply. She hadn't thanked him for the house, or for Mr. Evans' visits. She hadn't asked after his sister or managed to explain about the letter she hadn't read. Or showed him the now moot contract her uncles had written. Now he was gone again.

Not an auspicious beginning to their marriage.

A Mr. Smith arrived two days later, down from London, to be their steward. He rented a room in the village's only boarding house, which fortunately seemed adequate to the task, according to Mary who mostly dealt with him. He also brought with him, for Elizabeth's use, a fine two horse carriage and the men to drive and care for it and the team. The conveyance wasn't as grand as the one Mr. Darcy used but very fine indeed. Mrs. Bennet immediately seized upon it as a means for beginning to call on the neighbors, several of whom she'd already contrived to meet.

With painfully slow progress, Elizabeth worked her way through Mr. Darcy's letter. It did, indeed, inform her of his impending arrival and his subsequent trip to Scotland. She wondered if he really thought she may not have received it, thought her too dull witted to understand it, or, she shuddered to think, now assumed she could not read?

Laboriously, feeling it should come from her own hand because he was her husband now and she his wife, Elizabeth used her right hand to scrawl her thanks for all he'd done. When she finished, it looked like a child had written it, which she supposed in a way was true. Her right hand had never learned to form letters and must begin as the hand of any child.

She considered adding a postscript apologizing for her poor handwriting but, with the first spark of her usual will she'd felt since the accident, balked. For one, it hardly seemed worth the effort. Her left arm would heal, and her right would no longer need to do the writing. More importantly, she would not embark into their union tendering excuses or justifications. Even as little as she knew of him told her that Mr. Darcy enjoyed giving orders and expected to be obeyed, a way in which she would not live. Beginning with apologies for not being able to use an arm she'd broken saving him would set a poor precedent. To avoid the temptation, she sealed the letter and rang for her maid, asking the girl to take the missive for Mr. Darcy to Mr. Smith, who would surely know where to send it, for the promised address in Scotland had not yet come…unless it had, and she'd forgotten.

Over the next several days, stacks of letters began to arrive. Apparently, Mr. Darcy had put announcements of their marriage in the London papers, giving Elizabeth's Kent address for the purpose of well wishes. So many flooded in that Elizabeth wondered what report of Mr. Darcy's character and standing could possibly be in the letter left to her by her Uncle Gardiner, but she hadn't the time or concentration yet to read it. Instead, she listened to her mother read her the letters that arrived, which Mrs. Bennet enjoyed so fully as not to even ask why Elizabeth didn't read them, and dictate her replies to Mary, who'd become quite zealous in her role as something akin to Elizabeth's housekeeper.

A particularly effusive letter from someone named Mr. Bingley stood out as Elizabeth's favorite, despite her mother's complaints about his bad handwriting and crossed out sections. She hoped her husband was as fond of this Mr. Bingley as he seemed to be of Mr. Darcy. If they could spend time with people as obviously cheerful and lively as Mr. Bingley, maybe they could learn to be happy together.

At one point, plucking up a letter, Mrs. Bennet squealed so loud as to make Elizabeth queasy with dizziness.

"Mother, whatever is it?" Mary cried, looking over from where she penned a polite thank you to someone none of them knew.

"This one is from an Earl. An Earl, Elizabeth. Your Mr. Darcy knows an Earl."

Elizabeth pressed her fingers into her uninjured temple, trying to push her mind back into place. Heaven help her if Mr. Darcy knew a Duke. Her mother would succumb to a fit and drive Elizabeth to madness with the inevitable caterwauling that would accompany it.

Mrs. Bennet fluttered the page. "An Earl," she murmured, even as she read. She let out another shriek. "He's a relation. Elizabeth, you've a relation who is an Earl." She ran from the parlor calling for her bonnet and the carriage.

No doubt, soon the entire village would know that Mr. Darcy had a relation in the peerage. Elizabeth kept massaging her temple and turned to Mary. She worked to muster a whisper, the sound of her own voice too loud in her ears with her head throbbing so hard and asked, "Mary, could you write to Papa to come take Mama home, please?"

Mary nodded, expression resolute and purposeful as she put pen to paper.

Chapter Nine

Darcy attempted to read as his carriage brought him ever closer to his holding in Scotland, but his concentration was ruined by thoughts of his wife and her relations. Mr. and Mrs. Gardiner had both seemed competent, intelligent, and even stylish in a properly understated way. Darcy's man had looked into them for him and found them to be quite as respectable as one could hope, what with Mr. Gardiner being in trade.

Of the Bennets, his man had found little yet. They seemed some sort of countrified gentry from an obscure corner of Hertfordshire called Longbourn, near the village of Meryton. Darcy's man had dispatched someone to go there, to investigate them more fully. Not that it mattered what he found. It was far, far too late.

He would have sworn Elizabeth seemed intelligent that night he'd offered for her, if reluctant. Now, meeting her mother, he wondered if that could be true. Had her actions in hindering Wickham not been noble, as he'd assumed, but rather born of a mind too dull to comprehend the consequences? That left her a good-hearted woman, still, but a lackwit.

Mr. Gardiner had suggested his sister, Mrs. Bennet, had received little education. He'd said nothing about Elizabeth being unable to read Darcy's letters with comprehension. And she'd been hardly able to sign her own name. The mistress of Pemberley, unable to write. Or do figures, he gathered, from Miss Mary's quick offer. At least one of the three women could do sums, and Miss Mary could obviously read, she quoted the Bible so readily.

But her looks…He'd rarely seen a woman as unfortunately plain as Mary Bennet. It might be better were she ugly. At least then her face would have some interest. Mrs. Bennet, too, showed no beauty. He'd no way to tell if her florid countenance had been pretty when she was young, but seeing Miss Mary, Darcy doubted it.

He scrubbed his hands over his face. He'd so hoped that when his wife's injuries healed, he'd find her to be beautiful. He was a Darcy. Master of Pemberley. He was meant to marry someone lovely. Elegant.

Intelligent. Well-read and well spoken. He should have paid her off. What in God's name had he done?

He arrived in Scotland in the perfect mood to deal with his erstwhile steward's scheming assistant, which he did with precision and efficiency. However, the man's arrest and prosecution seen to, Darcy found the estate in much greater disarray than he would have guessed.

He needed a new steward. That much, he'd concluded before arriving. What he hadn't realized was how much work it would take to put the property right before selecting one. With the old steward gone and the ledgers in disarray, no one but Darcy knew the estate well enough to make the decisions that needed to be made. Once order was restored, then he could bring in a new steward.

He settled into the house the steward had used, wishing he'd hired a young, married man the last time, rather than an elderly arthritic one. Then there would have been no dictations, and his family would have notified Darcy of his demise. As it was, it would take ages to put the estate right. In resignation, he got started.

For days, Darcy sat in the tiny office on a chair not quite large enough for him, his back to a narrow window that didn't permit enough light to stave off the need for candles, going over the account books with care. His neck muscles cramped from so many hours in the same position. His eyes protested the abuse. He considered that improvements should be made to the house before he could hope to get a younger man with a family to move in.

Something else he would need to see to before he could return to England.

A tentative knock brought his head up. One of the footmen stood in the open doorway with a tray of letters, looking meek. Darcy's dark mood upon his arrival and his subsequent ousting of his old steward's assistant in a rather dramatic and unceremonious manner seemed to have put a mild fear of him in the remaining staff.

"Yes?"

"Letters, sir. You like them to be brought immediately."

"Yes, I do. You may leave them."

The man scuttled in, put the tray on the corner of the desk, and scuttled away.

The top letter was an expense report from Mr. Smith, the steward he'd sent once he'd realized he couldn't trust his wife to manage her household. The next, a report from his man in London saying they'd had no luck yet proving that Wickham had sabotaged the bridges or accosted Darcy at gunpoint. After that, the address penned in Mr. Smith's hand, came a letter from his wife. The single page, scrawled in embarrassingly childish writing, held thanks for all he'd done and a brief inquiry after the welfare of his sister.

Darcy imagined either the mother or the sister had insisted that Elizabeth pen the missive, realizing thanks were owed. Darcy wrote a brief demurral back, trying to use small words that Elizabeth would be able to decipher, and made no mention of Georgiana. Compulsively, he then put Elizabeth's letter in a drawer. It seemed inappropriate to burn his wife's letters, but it was inappropriate to leave them where others could see them. More than the content, her childish writing would embarrass him.

How could he install Elizabeth as mistress of Pemberley? Yet he must. He could not leave her in a rented home in Kent forever, and the alternative was to take her to town. He'd be the laughingstock of London. Frustration welled at how a single, unchangeable mistake looked fit to mar what had until now been a well lived life. Tamping that down, he took up the next letter.

Written on much finer paper and in a lovely, flowing hand, the missive was from his sister, one of quite a few to arrive since he'd reached Scotland. Georgiana wrote with thoughtless frequency, her letters filled with frivolities. About letters written to her by school friends or relations. Long walks, novels, and riding in Rosings Park. And, of course, endless pleas for him to hire her a new companion and install her in London, especially since Anne's usual companion, Mrs. Jenkinson, had been permitted time to visit her family for so long as Georgiana remained to keep Anne company. His sister went on at length about her feelings on being Anne's companion and not having one of her own, to which he wrote back that his man in London had orders to find someone suitable. Darcy would interview several very carefully vetted candidates once he settled matters in Scotland.

His correspondences, such as they were, seen to, Darcy returned to the ledgers, absently rubbing his neck to alleviate the tension there.

His days progressed like this, with little to interrupt or change them, as he went over the books and visited the farm workers. After two more weeks, interspersed with Georgiana's all but daily missives, another barely legible letter arrived from his wife. It spoke of her father's visit, her mother's departure and the arrival of another sister. This one she called Kitty, which evoked a wince as Darcy read. Of course, the vulgar sort of family into which he'd married would thusly shorten the very elegant name of Catherine. Likely, this Kitty's full name stuck in their uneducated craws.

The mention reminded him that he'd not yet taken the time to meet Elizabeth's paternal parent or even learn the names of her other sisters. When he wrote back, he would inform her that he would like to meet Mr. Bennet and ask for the names of the other two Bennet girls. Hopefully theirs would not be so ordinary as Mary or so silly as Kitty.

Elizabeth's letter concluded, in her painful scrawl, with a line about an upcoming topic to be posed to the House of Lords and another giving her opinion on a lofty Greek volume. Darcy read those with a second wince, this time for his own behavior. In his previous, admittedly terse, message he must have somehow conveyed his disappointment. He wondered from whom his wife had sought the final two lines in her effort to please him? Likely Mr. Smith. Darcy's man in London had recommended Smith in view of his intelligence and the expense reports Smith sent weekly concerning the rented house in Kent were in a neat hand, cogent, and with correctly tallied lines of figures.

Tempted as he was to toss this new letter from his wife into the grate, he shoved it in the drawer he'd designated for her letters. He doubted he would ever want to look at them again but he could always burn them later. For now, he would keep her letters as he kept all letters. Before adding her newest, he took out her first letter again. The handwriting on the latest letter had improved. Maybe she'd sought lessons? That, at least, showed a willingness to learn.

With his wife's correspondence and another of Mr. Smith's reports also came a letter from his man in London, which contained his report on Mr. Bennet of Longbourn. The man conveyed Mr. Bennet as quite respectable and his holdings as well managed, adding that his daughters were pretty and sought after in the community. Darcy read it twice, certain the fellow must have it wrong or be a sycophant of the worst sort. The Bennet women he'd met were unattractive and dull. Why should the other three be any different?

Additionally, the letter confirmed that the woman Darcy had married was Elizabeth Bennet, who'd been traveling with her aunt and uncle, the Gardiners. Darcy read that twice, as well, aware of a small, almost desperate hope he'd harbored that the scenario at the bridge had, after all, been a scheme of Wickham's. A scant hope, true, in view of how badly injured Elizabeth had been but Darcy wouldn't have put it past Wickham to throw her down the hill with no regard even if they colluded. With a sigh for what couldn't be undone, Darcy stowed the report and returned to ordering his holding.

About a month after Darcy's arrival in Scotland, there came a knock on the frame of the open office door that held no meekness at all. Darcy jerked his head up to take in his cousin, Colonel Fitzwilliam, framed in the doorway.

"Richard," Darcy greeted, immediately cheered. "What brings you?"

"Darcy." Richard came in, rendering the small room even smaller, and settled into the single wooden chair across from the desk, making it creak. "My answer will drop that smile from your face. Aunt Catherine."

Darcy's brows drew together.

"Told you," Richard said with a chuckle.

"What does our aunt want that is so dire she must involve you?"

"First, I have not yet offered my felicitations in person. I wish you well in your marriage."

That only deepened Darcy's frown. "I appreciate that."

Richard eyed him for a moment but, rather than press the topic, said, "Aunt Catherine and Anne are livid. All they have from you and, I believe Georgiana, is what I do, that this Miss Bennet saved you from attack by a highwayman, was injured and compromised in the process, and you had no choice but to marry her."

"That is an accurate summary," Darcy said, voice as devoid of emotions as he could make it.

"So you had no choice but to wed this stranger?"

"I did not see one at the time and now the deed is done and cannot be undone."

Richard cocked an eyebrow. "So, you wish it could be?"

Darcy wouldn't concede that, not fully and not even to his favorite cousin. "I admit that I always assumed I would choose my wife."

Richard considered that. Words a touch tentative, he said, "Aunt Catherine believes you may have been given false information about the woman. She investigated. You should know, one of the local servants here is in her pay."

"Aunt Catherine is spying on me?"

"Come now, that can't surprise you."

Darcy shook his head dismissively.

Richard nodded in grim acknowledgement. "Her spy has informed her that your wife's letters are illiterate. Conversely, Aunt Catherine's inquiries reveal that Miss Elizabeth Bennet of Longbourn is intelligent, well read, well versed in the classics, which her father taught her, and aware of what is transpiring in the world." Richard cleared his throat, grimaced, and continued, "Our aunt feels that the illiterate letters may be the result of someone else pretending to be Elizabeth Bennet. If so, that would be grounds for annulment."

Darcy's jaw tensed with chagrin at having his secret, guilty hope echoed by his aunt. "You may inform our aunt that her concerns are misplaced. I had my own people look into my wife and her relations. The woman I married is Elizabeth Bennet."

"Yet you do not deny the report of illiteracy?"

Darcy refused to either confirm his wife's shame, a correctable inadequacy, or to lie. "Whatever else may be, the fact remains that Elizabeth almost certainly saved my life, with no hope of benefit to herself and at great personal risk."

"Still, even if she is who she says, if she was misrepresented to you, that could be grounds for an annulment with a properly, ah, sympathetic priest. I'm certain one could be located."

"Where would that leave Elizabeth?" Darcy countered. "Compromised, married, and cast aside?

"So you will fall upon your sword?"

Darcy sat up straight, every muscle rigid. "I will do what is right. She is my wife. I will not seek an annulment."

"Ah, that famous Darcy pride."

Darcy glared across the desk at his cousin.

Richard shrugged, uncowed. "Yes, well, I told our aunt you must see things that way or you wouldn't have married the girl and remained married to her. Now, my message is delivered, so let us put that nonsense behind us." He leaned forward and tapped the desk. "What are you doing here in Scotland? Georgiana is about ready to disown you."

"It's this mess with my former steward," Darcy began. That, he was ready to delve into in considerable detail.

They carried the discussion of Darcy's Scottish holding into dinner, kept it up over brandy, and began again the following morning. Happy for a reason to take a break from the endless ledgers, Darcy spent the next day riding his holding with Richard, meeting tenants, and assessing the state of the land. By the time they returned to the steward's house for a late tea, Darcy felt confident that improvements were required for more than the house in which he stayed. He would arrange for work to be done on the workers' cottages as well.

It wasn't until they sat in a small parlor with their port that evening that Richard said, "Not that sheep aren't fascinating, but now that we're past our aunt's machinations and your temper has, hopefully, cooled on the subject, I wouldn't mind if you told me about your wife. I assume she is brave?"

Darcy's pride balked at admitting he worried she was not, but with whom could he discuss his doubts if not Richard? Sharing Elizabeth's failings with a sympathetic listener might make them easier to bear. "I cannot tell if she is brave or foolish."

"We are all both, I would say."

He shook his head. "Rather, I cannot tell if she risked her life to save mine because she is noble of spirit, or dim of wit."

"Ah," Richard said, brow furrowing. "Maybe if you gave me more detail?" He held out a cautionary hand before Darcy could rebuke him. "I ask for me, to keep between us, not for our aunt."

Rather than insult his cousin's honor, Darcy must accept his assurance. "There is little more detail to tell. Someone had sabotaged the two main bridges between Rosings and Ramsgate. Having traveled the route so many times as a lad, I knew of a third, local way. A narrow road that crosses a ravine, then follows said ravine a ways before twisting into the forest and to the next village over."

Richard nodded. "I believe I crossed that bridge once, riding. Not really a roadway for carriages."

"No, but I felt that, knowing the way, I could guide my driver on, so I climbed up beside him and we set out."

"So you were in the perch?"

"I was, yes. Quite vulnerable when a masked man stepped into the road as we crossed the bridge and aimed a pistol at our horses."

"At the horses?"

Darcy nodded. "I do think that was his aim, although I suppose it's difficult to say." Should he mention that the man's eyes, his yowl, had seemed so like Wickham? "When the railings were later checked, they'd been sabotaged. I can only conclude that the goal was to scare the horses into taking us over. Less opportunity for anyone to believe we'd been murdered, I suppose." He frowned, wondering if that was true. "Regardless, a woman rushed from the trees and ran at him, shouting, and pushed him as he shot, ruining his aim. He then threw her down the ravine and ran off."

Richard stared at him, port glass held loose and forgotten in one hand. "That is an amazing story."

"Yes, well, it was an unusual occurrence."

"And you wonder if she thought before acting and did so regardless, or acted without thought, diving into danger and possible ruin without a care for consequences."

Relieved that Richard comprehended so well, Darcy nodded. "Yes. Precisely."

"Have you asked her?"

Darcy answered that with a frown.

"I see. Well, that would be my first recommendation to you." Richard's gaze grew abstract, thoughtful. "Two bridges sabotaged, and the railing on the local pathway."

Darcy nodded, although he didn't think his cousin attended him.

"This bandit obviously wanted to funnel traffic his way, where he could hope to catch travelers alone on an obscure road, but the traffic he could hope for would be local and thus not as rich as one might expect elsewhere." Richard shook his head, his frown not easing. "But why sabotage the railings? Why kill you rather than rob you? And leave so much visual evidence, to make any subsequent travelers wary?"

Darcy sipped his port, unwilling to comment.

"I should look into this matter more. Investigate the site. The other two bridges. Am I correct that a man died at one? Maybe he was robbed in a similar, disastrous way to how the gunman attempted to rob you."

That was too much. Richard's interest rendered Darcy's silence a lie. He set his port down on the low table between them. "It was George Wickham."

Richard's gaze focused on Darcy with sharp intensity. "I beg your pardon?"

"I have no proof, but I'd swear the masked gunman was Wickham and the entire event orchestrated to keep me from getting to Georgiana."

"That begs further explanation."

"He was eloping with her. I arrived as they were departing."

"My ward nearly eloped with George Wickham, and you didn't think to tell me?"

"Our ward. Jointly. She got into the carriage, but I stopped them before it went anywhere."

Richard eyed him a touch sardonically.

Darcy took back up his glass. "Well, I've told you now. Did you expect me to record the incident in writing?"

Richard's ire dimmed. "No. No, of course not." He sipped his port. "May I assume you're seeking proof that it was Wickham?"

"I am, but meeting with no success. My coachman confessed to having no idea who the man might be, though he has briefly met Wickham. I've hired the runners to investigate it, but so far no, no proof. We couldn't follow the gunman when he ran since the woman, that is, Elizabeth, was at the bottom of the gully, needing help. You know Wickham. He'll have an alibi. Nor can I mention my belief that he had a motive, since that would mean admitting that he was seducing Georgiana."

"Seducing?" Richard sputtered.

"She assures me it didn't go that far."

"Yes, well, now I understand why you had to let her governess go with such alacrity and why you had to leave her with Aunt Catherine, and I can even extrapolate why your decision to marry needed to be made so quickly, as you had to leave the woman who'd saved you in order to collect Georgiana."

Darcy nodded, relieved. He should have told Richard the whole of it straight off. Richard always understood.

As if to contradict that thought, Richard continued, "But what I don't understand is why you, a new husband, are hiding in Scotland counting ewes."

Darcy scowled, having nothing he wanted to say to that.

Chapter Ten

Wickham's mind roiled as he strode down the alleyway that would bring him to the kitchen door of Mrs. Younge's boarding house. He didn't wish to go in through the front, hoping to see her without anyone else the wiser. Darcy had set people asking questions. Pointed questions about Wickham's character and his whereabouts on certain dates. Even though Wickham had donned a farmer's hat and covered his face with his scarf before stepping from the trees, and stood across a bridge from him, somehow Darcy had guessed who'd pointed a gun his way.

No, at the horses. He could honestly swear that he hadn't expected Darcy to be visible. A magistrate would see he spoke the truth in that. Why would the great Mr. Darcy of Pemberley be riding beside his coachman, after all?

Better still, it had been at a bird. That's what he would tell people. A crow whose death would save crops. He was practicing his shooting and saw a likely target, for the good of the community. He wasn't looking beyond the bird, and he'd had his scarf up against the dust blown off the dry dirt road.

It was good to have an alternative explanation because the high and mighty Darcy wanted retribution, but it would be even better to have an alibi. Hopefully, Mrs. Younge would place him in Ramsgate, but with the runners looking into him, having people able to connect him with Mrs. Younge was to be avoided. Who knew what her tenants and staff would say, and to whom?

But going to her was worth the risk. Try as he might, Wickham couldn't come up with a way to halt Darcy's inquiries, but Mrs. Younge was the only person who could implicate him or save him. Wickham had left her with a warning. He wished to make certain she hadn't forgotten that warning carried with it a threat.

He wrinkled his nose as he traversed the narrow alleyway, trying to avoid getting anything too revolting on his boots. Despite a lack of funds, he'd had them shined only yesterday. Appearances were of the utmost when your comforts were earned through charm.

He reached the kitchen door to the delicious odor of stew and grinned. He'd timed his visit in the hope of finding her in the kitchen, both to avoid being seen and to get a free meal. He stepped in without knocking to the startled countenance of a young woman in an apron. Her mouth hung open and a wooden spoon dangled from her hand, ready to drop into the pot she stood before. The aroma of fresh baked bread washed over him, mingling with that of the stew, making his mouth water.

"You aren't Mrs. Younge," Wickham said with a charming smile, calculated to put any young woman at ease.

"No, sir. Missus is in her office, sir."

Pretending a familiarity he didn't have, he posited, "Is she? That would be the second door down the hall, on the left?" He pointed across the kitchen to the far doorway.

"It, ah, it's the little room immediately through there, on the right, sir."

He chuckled, pleasantly rueful. "Silly me. I'm forever confusing my left and right." He strode across the kitchen, all confidence.

The cook watched him but made no protest. With a parting smile, Wickham went into the hall, pleased he'd escaped giving a name. Before anyone else could sight him, he ducked into the indicated room and closed the door behind him.

Mrs. Younge looked up from the ledger before her, pen poised. She grimaced and blotted ink from the tip, then set the pen aside and capped the well. "Mr. Wickham."

"Mrs. Younge." He dropped into the small chair across from her desk, where he imagined household staff sat while being berated or praised. "I came to check on you. How do you fare?"

"I *was* perfectly well."

She was determined to be unpleasant, then? Should he bother to charm her?

"I take it you've heard the news," she continued. "Though why that would bring you to me, I've no idea."

"News?" he repeated in unfeigned confusion.

"Yes. Of Mr. Darcy's nuptials." She studied him a moment. "It was in all the papers. At least, the respectable ones."

As if he'd squander coin on buying papers or time on reading them. "Darcy married? His cousin Anne de Bourgh?" Had one of Wickham's

90

dreams come true? Though it mattered little if he couldn't wed Georgiana.

"No. An Elizabeth Bennet. Of Hertfordshire."

Wickham stared at her, unable to comprehend the words. "Elizabeth Bennet?" He had no idea who that was. He knew everything about Darcy. How could Darcy marry someone of whom he'd never heard? "Who is Elizabeth Bennet?"

"I've no idea. I assumed you would."

Wickham shook his head. He'd hoped for Miss de Bourgh, and entertained the possibility of Caroline Bingley, sister to one of Darcy's closest companions. Wickham considered her a lesser option as she would never be susceptible to his charm, being an even bigger snob than Darcy, and she looked to have strong childbearing hips. "Bennet, from Hertfordshire, you say?"

"Yes, but as that's not what brings you, it's of no import."

On the contrary. It was very important to him. The trouble with Darcy was that there were few people for whom he truly cared, which made it difficult to find a weakness. This new wife was an opportunity. Wickham must know all he could about anyone close to Darcy to succeed in getting what was his by right. What was owed to him. More than that, a wife might provide some means by which to halt Darcy's inquiries into where Wickham had been when the bridges were sabotaged.

But Mrs. Younge was correct. That wasn't why he'd come. "People have been asking questions about me."

She frowned. "People?"

"Bow Street Runners."

Her eyes went wide, as well they might. The runners were not to be trifled with. "And that concerns me why?"

Wickham leaned forward, showing all his teeth. "Because you may believe you know things about me. Things I may have done. I came to make sure you aren't repeating your beliefs to anyone."

Her features pinched together. "Certainly not."

"Good, because I know that you cheated Darcy, and you conspired with me. Don't forget that."

"Are you saying that if I mention my…possible suspicions, we will call them, in regard to anything to do with the bridges in Kent, you will reveal that I cheated Mr. Darcy out of a few pounds and helped you to convince his sister to elope with you?"

Wickham leaned back, folding his arms over his chest and relaxing his gritted smile. "You understand me so well. That's why we get along."

"Oh, I understand you, to be certain." She tapped her desk with one fingertip. "Now you understand me. My friend still has your signed agreement. If you attempt to harass me again, I will see that contract handed over to Mr. Darcy and I will tell him everything I know about those bridges, my own hide be damned. Am I clear?"

Wickham sat forward again, scowling. "Keep in mind that accidents like that bridge don't only happen in the country, Mrs. Younge."

"Are you threatening me?"

"I'm reminding you what I am capable of."

"Very well. Consider me reminded and go. We are done here."

They would have been, his threat delivered, but now that he knew about Darcy's marriage, he required funds. He must go to Hertfordshire and learn all he could about these Bennets. He didn't like unknowns in Darcy's life, and he needed to explore their potential. He may find a chink in Darcy's armor. Who knew? In marrying countrified nobodies, Darcy may have opened himself to further machinations.

Wickham could only hope so, as he hadn't found another opportunity since he'd nearly claimed Georgiana as his wife.

"I said we're done, Mr. Wickham."

"We are if you give me ten pounds."

"I beg your pardon?"

"Ten pounds and I won't be back to trouble you." That would get him started at the tables. He could win what more he required.

She studied him in that hard, cold way of hers that always put him in mind of his and Darcy's tutors. He assumed that was why Darcy had selected her to watch over Georgiana.

"I think not."

That surprised him. She'd hired a cook. She was obviously doing well. She could spare ten pounds. "I beg your pardon?"

"I am not giving you ten pounds."

He gave her a wicked, smug grin. "You want me to return." He knew his charms had worked on her.

"On the contrary. Firstly, I do not have ten pounds here. As I told you, I employ a bank. But more importantly, if I truly believed that giving you ten pounds would rid me of you for all time, I would not hesitate to secure the funds for you. But I do not believe that. Giving you money would only ensure you return, likely with greater and greater frequency."

Wickham pushed to his feet. He didn't need to sit there and take insults from her. "If my word is not good enough for you, then we are done, madam."

She let out a sigh. "If only I could believe that."

"You may," he huffed and stamped from the room.

Back in the hall, he composed himself. He shouldn't permit Mrs. Younge to aggravate him. She would come around. She'd kissed him willingly enough that one time, after all. He was a good looking fellow. Affable and entertaining. Women enjoyed his company.

Regardless, he'd issued his warning. Now it was time to go, but not before he charmed bread and stew from the girl in the kitchen.

He ate as large a meal as he could finagle, which was the least Mrs. Younge owed him, seated on the back stoop in case she entered the kitchen. He'd also wheedled a mug of ale from the girl, pleased to finally have the drink Mrs. Younge had denied him all those weeks ago. When he finished, he brought the bowl and mug back in, after listening to ensure the cook was alone, so as to be well thought of. The cook dimpled at him so much, he felt certain she'd feed him again if he returned.

Leaving the alleyway behind Mrs. Younge's boarding house, Wickham started the long walk back to the little room he'd rented in a far less prosperous area of London. The day was hot. His slow pace gave him plenty of time to rail against Mrs. Younge and her unfair treatment of him.

Once that topic ran its course in his thoughts, he moved on to his favorite litany. Everything that was right in his life was due to Mr. George Darcy. Everything that was wrong was due to his son, Fitzwilliam Darcy, who'd inherited his father's property but not his obligation to care for his godson.

But Wickham would have his revenge. He would have what Darcy owed him.

On that thought, he changed his course. He didn't need to go back to his dingy little room, the room to which Darcy had relegated him when he'd interrupted the elopement. He needed the finer parts of town. A woman to charm whose fancy bracelet might accidentally slip from her wrist, or a gentleman in need of a wager or two to alleviate the heaviness of his purse. Even something he might pinch from a window thrown wide in a desperate attempt to let in a cooling breath of air. Anything to get him to Hertfordshire and these Bennets.

He would study them. Meet them. Ingratiate himself. The Bennets would have a weakness and whatever that weakness was, Wickham would exploit it. He would find a way to make Darcy call off the runners, and to get what was owed to him.

Chapter Eleven

Elizabeth sat on the sofa in the front parlor of the home her husband rented for her, giving a respectable impression of calm reading. Kitty, seated in an armchair to her left, appeared to be in all actuality embroidering while Mary, on the other end of the sofa, held a book. Elizabeth suspected her middle sister also made a pretense at reading, rather than a reality of it, for they both awaited Mr. Evans with considerable impatience, though for vastly different reasons.

Two months had passed since the would-be bandit had pushed Elizabeth down the side of the gully. No more outward signs of the attack were in evidence, save the splint Mr. Evans would remove when he arrived. Better still, her bouts of dizziness and lapses in memory seemed to have dissipated. At least, she hoped so. They'd grown less and less frequent, but she couldn't be entirely certain of never succumbing to the experience again.

With what she knew to be wicked glee, she looked forward to writing to her husband. After her first letter written with her off hand, she'd worried about legibility and wondered if she should swallow her pride and dictate to Mary. Then Mr. Darcy's reply had arrived, terse, almost exclusively monosyllabic, lacking any actual information, and written in an impeccable, bold hand. Studying his truncated reply to her attempt at communication and pleasantness, which had been managed through considerable diligence and actual suffering, Elizabeth had begun to suspect he thought her dull and illiterate.

She'd pondered what she knew of her husband, aside from that he seemed tall, attractive, and stern. She knew that he had relations in the peerage, both from the letters of well-wishers and because she'd finally read her stack of letters which, among Jane's well wishes and her father's sympathies, had contained her Uncle Gardiner's report on Mr. Darcy. Those pages had revealed Mr. Darcy to be wealthy and very respectable. Elizabeth had assumed the former, given the ease with which he'd procured a special license and rented and staffed a house for her, and guessed the latter, because it would take a respectable man to have done right by her as he had.

Which, all told, made him the sort of man who could expect to do far, far better than the daughter of a country gentleman with practically no dowry and ties to trade, as he undoubtedly thought of her. Something his letter showed he felt keenly.

An idea which had somewhat enraged her, especially as she'd been in both mental and physical distress. She hadn't set out to risk her life and upend her future for him. She hadn't asked for any of this.

Not that he needed to live in a state of perpetual gratitude. After all, he had saved her as well. But he could at least suspend judgment of her until she recovered.

She'd tested her theory that he thought her addlebrained with her next letter, deliberately including topics which would hold interest for a man like Mr. Darcy. Again, he'd been brief and uninformative in his reply, and used simple words. After that, her judgment confirmed, tormenting him with her awkwardly penned missives had become a form of entertainment for her.

Now, however, the game had begun to sour, for she didn't really wish her husband to feel her beneath him in intellect, as her father did her mother. Elizabeth had seen how that sort of inequality could harm a marriage. Besides which, she had something important to convey in her next letter. The banns had already been read once. Mary and Mr. Evans were to wed in two weeks' time.

A knock sounded.

Mary's head came up, her brows drawn into a vee. "He's early."

"He must be eager," Elizabeth said with a smile for her.

One of the maids appeared in the parlor doorway. "Are you home to Mr. Smith, Mrs. Darcy?"

Elizabeth hesitated longer than she normally would have before nodding, taken off guard by which gentleman called and still not accustomed to being addressed as Mrs. Darcy, even after nearly two months. "Certainly. We're always at home to Mr. Smith."

The man her husband had hired to oversee a household that Elizabeth ought to be overseeing and which Mary did oversee, Mr. Smith was intelligent, quiet, and dreadfully smitten with Kitty. The maid went back out to take his coat and Elizabeth looked over to find that Kitty still stitched, face down but cheeks pink and rounded with a smile.

Mr. Smith entered, whip thin but managing not to be too stork-like, and bowed. "Good afternoon Mrs. Darcy, Miss Bennet, Miss Kitty. I hope I am not disturbing anything?"

"Certainly not," Elizabeth said. "Please, sit." She resisted her mother's usual gambit of pointing out the obvious, that an empty chair stood beside the one in which Kitty sat. "I'll send for tea." Looking past him, Elizabeth nodded to the maid who'd let him in and who waited for precisely such a request.

The girl curtsied and slipped away. Mr. Smith entered and indeed sat beside Kitty, who'd regained her composure. Smile demure and cheeks holding only a trace of rosy hue, she looked up from her work to stare at him.

"I trust all is in order with the books?" Elizabeth said as it became apparent that Kitty and Mr. Smith were incapable of speaking to each other.

Mr. Smith turned to her. "All is in perfect order, Mrs. Darcy." That assurance delivered, he went back to gazing on Kitty.

"I didn't actually doubt," Elizabeth said. "I know Mary has a good head for figures." What more could she say? "I will be taking the books over after today, so I'm afraid you'll have to speak to me about them each week from now on. Mary has been a tremendous help, but the splint is coming off my arm today," and her head seemed sound again so she felt certain she wouldn't miscalculate the figures, "and I do think it being my house it should be my responsibility."

She ceased talking, to more silence. Would no one else speak? Was this what had driven her mother to babble? One sister dumbstruck and the other staring at the doorway while holding a book, not attending to Elizabeth's words at all?

She wished Jane were there. Jane would speak. Mrs. Bennet had denied every request thus far, however. Once she'd learned that Elizabeth now possessed noble connections, she'd forbidden, in her words, 'her two pretty daughters from being squandered on some small town in Kent when Elizabeth could introduce them to little short of royalty.'

"Yes, that is right. I'd heard you're to have the use of your arm back today," Mr. Smith finally said, dragging his attention from Kitty for long enough to utter the words.

"I am, and I'm terribly looking forward to it." Elizabeth paused again, waiting, but no one else spoke. She suppressed a sigh and returned to pretending to read. It was rude, but so was forcing her to carry the whole of the conversation.

Two maids came in with trays and started setting out the tea service. A knock sounded at the door, causing one to hasten off. She returned with Mr. Evans which brought Mr. Smith to his feet and commenced a swirl of easy greetings, everyone being well acquainted.

When the greetings finished, Mr. Evans directed his attention to Elizabeth. "I believe we should remove the splint in a room where soap and water are readily available. You will want to wash up after."

"Certainly." Elizabeth moved to join him by the parlor door, then turned back to say, "Mary, could I trouble you to accompany us? In case Mr. Evans requires any assistance." She then added to one of the maids, "If you could remain with Kitty and Mr. Smith until we return, please?"

The maid nodded. Mary gave Elizabeth a grateful look and rushed over to stand on Mr. Evans' other side. Elizabeth, feeling she'd done all a good chaperone could to facilitate unions, happiness, and the proper preservation of reputations, led the way from the room.

Mr. Evans was correct that Elizabeth wished to wash up. Her arm, while whole, felt weak and tender. It also appeared overly slender and white to the point of a sallow cast. She sent Mary and Mr. Evans back down to the parlor while she scrubbed at skin long compressed in darkness and decided a shawl was desired to hide as much of her arm as possible.

She hoped it would be in a more normal state by Mary's wedding, and by the time she saw her husband again...whenever that might be. He'd been aggravatingly vague about that and about his business in Scotland. Like as not, he'd decided her too dim to be able to count days and so did not trouble to explain. Trying to shake the aggravation that thought caused, she returned to the parlor, halting for a moment in the doorway.

Kitty and Mr. Smith held their tea and saucers, turned in their armchairs to face each other. Mary sat with Mr. Evans on the sofa, both straight backed and proper, not anywhere near the center where they might touch, but looking like cats who'd discovered how to open the larder. Both couples chatted amiably and animatedly, Kitty and Mr. Smith about travel and Mary and Mr. Evans about husbandry.

Elizabeth sighed. She did not in the slightest begrudge her younger sisters their obvious happiness. She simply wished she could have what they'd found. Even have had the opportunity, the mere chance, to have what they'd found. Elizabeth had lived her whole life in the same place with the same scant few young men, none of whom had ever sparked an inkling of interest.

This trip with her Aunt and Uncle Gardiner had been her first grand foray into the world. Yes, it had ended with her wedded and creating opportunities for her sisters, which she supposed had been the aim of her mother in encouraging the venture. Maybe even the aim of both of her parents and the Gardiners. Elizabeth wouldn't even have objected if told her wedding a wealthy, respectable gentleman was how the trip was fated to end.

Yet she couldn't help but feel as if she'd missed out on something. Something precious. Irreplaceable and irreplicable.

She wished Jane could visit, or that she might visit Jane. Maybe she could. It was not as if her husband needed her here, in Kent, specifically. Or anywhere else, for all she could tell. Nor had he forbidden her to travel. He probably didn't believe her capable of hitting on the idea.

"Lizzy, how is your arm?" Kitty asked brightly.

"Come have tea," Mary added. "Whyever are you hovering in the doorway?"

Elizabeth mustered a smile and went in. She sat on the sofa opposite Mary and Mr. Evans, near Mr. Smith's chair, and made a production of being able to pour tea. Her arm shook.

"It will take some time to fully recover your strength in that arm," Mr. Evans advised, seeing her tremble as she poured.

"I expected as much." Elizabeth placed the teapot down with care, glad everyone else had already been served so the pot wasn't that heavy.

"Don't rush the muscles," Mr. Evans continued.

"Never fear, sir. I will do nothing to jeopardize my recovery."

"And I'll still be here for two more weeks," Mary said to Mr. Evans. "I'll look after her."

"You are very considerate."

Mary pinked at his compliment.

"And I'm not going anywhere," Kitty said firmly. She cast a look askance at Mr. Smith, who smiled back.

"Yes, well, no one is departing until after the wedding, to be certain," Elizabeth agreed.

"Do you think Mr. Darcy will attend the celebration?" Mr. Smith asked.

Elizabeth took a sip of tea, finding the cup not too heavy, and replied, "Now that the use of my arm is restored to me, I will write to him and invite him. We are, after all, having the wedding breakfast in his house."

Mr. Evans appeared alarmed. "You haven't told him yet?"

"I wanted to be able to write with my good hand when I impart the news."

Mr. Evans made a fussy, tsking sound. "Mr. Darcy is a distinguished gentleman. He may not wish us to hold a gathering in his home."

Elizabeth struggled not to show the annoyance that comment sparked, hardening her smile in place. Her husband had spent less than two hours there when they married, and not been back since. What did he care if she threw a wedding breakfast? "Mr. Darcy gives me a generous allowance." Of which she'd spent very little. "A wedding breakfast for Mary and you fits very easily into that budget."

"It does," Mr. Smith added.

His affirmation only annoyed Elizabeth more. She should be able to keep her budget without someone overseeing it. Maybe not at first when she wasn't well and couldn't even do arithmetic, but months had passed since the incident. In that time, Mr. Smith had found not the slightest error in the handling of the household. Even if Mary had tallied the figures until now, Elizabeth had proven she could manage the home her husband rented for her quite well. Did he expect Mr. Smith to oversee her forever?

"Thank you again for hosting our wedding breakfast, Elizabeth," Mary said, eyes shining. A blush crept up her cheeks. "I'm looking forward to it."

"It's going to be very enjoyable," Elizabeth said, seeking equanimity.

Kitty nodded her agreement. "I do wish Jane and Lydia could come, though."

"I do as well." Mary pulled a face, somewhat belying her words. "Actually, I do not, if it would mean Mama coming. It is terrible of me to say, but I should rather marry without her here."

"Now dearest," Mr. Evans said. "You must honor your mother."

"I do." Mary looked down to study the hands she twined in her lap.

"She does," Elizabeth agreed. She added a smile to her next words. "It's simply far easier to honor Mrs. Bennet from afar."

Kitty laughed, Elizabeth joining her, and Mary managed a small smile.

Elizabeth tried to keep the cheer of that moment with her as tea progressed, and into the remainder of the afternoon. She must attempt a pleasant frame of mind when she wrote to her husband. When she mentioned the wedding, should she ask him to bring his sister? Elizabeth would like to finally meet her.

Chapter Twelve

Darcy walked up to the steward's house with a sense of satisfaction. After Richard left, Darcy had relocated to a nearby inn and then reordered the home. The house had only one usable bedroom when he'd arrived, but the purchase of another bed coupled with the sale of a huge armoire made it clear that the second room could be a bedroom. This, among other changes, had allowed him to attract a younger man with a wife and children, aged six and four. Slightly over a week ago, the family had taken possession. Now, Darcy had come to go over his new steward, Mr. Callington's, first week of work. Reaching the freshly painted front door, Darcy knocked.

The door swung open not to a servant but to an attractive young woman, soberly yet elegantly dressed. "Mr. Darcy?"

He nodded, realizing she must be Mrs. Callington. Even his steward had been privileged to select his own wife and had found a lovely and elegant woman. Taking in her poise and the intelligence in her eyes, he imagined she wrote and read quite well.

She backed into the entrance hall with, "I'm Mrs. Callington and, sir, I would like to take this opportunity to thank you for offering my husband this position and for the use of this home." Her eyes shone with happiness and sincerity. "It's truly wonderful. Almost too magnificent for us, I daresay."

Darcy went in with a dip of his head.

"Mr. Callington is waiting in his office." She turned, leading the way, but looked back with a smile to add, "I imagine you already know where it is."

They reached the office, the door waiting open. Mr. Callington lifted his gaze from the ledger before him, expression welcoming, and stood as Darcy went into the room.

"If you'll excuse me," Mrs. Callington said. "I should leave you to your work, and it's time for the children's writing lessons."

"Writing lessons?" Darcy repeated. Did he have their ages incorrect? "Even the younger?"

Mrs. Callington nodded. "My mother believed in accustoming young hands to a pencil early. It worked well for me, so I continue the tradition with my children." She gave her husband a fond smile, dipped her head to Darcy, and left.

If only Elizabeth's mother had been similarly trained and had passed the skills and idea on to her offspring.

"Mr. Darcy. Do come in. Please, sit. Which side of the desk would you prefer? Can I send for anything?"

Darcy pressed thoughts of his plain, illiterate wife from his mind as best he could. "This is your home now, Mr. Callington. This side of the desk will do well for me."

Darcy and Mr. Callington settled into their work, Darcy finding the man's decisions sound and his arithmetic flawless. He also had good handwriting. Darcy did sight one small error in spelling, goods marked as *recieved*, rather than *received*, but it wasn't repeated, and Darcy forwent pointing it out. Overall, he was quite pleased. With the Callingtons, at least.

On the ride back to the inn, he couldn't help dwelling on his wife. Writing lessons. Simple, routine lessons in how to craft and read letters. Should he offer them to her? Insist on them? He'd heard it was far more difficult for an adult to learn to read and write, and all knew the English tongue, noble though it was, held many pitfalls when adapted to the page. As Mr. Callington's error proved.

Darcy's carriage rolled to a halt before the inn. He frowned. His wife's spelling was impeccable. Did her more educated younger sister spell for her? But then, why not simply write for her?

He returned to his room to find Stevens hard at work on his boots, polishing them to a bright shine, and waved him back onto his stool as he made to stand. Darcy went to the desk near the window and took out Elizabeth's last letter.

Moving to stand in the window for better light, he studied the page. Her sentences showed definite complexity. If he considered them, rather than skim the page in disgust, her ideas were thoughtful. The handwriting was atrocious, but he could swear it was an improvement over her earlier letters. He pulled out another, compared them, and decided there was noticeable progress.

Going back to the desk, he pulled out a bundle of Georgiana's correspondences. Her handwriting was, of course, perfect, but her communications held no ideas. She rarely mentioned her studies. She instead prattled on about meeting neighbors, riding, walking, and practicing dancing. Her life was entirely frivolous. He really should find her a new companion. Take her in hand.

Taking up Elizabeth's latest letter again, he suddenly wondered if she was left-handed. If so, why wouldn't she have said as much? Not to tell him seemed deliberately…what? Mean? Misleading?

He frowned down at the page. He'd thought her keen of mind when they first spoke, when she woke in the inn room. Intelligent, reasonable, and calm. When he'd returned with the special license, he'd found her confused, almost dazed seeming, the lump on the side of her head so swollen that she hardly appeared human. Maybe she hadn't read his letter about that morning and hadn't mentioned being left-handed because she was confused? A blow to the head could have such consequences.

And he'd never asked. He sought back. Had he ever enquired about her health in his brief replies to her?

Stevens set one boot down and reached for the other. "Today's mail is there," he said, obviously trying to guess the impetus behind Darcy digging through the desk.

Darcy folded his wife's last letter and took up the small pile, shuffling through. His man in London. His sister. His Uncle Matlock. And…a letter in an unfamiliar hand.

He cracked the seal to find Elizabeth's usual salutation penned in firm, sweeping strokes. She opened with a cheerful mention of the removal of the splint and the return of the ability to write. Relief swept through him, so strong that he sank into the chair at the desk. He hadn't married an illiterate idiot. He wouldn't have to install a simpleton as matriarch of Pemberley. He squeezed his eyes closed, giving thanks.

And opened them to read on, finding that his wife meant to host a wedding breakfast in the home he rented for her. Her sister, Miss Mary, was wedding Mr. Evans.

Darcy's relief vanished in a surge of mortification. Mr. Evans? The surgeon he paid to look after her injuries? He wasn't even a doctor, but a lowly surgeon. A man Darcy would have to call brother. What the devil was going on in Kent in his absence?

That was the crux, was it not? His absence. Georgiana's studies were being neglected, which meant he was failing as her guardian. His wife was hosting a surgeon in a home he rented, permitting the man to court her sister, and celebrating their wedding. And where was he during all this?

Hiding in Scotland.

Darcy straightened in his chair. "Stevens, make ready. Tomorrow, we return to England."

"Certainly, sir." Stevens' even tone couldn't hide his relief.

Darcy would be annoyed that his valet should judge him, but Stevens was correct. Darcy should be in England. He must take his wife and sister in hand, even if he'd no idea how. He knew very little about young women, which they both were. Girls, practically, especially his sister.

He dropped his gaze back to Elizabeth's most recent letter. She did sound intelligent, something he could see now that her handwriting had improved. He might hope that she could help him with Georgiana, or he would have, until learning she'd permitted her sister to become engaged to a surgeon in a nowhere little town in Kent.

Who could he consult on how to manage his wife and sister? His mother had been dead for many years. His Aunt Catherine, he knew, would prove unreasonable. He had enough letters from her already to be quite aware that she considered him an oath breaker for not wedding his cousin Anne, even though he'd never proposed to her. He knew his stubborn aunt well enough to realize that she would take any opportunity to mold Elizabeth into a proper mistress for Pemberley as a chance to punish her for wedding him. He had an aunt and female cousins on the Fitzwilliam side, but they, as members of the peerage, had so far supported his Aunt Catherine's view, although not as vehemently.

Bingley. His friend Charles Bingley, whom he hadn't seen in some time due to his defection to Scotland, had two very proper sisters. Bingley came from trade, but his sisters had conformed so well to genteel life that they'd impressed Darcy to the point where he had, for nearly half a minute, given consideration to wedding one. Oddly, even in view of the disastrous state in which he now found himself, he wasn't sorry that he had not. Despite their poise, he couldn't see finding happiness with either.

Bingley's sisters, one of whom was married now to a respectable gentleman from a good family, would be excellent role models for Elizabeth and Georgiana, and Darcy would enjoy seeing Bingley again. He was a good friend and easy enough in personality to excuse social ineptitude in Elizabeth. Darcy would invite Bingley and his sisters, and the elder's husband Mr. Hurst, to Pemberley.

Or hadn't Bingley written about seeking a country estate of his own? Darcy dropped his gaze to the piles of read letters again. Yes, Bingley had definitely said something about renting in the country. Darcy would encourage that instead. Once Bingley found a property, Darcy would seek an invitation. Better Elizabeth should be molded more before going to Pemberley. Bingley would be tolerant of her errors and his sisters would keep quiet about them to please Darcy.

That decided, Darcy wrote to Bingley with said encouragement and the news that he would return to London soon. The following morning, he departed for Kent. He would collect his wife, ensure no trickery was involved with her return to intelligence, and then they would, together, claim Georgiana. While retrieving her, Darcy could also attempt to placate his aunt and cousin.

They made better time than Darcy hoped, for he wished to avoid Miss Mary and Mr. Evans' nuptials, but there was nothing to be done about fine weather and good roads. Still, the morning they would arrive, Darcy lingered longer than usual over his breakfast, hoping he would find the union carried out and the celebration over by the time he reached Elizabeth. In truth, he could have arrived at the house he rented for his wife the evening before but had halted early instead.

When they turned onto his wife's street, he saw carriages before her rented house. Darcy swallowed his annoyance and didn't direct his driver to carry on past. He disembarked and went to the door, mastered the urge to knock, for he rented the home and his wife lived there, and went in.

Guests filled the front parlor and the dining room, the door that adjoined them full open. The remains of an elegant spread cluttered the sideboard, paid for by him. People sat at the table eating and talking, or stood and sat in small clusters in the parlor. Good cheer and animated exchanges abounded. Darcy scowled, the expression half for his own lack of foresight. He should have realized that wedding celebrations could last for hours.

He saw no sign of Mr. Evans, the former Miss Mary, nor anyone who echoed Miss Mary's plain looks. Presumably, the newlyweds had already departed to take up residence in Mr. Evans' home, wherever that was. Certainly, on a less respectable street, this being the finest in the little town.

He also sighted no one with evidence of bruising or cuts on their face. Logically, he knew Elizabeth would have healed by now but swollen faced, purple and scratched was how he recalled her. With chagrin, he realized he'd nothing to go on, but a timeworn recollection of Mary's looks and the memory that Elizabeth had dark hair and brown eyes.

In truth, the only familiar face among the crowd of people in Darcy's rented home was Mr. Smith's. He sat at one corner of the table in conversation with a rather attractive young woman Darcy didn't know. Her hair was too light for her to be Elizabeth.

Smith being the only person identifiable to him, Darcy weaved through the throng to reach the man. He received many curious looks, the guests in his home obviously wondering who he might be, unannounced and grim. Smith, absorbed by the attractive young lady, didn't look up when Darcy came to stand beside his chair.

At the other end of the table, a woman stood, her smile and the intelligence that gleamed in her brown eyes rendering her quite charming. She moved around the table, revealing a form both graceful and fit, and extended a hand to him. "Mr. Darcy. How good of you to join us. We'd hoped you would."

Could this be Elizabeth? This lovely, elegant creature whose eyes danced with mischief?

His hand met hers, clasping it, though he'd no recollection of deciding to do so. She applied a gentle, reassuring pressure as she came to his side. Chairs scraped back, other people at the table standing. All about him swarmed a sea of convivial, curious eyes. Darcy worked not to scowl. He'd come to collect his wife, not to socialize with insignificant villagers he would never have cause to encounter again after he took Elizabeth from here.

"Allow me to introduce my family and neighbors," the woman said, all but confirming herself to be his wife. She went through the crowd, introducing everyone and ending with, "And this is my husband, Mr. Darcy."

This was met with greetings and jubilation a fraction shy of a cheer. Obviously, the community here had become fond of his wife. Had they thought he wouldn't return for her?

Once the excitement of his arrival diminished, Elizabeth turned to him. "There is plenty of food. Would you like to join us?"

To eat the food he'd provided? He didn't truly wish to but supposed he must. He went to the sideboard to fill a plate then took it to the table. Elizabeth did likewise, taking little and sitting beside him. Seeing some of those about him consider taking the seat on his other side, Darcy angled in his chair to face her and began eating, to discourage conversation.

"Did you have a pleasant journey?" Elizabeth asked.

Darcy halted his fork, with which he'd procured a piece of chicken, and said, "Very." He put the cold meat in his mouth and chewed it very thoroughly.

The next half hour progressed in a similar fashion, Darcy eating more than he was inclined to in order to avoid conversation. The celebration, which had already carried on deeper into the day than Darcy would have expected, died down and broke apart. Finally, the only two people who remained were the pretty young woman, who'd turned out to be Elizabeth's younger sister Kitty, and Mr. Smith. Feeling that small group little enough imposition, Darcy stopped eating and they moved to the parlor, closing the adjourning door to the dining room while the staff cleared up.

Silence drew out for a moment and then Elizabeth, who'd alighted on the sofa on which Darcy sat, asked, "Would you like to see the account books? I've been showing them to Mr. Smith."

Darcy looked across to the other sofa, where Mr. Smith sat with Miss Kitty and asked, "Is there anything in them of which I should be aware?"

"No. They are as I reported."

Miss Kitty coughed slightly, giving Mr. Smith a meaningful look.

Smith swallowed and said, "It pleases me to inform you, Mr. Darcy, that Miss Kitty Bennet has graciously consented to be my wife. I have permission from her father. The banns have been read once."

Another sister married beneath their father's station? Another unfit relation to call brother? Darcy frowned. "That is your business. I will be taking my wife with me tomorrow."

"Tomorrow?" Elizabeth said sharply. "That gives me no time to bid anyone farewell, and what of Kitty? She can't be left alone here. I am her chaperone."

Darcy turned his frown on her. "Did you not see everyone you know in this town this morning?"

"Well, yes, but I didn't realize I would be leaving tomorrow."

"And can your sister not stay with Mrs. Evans? She is married and fit to be a chaperone."

"Elizabeth can't go," Miss Kitty put in, voice touched with dismay. "The banns were already read once and we're to be married and Elizabeth is to host the breakfast, as she did for Mary."

Ignoring her, Darcy reiterated to his wife, "Can she stay with the Evans? Can they host a wedding breakfast?"

"To that, as well, I must reply yes, but also under protest. Mary wed only this morning. She and Mr. Evans should be permitted time alone together before taking on a house guest. Furthermore, I would like to be at my sister's wedding."

The banns had been read once? Darcy wasn't lingering in this village waiting for more Bennet sisters to descend, meet inappropriate gentlemen and be married, with celebrations he paid for. "I will consider your inclinations, but you should be ready to depart tomorrow."

Elizabeth's mouth pressed into a hard line.

"I, ah, should be going." Mr. Smith stood. "I'll, ah, have the books ready for your final approval first thing tomorrow, Mr. Darcy, in case you do, ah, depart."

Kitty Bennet surged to her feet. "I have letters to see to," she muttered and walked from the room with Mr. Smith.

Whispered voices in the entrance hall reached him, Miss Bennet's aggrieved and Mr. Smith's conciliatory, but Darcy couldn't make out the words. He turned to his wife and found that she wore a frown. On her, the expression proved somewhat daunting.

Chapter Thirteen

Elizabeth studied her husband, who'd dampened the celebration of Mary's union and chased Mr. Smith from the house and Kitty to her room. A man whose very posture evidenced his feeling of superiority over the rest of them.

Mr. Darcy cleared his throat. "Will you show me the house?"

Trying to master her anger, Elizabeth did. She showed him every room except Kitty's. Over the course of the tour, Mr. Darcy arranged for his valet to sleep in the best servant's room, ousting the cook. He also had his belongings put in the room adjoining to hers.

Elizabeth wondered what he thought would come of that. He'd every right to expect marital relations. They were, in fact, long overdue. In her present mood, however, she very much hoped he contemplated none. In view of his arrogance and highhandedness, she'd no desire to be touched by him.

When the tour concluded in the entrance hall, he turned to her. "I have given your request thought. Move your sister in with the Evans this afternoon. We're leaving tomorrow morning." Presenting Elizabeth with his back, he started up the steps.

She glared at his ascending back through narrowed eyes. That definitely decided things. They were not going to be engaging in any sort of marital relations anytime soon. She was too angry with him.

He would ignore her for months, answer every letter with as few words as possible, and then arrive unannounced and reorder her life? He was even more entitled than she'd feared. What would she do, living with such a man? Because, apparently, he'd finally decided that live with him she would.

She waited until he reached the top step and called, voice insincerely sweet, "Mr. Darcy, you've yet to tell me where we're going."

He halted, his shoulders tensing. He turned with yet another of his domineering frowns. Was the trouble that she wasn't permitted to know, or that she chose to have a conversation from opposite ends of a staircase? Because the latter had been calculated to aggravate him. A small reprisal for her sisters, her guests, Mr. Smith and the cook.

"We will go first to my aunt, Lady Catherine de Bourgh, of Rosings Park, to collect my sister, and then to London."

Smile benign, she replied, "That sounds lovely," and then stared at him until, frown deepening, he turned and disappeared down the hall.

Well, she'd enjoy London, she supposed. It would also be nice to finally meet this sister of his, Miss Georgiana Darcy. All Elizabeth knew about her so far was that she was important enough for Mr. Darcy to race off to her instead of remaining with Elizabeth, and that her husband preferred not to mention his sister in his letters. Not that he ever mentioned much of anything in them.

Elizabeth sent for the carriage to take Kitty's things, then went up to start her sister packing. She would need to pack her own cases as well but it wouldn't take long. Most of her clothes were still at home. At Longbourn, which was no longer her home. The closest thing she had to a home was here, a house she suspected that she would never again live in. She didn't have a home.

She would need to meet with the staff, tell them the news, and provide each with a small severance. Fortunately, she had the funds on hand. The one thing her husband did seem to be generous with was his money, which made her feel better about the never-signed marriage settlement, now only useful to augment a fire, to which she'd relegate it when she gathered her things.

First, however, she collected the funds she'd set aside for Kitty's wedding breakfast and walked to Mary's new home, which stood but one street over. Being a small village, there were few streets, but Mr. Evans owned a well-kept house with a large garden on the second most prosperous. Elizabeth's knock brought a maid she recalled from other visits.

"Mr. and Mrs. Evans aren't at home to anyone today, Mrs. Darcy."

"I know." Feeling wretched for intruding, Elizabeth nonetheless said, "But could you ask my sister for the barest moment of her time. It's concerning Kitty."

The maid pursed her lips but nodded. She closed the door, not even inviting Elizabeth into the entrance hall. Aware intrusion was not wanted and that passersby could see her on the stoop, troubling the newly married couple, Elizabeth kept her back straight, her gaze on the door before her, and tried not to fidget.

The door opened again and the maid gestured her in. "They're in the back parlor, Mrs. Darcy."

"I know the way," Elizabeth assured her. Enamored with Mary, Mr. Evans had invited them over on numerous occasions.

As she walked down the hall, Elizabeth felt a pang of sorrow. Once she'd recovered from her injuries, she'd begun to enjoy her life in her rented home. She had a carriage, funds, and little responsibility, coupled with the respectability of being a married woman. She, Mary, and Kitty had entertained often and been frequent guests about town.

Of course, it had always been meant to end and would have soon, regardless. Mary would withdraw for a time after her wedding and Kitty and Mr. Smith were to move to London, where he normally resided when he wasn't elsewhere on Mr. Darcy's business. They would have remained until Elizabeth left, but no longer. That would all happen rather more abruptly, was all.

As she neared the parlor, she could hear Mary talking cheerfully. Mr. Evans replied, and Mary laughed an unfettered, happy laugh Elizabeth had rarely heard. She smiled for her sister but couldn't help the sadness that washed through her at the sound. Somehow, Elizabeth doubted Mr. Darcy would ever make her laugh that way. He probably thought laughter was an evil.

"Elizabeth," Mary greeted when she entered.

"Sister," Mr. Evans added, standing until Elizabeth sat. "What brings you?"

"On our wedding day," Mary added.

"I am sorry to interrupt." Elizabeth put as much sincerity as she could muster into that apology, knowing she was about to extend that interruption tenfold. "It's about Kitty."

"So you told our maid," Mary said. "Is something the matter?"

Elizabeth shook her head. "Not as such." She attempted to contain the wince that came with her next words. "Mr. Darcy has arrived and decreed that we must leave come morning. Kitty wishes to remain so the banns can finish being read and she and Mr. Smith may wed, as planned."

Mary scrunched her face. "And Kitty cannot remain in that great big house living alone."

"Precisely."

Mary issued a huffing sigh. "But we've been married mere hours."

"Now, now, dear," Mr. Evans said. "Kitty is family and needs must and all."

Mary turned a fond smile on him. "I know. I didn't say she can't come. I'm simply letting Elizabeth know what I think of the idea."

"I can well imagine what you think of the idea," Elizabeth said, working not to add what she thought of it, and of her husband for demanding it. "I also have this for you." She proffered the funds.

Mary stared at the money. "We can support Kitty without your assistance, thank you."

Elizabeth shook her head. "It's what I'd set aside for her wedding breakfast. It would be wrong for you to have to pay when I said I would."

"Does Mr. Darcy approve of you giving that to us for a wedding breakfast I'm assuming he will not attend?" Mr. Evans asked.

Elizabeth didn't care. "Mr. Darcy provided me with funds on which to live and to do with what I saw fit. I saved this from those funds for the purpose of Kitty's wedding breakfast." She set the money on the table.

Mary looked at her husband and shrugged.

"Very well," Mr. Evans said stiffly. "It is considerate of you."

"Thank you," Elizabeth said, relieved at their fairly easy capitulation. She stood, necessitating Mary and Mr. Evans do as well. "Kitty will arrive this afternoon."

"This afternoon?" Mary repeated with clear dismay.

"As per Mr. Darcy's orders," Elizabeth replied dryly.

"Mr. Darcy is a well-respected gentleman," Mr. Evans said with a touch of severity. "His aunt is Lady Catherine de Bourgh of Rosings Park."

"Yes," Elizabeth agreed, annoyed with the reverence in Mr. Evans' voice. "I am aware. Is there any time that is preferable for Kitty to arrive?"

"The later the better," Mary said and came around the low table that stood between them. "Travel well." She wrapped Elizabeth in a hug and whispered into her ear, "And I wish you luck in dealing with your husband."

Elizabeth hugged her sister tighter, then released her and made her farewells.

She returned to find Kitty mostly packed, so she helped her finish. As Elizabeth expected, packing her possessions didn't take long either. With little help for it, she sent Kitty to the Evans. Elizabeth spent the remainder of the day meeting with the staff and putting the home in order for departure, then ate a nearly silent meal with her husband, thankful that the cook had accepted both being ousted from her room and, the following day, the house, with good enough grace to prepare edible food.

After dinner they retired to the parlor. Mr. Darcy sat in a chair by the fire and took up a book, flipping it open to a marked page.

He wasn't even making a pretense of talking to her. "Will any of the staff here come to Rosings Park with us?"

"No."

No explanation, no consideration of her needing a maid. She waited until he turned a page. "Do I have to do anything about the staff or the closing of the house?"

"No." He continued reading.

Elizabeth studied him for a moment and then declared that her head ached which, in truth, it did. She went to her room and locked the door leading to his and the one into the hall, then readied for bed.

If he tried either door during the night, she didn't hear.

As she unlocked the hall door in the morning, she was aware the servants would find no signs of her being in her husband's room or of him being in hers. She rang for her maid, embarrassed by the lack of evidence of marital relations. Wryly, she realized she would also have been embarrassed by the presence of such as well.

"Help me ready for the day," Elizabeth asked when her maid arrived. "My husband strikes me as the sort of gentleman who, when he says we will leave in the morning, truly means morning."

"Yes, missus, and may I say, we're all sorry to see you go. It's been an honor serving you." The young woman dropped her gaze to the floor, fingers woven together before her.

As Elizabeth had already given her a generous parting sum the day before, all she offered was, "Thank you."

Her supposition about an early departure proved correct, for they left not long after they had consumed their breakfast. It wasn't until she stepped from the house for the final time that Elizabeth realized she'd left the door locked between her room and Mr. Darcy's. She felt the heat rise to her face when she thought of the maids discovering this, even though she would probably never see them again.

Moments later, Elizabeth sat in Mr. Darcy's carriage, much finer than the one he'd procured for her use while she remained in Kent, which she'd thought very fine indeed. Mr. Darcy's personal conveyance seemed almost to glide over the roadway, while a second, smaller carriage, the one she had been using, followed with his valet and most of the cases. Elizabeth watched the familiar little town and the surrounding countryside drop away, then sat back to study her husband, who once again held a book.

He was undeniably handsome with a strong jaw, dark lashes and eyebrows, and aristocratic features. She had no trouble believing he had relations in the peerage. Finely built, too, with broad shoulders in no need of padding and long, well-turned legs. She glanced down at the rich fabric beneath the hand she rested on the seat and added exceedingly wealthy to the list of his good traits.

But those strong features of his were so often arranged into a dour look. His squared jaw too often at an arrogant tilt. His voice so very accustomed to issuing orders that were instantly obeyed. She did not think, had she met him under normal circumstances, that she would like him overly much. She couldn't imagine how she would get through a night of marital relations when the time came that he insisted on them, let alone years of marriage.

She pursed her lips. Well, she must try. Wealth and looks were, sadly, not traits in which Elizabeth put much stock, nor ones she would have used to select a husband, so she must find some laudable characteristics in him. There had to be something she could like about Mr. Darcy.

"What are you reading?" she asked into a silence broken only by the slight creak of the carriage and the sounds of hooves and birdsong drifting in the open windows.

Mr. Darcy looked up. "*The Farmer's Tour Through the East of England* by Arthur Young."

Something her father might have read but Elizabeth hadn't. "Is it interesting?"

"He reports that the soil in Hertfordshire is 'the worst soil a farmer can occupy.'"

Her husband would rather read about soil than converse with her? And what to say to that? He must know her to be from Hertfordshire. They'd never spoken of it, but he had her father's address. Was his comment about the soil in Hertfordshire a subtle insult? "And that is…interesting?"

"No."

Laughter burst from her, and she brought a hand to her mouth to push it back in. At least, if he chose to be laconic, he also chose to be honest. Dropping her hand she asked, "Then why read it?"

He studied her for a long moment and then marked his place and closed the book. "I must apologize for my behavior yesterday upon my arrival. I had your letter, of course, but I did not expect to find you in the midst of a celebration. I was in no mood to humor a house full of people beneath my station, but good manners should have dictated I do so."

People beneath his station? Elizabeth supposed that included her. And what about his behavior after the majority of the guests departed, which she considered far worse? Quite a few replies leapt to mind but she didn't wish to have a strained trip to Rosings Park. "I appreciate you taking the effort to say that."

He considered her words, likely aware that they didn't constitute an acceptance of an apology. Nor had she meant them to, as his statements had done more to offend than mollify. Elizabeth added nothing further, uncertain behind what topics lay pitfalls and determined to at least like Mr. Darcy no less by the time they arrived at his aunt's than she had upon setting out. After an interminably long moment, he reopened the book. Relieved, Elizabeth turned back to the scenery.

When they finally rolled up Rosings Park's drive late that afternoon, Elizabeth took in exquisitely manicured grounds and resisted the urge to stick her head out the window to view the manor house. They finally rounded the top of the drive and came to a halt before an enormous, ornate building. It was grand, modern, and large enough to make the home she grew up in seem like a cottage. Elizabeth firmly remembered to keep her mouth closed so as not to appear a gaping rustic and allowed a liveried footman to hand her down from the carriage.

Inside, the entrance hall proved equally grand. A glittering chandelier hung a dizzying height above, illuminating silk clad walls hung with pictures in elaborate gilded frames, and a sweeping staircase wide enough for a carriage. Greeted by the staff, who looked down their noses at her, she and Mr. Darcy were shown to adjoining bedrooms and advised that they'd arrived in time for dinner.

Elizabeth rang for a maid while she waited for her luggage, though she already knew she had nothing fine enough for dinner with Lady Catherine de Bourgh and her daughter. Familiar with how Mr. Darcy dressed, she suspected she didn't have anything as nice as Miss Darcy would wear, either. Well, she hadn't had the opportunity to have finer gowns made up. If the three women she was about to meet held that against her, they weren't people Elizabeth truly wished to know.

At least, that's what she told herself and made every effort to believe.

Her cases were carried in by more liveried servants. Once the footmen left, she washed up and donned her best gown. When one of Rosings' maids finally arrived to assist her, Elizabeth sat at the dressing table while the girl, who kept sneaking looks at her face rather than concentrating on her curls, set to arranging her dark tresses. She'd only one decorative pin, glinting with a lovely blue stone, so the end result of the girl's work proved rather underwhelming.

Elizabeth mentally reiterated that she was not here to impress Lady Catherine or her daughter, or even Miss Darcy. If they thought her underdressed, she didn't care.

She did care, however, about the girl's continued scrutiny. Standing, Elizabeth turned to her. "Will I do, do you suppose?"

"You look quite lovely, missus."

"No food caught in my teeth or stray spiders in my hair?"

"Missus?" the girl asked, confused.

"I'm trying to ascertain why you keep staring at me."

A blush rose in the maid's cheeks and she dropped her gaze. "No reason, missus."

"I know I took a bump on the head some months ago but it didn't addle my brains." At least, not for too long. Gentling her tone to reassure the girl, Elizabeth continued, "I'll have the truth, please."

The maid darted a look up. "It's only a…a rumor. What they're saying below stairs. One of the girls here got a letter from her cousin, brought by Mr. Darcy's tiger, and her cousin was on your staff where you were living."

Elizabeth drew her brows together, trying to recall anything she'd done to necessitate so many darted looks, but couldn't. "What rumor?"

"Oh, I couldn't, missus."

"Truly, you could. I won't be angry. You didn't start the rumor, after all."

The girl looked up at that, eyes wide. "No, missus. I wouldn't."

"Well then." Elizabeth caught her gaze and held it, waiting.

"It's only, they're saying you, ah, that is, that your marriage has not been, ah…" The girl's whole face went red. "And you're so pretty and you seem pleasant, and I don't see how that can be the case, is all, missus."

"I see." Elizabeth pursed her lips. Apparently, Mr. Darcy was deemed irresistible enough that his disagreeableness didn't factor in. "Thank you for telling me." She hadn't realized her marital relations were so interesting to the staff, but then, servants did gossip. "Mr. Darcy has been in Scotland since we married." And then been too overbearing to countenance.

"Yes. Certainly, missus." The girl fixed her gaze on her tightly clenched hands.

"Very well, then." Elizabeth took one final look at her reflection, decided that she did appear rather pretty, sucked in a deep breath, raised her chin to a non-apologetic angle, and went to the door.

Mr. Darcy waited in the hall, resplendent in dark evening wear, and the breath went right back out of her. Perfectly groomed and not yet frowning, he was dauntingly handsome. He offered his arm and Elizabeth went to him.

No one could fault him as a physical specimen. The way her heart pounded when she placed her hand on his arm was testament to that. If he would simply not speak, maybe Elizabeth could make some headway into wanting those all-important marital relations.

"You look lovely," Mr. Darcy said with apparent sincerity as they walked down the hall.

"I'm certain I will be underdressed but this is the best I have." She resisted the urge to add that much of her wardrobe remained in Longbourn. A valid sounding excuse, but one that hid a lie. Even if she had every last one of her gowns from her home…her former home…she wouldn't have anything fancy enough for dinner at Rosings.

He paused at the top of the staircase and turned to her. "Somehow, I did not realize what a magnificent neck you have."

Neck? Elizabeth raised her eyebrows, aware that his gaze dropped from hers to sweep down the length of her throat, take in her collarbones, and dip lower.

He brought up a hand to graze his fingers down the arc of her neck, then over to the hollow at the base. "I would like to see a diamond here." He frowned slightly. "No. A sapphire." He glanced at her hair. "You like blue."

She nodded, worried that if she spoke her voice would come out a breathy whisper, and concentrated on not trembling under his warm, strong touch. The idea of marital relations seemed more plausible by the moment.

He dropped his hand and offered his arm once more. They descended the grand staircase and Elizabeth attempted to lose herself in admiration of Rosings' splendor. She would not walk into a room full of Mr. Darcy's relations with thoughts of him touching her again at the forefront of her mind.

Fortunately, the house was large and the drawing room they sought rather far away. By the time they entered, arm in arm, Elizabeth had regained her equilibrium. She went in head high and calm, ready to face the women there.

All three sat opposite the door, the eldest on a grand chair and the younger two at opposite ends of a sofa. The older woman, presumably the vaunted Lady Catherine de Bourgh, wore a ponderous frown that put any of Mr. Darcy's glowers to shame. One of the younger mimicked her but the other smiled. Elizabeth hoped fervently that the smiling one, who looked of an age with Elizabeth's youngest sister, Lydia, was Miss Georgiana Darcy.

Whomever she might be, she wore a diamond and emerald necklace that certainly cost more than all the jewelry Elizabeth owned, and still would even if Mr. Darcy bought her a sapphire. In fact, Elizabeth suspected the smiling young woman's necklace was worth more than all the jewelry she, her sisters and her mother owned put together.

Mr. Darcy proceeded with introductions revealing, to Elizabeth's relief, that the youngest and most pleasant appearing of the women was indeed Miss Darcy. As Mr. Darcy spoke, Lady Catherine studied Elizabeth like someone would a bug under a magnifying glass. Out of annoyance with that, when the time came, Elizabeth offered the woman a dip of her head, rather than a curtsy. They were, after all, family.

Once the formality of introductions concluded, Lady Catherine raised her ponderous chin and said, "If you turn over your fellow conspirator, I will see most of the charges against you mitigated."

Elizabeth blinked, confused. "Charges against me? Fellow conspirator?"

"Yes. The man who actually pointed a gun at my nephew. The one in the mask who ambushed him. He's who I want to see hang." Lady Catherine leaned forward. "Tell me his name."

Elizabeth shook her head. "I have no idea who he was. Why would I?" Was Mr. Darcy's aunt implying that Elizabeth had been thrown down a hill on purpose? For what? Money?

Miss de Bourgh, who'd yet to speak, sniffed in disdain.

"You know very well who he is, and you will tell me," Lady Catherine barked.

Certain now of what allegation was being laid against her and coldly angry, both at Lady Catherine for accusing her and at her husband who wasn't defending her, Elizabeth dropped her hand from his arm. "I have absolutely no idea who the man with the pistol was, or is. My only interaction with him was to try to keep him from committing murder."

Miss de Bourgh sniffed again and said, "Oh, nicely done. You should be on the stage. Or were you?"

Lady Catherine scowled at her daughter before aiming the expression at Elizabeth again. "You expect me to believe that two bridges were out and another sabotaged, and a man lay in wait for Darcy, and yet there was no conspiracy? Ridiculous. Ludicrous. Impossible."

Back rigid, Elizabeth replied, "I have no control over what you choose to believe, Lady Catherine, but I will not confess to a conspiracy of which I am not aware and in which I have no part."

"And we will not have liars under our roof, will we, Mama?" Miss de Bourgh said.

Lady Catherine peered along her nose at Elizabeth. "Indeed not."

Miss Darcy looked from person to person with wide eyes, smile gone.

Elizabeth was about to pivot, having no desire to remain in the same room with such horrible persons, when her husband's hand settled on the small of her back. She glanced up at him to find him looking at his sister.

"Georgiana," Mr. Darcy said calmly, "I am sorry for the sudden change of plans, but I must ask you to gather your possessions. It is late, and the horses are tired, but there are several inns nearby, any of which I believe will suit us well enough." His hand leaving Elizabeth, he turned to his aunt and bowed. "Lady Catherine. Anne. I wish I could say it was a pleasure. My wife, sister, and I will depart now."

Miss de Bourgh shot to her feet. "Leave? You will not. Not until we resolve this issue." She waved a hand at Elizabeth.

"I see no issue," Mr. Darcy said stiffly. "Nor will I remain here and allow my wife to be insulted."

A wave of relief and gratitude went through Elizabeth.

Miss de Bourgh jabbed a finger at Mr. Darcy. "You were engaged to me, and you married this person."

"We were not engaged."

"We were," Miss de Bourgh screeched.

He ground his teeth together but still spoke with calm as he said, "I never asked you to marry me."

"Because it was understood. No proposal was needed."

"The point is moot. Elizabeth and I are married."

"No, you aren't." Miss de Bourgh scowled at Elizabeth. "Not really. You are not Elizabeth Bennet of Longbourn. That is a valid reason for the marriage to be annulled."

"I beg your pardon?" Elizabeth didn't know how to prove she was herself, but she felt certain she should not have to. "And you don't even like her," Miss de Bourgh went on, speaking to Darcy over Elizabeth. Expression smug, she added, "You didn't even avail yourself of her last night."

Miss Darcy gasped, going pink, as shocked as Elizabeth felt, though she worked not to show her outrage and surprise.

"Anne," Lady Catherine barked. "That is inappropriate." After reprimanding her daughter, Lady Catherine turned her narrowed gaze back to Elizabeth. "But Anne is correct. You are not Elizabeth Bennet. I have overwhelming evidence. You are a semi-literate nobody who contrived to take someone's identity. I have no idea why you picked Elizabeth Bennet, since she is not an appropriate wife for my nephew, but perhaps you simply wanted someone respectable enough so that Darcy wouldn't hand you a few hundred pounds and be done with her. You picked a real person who probably is traveling with her London relatives. You knew she wouldn't be available. I'm surprised you haven't absconded with the money Darcy gave you. You must have known your impersonation would eventually be discovered."

"Semi-literate?" Elizabeth repeated, an inkling of what had transpired growing in her.

Miss de Bourgh sniffed again. "Yes. Your letters are illiterate scrawls. My agent could hardly read them."

"Your agent?" Elizabeth's husband and his aunt chorused in matching surprise.

"What do you know of agents?" Lady Catherine continued with a quick glare for Mr. Darcy.

Miss de Bourgh turned an impatient look on her mother. "I paid someone in her household as well as someone in Scotland. You can't be angry. I took the idea from your letters with your spies and that conversation you had with Richard."

"Anne," Lady Catherine repeated, this time sounding a touch strangled. "You cannot do such things."

Elizabeth appreciated the sentiment, thinking of the note carried by Mr. Darcy's tiger and the very personal revelation therein. She willed the heat away from her face. She would not give Miss de Bourgh the satisfaction of winning such strong emotion from her.

"Why?" Miss de Bourgh asked her mother. "You bribe servants in other people's households all the time."

The skin about her lips white, Lady Catherine replied, "But I do not admit to their faces that I do."

"Enough of this," Mr. Darcy stated, voice cold. "Elizabeth, Georgiana, come. We're leaving."

Georgiana popped to her feet and scurried across the room. Mr. Darcy offered his arm to Elizabeth again. With a grave expression she hoped masked her elation at his defense, she put her hand on his sleeve and permitted him to escort her from the room. Miss Darcy walked, head high and eyes bright, on her other side.

Chapter Fourteen

To Darcy's relief, his wife easily matched his long stride despite her shorter stature. He'd no desire to mince steps as he left the drawing room that held his cousin and aunt. Spy on him, indeed. Air their marital relations, or lack thereof, before his sister and their staff. Proclaim her supposed lack of education for all to hear. Read his wife's letters to him, an invasion of privacy. Outrageous.

But how? Stevens could read and write, but he couldn't be bought. Darcy doubted his coachman or tiger could read, much less read Elizabeth's badly written letters. That only left the servants in Scotland. There was nothing to be done. They had been temporary and thus beyond his retaliation.

And what of this news about his marital relations, as unfit a topic for drawing room discussion as ever he'd heard. How could word have reached Anne so quickly? Again, Stevens wouldn't spread gossip. Could Daniels know such a detail? His coachman didn't gossip with maids. Which meant…his tiger? If the boy was at fault, Darcy would see him fired with no references or pay.

"He thought he was simply passing a letter between cousins," Elizabeth said softly. "He meant no harm."

Darcy darted a look at her as they reached the staircase. They started up, Georgiana still beside them, and he asked, "Pardon?"

"You muttered, 'my tiger.' I assume by your rather dire expression that you mean to reprimand the boy at the least. He's not at fault. One of the maids procured for the house you rented me is a cousin to one of the maids here. I'm sure they've exchanged many letters, almost certainly funded by Miss de Bourgh and your aunt, but this latest the young woman asked your tiger to carry for her. I have no thought that he knew what the letter contained."

She said this all in low, even tones as they ascended the staircase. The part of Darcy's mind not simmering with anger was impressed she could walk so quickly, with such grace, as to effortlessly keep up with him, while speaking and not seeming out of breath. When not recently thrown down a hill, his wife appeared quite hale.

She also seemed commendably calm. He could hardly contain his anger.

"How do you know all this?" he asked, halting at the top of the staircase.

She quirked a smile. "I gossiped with one of your aunt's maids."

He stared at her, uncertain what to say to that.

Georgiana turned to Elizabeth and held out both hands, which were instantly claimed. Squeezing them, Georgiana said, "I'm so very pleased to finally meet you." She released Elizabeth with a smile. "I'll ring for maids. I am so glad we're leaving here." Releasing Elizabeth, Georgiana hurried away.

Darcy turned from his sister's retreating form to find his wife studying him.

"Your aunt did make a fair point," Elizabeth said, keen gaze locked on his. "One I should have recognized much sooner. I'd thought the gunman simply bent on robbery, but it is rather a coincidence, both main bridges between you and your sister being out and a third, less well known or traveled option, sabotaged, with a man waiting there to shoot at you."

Now was not the time or the place for that discussion. "Georgiana will have rung for maids. You should oversee the packing of your possessions." Not that he'd seen anything of hers other than the topaz hairpin that shouldn't be replaced.

"I have a right to know," Elizabeth said firmly. "I nearly died."

"Very well." Darcy cupped her elbow, steering her down the hall and into his room.

Stevens, who was unpacking Darcy's belongings, looked over as they entered, but instantly covered his surprise.

"We'll be departing as soon as we're packed, but we need a moment," Darcy said.

His valet nodded and left, probably to his own room, where like as not he'd pack his own things.

"So, you do know the man who attempted to shoot you," Elizabeth said.

Looking away from her piercing eyes, Darcy's gaze caught on the oversized, archaically ornate bed. An image of Elizabeth there, dark locks fanned out across the coverlet, a smile on her lips, flashed in his mind. Giving his head a slight shake to banish that thought, for now, he focused on her as she was, fully clothed and standing before him with an expectant expression.

"I left so precipitously after your fall—"

"Pushed. I was pushed."

"Yes, well, I left because I feared that indeed, I might know that man. He was masked and wearing a hat, as you saw, and didn't even speak other than to yell, but if it was who I believe it to be, I've known him the whole of my life and even his eyes were enough to tell me his identity."

He drew in a breath. Should he tell her of Georgiana's near disaster? He'd told Richard, as her fellow guardian. Elizabeth was his wife. Georgiana's sister now. She had a right to know. If she proved competent enough to chaperone Georgiana in society, she would need to know.

"I arrived in Ramsgate to find Georgiana in the act of eloping. It is my belief that the man she meant to run off with sabotaged the bridges and tried to either delay or possibly kill me so that he would have time to abscond with my sister."

Elizabeth's eyebrows had crept higher and higher as he spoke, and now conveyed incredulousness. "But, someone died, did they not? On the northmost bridge. And you believe he truly did wish you harm. This man was willing to commit murder for…love?"

"Love?" Darcy couldn't hold back a bark of bitter laughter. "No. Georgiana's dowry is thirty thousand pounds."

The shock in Elizabeth's eyes gratified him. A small part of him had still feared…but no. She'd nothing to do with Wickham's plot. His aunt was clutching at straws.

"If you know who sabotaged the bridges, why have you not brought charges against him? A man died," she reiterated.

Darcy pressed a hand through his hair, his gaze going to the clock on the mantel. The longer they remained, the longer his aunt had to formulate retribution for how he'd spoken to her.

"Or is a cart driver beneath your notice?"

He snapped his attention back to his wife. Anger glinted in her eyes. "Even though I've no proof that the man who attempted to abscond with Georgiana is the same man who sabotaged the bridges, I arranged a small pension for the man's wife and children," he said, more sharply than he intended.

"You did?"

Her surprise at that shouldn't rankle so much. After all, she'd no way to know that he was a man who would take such steps. She might guess, though, based on how responsibly he'd behaved regarding her wellbeing. "Yes. I did."

"That was very good of you." She drew in a breath. "It doesn't explain why no charges have been brought."

"Because I have no proof. Nothing beyond my guess based on the man's eyes seeming familiar. If you saw the man who pushed you again, could you swear to his identity?"

She pressed her full lips together, then shook her head. "Probably not, but you have the proof of him attempting to run off with your sister."

"You would have me ruin Georgiana on the chance a magistrate would take her near elopement as enough evidence that the same man sabotaged the bridges and pointed a pistol at me?" He shook his head. "My man in London has set the runners on it. If there are sufficient grounds for charges to be brought, they'll find them. As it's been some months and they have not, I've lost hope."

She nodded slowly. "If there isn't enough evidence for the man to be convicted, I can see why it would be pointless to risk Miss Darcy's reputation."

"Thank you. Now, please, will you go see that your possessions are properly packed?" Which would allow Stevens to return to stowing Darcy's.

"Yes and, thank you."

"For?"

She reached up, tentative, and lay a soft hand along his jaw. "For championing me against your aunt and cousin."

Darcy covered her hand with his, holding her warmth there. "You are my wife. To disrespect you is to disrespect me."

"I see." She slipped her hand free and left his room.

Darcy stared after her, wondering what he'd said wrong now.

It took longer than he liked, but with lanterns hung on the carriages, they finally left Rosings. They reached the first inn in good time, Stevens going in to arrange their rooms. He returned with surprising speed, shaking his head. Rather than orchestrate unloading their bags, he told Darcy there was no room.

That surprised Darcy but the next inn wasn't far. Still, traveling slowly to spare the horses and for safety in the dark, the journey took longer than usual. Again, Stevens went in and again, he returned shaking his head.

Darcy scowled at him out the carriage window. "Full?"

"Exactly as the last, sir, and the innkeeper mighty nervous about it, too."

Frowning at that, Darcy directed them on to the next inn. This time, he alighted and entered, Stevens following, but was told the same thing. No rooms were available. As Stevens had noted about the previous innkeeper, the man running this establishment seemed nervous, staring at the floor as he spoke and toying with the corner of the registry book, which stood closed on the counter.

Darcy returned to the carriage and took his place beside Elizabeth with a frown, aware his driver awaited orders.

"Full again?" Elizabeth asked.

Darcy nodded. "I find the odds slight." He knew he should have wrung more haste out of their party in departing Rosings. He'd given his aunt too much time to plot.

Elizabeth nodded her agreement. "Maybe we should veer from the road back to London."

"Why would that matter?" Georgiana asked, where she sat across from them.

That was a good thing about having his sister with them, Darcy mused. Elizabeth sat at his side rather than across the carriage from him. It surprised him how pleasant it was to have her there.

"Changing our route shouldn't matter," Elizabeth was saying to his sister. "That is, if this were coincidence, but I suspect that Lady Catherine paid off all the nearest innkeepers to keep us from finding rooms. Who knows how far along the London road she's ordered her men to travel? They'll be astride on fresh mounts. We'll never pass them up."

"Not Lady Catherine," Georgiana gasped, eyes going wide. "Anne. Miss de Bourgh. I'm never going to call her Anne again, even though she is my cousin. Before we left, she came by my room. She was all smug and spiteful looking and she said, 'Have a nice night traveling.' I found it strange, but I didn't think anything more of it, until now."

"That does seem to indicate her." Elizabeth turned a questioning look on Darcy as she spoke. "Could she do that? Would she?"

"She was very angry about your marriage," Georgiana said. "She's been ranting and raving for weeks. I'd started avoiding her so I wouldn't have to hear about you breaking your word again."

Elizabeth looked from his sister to him, then asked, "Did you break your word?"

"Certainly not," Darcy snapped, offended.

She dipped her head. "My apologies. Can you explain to me about your non-engagement, then?"

He supposed he must. "My mother and Lady Catherine were sisters. They wanted to keep as much wealth in their line as possible and decided that the best course would be for me to marry Anne. Miss de Bourgh. But I never proposed."

Eyes narrowing slightly, Elizabeth asked, "Did you object? Had you ever made it clear to Miss de Bourgh that you would not marry her? She's old to be unwed, especially with her fortune. Has she been waiting for you?"

Wishing he didn't have to admit it, Darcy said, "I never made a show of objecting." He was warping the truth. With a grimace, he clarified, "I always considered the union a possibility."

"Giving her some justification," Elizabeth said.

"Justification to be angry, perhaps, but not to do this." He gestured out the window at the inn.

"Sir?" Stevens, who still waited outside, asked, seeing Darcy look out the window. "Should we move on to another inn?"

"Ask Daniels to take the next turn off the road from London. I don't care which it is. We need an inn along a different route."

"Yes, sir," Stevens said and passed the order along to both drivers.

They left the main roadway and found an inn, which turned out to have two rooms. The establishment wasn't as nice as Darcy would have liked, but it would do for his tired people and even more tired horses. He ended up giving his wife and sister the bigger room and sharing the smaller with Stevens. To his surprise, he found he resented being separated from Elizabeth.

She'd demonstrated both poise and intelligence that evening. Strength, as well, and calm. Traits he lauded in anyone and definitely wished for in a wife. Putting aside the months during which he thought he'd married an uneducated, possibly unintelligent and illiterate, fool, he liked what he knew of Elizabeth. His impression of her mother hadn't been very favorable, but the two younger sisters he'd met had behaved well. The elder of the two seemed capable and calm, the younger pretty and reasonable. Perhaps if he'd taken more of an interest, he could have seen them to unions with men more appropriate for him to call brother, but he'd made himself unavailable.

He'd definitely liked the Gardiners, despite their being in trade. The favorable impression they'd made had played a significant role in his decision to offer for Elizabeth. His reports on the remainder of the family claimed the father to be a true gentleman and the other two sisters attractive and pleasant. He would have to see if he could pave the way for them to marry better than Mary and Kitty had.

Elizabeth must also be good with money. Smith had claimed as much but Darcy had assumed her sister Mary to be behind that. Then, when he arrived and found that Elizabeth had taken charge of the books, he thought perhaps Smith had assisted her because he was smitten with the sister. Now, after spending a little time with Elizabeth, he began to see that she indeed possessed the keen mind he'd first thought.

He'd given her an allowance. Not a large one as he'd been uncertain what she would do with the funds. From that, she seemed to have saved enough to host not one, but two wedding breakfasts which, insofar as he could tell, included half the town. She clearly hadn't spent frivolously, though he wished she'd allocated some of the money to clothing. Every gown in which he'd seen her was barely respectable and certainly not suitable for the wife of Darcy of Pemberley.

Well, they would be in London soon. He would see her respectably clad. If Bingley hadn't found a place to rent yet and left for the country, Darcy would prevail upon Miss Bingley and Mrs. Hurst to help dress Elizabeth. Once she had new gowns, they could donate everything she owned now to charity.

That decided, and still wishing that chivalry hadn't dictated giving the nicer room to the ladies to share, Darcy drifted off to sleep.

Chapter Fifteen

The evening after their departure from Rosings, ensconced in his bed in Darcy House, Darcy thought to find sleep an easy companion. Instead, though a dearth of light prevented actual sight of it, his gaze fixed on the door that adjoined his room to his wife's. In all the years since he'd become master of Darcy House, that door had meant little to him. Less than a window. No more than the wall in which it was set. Now, his entire being cried out for him to fling it open.

To his relief, after the several days they'd now spent together, he found Elizabeth exquisite. Those eyes that often gleamed with something akin to mischief, framed in dark lashes. Her bowlike lips, fortunately fully healed and plush. The graceful curve of her neck, swanlike. So very delicate, like all of her except her mind and will.

He ached for her.

But what if he made the attempt to go to her and the door proved locked, as had the one that linked his room to Elizabeth's at the rented house in Kent? He liked to imagine that had been forgetfulness on her part. That the door in Kent was routinely locked and she, unaccustomed to his presence and with the sore head she'd claimed, had forgotten to unlock it.

Or his wife had locked that door with purpose, in a clear sign that she did not wish his attentions. If he tried this one, here and now, he might find the answer, but he balked at confirmation that Elizabeth did not want him.

Worse, what if the door opened but only out of a sense of duty? The thought of executing his marital rights on an Elizabeth who lay there, permitting him without participation, curdled all desire. Yes, he was wedded, and a wedded man could expect certain pleasures, but Darcy would find none where his wife didn't.

He needed her to welcome him into her chamber. Better yet, to seek him, so he knew for certain that she wished for his attentions as much as he wished to apply them. They'd come close in that moment in

Rosings, when she'd touched his face, but then she'd withdrawn. All because he'd said her honor was as precious to him as his own.

No. He'd said something else. What, he couldn't recall, but he'd meant that her honor was as precious to him as his own. It saddened him to suspect that she'd heard something different.

Turning his head so that he stared at the darkness above rather than the darkness that cloaked the door to Elizabeth, Darcy pondered their interactions. All his interactions, really, for he found he generally had two types. Those few people with whom he was close, like Richard and Bingley, heard the words that left Darcy's mouth and comprehended the meaning behind them. The remainder of those with whom he dealt heard the words, and were like as not put off as Elizabeth had been, but didn't permit their annoyance to show. They craved his money and influence too much to risk his ire.

Elizabeth had his money and influence. She'd no need to pretend a lack of offense. Therefore, he must somehow bring her into that smaller, more select group. He stared up at the dark ceiling, turning that impossible seeming task over in his head.

How did a man contrive for his wife to understand him?

He knew many married men, of course. He could not think of a single one who'd achieved that blissful state of understanding. He'd no idea from whom he might seek advice on the subject.

Darcy's mind roiled on thus through the night, during which he snatched little sleep. He woke restless, and groggy. Later than he normally might have but still early by London standards. In no mood for breakfast, he dressed for riding. The morning proved cool, as they ventured into autumn, and he soon rode the still sparsely populated lanes of Hyde Park, his mood improving with each stretch of his horse's legs.

"Darcy," a familiar voice called.

He turned his mount to watch Charles Bingley riding up with a wide smile. Darcy dipped his head as the other man drew near. "Bingley."

"I heard you were back in London. I'd planned to call this afternoon."

"Then you would have missed me. I'll be out for much of it, I suspect." At some point during his restless night, he'd decided to meet with each of his sister's instructors to ascertain where she stood with her education. He couldn't meet with the ones in Ramsgate, of course, but Georgiana hadn't been there for long. Her London instructors would do.

"It's good fortune that I found you now, then," Bingley, always affable, rejoindered. "I'd hoped for your advice on that country estate notion of mine, as you've encouraged the pursuit. Have you breakfasted?"

Darcy shook his head. "I have not."

"Come. Dine with me and I'll show you the listings my man sent over. There's one in particular that I think would do well and offer interest to you."

"To me?"

Bingley nodded. "I will show you."

They returned to Bingley's London residence to find Miss Bingley, who kept house for him, sitting down to eat. She greeted Darcy with warmth but without the usual glint of avarice in her eyes and he realized that here lay a benefit of being married. Women could no longer look on him as a commodity to be acquired.

While they ate, Bingley, who possessed impeccable manners but an easy nature that permitted a certain lack of stringency, had the listings brought in. He spread them out on the table, permitting Darcy and Miss Bingley to peruse them with him.

"Ah ha," Bingley exclaimed, tapping one. "Here it is. Netherfield Park in Hertfordshire." He turned a look of question on Darcy. "It's near a place called Meryton. I believe that's the village you mentioned as nearest to your wife's family's estate?"

Darcy nodded. "It is."

Bingley held out the page. "What do you think of the place? Quite large, with the number of rooms listed, and the park sounds extensive."

Darcy took the listing and ran his gaze down the catalog of qualities and specifications. "Fully staffed," he noted. When he finished his inspection, he offered the page to Miss Bingley.

"It seems more than adequate," she said after reading.

"On paper," Darcy cautioned.

Bingley nodded. "Yes, well, I won't rent the place unseen, worry not, but the real question is, would the location suit you, Darcy? You know I plan to invite you."

Darcy sipped his coffee, noting that Bingley's staff made an excellent brew. Did it suit him? He would like to come to know his wife's relations better, even if her mother had seemed, on their brief meeting, a bit inane. "Yes," he finally said. "But do not lease it on my behalf. A visit to Hertfordshire is in order but I will endeavor to reside with my relations, to come to know them better. Only lease the place if it pleases you."

"I'm certain one countrified corner of England is much the same as another," Miss Bingley said, gaze scanning the listings. "Netherfield Park is only a half day's trip to London, which means we can go back and forth if need be. At least if Charles takes it, we can be assured of some decent company."

As she said this without her usual fawning, Darcy had to assume she meant the compliment. The difference in her demeanor pleased him. He'd never been comfortable with Miss Bingley's aspirations involving him. "That reminds me, Miss Bingley, my wife's wardrobe is unfortunately rustic. I don't imagine she's had the opportunity to become familiar with London shops. If you and your sister could offer guidance it would be most appreciated." He wouldn't malign Elizabeth with the admission that he also worried she hadn't any sense of style or taste.

Miss Bingley's eyes gleamed with a new form of avarice, revealing her love of shopping, or possibly she reveled in the chance to dress Mrs. Darcy of Pemberley. "Louisa and I would be pleased to assist."

Darcy dipped his head to acknowledge that. "Thank you."

"Do you suppose there's an orchard?" Bingley said, taking back up the Netherfield listing. "I can't remember the last time I plucked an apple right from the tree and they should be ripe soon."

"I've no idea," Miss Bingley said with a roll of her eyes.

"There's likely to be," Darcy assured him and took another sip of coffee.

They looked over the other listings and discussed rates and the positive and negative aspects of renting a place that came staffed. Finally, Darcy realized the hour drew near luncheon and excused himself, wishing he hadn't been so caught up. Elizabeth would believe him to be avoiding her. He hadn't even advised the staff of anything more than that he was going riding.

He returned to Darcy House to find that his wife and sister had taken the smaller carriage to visit the Gardiners. He liked and respected the Gardiners but wondered if their acquaintance would make it more difficult for Georgiana to take when she came out. Then again, Bingley's family had connections to trade, most notably his own deceased father, and he and his sisters did well enough. A greater worry might be Darcy's new brothers, a steward and a surgeon. He hoped he could see the remaining two sisters better married to balance out those connections.

With his wife and sister out and having lingered over breakfast with Bingley and Miss Bingley too long to be ready for lunch, Darcy called for his carriage, pleased that Elizabeth had been courteous enough to take the smaller. He'd neglected his duties to Georgiana while in Scotland and was resolved to do so no longer. He set out to visit her instructors to ascertain the progress of her education, a task he anticipated would be easy to accomplish. Despite Mrs. Younge's nearly disastrous guardianship of Georgiana's virtue, she had kept precise records of his sister's education.

He called on her drawing instructor first and was shocked to discover that he'd only given Georgiana lessons half as often as Mrs. Younge had recorded. He went next to her instructor in Italian and found that four times a week Italian lessons were only twice a week. The pattern was the same for all the lessons Georgiana took. He wondered what she'd been doing with her free time. In Ramsgate she'd spent much of her time with that family, the Milfords, but he recalled no such acquaintances of hers in London.

Come to think of them, he wondered that she hadn't mentioned the Milfords since he'd removed her from Ramsgate. True, they'd remained, and she'd been living with Aunt Catherine, but Georgiana's letters had contained almost every inane detail of her days. She'd written at length about the content of letters from school friends. Why not mention the Milfords?

Had she feelings for their son, as he'd begun to expect, and the young man's engagement turned her into Wickham's waiting arms? That would be a relief in a way. More understandable than his sister actually developing a romantic attachment to George Wickham. Darcy would have to remember to ask after the Milfords to better ascertain Georgiana's feelings.

Darcy returned home and went to his office, taking down the ledger where he recorded Georgiana's upkeep. Though he'd expected as much, he still scowled as he read the entries that confirmed he'd definitely paid for double the lessons that his sister had actually received. Obviously, Mrs. Younge had kept the difference.

He frowned at the ledger. He should track the woman down and see her punished. She'd embezzled from him and nearly ruined his sister and…and that was the crux of it, was it not? Any action he took against

Mrs. Younge would make him appear a fool at the least, and ruin Georgiana at the most. And for what? To salve his pride and reclaim a sum that meant little to him?

He slapped the ledger closed and stood to shove it back onto the shelf behind his desk, then glared at the spine. His man had sent over the list of candidates for Georgiana's companion. Should Darcy review them? Ideally, his wife would oversee his sister's education, but he had no means by which to ascertain Elizabeth's capability to do so.

He needed to come to know Elizabeth better. He hadn't even asked after her when he returned from visiting Georgiana's instructors. He wasn't accustomed to having anyone to ask after.

Turning from the offending ledger, he rang for a footman. One appeared almost immediately. "Is Mrs. Darcy at home?"

"Yes, sir. She and Miss Darcy are in the blue parlor."

"Thank you."

The blue parlor, large and containing the pianoforte, generally served bigger gatherings. As he drew near, he heard music spilling out and quickly ascertained why the two elected to be there. Georgiana's voice, well trained and carefully modulated, added words to the music. A sweet contralto joined her, drawing a smile. Elizabeth's singing voice held every bit, if not more, melodious beauty as her speaking one.

He turned into the parlor to find them side by side at the pianoforte, both playing and singing, and halted. They were so absorbed as not to notice his presence, so he propped a shoulder against the doorjamb and waited, reveling in both their performance and camaraderie.

When they finished, Georgiana reached for the music and flipped back a few pages. "You misplayed several notes here." She tapped the page.

"Yes, I definitely did," Elizabeth agreed, studying the score. "Let me try them again."

Elizabeth practiced the section several times, then they played a few bars together. Although he liked that they were getting along so well, Georgiana's superior skill did not bode well for Elizabeth overseeing her education. At least he now knew that his wife played well enough to entertain company and sang well enough to please even his Aunt Catherine.

Not that he expected that opportunity to arise anytime soon.

He strode into the room. "That was a splendid performance."

Both women turned to him. After a moment, Elizabeth mustered a smile and a nod of greeting. She rose with smooth grace, Georgiana coming to her feet a moment behind.

Elizabeth crossed the room. "Mr. Darcy," she said when she reached him. "We did not realize you'd returned."

"Fitz," Georgiana greeted.

Sorrow touched him. He recalled a time, when Georgiana was a child, when she would greet him with genuine joy, something she did no longer, and which he had no idea if Elizabeth would ever do. "Yes. I finished my afternoon outing perhaps an hour ago." To Elizabeth, he added, "I apologize for missing breakfast."

"You've no need to apologize. Your comings and goings are not for me to dictate."

But he wanted them to be. Or at least, he wanted Elizabeth to care where he was. To have an opinion on what he did. Anything to show she regarded him with more interest than a passerby on the street. "You left word that you went to visit your aunt and uncle. They are well?"

That won a smile. "They are, as are my cousins."

He nodded, though if he'd known that the Gardiners had children, he'd forgotten.

"They're fabulous, Elizabeth's cousins," Georgiana put in. "Such well-behaved children, and enthusiastic conversationalists, no matter that the oldest is hardly nine." She smiled at Elizabeth. "Mrs. Smith is very nice, too."

Elizabeth returned Georgiana's smile, seeming pleased, then turned back to him. "I hope you don't mind, but I ordered two new gowns. Aunt Gardiner helped me, and Kitty came along."

He hadn't considered that the Smiths lived in London. Would Elizabeth wish to call on them? He imagined so. Would she bring his sister?

Darcy had no idea where Smith lived but he couldn't imagine anywhere suitable for Mrs. and Miss Darcy to visit. He resolved to offer the Smiths use of one of the houses he owned. He must have somewhere that would be free soon. If not, he would buy a place. He wouldn't have his sister dragged off to who knew where.

As to Elizabeth's wardrobe, he hoped Mrs. Gardiner hadn't steered Elizabeth too far astray, doubting a woman whose husband was in trade would know where Mrs. Darcy should shop. "I've taken the liberty of asking Miss Bingley and her sister, Mrs. Hurst, to call. I thought they might help you navigate London fashion."

Standing beside Elizabeth, Georgiana grimaced.

With the slowness of someone choosing their words with care, Elizabeth responded, "That is thoughtful of you." A genuine smile turned up her lips. "Would they be relations to Mr. Bingley? I recall his letter commending our union as by far my favorite. Will he call as well?"

A pang of pure jealousy stabbed through Darcy. She would smile like that for one of Bingley's letters but show no warmth to him? He drew in a breath, mastered the unwelcome emotion, and said, "I'm certain he will. In fact, he is looking into leasing an estate in Hertfordshire, near Meryton, so we may all congregate in the country while we visit your family."

"We will visit my family?" Her smile was for Darcy this time. "I should very much enjoy that." Her brow furrowed. "Would the property of interest to Mr. Bingley be Netherfield Park?"

"The same."

"It is a lovely property."

"Then I am certain he will take it. He journeys to inspect the grounds and house soon."

"I look forward to meeting him, here or in Hertfordshire."

"Will I get to go, too?" Georgiana asked.

Darcy frowned at her. "You must. I have not taken on a new companion for you."

Georgiana tossed her curls. "I don't require a companion. I have Elizabeth."

Darcy looked from one to the other, uncertain how to respond to that.

After a silence that dragged on for too long, Elizabeth quirked an eyebrow. "Is Mr. Bingley married?"

"No," he replied, relieved by the change in topic.

Mischief brightened Elizabeth's brown eyes to a shade of dark honey. "The neighborhood will be quite pleased to have him."

Darcy recalled she still had two unwed sisters. It occurred to him that Bingley would make a fine brother. Perhaps not quite the connections one might aspire to but being Darcy's closest friend outside Richard more than made up for that.

Elizabeth touched his sleeve, recapturing his attention. "I hope you do not mind, but I had a bit of the household money from Kent left, which I used today for the gowns, but I will require more funds if I am to shop with Mr. Bingley's sisters."

He minded only in that he should have seen that his wife had money for new dresses. "I'll see that you have more money tomorrow."

"Thank you." Features smoothed of expression, she asked, "Will I be managing this household?"

His gaze flicked to Georgiana, who listened avidly. "Yes." He could always take that task away from her if she mismanaged it. Because it must be said he added, "But I am going to instruct the housekeeper to come to me if she thinks you are doing something wrong."

Somehow that, a statement he felt certain would resurrect a gulf of distance between them, elicited only relief. "Good. I don't want to err inadvertently."

"I'm certain you won't," Georgiana said cheerfully.

Elizabeth turned to her. "But I am not certain. My mother trained me to manage a household but most of my practical knowledge comes from a dear friend of mine, Charlotte Lucas, whom you will meet in Hertfordshire and who's no experience with a London residence. I managed quite well in Kent, but that household was small compared to Darcy House. I shouldn't want to blunder into any errors before I learn, or to put the housekeeper in the untenable position of deciding between obeying me or reporting a misstep to your brother."

Far from offended by what could be construed as a reprimand, Georgiana touched Elizabeth's arm, expression warm. "You're so thoughtful."

Elizabeth chuckled. "I rather find it practical but laud me as you see fit."

His sister laughed and Darcy began to revise his fear that Elizabeth couldn't manage Georgiana.

"Sir?"

Annoyed by the interruption, Darcy turned to find his butler, Edwards, in the parlor doorway.

Chapter Sixteen

Reminding himself that the man was simply doing his job, Darcy asked Edwards, "Yes?"

"Colonel Fitzwilliam inquires if you are at home."

"Richard?" Georgiana exclaimed.

Trying not to feel jealous that Richard still received an enthusiastic greeting, Darcy turned to Elizabeth. "I would like you to meet him."

"He's our cousin," Georgiana added. "One of our good cousins."

"Georgiana," Darcy said sharply.

"Richard?" Elizabeth repeated the name, frowning. "Did not Miss de Bourgh say something about a Richard and Lady Catherine discussing spying on us?"

"Oh," Georgiana exclaimed. "But that wasn't Richard. I mean, it was him." She glanced at Darcy. "Elizabeth probably thinks our cousins are all like Anne. Richard isn't."

"Even if he discussed spying on us?" Elizabeth asked.

Georgiana nodded emphatically. "Even if. He wasn't a party to the spying and did not approve. You'll see. You'll like him."

Undoubtedly, she would. She would like Richard, and Bingley. All of Darcy's closest friends. Everyone, it seemed, except him. "I have every belief in Georgiana's interpretation," Darcy said.

Elizabeth nodded. "Then perhaps we should move to the front parlor and call for tea?"

Darcy turned back to Edwards. "As my wife says."

"Very good, sir."

They adjourned to the front parlor and Richard was shown in, and greetings exchanged, Georgiana's enthusiastic and Elizabeth's neutral. They all sat, and Darcy realized it would be the first time he witnessed his wife serve tea. It relieved him that Richard was the guest. If Elizabeth's manners proved in need of improvement, Richard would never make mention to anyone.

"I was surprised to hear you're in town," Richard said while they awaited the tea service. "I thought you were to remain at Rosings for several days."

Darcy exchanged a glance with Elizabeth. She gave a slight nod, which he took to mean that he should decide how much to reveal. "We found ourselves less than welcome."

"Less than welcome?" Richard looked to each of them in turn. "I wish you would speak plainly. I have an urgent summons to present myself to our aunt. I'd like to know into what disaster I'm commanded."

Georgiana gasped, drawing all eyes. "She's going to make you marry Anne."

Richard's eyebrows shot up. "Marry Anne?"

"Rather, Miss de Bourgh," Georgiana clarified. "After what she did, I vowed not to call her Anne anymore."

"What did our cousin do?"

Darcy grimaced, more over being required to repeat the sordid event than worry over Richard knowing. "She had some unflattering words for me regarding my union with Elizabeth."

"And Aunt Catherine accused Elizabeth of plotting with the gunman," Georgiana added.

Elizabeth remained silent, expression bland, but Darcy read a flicker of anger in her eyes. He imagined it directed at his relations who were not in the room, rather than those who were.

"Did she?" Richard smiled slightly. "I know you're rich, Darcy, but, if you don't mind me saying," he nodded to Elizabeth, "even after such brief acquaintance, I deem you too intelligent to risk death for profit."

"I would never prevent you from saying as much, but your aunt took a different view. She seems to believe I sustained more injuries than I'd expected, marking me not only a conspirator, but a liar and unintelligent."

"Not a tumbling artist, then?"

Elizabeth smiled. "Apparently not a good enough one."

"Elizabeth nearly died," Darcy said with a seriousness that drained any burgeoning mirth from the room. He cleared his throat and continued, "I see no reason to attempt a repetition of the details. Suffice to say that Aunt Catherine and Anne behaved unacceptably, and we left."

"That's not so surprising as I would like." Richard studied him for a moment. "It doesn't explain the urgent summons." He turned to Georgiana. "Or why you believe our aunt will press me to marry Anne."

144

"Before Elizabeth and Fitz arrived, Miss de Bourgh was harping about how unfair it was that my brother married a nobody and that there should be consequences to their broken engagement."

"We were not engaged," Darcy said sourly.

Georgiana shrugged. "I know. So did Aunt Catherine. She asked Miss de Bourgh if you had proposed. She said no, but that everyone knew you were supposed to marry her. Aunt Catherine said that they would take their revenge by making life unpleasant for Elizabeth. She said that she would show the world that Mrs. Darcy entrapped her husband and was unworthy of him." Georgiana scrunched her features in distaste. "She said that she would make you both regret marrying and that you would hide in the country."

"I received much the same rant," Richard said. "I believe it ended with, 'Darcy will rue the day he married that country trollop. He'll know shame for failing to fulfill my sister's wishes.'" He cast a quick look at Elizabeth. "Begging your pardon, Cousin."

Expression mildly amused, Elizabeth shrugged.

Conversation paused as the tea service arrived. Once the maids left, Elizabeth began to pour, serving Richard first as their guest, her every movement elegant and precise. Darcy felt the relief of another worry lifted.

"But that still doesn't answer why you believe our aunt wishes me to marry Anne," Richard said, accepting his tea.

Georgiana leaned forward. "When we left Rosings, Miss de Bourgh told me that I would have an unpleasant trip to London, and then we found all the inns along the London route mysteriously full."

"And the innkeepers on edge," Darcy added.

"You believe Anne paid the inns along the route to London to turn you away?" Richard sounded a bit incredulous.

Georgiana nodded. "The moment we turned from the road to London, at Elizabeth's suggestion, we found an inn with room."

Two rooms, as Darcy recalled, and neither shared by him and his wife, who handed him tea prepared to his liking, although she hadn't asked his preference. It pleased him to realize she must have inquired from the staff.

Richard looked between them all again. "And now Aunt Catherine wants me to marry Anne?"

"I may be misjudging the individuals involved as I do not know them well," Elizabeth said. "But I believe what Georgiana is suggesting is that Lady Catherine worries word of Anne's, and possibly her own, behavior will come out and that she will find it difficult to convince anyone to take her daughter."

Darcy nodded his agreement. "At least, anyone who would treat her well."

"She's a monster," Georgiana said and reached for a small cake without waiting to be served.

"A monster who will inherit Rosings," Darcy noted.

"Indeed," Richard said. "And consider her circumstances. Lady Catherine surrounds herself with flatterers and sycophants. Those who aren't praising Lady Catherine are praising Anne. She's never allowed to do anything or express any ideas. She's been taught that she's better than anyone she meets regularly, except her mother."

"She meets you," Georgiana said. "Surely the son of an earl is better than the daughter of a baron."

"I defer to Lady Catherine, since she is my hostess and my senior."

"Has Miss de Bourgh had much interaction with people who are her age and class?" Elizabeth asked.

Darcy exchanged a glance with Richard. "Only with one cousin."

"Who hasn't visited in years, since Lady Catherine quarreled with my brother's wife," Richard added. "Lady Catherine doesn't like deferring to the new countess."

"And she hasn't been to school or had contemporaries as friends?"

"No," Darcy replied.

"Not only that, hardly anyone visits Rosings who interacts with her." Richard appeared glum, considering his own words. "When I visit, I now and then have a conversation with her. She said last time that she talks more with me than with anyone who isn't in her household. I only visit once a year."

"Assuming she isn't exaggerating, it is no wonder she is strange," Elizabeth said. "I admit my interaction with Lady Catherine was brief, but if Miss de Bourgh imitates her mother's behavior, she will have difficulty making friends."

"She is usually more reasonable," Darcy protested.

"Is she?" Georgiana asked, voice thick with sarcasm. "You didn't have to live there for months while you were in Scotland."

"Well, then," Richard took another sip of tea. "If we are correct about Aunt Catherine's fears and her plan, I believe I will marry Anne."

"What?" Georgiana exclaimed. "Why?"

"For Rosings?" Darcy asked, surprised Richard would be quite so mercenary.

"For Rosings and for Anne. There is no way to take Anne away from her mother except through marriage. No one with any authority would think Anne is badly treated. Lady Catherine showers money on her and gives her everything she asks for. Her governess never taught her accomplishments, but she does have a basic education, so there's no neglect to claim there."

"But you are giving up the possibility of marrying someone you love," Georgiana protested wistfully.

Richard chuckled. "But do you know, I always expected to fall in love with a woman with at least fifteen thousand pounds? Having a large dowry makes a woman very lovable. But such women are rare."

"There's Miss Bingley," Darcy said with a straight face.

"Miss Bingley would need more than Rosings for me to marry her."

"Isn't Miss Bingley who you suggested I take advice from?" Elizabeth asked with obvious confusion.

"Advice on fashion," Darcy clarified.

"She is very fashionable," Richard stated in agreement.

"And dreadful," Georgiana mumbled, then popped another tiny cake in her mouth.

"I see," Elizabeth said. "Well, I will meet her, with your words in mind, and form an opinion of her."

"Do you really think Aunt Catherine will let you marry Anne?" Georgiana asked Richard as she reached for more cake.

"That's the beauty of it. I suspect she will ask me to do it."

Darcy suspected that as well. He also understood Richard's decision to accept. He only hoped his cousin fully comprehended what he was getting into.

"There is one other reason I came by," Richard said, looking from Darcy to Elizabeth. "I have your version, Darcy, of how the two of you met, and Aunt Catherine's for that matter, but I cannot imagine either being what you wish put out into the world?"

Georgiana paused in the process of reaching for another cake. "I'd like to know, too. You told me that Elizabeth fell down a gorge while stopping your carriage from going in, but Aunt Catherine said there was a man with a gun."

"Yes, well..." Realizing his sister had a right to expect the truth, Darcy reiterated the event, leaving out any mention of Wickham or notion that the man with the gun was anything more than a common highwayman.

"Oh," Georgiana breathed when he finished. She turned to Elizabeth. "You were so brave."

Elizabeth grimaced. "I'm not certain. I had precisely enough time to realize that I was putting myself in grave danger but not enough time to hit upon any other way to prevent the attack. In retrospect, it seems rather a foolish thing to have done. The man may well have missed, or your brother and the driver may have managed to control the horses."

"There are always maybes in such situations," Richard said with the authority of a man who'd seen combat on the Continent. "You were brave. You acted quickly and decisively to do what needed doing, and I for one am very grateful." He grinned. "I'm passingly fond of Darcy, for all he's a bit stern much of the time."

Elizabeth's cheeks suffused with pink. "That is kind of you to say, yet none of it answers your question."

"We should tell the truth," Darcy said, aware that his tone bolstered Richard's claim that he was often stern.

"It's very romantic," Georgiana added.

Giving him a piercing look, Richard said, "I believe the truth but with a little less detail."

Elizabeth nodded, the gleam in her eyes echoing Richard's. She darted a quick look in Georgiana's direction while Darcy's sister took more cake. "The full truth begs for people to ask questions."

"Yes," Georgiana said, oblivious to the strain in the others. "Like who the highwayman was and why he hasn't been apprehended."

Even though most highway robberies did not result in apprehended highwaymen, Darcy realized they were right. Georgiana didn't even know about the other bridges and the dead man, and already had questions. Unlike his sister, many others would have heard about the bridges and the wagon driver. Facts would be strung together. Ones that might lead to questions about who wished to keep Darcy away from his sister and why. "We will tell the truth, leaving out the highwayman."

"And the risk to you," Elizabeth said.

Darcy cast her a quick look. "That will leave you falling down a hill for no reason."

"I am willing to appear the hapless female in this." She gave him a smile, the warmth of which surged through him. "It is enough for me that you know the truth." Breaking their locked gaze, she turned to include Georgiana and Richard. "All of you."

Darcy shook his head. Too many people already knew the events of that day to hide them now. "Considering the number of people who heard the story about the highwayman, I think we must stay with the truth."

Elizabeth appeared thoughtful, then sighed. "You are correct, of course."

Darcy was again pleased, but not simply by her agreement. This was not an obedient wife accepting her husband's view, but an intelligent person who understood and agreed with his logic. Maybe he was making some headway in achieving her good opinion.

"That is all very well," Richard said. "And I agree. However, we need not press the truth on others."

Elizabeth nodded. "A fair point." She looked to Darcy, as if seeking his agreement as she continued, "If others bring up the highwayman, I won't deny it, but my version of the story will speak only about the fall."

"Mine as well," Georgiana said firmly, as one resolved. "Though I will do my best to avoid the subject entirely."

"There was a soldier I knew who had a head injury," Richard said. "He didn't remember anything that took place immediately before the injury, although he recovered. The doctor who treated him said this was common with head injuries. Mrs. Darcy can pretend she doesn't remember the fall and I suspect Darcy can handle any inquiries."

Elizabeth looked to Darcy again and asked, "Is that what you wish?"

"If it makes it easier for you, yes. If it makes it harder, no."

"It will make it easier," she said, smiling at him.

Darcy returned her smile.

"Georgiana, you need to watch your brother and new sister. They are so busy agreeing with each other that they may make bad decisions." Richard set down his tea. "Very well, then. Thank you for the tea and the information. I am off to prepare for my journey to Rosings tomorrow."

"Safe travels," Darcy said as everyone rose. He refrained from adding a wish for luck. Richard, being Richard, wouldn't need any.

Chapter Seventeen

Elizabeth spent the next several mornings seated across the desk from Mrs. Flynn, Mr. Darcy's housekeeper, in her spacious office off the kitchen. They went over the household accounts for Darcy House in detail. The house was well run, which she'd expected, and Mrs. Flynn convivial, something for which she'd hoped. They discussed the reasons behind various expenses and decisions. Mrs. Flynn listened to Elizabeth's few tentative suggestions and either acknowledged that they were valid and should be attempted or explained why not.

In truth, the house was run much the same as Longbourn, though on a grander scale. One her mother would envy, even if Mrs. Bennet wouldn't be up to the task. In contrast, Elizabeth suspected that her friend Charlotte would have no trouble running such a household. She made mental note of various questions she might direct to Charlotte in her next letter.

On the third such morning, after several hours of tea and work, Mrs. Flynn closed the account books with a smile, her signal that she had other duties to which to attend. "If it pleases you, Mrs. Darcy, may we halt for this morning?"

"Certainly, and I thank you for your time." Happy to have found such a strong ally in the housekeeper, Elizabeth felt a spark of hope as she said, "You are so kind to me, Mrs. Flynn, in giving your time so freely. May I ask, do you know the housekeeper at Pemberley? I hope to find her as helpful and competent as you are."

Appearing surprised by the question, Mrs. Flynn replied, "I know Mrs. Reynolds slightly and am flattered to be put in the same category she is."

"Then I'm certain I'll get along with her," Elizabeth said.

Elizabeth left the housekeeper's office wondering at the impetus of Mrs. Flynn's reaction. Did she hold Mrs. Reynolds in high esteem, or Pemberley? Perhaps both? Did her surprise stem from the idea that anyone would think Mrs. Reynolds kind or that anyone would think her unkind? Traversing the wood paneled halls of a house that still felt nothing like home to her, Elizabeth supposed she would find out in due course.

She went to find Georgiana because her husband had tasked her with practicing pianoforte with his sister every day. He'd couched the request as her helping him with Georgiana's studies and accomplishments, but in view of Georgiana's proficiency, Elizabeth suspected a different motive. She was the one Mr. Darcy wished played better. Assigning her practice with Georgiana was undoubtedly her husband's version of diplomacy.

Rather than be offended, Elizabeth chose to be amused. Firstly, because she did need to practice more. More important, however, was Mr. Darcy's lack of subtlety. If the exchange over pianoforte practice indicated the level of artfulness of which her husband was capable, they would get on together well indeed. She had no wish to spend her life with a conniving man, even if that sometimes led to bluntness on his part.

She and Georgiana still practiced, the duet on which they were working coming along quite well, when Darcy House's butler, Edwards, arrived in the doorway. "A Mrs. Hurst and Miss Bingley are asking if you are at home, Mrs. Darcy, Miss Darcy."

"No. At least I'm not at home," Georgiana said before Elizabeth could reply.

Elizabeth swiveled on the piano bench to look at her. "Aren't these people friends of your brother?"

Georgiana pulled a face. "Yes, but tell them I must work on my Italian."

"Only if you introduce them, and politely and with an appearance of reluctance, give your excuse and actually work on your Italian."

Georgiana heaved a sigh, reminding Elizabeth of her youngest sister Lydia who was a similar age, and said, "Very well. If I must."

Not permitting her amusement to become a smile, Elizabeth replied, "Yes. I believe you must." She stood from the bench. "We will meet them in the jade parlor, thank you."

Edwards nodded and strode off.

Georgiana stood as well, closing the fall over the keys. "Miss Bingley will look down her nose at your gown," she said as they crossed the room.

Elizabeth glanced at her dress, still one of her old garments. The new gowns she'd ordered with Aunt Gardiner's assistance would be ready soon but until they arrived, she'd nothing to wear but what she had. "Are Mrs. Hurst and Miss Bingley not Mr. Bingley's sisters?" She couldn't imagine the relations of the man who'd written such a lovely letter wishing them a happy union to be anything but pleasant.

"Yes."

Georgiana offered no more as they went to the jade parlor and Elizabeth didn't ask. It didn't do to gossip in hallways. She would meet the ladies momentarily and could form her own opinion.

They reached the parlor shortly before two tall, very fashionably gowned women were shown in. The younger of the two did pause slightly in her step at the sight of Elizabeth, and exchanged a look with the older, but they came forward with smiles as Georgiana made introductions. Elizabeth had to admit that at first impression she would prefer to dislike the two, but she attempted to master that.

"It is a pleasure to meet you both," Elizabeth said when Georgiana finished. "Should I send for tea?"

"Not for me, please," Georgiana said, turning a deprecating smile on Mrs. Hurst and Miss Bingley. "My brother is certain that my studies suffered this summer while I resided with my Aunt Catherine, Miss de Bourgh being older and no longer in need of tutors. He's designed quite the strict daily regimen for me." She added a beleaguered sigh that Elizabeth felt a touch overdone.

"We will miss you, dear Georgiana," Miss Bingley said. "But this will give us more time to come to know Mrs. Darcy."

"Charles sends his warm regards," Mrs. Hurst added.

"Thank him for me." With that, Georgiana pivoted and fled the room.

The two women refixed their attention on Elizabeth, who smiled. "Shall we sit, then?" They did and she called for tea, then opened with, "I've not spent much time in London, but I believe it's unusually warm for the time of year?"

Miss Bingley nodded. "Charles said Mr. Darcy mentioned something regarding that, which is why we've come."

Unable to resist, Elizabeth schooled her features and said, "Because of the unseasonable heat?"

Miss Bingley exchanged another look with her sister, this one a clear bid for patience. "No, Mrs. Darcy. Because you've not been much in London." She made a sweeping gesture, encompassing Elizabeth. "Your gown tells that story quite well. Louisa and I should be honored to educate you in London fashion. We could make a day of it. Tomorrow, or the following?"

"That is very kind of you. If you can spare the day after tomorrow, I have commissioned some new gowns and they will be ready tomorrow. That way, I won't be too much of an embarrassment when I shop with you."

Mrs. Hurst's shoulders dropped with relief. "That would be ideal."

Miss Bingley cast her sister a warning look. "No one expects you to have London fashions the moment you arrive in town. However, the day after tomorrow suits us well, does it not, Louisa?"

They then embarked on a back and forth about where Elizabeth should shop. It amused her to hear some of the locations she and her aunt had visited mentioned, the main exception being the cordwainer. She and Aunt Gardiner had sought one who specialized in boots, at Elizabeth's request. She knew she would need slippers as well but had very much wished for new walking boots.

The fashion dialog between the two sisters took them well into the serving and sipping of tea, both women becoming far more relaxed than when they'd arrived. Elizabeth worked to rescind her initial dislike. They were snobs, but not on the level of Lady Catherine. She suspected that was because Mr. Bingley's sisters wished to be seen as good people as well as fashionable. Lady Catherine raised her daughter to believe both of them were better than anyone other than royalty and above any petty things like genuine goodness.

At the end of a lengthy debate between the top two milliners in London, Miss Bingley turned to Elizabeth. "Mrs. Darcy, if you do not mind me saying, rumors abound over how you and Mr. Darcy met. One is so outlandish as to say you saved his carriage from tumbling into a ravine."

Elizabeth smiled. "That does sound outlandish, doesn't it? Precisely the way a story might come out once passed through the lines of gossip."

Both women chuckled.

"What did happen?" Mrs. Hurst asked. "Every account has some element of the extraordinary."

"Not that we permit the repetition of tales," Miss Bingley added with haste. "Not when we can prevent it."

Elizabeth dipped her head to acknowledge that, though she doubted the truth of Miss Bingley's declaration. She conjured the carefully truthful words she'd prepared for such occasions in her head and said,

"Mr. Darcy saw me tumble down the side of a gully and came to my rescue. I'd been out walking but the girl who'd come with me became scared and ran away. Mr. Darcy saved me."

"You poor thing," Mrs. Hurst said with no sympathy in her voice. "That must have been dreadful."

"I cannot truly say. I hit my head and was rendered unconscious, so I don't recall any of the most dreadful bit." Only waking alone and afraid in an unfamiliar place with a stranger.

"You were unconscious?" Miss Bingley echoed in surprise.

"Yes. I also broke my arm and several ribs." Elizabeth grimaced. "Truth be told, my face was so scratched and swollen, I doubt Mr. Darcy even knew what I looked like when he offered for me."

"That's horrendous," Mrs. Hurst said with much more feeling.

Elizabeth wondered to which part of the statement the other woman referred.

"What of your companion?" Miss Bingley asked. "How could she simply abandon you?"

"She was only a girl," Elizabeth had already decided that Lucy could bear some blame but shouldn't carry much, as the man they'd seen had a pistol. "Borrowed from the local inn."

"Local inn?" Suspicion sparked in Mrs. Hurst's eyes. "That's right, you were in Kent, were you not? Even though Charles assures us that your family is in Hertfordshire."

Elizabeth decided that Mrs. Hurst didn't know how much it hurt to be pushed down a hill. No amount of wealth could be worth the possibility of a broken neck and the reality of the injuries she'd suffered, yet people would insist on believing she'd somehow singled out Mr. Darcy, tracked him to Kent, and flung herself down a hill in front of him. "Mr. Bingley is correct. I was with my aunt and uncle."

Miss Bingley gave her sister a quelling look. "Do your aunt and uncle have an estate in Kent?"

Elizabeth suspected Miss Bingley only asked to make up for her sister's borderline impoliteness. However, she knew revealing that her aunt and uncle were in trade in London would only make the other two women uncomfortable. Tempting as that was, she merely said, "No. We were taking a pleasure trip." She smiled at both women. "Am I correct in recalling that Mr. Bingley is considering leasing an estate in Hertfordshire?"

"He is," Mrs. Hurst said. "He is there now inspecting the holding."

"Otherwise, he would be with us," Miss Bingley added. "He does so enjoy visiting with Georgiana."

"Not with my husband?" Elizabeth asked.

"Certainly. Charles and Mr. Darcy are great friends."

"I look forward to making your brother's acquaintance on his return." She gestured to the table. "More tea?"

They declined. After a touch more inane banter and an agreement as to when they would arrive in their carriage to take Elizabeth to shop in two days' time, Mrs. Hurst and Miss Bingley departed. Feeling it to be her duty both as Georgiana's chaperone and, in a way, to the women of Meryton, Elizabeth then went to find her sister-by-marriage to seek clarification on her relationship with Mr. Bingley. Not because she knew of any reason for the match to be wrong but because her obligations to various parties demanded greater knowledge.

She found Georgiana in the library, an array of books spread out atop the table at which she sat. Pen in hand, she looked up from the novel she diligently translated as Elizabeth sat across from her. "Have you come to check my work?"

"I wish that were the case," Elizabeth replied. "It would mean I speak Italian. Alas, you must await the verdict of your instructor."

Georgiana smirked and blotted her pen.

Elizabeth realized the dearth in her knowledge was already known and that Georgiana had simply wished to test whether Elizabeth would pretend. The girl definitely needed taking in hand. Not too firm a hand but at least some gentle guidance.

"They have left?" Georgiana asked, laying down her pen. "It's safe for me to leave this room?"

The subject which interested her broached, Elizabeth embarked on a circuitous route. "They seemed pleasant enough. What is it about them that you find so off-putting?"

Georgiana scrunched her nose. "They're so proper and so stiff, and they gush about how wonderful I am but notice every little error I make. And they talk about others behind their backs, which makes me wonder what they say about me. I'm not perfect."

"That does sound disagreeable." Elizabeth waited, hoping for more. In her experience with her sister Lydia, pushing led to less forthrightness than silence.

Georgiana picked her pen back up and put it down again, then blurted, "And they're always machinating."

"Machinating?"

She nodded. "Mr. Bingley truly likes Fitz but his sisters, I don't believe they've ever even considered if they like my brother. They simply like being in his sphere." She shrugged. "I've seen it so many times in my life. It used to happen with my school friends. I would think they wanted to be my friends but really, they wanted to be friends with a Darcy."

"I see." That did sound difficult, and Elizabeth could see what Georgiana meant about Mrs. Hurst and Miss Bingley not caring, or even considering, if they bore Mr. Darcy any genuine affection. She imagined they regarded her much the same way.

"And they're always trying to push me and Mr. Bingley together." Georgiana pulled a face.

"And that is not something you would consider? I gather that Mr. Bingley is a kindhearted gentleman."

Georgiana shook her head as Elizabeth spoke. "He is. He's amazingly nice and truly not an unattractive fellow."

"Then?" Elizabeth cocked an eyebrow.

Georgiana took up the cap for the inkwell and turned it in her fingers, causing Elizabeth to hope no ink wet it. "He's too nice. When you meet him, you'll see what I mean. He's simply…he's too nice. I don't know any other way to put it."

"Nicer than your cousin, Richard?"

"Our cousin," Georgiana corrected absently, still fidgeting with the inkwell cap. "Yes. By far. Fitz is nice. Richard is nice. They're still…I don't know." She pursed her lips. "Do you know anyone who, if you walked up and took the food right off their plate and ate it, would apologize to you for it?"

"You mean, say, 'I'm sorry. I should have thought to offer you some,' or some such?"

"Yes." Georgiana nodded emphatically. "Like that."

Her sister, Jane. "Yes. I do."

Relief touched Georgiana's sudden smile. "Well, then, you know what I mean. That's how Mr. Bingley is and it's infuriating. If I don't speak to him, he apologizes for not being a good conversationalist. If I do speak to him but attempt to be aloof so as not to be seen as encouraging affection, he apologizes for not being more entertaining."

"Perhaps he is trying to be kind to you to win your regard?"

157

"No. He's like that with everyone, about everything. It works well with Fitz because my brother has a habit of saying the wrong thing and offending people, even though he truly doesn't mean to. Mr. Bingley doesn't care, though. I'm not certain he even notices. You could walk up to him and slap him across the face for no reason, and he'd apologize."

"I see. Well, now that I know your feelings in the matter, I'll endeavor not to encourage Mrs. Hurst and Miss Bingley's ambition in that area. And I certainly won't slap Mr. Bingley." The last made Georgiana smile.

"It's not that I dislike him," Georgiana said hurriedly as Elizabeth made to rise. "He's very nice and a happy addition to any occasion, and he always dances with me if there's any dancing when they come for dinner, which there always is because Miss Bingley plays. I simply don't feel, well, that way about him." She frowned slightly. "I do not believe he feels that way about me, either. He's nice to everyone."

"I understand," Elizabeth assured her as she stood, though she didn't think it boded well for Georgiana that she didn't like men who were 'too nice.'

Georgiana smiled, looking up at her. "You have unmarried sisters still, do you not?"

Elizabeth nodded.

"One of them should marry him. Then Mrs. Hurst and Miss Bingley will have their tie to my brother and maybe then I can get along with them."

Elizabeth chuckled. "I'll see if I can work that out for you." Unbidden, her thoughts went to Jane.

Chapter Eighteen

Going by the name Mr. George Wiekran, Wickham used forged papers making him a landholder and obtained a lieutenant's position in the local militia about to be stationed in Meryton. He then charmed his way into being the officer that his new colonel, Forster, sent on ahead to begin community relations and to arrange accommodations for their unit. An assignment that came with a pleasantly weighty entrustment of funds.

His success in creating a plausible reason to be in the village near where the Bennets lived pleased him. He'd expended considerable charm, effort and even some of his meager funds researching where the Bennets lived and coming up with his cover for being there. Mustering the funds to buy the paperwork had been difficult and had required a few risky thefts, but he didn't mind being steadfast and dedicated when it came to getting retribution from Darcy. Besides which, though the inquisition had become more a trickle than a torrent, being Mr. Wiekran in a local militia afforded the additional comfort of not having to worry as much about the runners Darcy had loosed to investigate him and the bridge incidents.

His first few days in Meryton, rather than seek arrangements for his unit, he wandered the town charming merchants and making new friends. He spent the money Colonel Forster had entrusted to him in shops and gambled freely, both to add to his appeal as an acquaintance and because Darcy would be paying the money back, one way or another. He didn't ask about the Bennet family. Not right away. He bided his time until the question could arise naturally so as to avoid suspicion.

Nearly a week into his stay in Meryton found him in the general store inspecting a length of leather he fancied for a new belt, until movement caught his eye. There, reflected in the small mirror beside a display of rather sorry looking bonnets, appeared the loveliest creature he'd ever beheld. Tall, sweet of face and demeanor, she entered with a maid in tow. That paltry chaperone would be easily worked around.

"Ah, Miss Bennet," the shopkeeper greeted, and Wickham went still lest his reaction betray him. "Have you come for your mother's order?"

"Yes, Mr. Basil."

Nodding, the shopkeeper disappeared into the back.

Wickham couldn't believe his good fortune. Surely, Heaven smiled on his work to gain retribution from Darcy. He'd hoped for a father or brother he could lure into gambling debts, or a bored matron he might seduce. Possibly a younger female relation to compromise. This fair creature, though, cried out for elopement.

And then, Darcy would have to call him brother. Darcy would be forced to accept him, ensure he and his bride had enough money on which to live, and to call off the Bow Street Runners. There was no way that Darcy would prosecute him. Darcys didn't disown their family members, only their godsons.

Before the shopkeeper could return, Wickham maneuvered to stand behind the woman and her maid, then turned his back on them. Confident in both his regimentals and his smile, he knocked a large pot off the nearest shelf.

Predictably, the women started, one letting out a shriek. He turned to apologize as they turned to look, making certain he collided with the inviting form of Miss Bennet. He jumped back, bumped the shelf again, and winced for show.

"My apologies," he said, hands held before him, palms out. "I am so sorry. How clumsy of me. I didn't mean to startle you, Miss..."

Her maid looked back and forth between them, eyes narrowing.

"Oh," Miss Bennet breathed, hand pressed to her pounding heart. "I am so sorry. Think nothing of it, sir. I apologize that I did not realize you were there."

"Wiekran," he said, bending to gather the fallen pots as if too distracted by putting right his mess to recall his manners or realize she hadn't asked. "Lieutenant George Wiekran."

She dipped her head as he turned from returning the jostled pots to their shelves. "Mr. Wiekran. Again, my apologies."

"Miss Bennet," the shopkeeper said, coming out, arms laden. "I heard an awful—Oh, Mr. Wiekran. Can I assist you, sir?"

"My apologies." Wickham added an ingratiating smile to his words. "I knocked over some pots. I've put them right." He gestured to the shelves. "I'm afraid I startled these two ladies." Would he secure an introduction or not? He'd given her every opportunity to offer her name. Most women would not be so proper or so resistant to his smile.

"Jane?" a voice called as the shop door flung inward. "Jane, are you in here? Oh, there you are."

The owner of that voice, a taller but obviously younger version of the beauty before him, strode forward, gaze raking him up and down. Wickham turned his smile on her. She lacked her older sister's almost otherworldly loveliness, but more than made up for that with the spark of mischief in her eyes.

Reaching them, she thrust out her hand. "I'm Miss Lydia Bennet."

Wickham took her gloved fingers and raised them to his lips, then applied slight pressure to them before releasing her, each move calculated to stir her young heart. "Lieutenant George Wiekran, at your service."

"And you can be of service right now, can't he, Jane?" Lydia smiled wide enough that the look would appear vapid, if he didn't read cunning in her eyes. "I'm certain the three of us can use a gentleman's assistance carrying home Mama's order. She always orders so very much. Am I not correct, Mr. Basil?"

"Ah." The shopkeeper looked from person to person, uncomfortable with his involuntary participation in introducing two unwed misses to a man. "There are quite a few, Miss Bennet. I was coming to tell you as much when I heard the crash, but I didn't know that you were here as well, Miss Lydia."

Lydia's smile evolved into a smirk. "You see? We are in desperate need of your assistance, Mr. Wiekran." She leaned forward. "Very desperate need."

Wickham nodded, tossing aside his burgeoning plan to seduce the older sister. Lydia offered a much easier target, and the prospect for a lot more fun. "It is my duty as a gentleman to come to your aid, Miss Lydia." Catching sight of three frowns he reined in his grin. It wouldn't do to have Miss Bennet convince any paternal parties to forbid Lydia his association.

He caught her puckish gaze again and amended that thought. Forbidding her his company might serve him perfectly well. But first, he would attempt the easy route of being welcomed in.

He turned to the shopkeeper. "Mr. Basil, if you could pack them up, I would be delighted to carry the ladies' packages for them."

Basil looked to Miss Bennet, who hesitated, then nodded. She turned to Wickham as the shopkeeper retreated into the back once more. "Thank you, Mr. Wiekran. Your assistance is appreciated. I'm certain Mama didn't recall quite how many items she'd ordered when she sent us without the carriage."

No carriage? He hid a grimace. "It's a splendid day for a walk." As if any day were, but if he must play beast of burden to get Lydia into his arms, he would. For now.

When the shopkeeper returned, Wickham took up several of the packages, leaving the remainder for the maid, who still regarded him with suspicion. He needed to keep at least one arm free, so he could offer it to Lydia as they walked, which he did. They set off through town, then out along a wide lane. Miss Bennet walked slightly behind with the maid, taking up some of her packages. Wickham sneered inwardly at how the woman coddled her servant.

Lydia prattled as they walked, as she had in the shop and all through town. Wickham didn't mind the lack of silence or the lack of need to carry one side of the conversation, but he knew from experience that her penchant for chatter would annoy him once he'd had her in his bed. It was always the case. Things that didn't trouble him about a woman became insufferable once he'd bedded her.

"It's such a fine day, do you not agree, Mr. Wiekran?" Lydia asked. "Of course, it is autumn and in Hertfordshire, autumn is the very best time of year. But then, our winters can be mild and quite fine, and spring is lovely. Do you care for summer? I don't like the heat, but I do prefer the gowns. Light and gauzy, and as low bodiced as you like to let out the heat." She batted her eyelashes at him as she said that.

As she must have intended, his gaze immediately dropped to take in her bosom, displayed nicely by a cloak closed at the throat but otherwise thrown open. She was correct to remind him of such a fine view for he hadn't looked his fill in the shop, under the wary eyes of her older sister and the maid.

"Not that I'm ever cold, so really I can do as I like with my gowns and Mama doesn't care. Lizzy used to but now she's married and doesn't live with us anymore, so she has no say in my dresses. Not that she ever ought to have. Really, the way she acted, you'd think she was the Mama."

He let her cheery voice wash over him, making no effort to comprehend the words or formulate obviously unrequired replies. As often as he liked, for he could tell it pleased her, he took his attention

162

off both her and the smooth roadway to stare at the plush swells rising from the low bodice of her dress.

"…and Netherfield Park is that way," she was saying, pointing. "It's been let at last. An unmarried gentleman is coming. A wealthy one." She breathed in deeply to heave out a dreamy sigh.

That caught his attention, both the deep breath and the words. "Oh? When is this wealthy gentleman arriving?"

More idiotic eyelash fluttering. "Why, are you jealous, Mr. Wiekran?"

"Very." He half closed his lids in a smoldering look that had brought far more proper ladies to his bed. "For you are the most beguiling, lovely creature I've ever seen, and I would have you all to myself, for all time."

She giggled in an overly vapid way and swatted his arm. "Oh, Mr. Wiekran, you are so naughty to say such things, but you needn't worry. Mama has Jane allotted for Mr. Bingley, the gentleman who's let Netherfield Park, and anyhow, I prefer a man who wears a uniform."

"Bingley?" If Bingley was coming, Darcy wouldn't be far behind. Like as not that too-good dullard had based his selection of a country home purely on being near Darcy. The two were infatuated with each other. Fast friends, acting as if Darcy didn't believe he was far too good for Bingley and as if Bingley actually cared for Darcy, rather than simply using him for his connections.

"Oh yes, Mr. Bingley. They say he'll bring legions of gentlemen up from London and that he has five thousand a year. Do you know him? Is he handsome?"

Those sisters of his would likely come too. Would any of them recognize him aside from Darcy? Wickham had encountered Bingley once or twice. He'd glimpsed the sisters and he knew Hurst. Hurst could be a problem. Darcy wouldn't be. He hated to socialize and wouldn't condescend to do so with any of the countrified gentry in the area. His snobbery made him easy to avoid. "I don't know him, no."

"Oh. That's too bad. I'd hoped you could introduce us."

Wickham refocused on Lydia. Trust Darcy to interrupt his attempts to seduce the girl, even from miles away. "Why would I introduce you to a wealthy gentleman when I wish to have you all to myself?"

That won him another bout of giggles and a second slap on the arm. "Oh, but you're terrible, Mr. Wiekran."

She had no idea how terrible. He imagined it would be fun to teach her, though.

When they finally turned up the drive, the packages he carried having grown annoyingly heavy over the course of the trek, Wickham took in the Bennets' estate of Longbourn with hidden glee. The lands and house, well maintained and perfectly adequate to a country gentleman, announced that Mr. Bennet must have enough resources to settle some amount of money on Lydia. Money that would be supplement for whatever he could wring out of Darcy through the connection of brotherhood. Money Wickham deserved for planning to put up with Lydia at least until he could augment whatever he received into enough to leave her and start over somewhere new as the wealthy gentleman he was meant to be.

More than that, though, Longbourn appeared so very ordinary. It must eat away at Darcy's soul to have married so far beneath him. Wickham only wished he knew why Darcy had done it.

"You will come in, won't you, Mr. Wiekran?" Lydia asked when they reached the top of the drive. "The least we can do is offer you tea for your trouble."

"Tea would be most pleasant, Miss Lydia."

"Splendid."

They stepped into an entrance hall so perfectly adequate as to rekindle his glee. He could imagine Darcy there, disapproving and awkward. Making the tiny space seem overly small instead of quaintly so. Wearing that condescending frown. Wickham pressed the packages he carried onto a waiting maid and began removing his outerwear. He was shown into a sunny parlor, the furnishings well-kept but neither up to current fashion nor respectable antiques. He continued his delightful imaginings of how it would pain Darcy to be in the space.

Miss Bennet excused herself, but the maid remained, as if Wickham would be foolish enough to kiss Lydia so soon and jeopardize his suit. Before Lydia could call for tea or either of them sit, Miss Bennet returned with a florid faced matron who bustled in with Lydia's same vapid smile. Wickham greeted her with great cordiality, pleased he wouldn't be forced to seduce her to blackmail money from Darcy but even more pleased to picture Darcy enduring dinner with this woman presiding.

After they were all seated and tea sent for, Wickham turned to her, hoping he might finally discover why Darcy had up and wed. Looking around, he couldn't fathom any reason but love and yet, he didn't believe Darcy capable of the emotion. After all, he clearly didn't love Wickham even though they'd been raised as brothers. No, Darcy would marry for wealth and connections, not affection, but he clearly had not. "Mrs. Bennet, you have two absolutely lovely daughters. You must be so proud."

"Oh, I am of Jane and Lydia, to be certain. My favorites, for all they aren't married."

"Mama," Miss Bennet murmured in mild reprimand.

"Favorites?" Wickham repeated with feigned innocence. "You have more lovely daughters about?"

"Not about. Married off," she said smugly. "Kitty married a steward and Mary settled for a country surgeon, but my Lizzy married Mr. Darcy of Pemberley. A very wealthy man."

"Indeed? She must be exceptional."

"She is not," Lydia said, scrunching her nose. "She's boring and short and judgmental."

Boring and judgmental would appeal to Darcy. "Oh? I cannot imagine a wealthy man selecting someone like that over you, Miss Lydia."

That won him a smile from both Lydia and her mother.

"Yes, well, he's never met me," Lydia said.

"When he does, we must hope he doesn't regret picking Lizzy too terribly," Mrs. Bennet added.

"Mama," Miss Bennet repeated, a touch louder this time.

Wishing they would provide the information he wanted, Wickham said, "Surely, if he is a wealthy gentleman, this Mr. Darcy married for love."

Lydia shook her head, eyes wide and dancing.

Mrs. Bennet mimicked the movement, jowls wiggling. "Oh no. It was an accident. Elizabeth accosted some man and fell into a gully, and Mr. Darcy took her back to town and did right by her."

Wickham feigned surprise to cover his elation. That woman, the one who'd spoiled his plans, she was Elizabeth Bennet? He'd hoped her dead, but this was better. Because of him, Darcy was shackled to this family? A family so far beneath Darcy and one which offered such an easy path for Wickham to bind himself to the Darcy line forever. He could hardly have planned his failure to keep Darcy from reaching Ramsgate any better if he'd tried.

The women talked on, mostly prattling about Bingley's upcoming arrival, requiring no encouragement from Wickham. He made a show of attending to their words, but his mind frolicked with images of Darcy's misery. Of his noble self-sacrifice. Falling on his sword, as it were, for

165

the dignity of some country girl, yet all the while actually doing it to salve his enormous pride.

After carrying the packages and having tea, it proved deplorably easy for Wickham to insinuate himself into the Bennet household. To cover Mr. Bennet's suspicions when he met the man, who proved too sharp for Wickham's liking, he spun a tale of bad luck accounting for both his education and his current poverty. In a matter of days, he had them all charmed, along with half of Meryton.

Everything was in place, but Bingley was coming, and Wickham suspected both Hurst and Darcy to arrive shortly thereafter, if not with Bingley. Just as in Ramsgate, Wickham needed more time but unlike Ramsgate, he felt certain he could avoid detection while charming the girl he planned to run off with. No need for sabotage. Only one to avoid anyplace Hurst or Darcy might go.

Fortunately, Hurst was lazy and Darcy too much of a snob to venture into most Meryton residences or gathering places. Certainly, Darcy wouldn't set foot in Longbourn if he could avoid it. Much as Wickham enjoyed imagining Darcy awash in crassness and a lack of luxury, the fact that his snobbery would make him shun his wife's relations was for the best. Wickham would have all the space he required to seduce Lydia into running off with him.

Chapter Nineteen

Elizabeth enjoyed her outing with Mrs. Hurst and Miss Bingley more than she expected and used the opportunity to quiz them about the books she'd seen in Georgiana's stack for translating. It turned out that some were French titles and some Italian, and that Elizabeth's inquiries pleased them, as they provided the opportunity for Mrs. Hurst and Miss Bingley to show their superiority.

The two sisters were snobs. Of that she had no illusions. She suspected that, were she not Mrs. Darcy, she would see a much different side of them. One that she wouldn't care for very much. As she was Mrs. Darcy, she accepted and appreciated their recommendations for her apparel, while working to hide her amusement at how similar their opinions were to those offered by her aunt...in trade.

Their only slip in their mutual veneer of civility came when Mrs. Hurst, atop many other such hints, said, "Miss Darcy should have come with us. We could point out to her Charles' favorite colors."

Elizabeth, patience stretched thin by an afternoon of such comments, replied, "I don't believe it would be at all appropriate for a fifteen-year-old girl who isn't even out to consider the preferences of any gentleman, except possibly those of her guardians."

"Oh, but surely, Georgiana will be out soon," Miss Bingley said with the slight condescension that often edged her voice.

"That, as well, falls into the province of Mr. Darcy and Colonel Fitzwilliam."

Mrs. Hurst, who'd been contemplating her reflection while holding up various shades of umber, turned to Elizabeth. "But surely you have influence." She offered a knowing look. "You're a new wife. You must have discovered the power of your wiles."

To cover a shock of both embarrassment and anger, for she'd discovered no such thing, Elizabeth snapped, "I do not believe bringing out my new fifteen-year-old sister is a good use of wiles. In truth, I am not certain of the morality of such tactics. A man and his wife ought to be able to engage in reasonable discourse on any and all issues that impact them."

Mrs. Hurst's eyes narrowed in anger but then she shrugged, chuckling. "I forget that, though married since summer, you are new to actual married life. You'll learn soon enough that men cannot be reasoned with, my dear. Only managed."

"Oh Louisa," Miss Bingley said on a sigh. "Let her linger in the first glows of love. You know they're fleeting and not to be repeated."

"True. So very true," Mrs. Hurst said and turned back to the mirror.

Elizabeth looked down to smooth the cloth she'd been admiring, a lovely sapphire that brought to mind the intensity of Mr. Darcy's expression as he'd spoken of buying her a necklace, which he seemed to have forgotten, and willed away a blush.

After the dress outing, she didn't see the two women for some days, which gave her much needed time for correspondences with Jane, Charlotte, and Mary, and for more visits with Aunt Gardiner and Kitty, who was in the process of moving to a much finer residence than Mr. Smith had when they'd first married. When Mrs. Hurst and Miss Bingley did next call, the butler announced that Mr. Bingley accompanied them. Elizabeth bade him put them in the jade parlor while she went to locate her husband. He'd never said as much but she felt he regarded Mr. Bingley with singular friendship and would wish to join them for tea.

She found Mr. Darcy at his desk going over ledgers, various stacks of letters arranged neatly about him. Engrossed in his work, Mr. Darcy appeared much as she'd pictured him over his long weeks in Scotland after they married. Standing in the open doorway watching him, it heartened her to see him so conscientious in the heart of London with the city's many distractions beckoning. It made her feel more valued to think he truly had been diligently at work in Scotland, not there simply to avoid her.

He'd removed his coat, the paneled room warm despite the winds of autumn swirling without. His hair fell less neatly than usual, as if he'd run his fingers through it without thought. His shirtsleeves were not rolled up, as she'd seen her father do to avoid getting ink on the cuffs. Elizabeth imagined that Mr. Darcy did not get ink on his cuffs. The ink wouldn't dare.

The tip of his pen moved down a list of figures, his lips silently counting, then back up again, then down. He pushed a hand through his hair and frowned.

"Is something the matter?" she asked.

His head snapped up, his frown vanishing into a smile. "Elizabeth." The smile disappeared. "Is something wrong?"

"That is what I asked you." She gestured to the ledger. "The numbers in that column seem to be thwarting you."

He glanced down. "One is missing, and another is too high. I didn't notice in the quarterly report because it holds only the sums, but these are by day."

She crossed the room, ready to retreat if he showed any sign of not wishing her to look at his ledger. Leaning over the desk to see better, she scanned the offending row. "The high number immediately follows the missing day. Could it be that someone simply combined the two?"

She looked up to find him staring not at her face or the ledger, but somewhere in between. Heat suffused her face and she straightened.

He cleared his throat, expression abashed, and looked down, then frowned. "Yes. That could explain it. The too-large number is about double what I would expect."

"Well then, that's likely what took place."

He met her gaze. "Thank you."

She shrugged. "What are those numbers?"

"Daily yields from one of the tenant farms."

"Daily yield?" During the harvest, tenants were usually too busy to report daily yields.

"I have a few tenants whose families have been there for generations but can't save. I let them give me a percent of their daily yield rather than quarterly payments. It saves them the trouble of marketing. I've had several other tenants go on that system because they are better at farming than selling."

"You go over all of them?" She had the impression his holdings were extensive. How long must that take?

"I select a few at random to double check the work of my stewards."

"That is very diligent of you."

"It is my duty to the people beholden to me to manage the land well." He marked the page and closed the ledger. "But you cannot convince me you've come to discuss milk production or crop yields."

"I did not. I came to tell you that Mr. Bingley and his sisters await us in the jade parlor, or me, at least. I am happy to give an excuse if you are not available."

Mr. Darcy reached to put up his pen and cap the ink. "I welcome the interruption." He stood and came around the desk.

"Your coat," Elizabeth said when he stopped beside her, regretting her own words as she quite enjoyed seeing her tall, handsome husband in his shirtsleeves and waistcoat. "And your hair. Here, let me." She reached up to run her fingers through his hair, ordering it.

As she brought her arm back down, he caught her wrist in a light grip, turning his face to kiss her palm but keeping his dark eyes locked with hers. A delightful shiver ran through her, weakening her knees. She opened her mouth without any real thought of what she might say, which didn't matter as her breath caught in her throat.

His thumb stroking up and down her palm he murmured, "I don't know what I said wrong, that evening in Rosings."

"Evening in Rosings?" She felt nearly as dazed as in the first weeks after the blow to her head.

"You touched my face, like this." He pressed her palm along his jaw, covering her hand with his larger one. "And I thought...that is, I hoped that was a sign that you'd begun to hold me in some affection. Then I said something foolish. Or insensitive. I know not which, only that I am prone to such errors, and you withdrew your hand and left me. You haven't touched me since."

Elizabeth struggled for the memory and claimed it but couldn't muster any of the ire his words had sparked then. "You said that to insult me was to insult you."

Lines of confusion marred his brow. "Why is that wrong?"

Each time he spoke, the corner of his mouth grazed her palm, threatening to eradicate thought. She drew in a deep breath, seeking the wherewithal to form an explanation. "I didn't want you to defend me because you took insult. I wished you to defend me for my sake, and because your aunt and cousin were wrong."

His eyes widened slightly as he absorbed her meaning. He recaptured her fingers in his. "You see? I am prone to such errors. Let me be clear now. My aunt and cousin were wrong, and I will always defend you for your sake."

Elizabeth stared up at him, hardly able to breathe. "Thank you."

Footfalls sounded in the hall. Unhurried, Mr. Darcy kissed her palm again, then released her. Turning away, he went back around his desk to take up his coat. He shrugged into it, then plucked a letter from one of the piles on the desk and slipped it into a pocket.

Darcy House's butler stepped into the open office doorway. He looked between them, expressionless, and said, "Mr. Bingley, Mrs. Hurst and Miss Bingley are in the jade parlor sir, madam."

"Thank you, Edwards," Mr. Darcy said. "We are on our way there now. Please have tea brought. See if there are any of those raspberry tarts left that Bingley fancies so much."

"Yes, sir."

Edwards left and Elizabeth and her husband set forth for the jade parlor. As she walked, Elizabeth stole glances at Mr. Darcy's impressive profile. Her palm tingled, the sensation both maddening and delightful. She worked not to blush, hoping their guests wouldn't guess...

What? That she'd helped her husband with a ledger and fixed his hair before he made an apology and kissed her palm? Hardly the stuff of gothic novels.

Yet the memory of it left her breathless.

Fortunately, she regained her composure before they reached the parlor. Seated within with the now familiar Mrs. Hurst and Miss Bingley was a gentleman with a round, cheerful face. He rose to greet them, revealing himself neither too very tall nor very short, and possessed of the sort of eager, engaging affability that had come through so readily in his letter. Unmistakably her brother, his cordiality illustrated how much lovelier Miss Bingley would look should she ever smile.

After apologizing for the delay, for which he took the blame, Mr. Darcy performed the introductions. Assessing Mr. Bingley, Elizabeth decided that he seemed the sort of gentleman everyone wished to have about. Kind natured, affable, and possessed of more wealth than hauteur. What interested Elizabeth most, however, was seeing her husband genuinely pleased to greet someone and relaxed in their presence.

"Well, Darcy, it's a fine place," Mr. Bingley said once they were all seated. He looked to Elizabeth. "I've rented Netherfield Park, you see. Splendid estate."

"Mr. Darcy told me you'd gone to inspect it. I'm pleased it met with your approval."

"Not only the estate," Mr. Bingley replied. "The whole neighborhood. Splendid. Meryton, splendid. Your father and Sir William Lucas—"

"So help me, Charles, if you say splendid again," Miss Bingley warned but her annoyance possessed a wry edge.

Mr. Bingley chuckled. "Well, they are. Mr. Bennet is a sharp one, let me tell you, and Sir William has met the King, you know."

Elizabeth did know. Sir William Lucas, father to her dear friend Charlotte, told the story at least once a fortnight. He would be overjoyed to have new ears into which he might impart the tale.

"And Sir William informed me that there will be an assembly next week," Mr. Bingley continued eagerly. "You and Darcy should come up to dance. I'm officially inviting you to Netherfield Park, to remain as long as you like. We will even hold a ball. The ballroom is quite splendid."

"Really, Charles," Miss Bingley groused, "one does not leave London to dance."

"And Caroline hasn't had an opportunity to settle the household," Mrs. Hurst added. "You must allow her a few days before filling the place with guests."

"I am perfectly capable of organizing some country manor," Miss Bingley protested.

"I know you are, dear," Mrs. Hurst said and turned to Elizabeth and Mr. Darcy. "And I am certain Charles meant that he is inviting the both of you and Miss Darcy."

"Oh, yes, Miss Darcy too," Mr. Bingley said with unwavering affability but, as Georgiana had advised Elizabeth, not a hint of any real interest. He didn't care if Georgiana joined them or not.

"That is kind of you, but I believe that, as I previously mentioned, we will seek lodgings in Longbourn," Mr. Darcy said, turning to Elizabeth with question in his eyes.

Apparently even if 'one did not leave London to dance,' Mr. Darcy did, much to Elizabeth's happiness. She nodded in answer to his look. "That would be pleasant. I haven't been home, that is, to my parents' home, since leaving for Kent with my aunt and uncle."

"It's decided, then," Mr. Bingley said enthusiastically. "Caroline and I will be off to Netherfield tomorrow. You and Hurst can follow, Louisa, or join us, and we'll see you there, Darcy, Mrs. Darcy."

"And Miss Darcy," Mrs. Hurst added.

Elizabeth felt nearly as delighted with the plan as Mr. Bingley looked. She hadn't troubled Jane to send her many of her belongings, knowing the expense would rile her mother, who preferred to allocate their funds to entertaining, and because she wished to go through her belongings before asking for them. Elizabeth felt a touch ungrateful thinking it, but she imagined many of her possessions, mostly clothing and accessories thereof, would seem a touch shoddy now and not quite fit for her new role.

More important than going through her left-behind garb, she wished Mr. Darcy to finally meet Jane and her father, and Charlotte. And to show him off to the neighborhood. From Jane's and Charlotte's letters, Elizabeth had the impression that half of Meryton didn't believe Mr. Darcy existed, even if Mrs. Bennet expounded on him to any available ear ad nauseam.

Tea arrived and she served, aware her husband watched her nearly to the point of ignoring their guests. His gaze, intent but lacking in judgment, stirred the continual desire to blush, which she ruthlessly suppressed. She wouldn't have his closest companions believe her an overly innocent ninny…even if she was still nearly as innocent as the day she'd married.

Once their guests departed, she turned to Mr. Darcy, who'd stood at her side as they made their farewells. "Thank you for agreeing to this trip. I've missed my father and older sister terribly." She smiled up at him. "And I will enjoy showing you where I used to walk. I know you prize Derbyshire but that will not stop you from appreciating the view from Oakham Mount."

Mr. Darcy smiled but reached into his coat to pull forth the letter. "I enjoy you thinking fondly of me, but it would be a lie not to mention that I have an ulterior motive for leaving London." He passed the letter to her.

Elizabeth unfolded it to read.

Darcy,

After leaving you I accepted our aunt's invitation to Rosings. In her usual style, she did little more than permit me to greet her before demanding that I take Anne to wife. You would have enjoyed her shock when, rather than accept with fervor, I declined on the basis of a lack of romantic affection. I know I enjoyed it. Aunt Catherine can look rather like a trout when caught off guard.

She recovered quickly, of course, and stated that she was offering me possession of Rosings upon her death, not Anne, but that marrying Anne was how I would secure that offer. I countered that wedding Anne would give me Rosings years from now and in the meantime, I would have a wife incapable of mixing in polite society. I believe that's when she realized that she hadn't brought me to Rosings quickly enough to keep me from speaking with you.

I can recount the details when next we meet, if you like, but let me assure you that I bargained like a horse trader and I feel I came out on top. Needless to say, Aunt Catherine is not pleased but she had little choice. Any man who would marry a woman as poorly behaved as Anne would do it only for Rosings, and once he had Rosings, he would have the funds and means to keep her locked away. Our aunt knows that I am one of the few people she can trust not to treat Anne badly.

She did claim two victories. First, she insists we wed by special license, presumably so I may not change my mind. Second, she demanded the right to allot the Hunsford living to anyone she likes. I know I will regret it, but I agreed. Her ego needs the salve of that revenge, or she will be as poorly behaved as Anne, if not worse, for years to come. Our aunt is most unforgiving once she takes offense.

Regardless, the agreement was drawn up and my attorney approved the details. We're to marry in London by week's end. Aunt Catherine and Anne do not wish me to invite you and your bride, but I am inclined to. I seek your opinion on if I should press the issue.

Wishing you and Mrs. Darcy the very best,

R.F.

Elizabeth lowered the letter. "If your aunt does pick someone awful for the parsonage, we should endeavor to mitigate that."

"I cannot see how we could contrive to."

She shrugged. "You never know. If he is aged, we might help Colonel Fitzwilliam find a skillful assistant. If he is young and unwed, we might help him make a match with a reasonable woman."

Darcy considered that. "He will be young. Younger than Richard."

"Why do you say that?"

"Aunt Catherine will want to find someone likely to torment Richard for the remainder of his days."

Elizabeth shook her head, expression bemused. "And you wish us to go to Longbourn so that we aren't in London to attend the wedding?"

"It is one of the reasons," Mr. Darcy replied, accepting the page back as she proffered it. "I also, very much, wish to make the acquaintance of your father and to meet your sister and Miss Lucas, as I can tell when you speak of them that they are important to you."

Elizabeth smiled slightly. "And what is important to your wife is important to you?"

He returned her smile and nodded. "Very much so."

"I am as pleased as you not to be in London to attend." Elizabeth might forgive Lady Catherine and Miss de Bourgh someday, but she certainly hadn't yet. It would take time to forget the other women's slander and vehement hatred.

Mr. Darcy studied her in that intent way again. "And after Longbourn, I thought we might travel to Pemberley? I wish to show you where I walk and my favorite views, too."

"I would like that." Would he kiss her? Her pulse raced with the surety that he would.

"Very well. I will make the arrangements." He smiled at her, then quit the parlor.

Elizabeth stared after him wishing she hadn't spurned him in Rosings and wondering what she must do to claim his kiss.

Chapter Twenty

Darcy decided it was a divine form of torture to sit in the carriage alongside his wife. To have her so near, yet out of reach. Not simply because she hadn't come to him yet but also because they weren't alone. Georgiana sat across from them, reading. The carriage rumbled up the road, drawing them closer to Longbourn and a meeting with the final and, insofar as Darcy could tell, two most important to Elizabeth members of her family. And, of course, to her mother and the youngest sister, who was Georgiana's age.

To distract from imagining Elizabeth in ways that were highly inappropriate to their circumstance of the moment, Darcy went back over Georgiana's lessons in his head. Now would be a good time to see if her increased time spent studying while in London was garnering any noticeably results. He deemed it an auspicious sign that the book she held appeared to be in Italian.

Knowing she could become belligerent if she felt judged, he opened with, "What are you reading, Georgie?"

She looked up, over the book. "You won't approve."

Darcy frowned. "It is an Italian novel, is it not? For practice."

"It is but you won't approve."

Darcy stared at her in confusion.

"Is it of a gothic bent?" Elizabeth suggested.

Georgiana lowered the book, expression mischievous. "It is, and I've French ones, too. Have you any idea how much more fun it is to practice French and Italian when I can read something like this?"

She was correct. He didn't approve. "Where did you get them?"

Georgiana rolled her eyes. "I couldn't say."

He wracked his mind, but she hadn't spent time with any acquaintances in London. Simply gone to her lessons and practiced pianoforte with Elizabeth. His wife had taken her to visit Mrs. Gardiner and Mrs. Smith, but Darcy couldn't conceive of either of them having such books. Georgiana must have acquired the books before he'd taken charge of her. They wouldn't come from their aunt or cousin. Possibly

Mrs. Younge, but she wouldn't spend the money. That left... "Did one of the Milfords give them to you?" Georgiana's acquaintances in Ramsgate had a daughter about her age, if he recalled correctly from her letters.

An odd smile curled her lips. "Why, yes. Missy Milford gave them to me. How astute of you, Fitz."

"I deem it a good thing you are no longer in the same town as them, then."

Her gaze narrowed. "Maybe they will come to London."

"We will not be back for some time."

"Tell me more about these Milfords," Elizabeth broke in, voice flat.

Darcy looked over to see an unusually stiff expression on his wife's face. Did she know the Milfords? Were they not fit companions for his sister?

Georgiana turned to her and the smug look she'd adopted dropped away. "They, ah, are a family I spent time with in Ramsgate."

"Are they?" Elizabeth's voice held an odd, sardonic edge. "And before you reply, keep in mind that I have three younger sisters."

Darcy studied his wife, thoroughly confused. What did younger sisters have to do with the Milfords?

Georgiana huffed and looked away, out the window. Silence drew out. Darcy longed to break it but he had no idea what transpired. Elizabeth kept a hard stare on his sister, which disconcerted him, but he'd learned from misjudging his wife in the past that he should allot her the benefit of assuming her intelligent and capable.

"Fine," Georgiana snapped, swiveling back around to glare at Elizabeth. "They aren't real. Are you happy now?"

"Somewhat."

"Well, I am not," Darcy cut in, still not completely certain what had happened between the two women but angry all the same. "What do you mean, the Milfords aren't real?"

Georgiana fidgeted with one corner of the book's cover. "They aren't real," she mumbled. "I, ah, made them up. Mrs. Younge said it would be the easiest way to have free time for, ah, to..." She trailed off with a grimace.

Darcy stared at his sister, horrified. "Everything you wrote to me about them?"

She shrugged, still looking down. "Made up."

He sat back, stunned.

Georgiana's head came up to reveal pleading eyes. "It didn't seem so terrible. You were happy. I was happy. It wasn't a bad lie."

"You wrote to me about them for months." His voice sounded strange to his ears.

"And the books?" Elizabeth said.

"From my instructors and they really aren't bad. They're meant to teach me. They picked ones that are only romantic not..." She made a vague sweeping gesture.

"They fill your head with nonsense," he snapped. The sort of nonsense that led reasonable young women to lie about acquaintances and attempt to elope.

A touch of stubbornness returned to his sister's face. "They're not much different from Shakespeare, Fitz."

Anger mounted in Darcy. At his sister. At Wickham and Mrs. Younge. At himself for being so stupidly blind.

"You may keep the books," Elizabeth said. "You will need them."

Darcy turned to her, hardly able to suppress his rage. She had no right to decide that.

She didn't seem to notice, her attention on Georgiana. "However, as you are not yet out and show little sign of being mature enough to be out, you will not be attending any events when we reach Hertfordshire."

Georgiana's mouth dropped open. "But the assembly...the ball...It's to be my first ball. You have to let me go."

"No." Elizabeth's tone brooked no room for argument.

Tears sprang up in Georgiana's eyes. "You can't tell me what to do," she cried and turned to Darcy, beseeching. "Tell her, Fitz."

Darcy pushed aside his anger with Elizabeth, agreeing with her verdict on Georgiana being out, if not on the books. "Elizabeth is my wife, and I am your guardian. She very much can tell you what to do."

"You could overrule her," Georgiana pleaded.

"I agree with her."

His sister sucked in air through her nose, fighting not to cry. "I hate you both."

Darcy stared at her, gutted by those four words.

"I daresay you do, today," Elizabeth said, voice mild now. "We can only hope you reconsider." She pulled a small volume from her cloak and opened it, dropping her gaze, by all appearances bored with the exchange.

Darcy wouldn't know otherwise if he couldn't see the tremble in her hands, which she quickly dropped to her lap so as to conceal the motion. Georgiana crossed her arms over her chest and glared at them. With no idea how to respond to his sister's anger, Darcy took his cue from his wife and pulled forth a volume of his own.

He'd begun to truly read by the time Daniels pulled off to the side on a particularly wide stretch of roadway, halting the carriage to rest the horses. A glance found Georgiana still sullen and glowering.

Elizabeth lowered her volume. "I believe I will stretch my legs while the horses rest theirs. Would you care to join me, Georgiana?"

"I can't. I'm not allowed out."

Elizabeth raised her eyebrows but made no further comment as she marked her place and pulled on her gloves. Ready, she turned on their shared seat to regard him. "Would you care to accompany me, Mr. Darcy?"

"Certainly." He donned his hat, disembarked, and went around to help Elizabeth down, only to find her already free of the carriage and looking up and down the roadway with interest.

She turned to him, smiling. "I don't believe I've stopped here before." She looked across the roadway and back. "Do we go up or down?" she asked, in reference to the gentle hill that rose to meet one side of the roadway and climbed upward on the other.

"Up," he said and offered his arm.

Darcy escorted her across the rutted dirt road, then assisted her over a low stone wall. They strode up a pathway almost certainly made by sheep, the wind in their faces. Elizabeth's expression contained a mixture of pleasure and interest, and he tried to imagine other women of his acquaintance, his stifled cousin or the prim Miss Bingley, taking delight in walking a sheep trail on a windy day.

They crested the ridge to a lovely view of pastureland full of all the interest imparted by hills and dales. Not, he decided, as verdant as Derbyshire, but still lovely enough in the golds and russets of autumn.

"I don't believe that Georgiana realizes her petulance only augments the view that she is not yet mature enough to be out," Elizabeth murmured, gaze on the view.

Darcy took in her perfect profile, already so ingrained in his mind…and heart. "You handled her well."

"Thank you. As I said, I have several younger sisters. One who is similar to Georgiana at her worst."

"You worried she would not obey you?" Turning fully from the view, he brushed a curl back from Elizabeth's cheek, merely for the excuse to touch her. "I saw you trembling."

She looked at him. "I am well versed in sulky young women so no, I did not fear that. My worry was that you would gainsay me, hampering my ability to exert future influence over her behavior, the heart of my role as her chaperone." Her lips quirked. "I am not well versed at handling a domineering husband who is accustomed to absolute rule over his world. Or at all versed."

Locks of her hair danced free in the wind, all the excuse he required to cup her face. "That is because you don't know that this domineering husband realizes he underestimated you atrociously at the start of our union, despite having ample illustration of your bravery and moral certitude. I am not always the quickest thinker, but I take pride in not repeating my errors."

Amusement brightened her eyes. "Yes. I daresay you take pride in many things."

Darcy frowned, certain he was being teased.

Elizabeth lay a hand against his chest, looking up at him with genuine warmth. "And I thank you for not contradicting me in front of Georgiana."

"You are welcome, but I am not certain she should keep those books."

"I am. When she brought them home, even though I had to endure the embarrassment of my inadequate pronunciations, I inquired about the titles to Mrs. Hurst and Miss Bingley. They both assured me the volumes aren't improper and that many Italian and French instructors use them, and similar books, to engage young ladies' minds. If Mrs. Hurst and Miss Bingley don't believe the books inappropriate, I can only conclude that they are not."

She'd done that? Of her own impetus? Engaged in the dedication and time necessary to note when his sister obtained new volumes and to investigate them?

Moments after revealing his intention not to underestimate her, he'd done so once more. Perhaps he did deserve to be teased about his pride. "Thank you." He studied her, hand still cupping her face. Hers rested on his chest, warm even through her gloves and his lawn shirt. Would it not be acceptable to kiss her? She was his wife.

"Fitz. Elizabeth," Georgiana called, voice loud and smug. "The horses are rested."

"She wishes to intrude," Elizabeth murmured. "She's exacting revenge."

"It's working," he said, dropping his hand. He urgently wished to take Elizabeth in his arms and kiss her until she clung to him, desperate to become his wife in more than name only, but not with his sister, Daniels and the tiger watching. Not to mention the second carriage, containing Stevens, two maids and another driver.

They went back down, and Darcy did his best to ignore his sister's expression of vindictive glee as he helped Elizabeth into the carriage. He went around to his side and climbed in.

Peeling off her gloves, Elizabeth said calmly, "I'm happy we're taking this journey. At Darcy House, I came under a false impression of your maturity, Miss Darcy, which could have led to an improper amount of trust and independence. I am now afforded a much better picture of what sort of relationship you and I will enjoy."

Georgiana gaped at her. "I thought we were friends."

"I hope we will be, someday, but I do not believe a friend is what you currently require, so I will forgo the pleasure for now."

Georgiana stared, expression revealing her hurt. Darcy wondered if Elizabeth's declaration had been a touch harsh but then, Georgiana had nearly eloped. She'd spent months lying to him about an imaginary family while never once mentioning that George Wickham was in Ramsgate, courting her. Mrs. Younge had obviously not been a guiding influence but rather a coconspirator, something akin to a friend.

They returned to their silent travel, Darcy once more delving into his book. By the time they reached Longbourn, he looked forward to Mrs. Bennet's chatter. He generally preferred silence but the mood in the carriage had become somewhat oppressive.

They disembarked before the manor house into a riot of movement and sound. Darcy was introduced to Mr. Bennet, who revealed where Elizabeth got her intelligence, and reintroduced to Mrs. Bennet, who fawned over him and insulted Elizabeth in every breath. Miss Jane Bennet turned out to be tall and possessed of the sort of demure loveliness that many men sought in a wife, but none of the spark that drew Darcy to Elizabeth. Miss Lydia Bennet was as loud as her mother and obviously in need of more guidance than anyone who currently resided with her cared to give.

When the greetings were finished and the others began their retreat indoors, Miss Bennet gestured Darcy and Elizabeth aside. Blue eyes wide and almost excruciatingly kind, she asked, "Did my most recent letter reach you before you set out?"

"The one about Papa's trout stock and Mr. Goulding's fishpond?" Elizabeth asked.

Miss Bennet shook her head. "The one about rooms. Mama put Miss Darcy in Kitty's bed, as she and Lydia are of age. I could go sleep in Mary's room and give you and Mr. Darcy our room, Lizzy. I've kept everything as you left it."

Darcy read the pleading in Miss Bennet's eyes but couldn't guess for what.

"Or Mr. Darcy could use Mary's room and I could share our room with you?" Elizabeth said, casting him a quick glance.

Miss Bennet nodded, reaching to capture Elizabeth's hands. "Only, I've missed you so. I didn't know, when you went away with Aunt and Uncle Gardiner, that you would never live here again."

Elizabeth squeezed her sister's hands. "I didn't either."

"Can Elizabeth and I not share Mrs. Evans' former room?" Darcy asked. He hadn't considered that he and Elizabeth wouldn't have adjoining bedrooms as they had at Darcy House, or the rental in Kent, or his aunt's, or Pemberley. He hadn't realized Mr. Bennet's home was quite so small.

Then again, did he really want the first time he shared a bedroom with his wife to be in her childhood home with her relations packed into rooms on either side?

"Mary's room is too small for two people," Miss Bennet said. "It will be hardly large enough for your use, Mr. Darcy." Miss Bennet looked between them. "There is a second, similar room across the hall, that we've always employed for guests. I thought your valet might sleep there but if you like you and Lizzy could take those two rooms."

"I see." He mustered graciousness. He'd waited months for Elizabeth. Soon they would be in Pemberley where he could apply all his will to the task of enamoring his wife. "You two should share your room. Mrs. Evans' former quarters and the like sized guest room will do well enough for me and Stevens."

Elizabeth released her sister's hands to turn and study him. "You're certain?"

He nodded.

Smiling at her sister, Elizabeth said, "Very well. It will be as you wish, Jane."

"Thank you, Mr. Darcy." Miss Bennet's eyes shone. "I will let Mrs. Hill know."

"Shall we go in?" Elizabeth said. "Might we take tea?"

"I'm sure that can be arranged," Miss Bennet replied. With another sunny smile, she turned and led the way.

Darcy followed with mild trepidation as to how this visit would progress. Among other hurdles, he expected Georgiana to make a fuss over not being allowed to attend the assembly or the ball. He did, however, anticipate a certain amount of enjoyment in the events themselves. The assembly would be his first opportunity to dance with Elizabeth, something he awaited with pleasure. Bingley would be there with his sisters and Darcy assumed that Miss Bennet, and likely Miss Lydia, would attend, giving him at least four other partners.

He also wished to observe Elizabeth among her family and acquaintances and, as he'd told her, to meet the people who were important to her and among whom she'd lived and grown up. In short, to learn all he could about his wife and the life she'd enjoyed. Every detail, because, he realized, everything about Elizabeth interested him.

Chapter Twenty-One

Unpacking in the room she'd always shared with Jane felt very odd. Jane had kept all Elizabeth's possessions as they were when she left with their aunt and uncle, and most of them seemed quite unneeded now. A bag with scraps of lace and trimmings of ribbons that she'd hoarded seemed somewhat pathetic. The gowns she'd felt not to be of sufficient quality for the journey with the Gardiners appeared hardly fit to give to the staff. Even the very walls, Longbourn itself, felt a bit shoddy and run down, and her mother's sense of décor was even more outdated and overly gaudy than Elizabeth recalled.

But then there were the dried roses tied with a cream ribbon and hung at the corner of their mirror, that she and Jane had cut the day they'd had a play wedding in the garden years ago. There was the little porcelain bowl that held their hairpins, flowers and flittering butterflies painted around the outside, that they'd saved months of pin money to buy together. And, Elizabeth knew, that should she choose to crawl under the bed, there waited a floorboard where she and Jane had carved their initials in a fit of giggles and mischief, marking this as their room.

It was strange, now that Elizabeth could no longer call this place home, what things proved to matter and what didn't. What she hadn't thought on since leaving and what she missed daily. Most of all, she'd missed her sister. Letters hadn't been enough. She wondered if she and Jane would ever be so close again as they'd been before now. It seemed sadly impossible.

When the day came, they took two carriages to the assembly, Elizabeth's parents joining them in Mr. Darcy's at his insistence. Watching her mother's awe and excitement at the fine conveyance, Elizabeth realized that she'd already become accustomed to the luxury. She couldn't decide if that should disturb her or not.

Upon arriving, they joined the others outside the building where the assembly was being held, waiting for the press before the doorway to clear. Mrs. Bennet immediately began regaling Elizabeth's father with details of the wonder of Mr. Darcy's carriage, as if Mr. Bennet hadn't ridden there in the conveyance with her. Elizabeth half turned away from them, to give the impression that she couldn't hear.

"…you'll meet him tonight, Elizabeth," Lydia was saying, catching Elizabeth's attention away from trying not to be embarrassed by her mother. "He's an officer and I'm going to marry him."

Elizabeth blinked, aware that she'd missed part of what Lydia had said. Her thoughts went to Jane's more recent letters. "Mr. Wiekran?" She asked, dredging the name from her memory.

"Yes, Mr. Wiekran. Who do you think I've been talking about? Really, Lizzy, I think you must have hit your head awfully hard if now you're hard of hearing."

Mrs. Bennet broke off her diatribe, apparently hearing Lydia as well, to say, "You aren't going to marry Mr. Wiekran."

Elizabeth raised her eyebrows. That hardly sounded like her mother. "Is something wrong with the gentleman?"

"He's perfect," Lydia said.

"Nothing is wrong with the gentleman," Mrs. Bennet said over her. "But he's only a lieutenant. Now that you're married to Mr. Darcy and with Jane sure to capture this Mr. Bingley, Lydia, being the prettiest by far, can do so much better than a mere lieutenant in the militia."

Jane's cheeks went scarlet. Elizabeth endeavored not to glance at her husband to gauge his reaction to her mother's unsubtle machinations.

"I love Mr. Wiekran and he's already talked to Papa and when he proposes, I will accept." Lydia's expression brightened. "He may even propose tonight."

"You did not give him permission without consulting me, Mr. Bennet?" Mrs. Bennet gasped.

"Not entirely." Mr. Bennet turned his gaze to the assembly hall attempting, as always, to avoid any discussion with wife or daughter that involved heightened emotions.

"You gave him permission enough, Papa," Lydia stated.

Deciding she would ask her father about that later, Elizabeth sought to defuse Lydia. "Surely there's no hurry for you to wed? Do you not wish to tour the countryside or to visit London?"

"You are welcome at Darcy House," Mr. Darcy stated.

Elizabeth cast him a surprised look.

"You see?" Mrs. Bennet cried. "You're welcome at Darcy House, and Mr. Darcy has connections to the peerage. The peerage, Lydia."

Elizabeth resisted the urge to cover her face.

Lydia tossed her head. "I refuse to be the last one married."

"But surely, something so important should be entered into with consideration?" Elizabeth suggested.

Lydia answered with curled lips. "I had letters from Kitty while she stayed with you so don't think you can fool me with this new story you wrote to Mama about Mr. Darcy saving you when you fell down and you falling in love. I know my George a lot better than you knew Mr. Darcy when you married him. I love him." She turned her glare on their mother. "I don't need a peer with all their fancy this-and-that and rules."

"George?" Mr. Darcy said sharply. "George Wiekran?"

"Do you know him?" Mr. Bennet asked, turning from his study of the landscape.

Mr. Darcy shook his head. "I do not know a George Wiekran, no."

"Then why did you say his name like that?" Lydia rolled her eyes as she spoke. "Did your husband hit his head too, Lizzy?"

Elizabeth looked to her father, hoping he'd curtail Lydia, but Mr. Bennet had already turned his attention away again.

"We can go inside now," Jane said brightly. "Oh my. Everyone is staring at Mr. Darcy's carriage."

As well they might be. Having seen Mr. Bingley's, Elizabeth knew that even with him attending the assembly too, her husband's carriage was the finest in Hertfordshire and the four matched bays were obviously of the highest quality. Somehow, that made her both proud and a touch embarrassed. She wasn't accustomed to people she'd known her whole life gawking at her.

Her mother and youngest sister both started for the assembly hall door with chins high and eyes gleaming, clearly sharing none of Elizabeth's reservations. Jane appeared blissfully cheerful, and their father amused. Mr. Darcy, as he offered Elizabeth his arm, wore a mask of stony indifference. In the past, Elizabeth might have taken that as him accepting the admiration of the countryside as his due, or even of disdain for those he saw as lower than him, but as she accepted his arm now, she wondered.

In London, they had few callers. Mr. Bingley and his sisters were the most frequent by far, followed by Colonel Fitzwilliam. Elizabeth didn't know if Lady Catherine and Miss de Bourgh might normally visit, but they certainly hadn't. Her husband, Elizabeth concluded, was a reserved, possibly even shy man, his indifferent façade carefully crafted to mask that.

They entered and Elizabeth needed only to follow the attention of nearly everyone in the room to find Mr. Bingley coming their way. His sisters accompanied him, as well as a gentleman whom Elizabeth didn't know but could only assume to be Mr. Hurst. Mr. Bingley smiled a wide, welcome smile, taking them in, until the moment his gaze alighted on Jane. Then, he nearly stumbled, features slackening with a familiar awe. Elizabeth had seen many men react similarly to Jane's beauty.

Not, however, her husband. A warmth unfurled in her at the memory of his perfectly polite but also completely un-enamored greeting of her older sister. Still on his arm, she looked up at Mr. Darcy and smiled, drawing a like expression in return, which served to enhance his already handsome face.

"Darcy. Mrs. Darcy. So pleasant to see you," Mr. Bingley said, hardly managing to bow to them before turning to Jane, expression eager.

Behind his back, his sisters exchanged a look.

Introductions commenced, Elizabeth keenly aware that every word said was garnered and repeated by the assemblage. Most of those listening made at least a pretense at their own conversations. Some openly gawked at the newcomers. The Lucases joined them, and Elizabeth had the pleasure of introducing Mr. Darcy to her dearest friend, outside Jane, the Lucas' eldest child Charlotte. All the while, Lydia stood on tiptoe, even though she was already taller than most women, scanning the crowd.

The musicians struck a telling chord and Mr. Bingley turned to Jane. "Miss Bennet, would you do me the honor of this set?"

"I should be most pleased to, Mr. Bingley," Jane said with a slight, pretty blush.

Mr. Bingley's sisters exchanged another look. Elizabeth felt they seemed pleased by their brother's obvious admiration, likely seeking a connection to Mr. Darcy through Jane. Elizabeth must reserve her approval, however, until she ascertained how Jane felt. As Jane was smiling and pleasant to everyone, she wouldn't know until she had time to ask.

Mr. Darcy dipped his head down, his breath caressing her cheek as he asked, "Elizabeth, will you dance with me?"

A delighted shiver went through her. She nodded, to prevent whatever sort of breathy whisper a verbal reply might emerge as. Odd, that she should be wedded for so many months and yet so thrilled for the opportunity to dance with her husband.

And dance they did, for Mr. Darcy partnered her for nearly every set. He gave her up only to dance with her sisters, Mr. Bingley's sisters, and Charlotte. Far from dismayed, the local community seemed pleased with how enamored Mr. Darcy appeared with her.

Appeared, Elizabeth wondered, or was? The way he looked at her that evening reminded her of his expression at the top of the staircase in Rosings, his eyes dark and intent. As if taking in every possible detail of her was the most, possibly the only, important thing in his world.

And she liked that look. She wanted more of that intensity.

At one point, while Mr. Darcy danced with Mrs. Hurst, Miss Bingley sidled over, punch in hand.

"Mrs. Darcy, may I say that your attendance is all that makes this outing bearable for Louisa and me?"

"You may say it, but I will never agree."

"No? Whyever not?"

"There is my husband, with whom you've had the pleasure to dance, and my sisters, and my dear friend Charlotte, who even now partners your brother."

"Your younger sister appears out of sorts, however, I should say."

They both looked to Lydia who stood beside Mrs. Bennet frowning in a way foreign to her young, pretty face, but which brought out her resemblance to their mother. So far, her Mr. Wiekran had not put in an appearance.

"Her favorite beau is absent." Which was likely for the best, although Elizabeth would reserve judgment until meeting the lieutenant. She pursed her lips, wondering why her husband had reacted as he had to Mr. Wiekran's name. She'd not found a quiet moment to ask him.

"That will always sour a lady's evening but she's young enough to expect many such infatuations to come." Miss Bingley sipped her punch and continued, "I am surprised Miss Darcy isn't in attendance, especially with your sister here. They seem of a like age." Her gaze went to her brother.

Ah, the vaunted connection. No doubt, Miss Bingley and Mrs. Hurst had hoped that a set or two between their brother and Georgiana would bloom into something more, since Georgiana was the closest tie to Darcy. "I deemed this evening and Miss Darcy an ill match."

Miss Bingley darted a surprised look Elizabeth's way. "You? Not Mr. Darcy?"

"My husband agreed with me."

"I do, as well. This countrified atmosphere is no place for a young woman of Miss Darcy's delicate sensibilities. I myself can hardly stand to be here and I've been out for years."

Much as Elizabeth resented Miss Bingley's snobbery, she let that stand, a lie between them. No good could come of admitting that Elizabeth deemed Georgiana's behavior unfit for Meryton society, not the opposite.

Looking over the room, familiar with every gentleman there, Elizabeth wondered if she'd been too severe with Georgiana. The assembly would be a good place for her to practice her social skills. Her gaze caught once more on Lydia, who never received proper discipline, but her mind went to Miss de Bourgh, who'd grown up a monster. Better Georgiana should be angry with Elizabeth now than turn out like her aunt or cousin.

"Your friend Miss Lucas is an excellent dancer."

Elizabeth smiled. "She is excellent at most things."

"And the daughter of a lady and a knight, even if one knighted for service, not lineage. It's surprising she remains unwed at seven and twenty."

"Is it?" Elizabeth asked, daring Miss Bingley to point out that Charlotte was remorselessly plain. When she didn't rise to the bait, Elizabeth added, "The families in this area have been blessed with more daughters than sons, I'm afraid. There is a notable imbalance in opportunities."

"Rumor has a militia about to arrive. Surely that will even the scales. Miss Lucas can find someone."

Elizabeth nodded but she doubted Charlotte would wish for a redcoat.

"Miss Bennet, however, must have higher aspirations than an officer," Miss Bingley continued. "With her beauty and your connections, you must have every hope she may marry quite well."

Ah. Now Elizabeth understood their conversation. Miss Bingley didn't wish Charlotte to get any ideas about her brother. She wanted the connection Jane brought to the Darcy line if married to Mr. Bingley. "I daresay Jane will marry for love and happiness over connections and wealth." She turned an innocent look on Miss Bingley. "We've connections in trade, after all. No matter how lofty Mr. Darcy is, there is only so much any of us can hope for Jane."

Miss Bingley's gaze narrowed over the rim of her glass as she took another sip of punch. Elizabeth wondered if that calculating look meant Miss Bingley was reprising her plans for Jane and Mr. Bingley, or seeing them as suddenly more viable?

"Do you?" Miss Bingley infused a world of unconcern into those two syllables.

Elizabeth wasn't fooled and if Jane's heart might become involved, best to have everything in the open so that no trouble could arise later. "Oh yes. My mother's family comes from trade. The aunt and uncle I traveled with when I met Mr. Darcy are in trade." A muscle at the corner of Miss Bingley's eye jumped at that and Elizabeth wondered if she'd ever be forgiven for stealing Mr. Darcy from his single female acquaintances. "My younger sister Kitty married one of Mr. Darcy's stewards and my sister Mary wed a country surgeon." She watched Miss Bingley digest that.

"Charles has mentioned the Smiths," she finally said. "It is a shame, but I suppose with five daughters some concessions must be made. And Miss Lydia is quite attractive. If she can be made to marry well, that would tip the balance."

"Indeed," Elizabeth said dryly but Miss Bingley gave no acknowledgement of hearing.

Fortunately, the set ended, and Mr. Darcy and Charlotte converged on them, Mrs. Hurst going to find her husband and Mr. Bingley once more seeking out Jane. The four of them chatted amiably until Mr. Darcy excused them so that he might dance with Elizabeth yet again. Even for the joy of Charlotte's company, Elizabeth had no desire to refuse her husband.

When they finally returned to Longbourn after a wonderful, if exhausting evening, Elizabeth forgot to ask her husband about his reaction to Mr. Wiekran or her sister Jane about Mr. Bingley. Instead, she fell into a deep and dreamless sleep, at peace in her familiar room.

Chapter Twenty-Two

She woke early and left Jane smiling in her sleep to go find Mr. Darcy, only to be told by Stevens that he'd gone out riding. Oddly sad to have missed her husband, Elizabeth sought out her father in his library, he being the only Bennet yet awake.

She knocked and let herself in to find her father seated behind his desk with a book. "Good morning, Papa."

"Lizzy. I've missed our morning talks." He lowered the book, marking his place. "You do realize that you were only to be gone for four weeks, not the remainder of your lifetime."

"So Jane pointed out to me," Elizabeth said as she crossed the room to sit.

"Yes. Jane and I both miss you."

Elizabeth permitted him that jab against her mother and youngest sister, desirous of a different topic. "How can one nearly give permission to someone to ask for one's daughter?"

"You refer to Lydia's statement about Mr. Wiekran."

Elizabeth nodded even though her father's words hadn't been a question.

Mr. Bennet appeared thoughtful. He opened a drawer, took out a page, and set it on the desk. He did not push it across to Elizabeth. "Mr. Wiekran has no money outside his salary. He admitted as much when he came to me for permission to propose to Lydia. He pointed out, quite reasonably, that nearly all my other daughters were married and one very well married. He asked for eighty pounds a year. If I get Mrs. Bennet to agree not to give them more than ten pounds a year in gifts, I suspect that will allow me to break even with what I spend on Lydia now."

"A militia lieutenant's salary and eighty pounds a year isn't much to live on," Elizabeth ventured. She wondered if this Mr. Wiekran was expecting her and Mr. Darcy to help support him.

"True, his militia pay isn't much, but to do him credit, he's living on it. I investigated, and he owes nothing to local merchants. I also assume he is trusted by his commanding officer as he's mentioned that he was sent ahead to organize quarters for his unit, which will arrive soon."

"Did he organize quarters for his unit?"

Mr. Bennet shrugged. "Not that I am aware of, but I have no reason to believe he will not."

"So, you agreed to his terms?" That still didn't explain Lydia's comment.

"We went to your Uncle Phillips to draw the agreement up but Mr. Wiekran insisted on writing out each copy himself, and on not signing until he has an attorney in London, a friend of his, look the contract over. He said this is because people often misspell Wiekran. His name is so unusual, that I understand him caring about it."

"An attorney friend in London? He believes you somehow mean to cheat him?" Was that why he feared to have his name misspelled as well?

Mr. Bennet shook his head. "I'm not certain. He said he was ignorant about law and that his friend will look over the contract for free. He insisted I sign, so that once he does, the contract will be valid."

Elizabeth asked, "You signed?" Somehow, that seemed a poor idea.

"Why not? The only incentive is eighty pounds a year and a quarter share of the interest on your mother's money after her and my deaths. He reasonably said that you would be well cared for, and your mother's money should be divided among those daughters who need it."

"I suppose that is reasonable," Elizabeth said reluctantly.

"I imagine the contract explains why he wasn't at the assembly." Her father finally pushed the page he'd brought out across the desk. "He must have taken his copy to London. This is mine."

Elizabeth leaned close. The terms were as her father had stated. His and her Uncle Phillips' signatures rested along the bottom. Her only criticism was that Mr. Wiekran wrote his name so that the e looked more like a c. She looked up to say, "You believe he rushed off to London in his hurry to marry Lydia?"

"Yes. He must have gone to London to meet his friend and not been able to return in time for the assembly."

"Possibly," Elizabeth agreed. "In which case, he should be back in time for the ball Mr. Bingley plans to throw."

"Ball?"

"Yes. We discussed it before leaving London. I imagine invitations will be going out soon." Elizabeth smiled. "It will be fun to see the inside of Netherfield Park's manor house. I don't believe anyone has held an event there since before I was out."

"You should tell your mother and sisters. They'll be pleased."

"I am waiting for Mr. Bingley to make it official. Miss Bingley may decide she needs more time to ready the household." Elizabeth tapped the desktop. "But enough of balls and weddings. Tell me how you are? How does the farm fare? How are the tenants doing this year with their holdings?"

They chatted about the properties that made up Longbourn, something which used to bore Elizabeth but which she'd missed. Her father had been going over his work with her for years, having no one else in the household who would listen and respond intelligently. Elizabeth's heart filled with a gentle pang of sorrow as her father spoke.

Finally, the household began to stir about them. Sure Jane would be rising and Mr. Darcy returning from his ride, Elizabeth made her excuses and went back to the front of the house, only to find Jane coming down the stairs.

"Good morning, Lizzy."

Elizabeth answered with a cheerful smile and soon they were breakfasting, their father and Mr. Darcy joining them. In some ways, Elizabeth felt as if she'd never left, so much of their meal appeared the same as always. Mr. Darcy's occasional, thoughtful contributions to their morning discussion of yesterday's paper with Mr. Bennet belied that, however. And if he found it odd that a gentleman might discuss the politics of the day with his daughters, he didn't let it show.

After breakfast, she and Mr. Darcy walked, sometimes chatting about the scenery she wished to show him, or her many walks with Jane or Charlotte. Sometimes in a silence that felt as pleasant and sustainable as any she'd known with her usual walking companions. She couldn't help but cast her husband many looks as they gamboled about the Hertfordshire countryside, the sky blue and the air crisp with autumn. He appeared genuinely interested in all she showed him and said, and her heart throbbed with the pleasure of his regard.

Though they'd left through the back gate of the garden they returned up the drive, arm in arm, Elizabeth having selected a circuitous route. At the top of the drive, a familiar carriage stood off to the side and a gaggle of people spilled from the front door. Elizabeth took in Mr. Bingley, Miss Bingley, Mrs. Hurst, Jane, Lydia, and Georgiana. From their animated faces, it appeared a cheery gathering and it pleased

Elizabeth to see Georgiana recovered from her displeasure at not being permitted to attend the assembly.

Mr. Bingley sighted them with a call and a cheery wave, and everyone turned to look down the drive. Georgiana's face went red, then white. Face stony she whirled, wordless, and stalked back into the house.

"She's not speaking to you," Lydia proclaimed as Elizabeth and Darcy joined the group. "Either of you."

Elizabeth shook her head. Could Georgiana not see that rushing away without even a farewell to their guests made her seem even less ready for society? "I see."

Lydia narrowed her eyes. "You aren't sorry you ruined the Bingleys' visit?"

"I can't see that I, or Mr. Darcy, have ruined anything. Miss Darcy's behavior is of her own volition."

"And nothing is ruined," Jane put in cheerily before Lydia could reply. "We were about to walk. That is, Mr. Bingley asked if I should care to walk with him and the others were to accompany us."

"Join us?" Mr. Bingley said cheerfully.

"Yes, do," Miss Bingley added, a request echoed by Mrs. Hurst.

Elizabeth, who never tired of walking, looked to her husband.

Mr. Darcy shook his head. "The post has come?"

"It has," Jane confirmed.

"You have two letters and so does Lizzy," Lydia added.

Happy to read letters with her husband, Elizabeth said, "Well, as we've letters and have only now returned from a morning of walking, we will decline but please, do not let us keep you."

Lydia looked over her shoulder. "Should I go get Georgiana?"

"Oh, do let us walk while the day is still fine," Miss Bingley said. "Clouds mass to the west."

Shrugging, Lydia nodded, and they all set out, Mr. Bingley's the only beaver hat in a sea of bonnets.

Elizabeth and Darcy went in to find a new paper and a stack of letters waiting in the front hall, Elizabeth readily sighting one from Mary to her atop the pile. After turning over their outerwear she sorted the remainder, handing Mr. Darcy a letter from his cousin and another from his man of business. Leaving the rest for other members of her family, she took Mary's correspondence, and, to her surprise, one sent to her from the newly made Mrs. Fitzwilliam.

They entered the parlor to find only her mother, seated in her favorite chair with her sewing. "Mr. Darcy. Elizabeth. The others have left for a walk."

Elizabeth went over and bussed her mother's cheek, then settled onto the adjacent sofa, Mr. Darcy joining her. "We know, Mama. We met them in the drive."

"Ah." Mrs. Bennet nodded. "That must be why Miss Darcy rushed back inside. You really must take her in hand, Elizabeth. You're responsible for her now. You must see her well married."

Was that glee in her mother's voice? Elizabeth mustered a grave expression. "Yes, Mama."

Apparently satisfied, Mrs. Bennet returned to her work. Elizabeth read her letter from Mary first, sometimes voicing bits aloud for her mother and Mr. Darcy, finding the pages full of tales from Mr. Evans' practice. Her sister always made the life of a fussy country surgeon seem very interesting, which it pleased Elizabeth to think meant that Mary was happy. She mentioned a brief trip to see the Gardiners and Smiths as well, with regrets that they'd missed Elizabeth and Mr. Darcy. Elizabeth regretted missing them, too, and was certain she'd be made to repeat those regrets after her next letters from Kitty and Aunt Gardiner arrived, but even had she known of the visit, she wouldn't have remained in London for Miss de Bourgh's wedding.

That in mind, she took up the second, much lighter letter. A single page, though of ridiculously thick paper. She broke the seal and read.

Mrs. Darcy,

I realize I am slow to write as much, but I wish to extend my apologies. I behaved in a reprehensible, hoydenish manner. I should not have slandered you or spoken harshly to Darcy. I definitely should not have paid off every innkeeper from Rosings to London to keep you from getting a room. That was petty and unworthy behavior for a grown woman. I extend my apologies and regrets in the hope we may one day amend our relationship.

I also wish you great joy in your union with Darcy.

Wishing you happiness and health,

Mrs. Anne Fitzwilliam

Slack jawed, Elizabeth looked up. "Mr. Darcy, you have a letter from Colonel Fitzwilliam?"

Her husband, who'd already set that missive aside to peruse the thick bundle his man in London had sent, looked over and nodded. "I do."

"Does it…that is, is there anything about Mrs. Fitzwilliam?"

He plucked up the letter and held it out.

Aware that her mother listened intently, Elizabeth handed him her letter from Mrs. Fitzwilliam.

Mr. Darcy scanned it, eyes widening slightly. "That makes sense." He nodded to the letter she held.

Elizabeth dropped her gaze to read, skimming until she came to the part about Mrs. Fitzwilliam.

Aunt Catherine and I continue to argue. Despite my desire for peace, I cannot permit certain misconceptions to survive. For example, Aunt Catherine's endless lauding of Anne's perfection as a wife, to which I could no longer contain the observation that Anne is very ignorant.

Our aunt, as you can imagine, took exception to that, forcing me to recount an incident from the previous evening. I'd taken Anne to dinner with a fellow officer and his wife. Anne didn't know what to say or how to interact. She tried to mimic Aunt Catherine's behavior, but a young bride cannot make sweeping statements or ask intrusive questions without giving offense. I must admit that I've rarely been so embarrassed.

As you may suppose, our aunt ignored my recounting of Anne's behavior and instead fixated on my statement that Anne had mimicked her to detriment, making every topic about her, as always. Aunt Catherine stated that she does not give offense. Again, I realize I should have deferred, but since Anne and I married, my patience for our aunt's behavior has worn thin. I informed her that she does give offense and that she would know as much if her rank didn't protect her from people's honest reactions.

This devolved into a rather heated argument in which Aunt Catherine insisted that she'd raised Anne well and had always acted out of a need to protect her. I pointed out that Anne hardly spoke to anyone before we married, let alone anyone her own age. I may even have gone so far as to accuse Lady Catherine of turning Anne into someone in need of protection, of socially hobbling her.

Regardless, good came of the argument. Lady Catherine is not speaking to me, for now, and Anne eavesdropped on our conversation, a habit of which I am trying to break her, but which worked out well. Since that incident, I've persuaded her to talk to me about her day and about what people do. I am frequently astonished as to her opinions. I see a few as coming from Aunt Catherine but others arise seemingly out of nowhere. You would be astonished by many of the things she thinks. Thank goodness she's willing to talk to me. I believe she is, slowly, changing.

Due to that belief, when she informed me that she meant to write to Mrs. Darcy, I encouraged her. I even went so far as not to read the letter she composed. I have hope it is reasonable. If it is not, I extend my apologies but please know that Anne is working to improve and so, attempt not to hold any offense her letter gives against her.

Wishing you and Mrs. Darcy the very best,

R.F.

"Yes," Elizabeth said, looking up. "That does make sense."

"What does?" Mrs. Bennet blurted, agitation edging her tone, no longer sewing.

"Mrs. Fitzwilliam wrote that she's beginning to like something her husband likes," Elizabeth hedged, impressed her mother had remained silent for so long as she had. "I was surprised."

Mrs. Bennet nodded, needle flicking back to life. "That does happen in some marriages." Wistfulness touched her words.

Elizabeth studied her mother, wondering what Mrs. Bennet would be like if Mr. Bennet were a little kinder to her. Elizabeth had endured nearly two months of her husband writing to her as if she were addlebrained. She'd found amusement in the experience but imagined that would fade if he'd continued the treatment. It disturbed her to consider such a deep flaw in her father.

Perturbed, she folded Colonel Fitzwilliam's letter and handed it back to Mr. Darcy, then stood. "I'll collect my writing box."

Despite Elizabeth's momentary disquiet, the afternoon passed pleasantly. Jane and Lydia returned, both cheerful but, for once, Jane smiling more broadly. They recounted their walk in so much detail that it should have been excruciating but Elizabeth, after so long apart from them, enjoyed the telling.

Later, when Elizabeth went up to the room she shared with Jane to ready for dinner, she found her sister already dressed for the evening, seated at the table before their mirror, arranging her hair.

Greeting Elizabeth's reflection with a smile, Jane said, "Good evening, Lizzy."

"Good evening. Would you care for help with that?"

Jane lowered her arms in relief. "Please."

Elizabeth came to stand behind her sister, accepting the proffered hairpins. "Did you have a nice walk with Mr. Bingley today?"

Jane's face melted into a dreamy look. "Oh Lizzy, I truly did. Have you ever met anyone so wonderful?"

At one time, Elizabeth would have said no, but now Mr. Darcy's visage sprang to mind and she simply smiled and let the question pass unanswered instead saying, "I'm glad you've met someone wonderful."

"And it's good that I think so," Jane said as Elizabeth began on her hair. "It was almost embarrassing how Miss Bingley and Mrs. Hurst threw us together, repeatedly asking Lydia to show them something down one path while suggesting I take Mr. Bingley down another. If I didn't like him so much, I would be shocked." She met Elizabeth's gaze again in the mirror. "Why do you suppose they're so intent on the match?"

"I believe they wish a permanent attachment to Mr. Darcy and his wealth and connection."

Jane appeared a touch crestfallen. "Oh. They like me because of you. Do you think that's why Mr. Bingley danced with me so often at the assembly and came to walk with me today?"

Elizabeth shook her head. "Mr. Bingley appeared smitten with you from the moment he sighted you, long before introductions were even made. You could simply have been a family friend when we entered but I believe he'd already fallen quite in love with you."

Jane's expression cleared of worry, but then her brow furrowed again. "I don't think they like Lydia or Mama, even if they kept asking Lydia to walk with them. Some of their comments make me think that if Mr. Bingley and I did marry, they would try to get me to distance myself from them. They brought up Mary and Kitty as well, asking all sorts of questions." She met Elizabeth's gaze. "They spoke highly of you and Mr. Darcy, and Miss Darcy, though."

Hands stilling, Elizabeth asked, "Do you believe Mr. Bingley agrees with them about Lydia and Mama?" And likely the Gardiners, Phillips, Evans, and Smiths as well.

Jane shook her head. "I don't believe so. He likes everyone."

Elizabeth smiled and resumed her work arranging Jane's enviable golden curls.

"I wish I could know if he is the right gentleman," Jane said after a moment.

"I think you already know," Elizabeth observed.

Jane blushed but said, "Maybe I will ask Mary or Kitty how soon they knew, next time I write. I shouldn't want to mistake infatuation for love and encourage a suit I'll regret encouraging. Especially in a friend to you and Mr. Darcy. That would be cruel."

"You'd take Kitty or Mary's advice over mine?" Elizabeth asked, half teasing, half hurt.

Jane dropped her gaze to the surface of the dressing table.

After a moment, Elizabeth realized what her sister must be thinking. "They were able to choose their husbands." Why did that statement hurt so when she'd finally begun to care for Mr. Darcy?

"They might have more insight into selecting a husband," Jane agreed reluctantly.

Elizabeth pursed her lips and kept pinning Jane's hair. She may not have been permitted a choice when she accepted Mr. Darcy but she'd come to value and esteem him. Surely, Jane and all of Meryton believed that after last night, watching her and Mr. Darcy dance together so often?

If her closest sister wasn't certain of the regard in which she'd come to hold Mr. Darcy, did that mean that he wasn't either? Was that why he'd yet to come to her bedchamber? Had he sensed her not very subtle rebuff when they'd first resided together?

Well then, Elizabeth would put that right. She couldn't quite imagine creeping down the hall to his room while her parents and sisters slept but she could begin to show him in other ways. And once they reached Pemberley, well…she'd be free to enter her husband's chambers at night. Not that she hadn't been in Darcy House, but now she realized that making their marriage real in more than name was something she not only would, but wanted, to do.

Chapter Twenty-Three

Outside the gate, Wickham paced the stacked stone wall at the far end of Longbourn's garden. He didn't like to be kept waiting. Wouldn't bother to wait for any girl, let alone a silly one like Lydia Bennet, were she not how he would get the funds and acknowledgement he deserved from Darcy.

Not for the first time, he cursed Darcy for staying at Longbourn and for deigning to attend the assembly. Both were unthinkable. The grand Mr. Darcy living in that single wing, cramped country home with the Bennets? Going to rural dances?

Why was Darcy playing the smitten husband for these people? Did his wife have some hold over him? A way to blackmail him, perhaps, or an error in his marriage contract that gave her rights to some of his fortune? There had to be an explanation for Darcy lowering himself this way and threatening to derail Wickham's plans in the process.

Wickham's pace increased, his anger at suffering more injustices from Darcy growing. He'd been hours away from proposing to Lydia. He'd charmed that fool Bennet and his attorney brother-in-law into giving him a document to which he could later add his real name. Mr. Wiekran would no longer exist. Or, if he did, Wickham didn't know the man.

He hadn't even been worried when Mr. Bennet mentioned Darcy's impending arrival. Not until the moment he'd learned that Darcy and his wife would stay with the Bennets. All Darcy had to do was sequester his snobbish self in Netherfield Park for long enough for Wickham to whisk the girl away, a letter giving him permission to wed her, and eighty pounds a year, in hand.

Then he could have returned with his new, thoroughly ruined, bride and started negotiating the terms by which they would be provided for by Darcy. A simple, easy plan. Just as with Ramsgate, Darcy had ruined everything. This time, Wickham hadn't even had enough warning to attempt to counter him.

A twig snapped and he jumped, whirling to face the gate. Lydia Bennet, her bonnet engulfed in a ridiculous number of ribbons and silk flowers, stepped through. Sighting him, a smile formed on her wide lips.

Much prettier than Georgiana's lips. He preferred the taste of Lydia as well. Smart in some ways, she always made certain to chew mint before meeting him, making her perfect for kissing.

"George." She rushed forward, hands extended for him to clasp.

He worked to thrust his hatred for Darcy to the back of his mind. He required a different sort of intensity to bring his plan to fruition. "Dearest. How I've longed for you. I live for these moments when we may be together."

She clasped his hands tight. "Then why did you not come to the assembly? I missed you so." She batted her lashes. "We could have danced, and everyone would have seen us together, especially Lizzy, and she'd be so jealous because she didn't even get to pick her husband and he's so cold and obviously doesn't love her."

"Why do you think that, dear heart? As one so in love, I cannot imagine others not knowing our bliss." He fought not to let loose a laugh at his own drivel.

Lydia's glowing eyes showed how she soaked up every ridiculous word. She dropped her voice to a whisper, even though they were alone, past the wall at the back of her family's garden, and said, "Because she's sharing a room with Jane. If he loved her, he would want her in his bed. And how can he love her when his sister hates her?"

"Miss Darcy is here?" Wickham asked sharply. Mr. Bennet hadn't said anything about Georgiana traveling with Darcy and his wife.

Lines creased Lydia's forehead. "She's sharing a room with me." Her lower lip jutted out, petulant. "Why? Do you know her? Mr. Darcy seemed as if he might know you but then he said he did not."

Wickham shook his head, mind whirling. He had to get Lydia away. That was paramount. But if he could get Georgiana as well...He couldn't marry her now. She'd never agree. Perhaps he could ransom her back? How far would Darcy's leniency for a brother by marriage extend? How much would he be willing to hush up to avoid attaching scandal to the vaunted Darcy name? He'd already covered up Georgiana's near elopement, made no public mention of Mrs. Younge's thievery, and let Wickham get away with the death of a wagon driver, all to avoid scandal. Surely, he'd pay a ransom for his sister's safe return and fail to press charges for that as well?

"George?" Lydia asked, looking truly worried now. "Do you know Miss Darcy?"

He shook his head again, focusing a smile on Lydia. "Dearest, did I, I should have forgotten her name and visage the moment I set eyes on you."

She preened, brow smoothing. "I should think so. She's gawky and plain."

"And you are elegance and beauty," he said, a plan firming in his mind. "But I have heard of her. This is…it's embarrassing. I shouldn't tell you."

"Tell me what?" Worry returning, she squeezed his hands. "You know you may tell me anything, George. I love you. I will always side with you."

He gazed at her with all the adoration he would give a pile of bank notes, which in a way she was. "When I was young, I lived near the Darcys, in Derbyshire. Everyone there knows them. They're a very important family."

Lydia sniffed. "They believe so, at least. I can tell."

Wickham nodded. "They used to let us onto their land in the autumn, after their servants harvested the best from their orchard, so we might collect the pickings." The truth was that the Darcys routinely let the people of Lambton, the nearest village, have first pick from a large swath of Pemberley's orchard, but he preferred his version. "A few autumns ago, Miss Darcy had wandered down to the orchard and was caught—" He broke off, expression pained.

"Caught what?" Lydia asked, entranced.

"I cannot. It's unfit for your ears, my love."

"You must tell me. I'm sharing my room with her."

He couldn't see how that made much difference but, after a long-agonized moment calculated to fully invest her in his lie, he nodded. "I suppose you must know."

"I really must."

He heaved a sigh. "She was caught in a compromising position with a young man."

Lydia gasped, eyes so wide they might pop from her head. "No."

"Yes." He drooped with feigned sorrow. "The young man ran off, arms about his head, before they could identify him, but they saw his hair. It was similar to mine. They rounded up several of us and she, knowing full well who the perpetrator was, pointed me out to spare her lover."

Lydia stared up at him, aghast. "But, they didn't make you marry her?"

"One so low as me for the great Miss Darcy?" He shook his head. "Not when they could use their money and connections to make it as if the incident had never happened. To make me disappear from their lives. I was cast out, my father made to forsake me and when he passed, his lands went back to the Darcys. Her lie hurt me. It hurt my family." Warming to his tale, he mustered a sheen of tears.

Lydia released his hands to place hers on either side of his jaw. "Oh, my poor George. How it must hurt you to find them here."

"So you see, Mr. Darcy does not know me or I him, but he would have recognized the name George Wiekran, though he'd never admit as much."

"But Miss Darcy gave no reaction to your name at all when I spoke to her about you."

"She probably never bothered to learn the name of the young man whose life she ruined."

Lydia rose up on her toes to kiss him. When she withdrew, she repeated, "My poor George."

He caught her hands, returning to a loving look. "But it all came out well, you see. It all led me here to you."

"Now I understand why you always say the name Darcy with such dislike."

He thought he'd hidden that from her. He would have to do better in the future. He couldn't have his wife knowing what he actually thought. "Yes."

"And why you didn't come to the assembly."

He nodded. "I'd thought to walk in, head high, for I've done nothing wrong, but then I remembered his fortune and his power. He's like to stop at nothing to prevent me from marrying his wife's sister."

Lydia frowned, lips pursed as she thought.

After a long moment, tired of waiting for her to come to the proper conclusion, Wickham added, "Of course, if Mr. Darcy knew the truth, that I was not the one discovered in the orchard with his sister, he would likely wish to make amends. They are known for being a reasonable family."

"Make amends?" Her gaze turned thoughtful. Calculating. "Do you mean, restore your family's lands to you?"

He sighed again. "I can but hope."

"But only Miss Darcy knows that it wasn't you in the orchard."

"Indeed, and if she'd any intention of setting matters right, she would have." He kept his features slack and sorrow filled, willing Lydia to come to the idea he wanted.

Her face took on a grim, firm look. "Then we must make her confess."

Perfect. A little more was all he needed. "But how? We cannot force Miss Darcy's hand. She has everything and we have only each other."

"We have truth on our side." Lydia's brow creased. "We could…"

"What, dearest?" he pressed, not hiding his hope.

"Well, that is, if we had her, we could make her write a letter telling the truth."

He could kiss Lydia for being so dedicated and ruthless. "Had her? I don't understand."

"Well, we could take her." She rushed on, full of appeal. "Don't you see? We would need something to hold over her. So, we take her and say we'll let her go if she tells the truth. She has so much, and you already said that Mr. Darcy's money can guard her reputation. No real harm will befall her."

He gasped in feigned shock. "But we would be kidnappers. Darcy would see me hung and you locked away, and with good reason."

Lines of concentration on her brow she turned from him, pacing. He let her, appreciating the sway of her hips each time she walked away. All else aside, it would be a pleasure to enjoy her fine figure on their wedding night. Or maybe before, if she proved susceptible to his advances once he had her away from here.

She turned back and rushed to reach for his hands. "We'll marry right away. In Scotland. Then you and Mr. Darcy will be family. He won't see you hang then, especially once Miss Darcy confesses. He'll see that we only did what we must to set things right."

"I don't know," he drawled while glee filled him. She'd been slow about it, but she'd come to the exact plan he wished, all of which suited him well enough. He didn't want a wife who was too clever. "How would we even take her?" He waited, expectant, for he truly didn't have a plan in place for that.

She crinkled her nose, thinking. "There's to be a ball at Netherfield. Everyone is going."

"We can't abduct her from a ball."

Lydia shook her head. "No, but Miss Darcy isn't going."

She might have mentioned that when she said everyone would attend. "She's not?"

"My sister said she can't be out yet because she's not ready and Mr. Darcy agreed. She didn't get to go to the assembly, either. I can say I'm not feeling well and stay at Longbourn with her, and then ask her to go for a walk." She studied his face, seeking approval.

"No," he said slowly, calculations spinning through his head. Georgiana was best controlled through her desire to disobey Darcy. "Darcy said she cannot go?"

Lydia nodded, looking confused.

"Say you won't attend the ball unless she can, too."

"But what if Mr. Darcy changes his mind, and then lets her?"

Wickham couldn't contain a derisive snort. "He won't. Darcy doesn't change his mind."

"So, I will say that, and she'll be grateful, and then we'll go for a walk?"

"You will say that, and she'll be grateful, and once everyone is gone, you'll confess that you have a friend with a carriage waiting to take you both to the ball. Tell her Darcy won't endure the shame of admitting she isn't supposed to be there once she is."

Lydia grinned. "That is perfect. You're so smart, George."

Smugness filled him. "I am, rather, aren't I?"

"And then we'll go to Scotland and marry and we'll make her write that note and I'll be Mrs. Wiekran and you'll have your lands back and I'll be wealthier than Mary and Kitty, at least. I won't be last in anything."

He brought her hand to his lips, kissed her, then said, "You will always be first with me, dear heart. Always."

She beamed at him, her perfect oval face lovely. It would be a pleasure getting brats on her, and he would. As many as possible, each one increasing his fortune. Mr. and Mrs. Darcy would never permit their nieces and nephews to live in squalor. That, plus the meager amount Lydia's father offered, plus whatever he managed to barter Georgiana for…it would all go a long way to making up for how Darcy had treated him thus far.

Yes. It would do. At least until he devised a new plan to get more from Darcy.

Chapter Twenty-Four

On the day of the ball, Darcy received a request to meet Bingley in Meryton. Perfectly content to leave a house full of bustling women, especially with Elizabeth saying she would take that time to visit Miss Lucas, Darcy complied. In short order, he and Bingley had left their mounts in the care of the cheerful lad at the inn and strolled the main street of the village.

It didn't take long, walking in silence while Bingley stared at nothing and sighed, for Darcy to realize that his friend had more on his mind than escaping the bustle of readying for a ball. He ventured, "Preparations for this evening are well in hand?"

"Yes. Caroline has outdone herself, especially considering how little time I gave her."

"Good."

They walked on, Darcy uncertain how he might bring Bingley to the point. He didn't wish to press but couldn't imagine his friend arranging their meeting for less than discourse.

Halting before a storefront, Bingley turned to him. "May I prevail upon you for advice?"

Darcy nodded. "You may."

"I wish to offer for Miss Bennet."

Satisfaction sparked in Darcy but he tamped it down. Bingley needed honest advice, not encouragement that stemmed from Darcy's selfish desire to see Miss Bennet and Miss Lydia, at least, well wed. "You have not known her long."

"You didn't know Mrs. Darcy at all."

"I am fortunate." Even if it had taken him time to realize as much.

"But she and Jane are sisters. Surely, with Jane, I would be as fortunate."

Darcy didn't miss how easily Bingley slipped into using Miss Bennet's Christian name. "But they are not the same person, and you have a choice."

Bingley's features were overcome by a mooning, dazed sort of smile. "I don't know that I do have a choice. Not from the moment I beheld her."

"Then ask yourself, what is the worst that might happen?"

"She might refuse me," Bingley replied without hesitation.

"I meant, rather, the worst that could happen if she accepts and you later find you don't suit."

"Oh, but Jane is the kindest, sweetest person I have ever known. I daresay if we didn't suit, I would never even realize it."

In view of Bingley's obvious devotion, Darcy didn't trouble to point out that regrets wouldn't be exclusive to him. Miss Bennet might have them, too. "And would you be able to live with the possibility that she may not love you so devotedly as you love her?"

Bingley turned to the shop window, frowning. Their reflections looked back, dim and overlaying the wares. The wind gusted and dead leaves rose behind them, a swirl of motion in the reflection and a rattle of detritus in Darcy's ears, then settled again.

"I love her so much that were she the least bit amiable, I believe I should be far happier with her than without her," Bingley said, voice quiet and sure.

"Then I believe you have your answer."

Bingley cast him a quick look. "Do you think she doesn't care for me?"

"On the contrary, I believe she does. We cannot know for certain, however, or be sure she would not marry you if she didn't."

Bingley relaxed into his usual amiability. "So, you believe she does care for me."

Darcy found Miss Bennet, with her perpetually pleasant expression, difficult to read but he rather felt Bingley already decided on his course. He tried not to dwell on how his advice might differ if he didn't wish for the connection and settled for, "I am certain there is no dislike, at least."

Bingley nodded, smiling, but his unfocussed expression spoke of a gentleman already picturing the proposal in his mind, not one attending to Darcy's cautious words.

Darcy shrugged, training his gaze through the shop window. A glint of blue caught his attention. "Let's go in."

"Inside?" Bingley asked, blinking.

"Yes." Darcy led the way, wishing for a closer look at the adornment that attracted him.

Before leaving London, he'd commissioned a diamond and sapphire set for Elizabeth, to be delivered to Pemberley. He eagerly awaited bestowing the pieces, especially the pendant, but that left him with nothing to give her now. He pictured how pleasant it would be to present her with a token of his affection. This afternoon, for the ball.

There was only one store in Meryton which was likely to have jewelry. Skirting the shelves of pots and place settings, bolts of inexpensive cloth and lengths of leather that marked the general store at the heart of Meryton, Darcy finally reached the store's small selection of jewelry. His eyes fell on a necklace which was an inexpensive but delicately filigreed arrangement of milky blue stones, cleverly ordered to form a sprig of small blue flowers strung through on a slender chain. While nothing about the piece spoke of great wealth, the craftsmanship was exquisite. The stones were placed with obvious care to give the impression that the sun's rays radiated down from the lefthand side in the mythical glade in which the flowers bloomed.

"Pretty thing," Bingley said, beside him. "But not what one would expect for the mistress of Pemberley."

"True." Not the sort of grand, diamond accented pieces he'd commissioned for his wife. The necklace lacked glamor. It wouldn't stun a room or fill others with envy at a glance. And yet, the more he studied it, the more he appreciated the sophistication. The perfect craftsmanship and obvious dedication.

Darcy straightened. Aware that the shopkeeper, at the front by the counter, had half an eye turned their way, he said loudly, "I'll take it."

The man came around his counter, hurrying over. He named a price that Darcy thought was very reasonable, adding, "Ah, and, meaning no insult, sir, but on cash only. I can't afford to extend any more credit this quarter."

"That is fine."

The shopkeeper noticeably relaxed and reached to collect the necklace with care. "If you'll come to the front, gentlemen, I have a box set aside for this piece. Included in the price." He grimaced. "The craftsman insisted. He said he'd not have me selling it to have it ruined by being shoved in some gentleman's pocket."

"I'm happy to take the box," Darcy assured him. He wouldn't have it ruined, either.

The shopkeeper started for the front of the shop, but Bingley held Darcy back. In a low voice, he said, "I know you don't haggle but as I'm here, I can get the price down for you."

Slightly affronted, Darcy replied, "That isn't necessary." The price was reasonable, so there was no need to haggle, especially since many shopkeepers lost more than what Bingley could hope to save due to lack of payment from his class.

Darcy went to the front of the shop, where the shopkeeper placed the necklace atop the counter and began to rummage about the shelves underneath.

Bingley came to lean against the counter in a show of casualness. "Extended too much credit, then? Sorry to hear that."

The shopkeeper looked up, winced, and adopted a put upon expression. "Aye. We poor working folk are always at risk. Every penny matters." He returned to looking for the box.

Darcy gave Bingley a quelling look.

Appearing not to see, Bingley said, "Well, there's always that risk between keeping customers happy and being taken advantage of. I daresay a bit of ready cash would help about now. Almost be worth more than the value of the bills, if your need is dire."

"Aye, it was a good customer, too. Always paid up in full until recently. Must have fallen on hard times though I don't see any indication of that." Ducked down out of sight below the counter, the shopkeeper's reply was muted. He popped up to add, "Maybe he overspent, knowing he's money coming in from Mr. Bennet soon."

"Mr. Bennet?" Darcy cut in.

"Aye. Whole village knows he's about to propose to the youngest Bennet daughter."

"You speak of Mr. Wiekran."

The shopkeeper nodded. "See? Even you know and I know you two are new hereabouts." His eyes widened. "But then, you must be Mr. Bingley and Mr. Darcy?"

Bingley smiled but Darcy could read his disappointment. The man was likely raising the price as he spoke. "I'm Bingley, yes, and this is Mr. Darcy."

A smile broke over the man's face. "Mr. Bingley, you've brought me so much business readying for this ball, and Mr. Darcy, everyone in town is gossiping over how happy you make our Elizabeth, I'm pleased to sell you the necklace at a discount."

"That won't be necessary." Darcy leveled a repressive look on Bingley until the other man nodded. "I insist on paying in full."

"They do say you're a good one, Mr. Darcy."

After concluding the purchase, Darcy and Bingley went their separate ways, Bingley glowing with happiness and Darcy in a less pleasant frame of mind than when he'd ridden out. As he rode back along the packed dirt lane, he tried to concentrate on the necklace and giving it to Elizabeth but his mind kept going to Mr. Wiekran. George Wiekran, who hadn't attended the assembly or visited Miss Lydia since Darcy's arrival and who'd suddenly gone from a good community member to one racking up debts. Darcy felt paranoid and foolish for entertaining the notion, but he couldn't shake the worry that Mr. Wiekran wasn't who he said he was, despite his knowledge that the first name of George and a two-syllable last name beginning with W were common occurrences.

There was nothing for it but to meet the man. Surely, that could be arranged. And if not, if the request scared Wiekran off, Darcy felt certain he would have prevented a tragedy in keeping Miss Lydia from accepting the man.

Upon returning to Longbourn, wishing for both quiet in general and a private word with his wife, Darcy left a message for her to seek him in Longbourn's garden when she returned from visiting Miss Lucas, and went out. The autumn weather proved softly warm even as the sun dropped lower, and he found his coat too hot for the pace at which he preferred to walk, but he walked regardless. Away from the bustling house and the noise there, glad that he hadn't visited when Longbourn held Mrs. Bennet and all five Bennet sisters. Darcy fully understood why Mr. Bennet chose to breakfast early and rarely left his library.

"Fitz," his sister's voice called.

Darcy turned to see her and Miss Lydia picking their way up the path in his direction. Both appeared determined and tension tightened in his chest. In the days since the assembly, his sister had moved from angry to sulking, and had only recently deigned to speak if he or Elizabeth were in the room. Georgiana's spite hurt, but Elizabeth had assured him it was within the normal realm of what the guardian of a fifteen-year-old girl must endure.

"Fitz," she repeated when she reached him.

"Georgiana. Miss Lydia." He waited, attempting to gauge their mood.

"We've come to talk about the ball," Miss Lydia said.

Darcy nodded, working not to betray a stab of panic. When would Elizabeth return? She would know how to deal with whatever was coming.

"You must let me attend," Georgiana said. "You can't truly mean to leave me behind while everyone else is there, dancing. It's not fair."

Fair? He frowned, trying to think how fairness played into his sister's recent bad behavior.

Miss Lydia crossed her arms over her chest, squeezed her mouth into a scowl and said, "And if you don't let Georgiana go, I'm not going either."

"That would hardly be my fault."

Georgiana glared at him. "It's *all* your fault. You agreed with Elizabeth when she said I couldn't go, and now if Lydia doesn't get to go and dance with her Mr. Wiekran, it will be all your fault."

Mr. Wiekran. If he were at the ball, that would be all the more reason to make sure Georgiana didn't attend. Not until Darcy met with the man and put his likely irrational fears to rest. He shook his head. "The decision is already made."

"But everyone else is going," Georgiana reiterated, voice going up an octave. "It's embarrassing, everyone thinking I'm not grown up enough to go to a dance hosted in the country, by the Bingleys."

"And yet you rarely hear such caterwauling from a grown woman," Elizabeth's voice said.

Darcy looked past Georgiana and Miss Lydia to see his wife coming up the path. His shoulders relaxed in relief. She gave him a commiserating smile.

"Now," Elizabeth said as she took her place by his side. "I daresay this idea to ambush Mr. Darcy without me present was Lydia's, but you should realize, Miss Darcy, that such tactics do not further your cause. Nor does screeching like a banshee."

"A banshee?" Georgiana screeched.

"You would prefer fishwife?"

Miss Lydia's hands flew to her mouth, trying to hold in a giggle.

"Agh," Georgiana growled, glaring at all three of them. Hands balled at her sides she whirled and stalked back down the path.

Miss Lydia dropped her hands, leveling a narrow-eyed look on Elizabeth. "You ruin everything," she spat out, then rushed off after Georgiana calling, "Miss Darcy, I'm sorry. I didn't mean to laugh."

The picture of calm, Elizabeth turned to him. "Your note said you awaited me in the garden but I daresay being rescued from them wasn't your reason for writing it."

He smiled for she truly had rescued him. He'd no experience with irate fifteen-year-old girls. Until recently, Georgiana had been a sweet and biddable child always seeking to make him proud. "It was not, but I thank you."

"Then you called me out here to enjoy the autumn air? I shouldn't mind a turn about the garden but then I must go ready for tonight. We've something elaborate planned for Jane's hair."

He caught a silken curl. "Not for yours?"

"My maid will fix my hair in a way that pleases me. Jane has only an overworked maid or an unhelpful sister to fix her hair."

Her words came out pleasant and even but standing so close, Darcy noted the uptick of her pulse. Did his nearness inspire that telltale staccato? Hoping so, he released her curl to smooth the backs of his fingers along her cheek. She turned her head slightly, leaning into the caress.

His own pulse kicking up, he glanced down the path to make sure their sisters had left, then recalled the necklace. Releasing Elizabeth, he drew the box from his coat. "I bought you this."

Her eyes, which had begun to drift closed, came fully open. "How very kind of you," she said as she accepted the box.

"You don't know what it is yet."

"I can guess it is jewelry, selected for me from you, and so I am certain it is kind of you." She drew the box open.

The warm glow of the lowering sun caught the delicate flowers, adding a blush to their creamy blue luminescence. The filigreed leaves gleamed. It pleased Darcy to see that by the light of day, the necklace proved even prettier than inside the shop.

"It's beautiful," Elizabeth breathed.

He looked up from the necklace to see a shimmer of tears in her eyes.

"Put it on me?" She proffered back the box.

He took it and she turned away. Putting the box in his pocket, Darcy grasped the two ends of the necklace in fingers that seemed too large for the delicate clasp. Reaching around her with one hand, he brought the chain about her neck and fastened it. He released the necklace and, unable to resist, slid his hands down the smooth arc where Elizabeth's neck met her shoulders.

She swayed backward, again leaning into his caress. A jitteriness built within him. Feeling as if he dared greatly, he dipped his head to kiss the back of his wife's neck. She gasped but didn't pull away, so he kissed that warm soft skin, scented with honey and lemon, a second time, lingering.

She moved then, but only to turn. One hand lightly touched the necklace as she gazed up at him in wonder. "Thank you. It is the most splendid gift anyone has ever given me."

He dropped his gaze, uncomfortable with such high praise. He should be giving her gifts every day. Costly, rare, wonderful gifts. "It wasn't expensive or planned. I went into a shop in Meryton, and it made me think of you."

"That is why it is so splendid," she said. "Because you saw it and thought of me. Do you think the expense matters to me at all?"

He shook his head. "No."

Her gaze traversed his face, her full lips turned up at the corners. "Do you know what, Mr. Darcy?"

"Fitzwilliam. Or Fitz."

She blinked, meeting his gaze. "Fitzwilliam."

A surge of pleasure went through him at the careful, wondering way she said his name. "What don't I know, Elizabeth?"

"That I love you."

If her name on his lips was pleasure, her declaration of love was ecstasy. "I love you, too," he said, hardly able to get the words out before their lips met.

Chapter Twenty-Five

Preparing for the ball was torture. Being at the ball was torture. In fact, every moment they lingered in Hertfordshire must be overshadowed with agony. After so thoroughly kissing his wife in the garden that they'd never noted the setting sun and had made everyone else late, Darcy could think of nothing but reaching Pemberley, where they might at last find privacy. As he looked about the crowded ballroom, decorated to London standards as a reflection of the strength of Miss Bingley's will and her skill as a hostess, Darcy contemplated nothing but how quickly they might leave come morning.

"Should we dance?" Elizabeth murmured, looking at him askance. "I do enjoy dancing with you."

Darcy knew his young wife didn't mean any innuendo. Normally, he wouldn't have heard any, but for the indecent thoughts regarding Elizabeth that paraded through his mind. "Certainly," he said, wondering how his wife wasn't similarly distracted.

He clasped her hand, felt the slight tremble and took in the flush that rose in her cheeks, and checked a smile. Perhaps their time in the garden had evoked similar ideas in Elizabeth after all.

They danced a set, Darcy attending to little outside watching his wife. He then led her away from their friends to a less crowded corner of the room. He'd no inclination to share her. Not even for a polite gavotte with Bingley or Hurst. Across the room, Bingley seemed similarly determined, sidestepping to cut off a young man who approached Miss Bennet, presumably to ask for the next set.

"Miss Bingley appears agitated."

His wife's words caused Darcy to glance around. Indeed, their hostess strode across the room in their direction, expression firm and unyielding. "If she wishes to make up a set, intimidation won't work."

"We do have our entire lives to dance together," Elizabeth countered but her hand told a different story, tightening on his arm.

"Mr. Darcy, Mrs. Darcy," Miss Bingley greeted when she reached them. "I must ask you to come with me."

"Both of us?" Elizabeth sounded surprised.

"Yes, please, and as discreetly as you can manage." She glanced about at the sea of watching eyes with mild disgust then turned and started walking.

Exchanging a confused look, Darcy and Elizabeth followed Miss Bingley back across the room and through a side passage. They wound deeper into Netherfield's manor house, lit sconces less frequent the farther from the ballroom they went. Finally, Miss Bingley pushed open the door to the kitchen. She didn't halt but instead led them across and out the back, into the garden.

A cloaked form hurtled at Darcy. He released Elizabeth to catch the figure, who collapsed against him with a sob.

"Georgiana?" Elizabeth gasped.

"I don't know what the trouble is," Miss Bingley said. "She had one of the maids fetch me."

"It's L-l-lydia. George t-took her," Georgiana sobbed.

"Mr. Wiekran?" Elizabeth asked in clear alarm.

"G-george W-wickham." Georgiana followed that with a wail, clinging to Darcy.

"George Wickham?" Miss Bingley reiterated. "Who is he?"

"A st-steward's son," Georgiana replied for him, giving him a pleading look.

"Is with Miss Lydia?" Miss Bingley cast a look over her shoulder at the kitchen door, but Darcy suspected her mind ranged all the way back to the ballroom. "I see. If you will excuse me, I must stop…that is, I must speak with my brother." Without waiting for an answer, she turned and hurried away.

"I assume even a connection to the Darcys isn't worth one to this Wickham?" Elizabeth asked, looking up at him in worry. "Who is George Wickham? Why would he take my sister?" She glanced in the direction of the ballroom as well. "I should fetch Papa."

Georgiana pulled free of his arms and turned to Elizabeth, scrubbing her hands over her tear coated cheeks. "George Wickham is the man I nearly eloped with."

Elizabeth gasped, gaze colliding with Darcy's. "The man who tried to murder you has my sister?"

"Murder you?" Georgiana squeaked.

Darcy took a steadying breath against the panic that ricocheted about them. "Elizabeth, please ask someone in the kitchen to fetch your father. Georgiana, tell me what happened, succinctly and from the start."

He thought Elizabeth might argue, wanting to hear what Georgiana had to say but, expression grim, she went to the kitchen door and through. Darcy looked at his sister, expectant.

Leaving off biting her lip, Georgiana said, "After you all left, Lydia said we could still attend the ball. She said that if we arrived dressed for a ball and started dancing that no one would question it and by the time you noticed we were there, it would be too embarrassing to make us leave so you would have to pretend we were to attend all along."

She stopped, sucking in air and Darcy held up a hand, seeing the kitchen door open. Elizabeth came out, nodding to him. Once she reached them, he said, "Continue."

"Lydia said her friend Mr. Wiekran would take us in his carriage because he knew we were grown women, not children, and he wasn't afraid of you, Fitz." Georgiana swallowed, seeming afraid herself. "So, we dressed, and we sneaked out through the garden and went to the back gate. A carriage was there, and Lydia went right up to it. A man inside leaned forward to offer his hand. He was careful not to stick his head out into the moonlight but I knew. I don't know how I knew but I knew it was George."

"Mr. Wickham?" Elizabeth asked.

Georgiana nodded. "So I ran back down the path. He jumped out yelling for me, but I didn't stop. I heard Lydia call to him and the carriage leave, but I didn't look back. I ran to the house and went straight to your housekeeper."

"Mrs. Hill?" Elizabeth looked about. "Where is she?"

"I told her what happened and that we had to come get you right away, but she wouldn't believe me. She did go with me and see the carriage tracks and check that Lydia is missing, but she said like as not Miss Lydia had changed her mind, her not being a self-sacrificing sort, and asked her gentleman to take her to the ball and I was jealous and acting out a-and—" She broke off in a hiccupping sob. "And that she wouldn't be fooled by a w-willful child into bringing me where I'd been ordered not to go. So I sneaked out."

"You came all the way here alone?" Darcy asked sharply. With Wickham out there somewhere likely intent on kidnapping?

Georgiana looked from him to Elizabeth and back with pleading eyes, fresh streaks of tears gleaming in the moonlight. "I didn't know what else to do. I had to come."

"How did you know how to get here?" Elizabeth asked.

"Lydia took me a couple of days ago when we were out walking. She showed me a short cut. I cut across the fields to be safe."

Darcy didn't find that much safer at all but at least the moon was nearly full to act as illumination and guide, and Georgiana wore sensible boots under a ballgown covered by a cloak.

Elizabeth put an arm about his sister. "You did well. You did the right thing coming to us and you were very, very brave."

"Did George truly try to murder my brother?" Georgiana sobbed.

"Shh. We aren't certain. Let me take you in and have someone make tea. I'm certain they can spare a maid for that."

She cast Darcy a scared, nearly panicked look that belied her soothing tone then led his sister to the kitchen door. As they neared, Mr. Bennet came out. Elizabeth paused to speak to him and nodded to Darcy. Her father looked past her, sighted him and rushed over while Elizabeth and Georgiana disappeared inside.

"What is this about Lydia being kidnapped?" Mr. Bennet demanded.

"I need to beg a mount from Bingley to go after them. I'll recount the tale while we find him."

"No. You'll tell me what has happened to my daughter on our way to the stable, where we'll take mounts and apologize to Mr. Bingley later," Mr. Bennet said firmly and started walking in the direction of Netherfield's stables.

Darcy hesitated a breath, realized Mr. Bennet was right, and caught up in two long strides. "Mr. Wiekran is a man named Wickham. He took Miss Lydia away in a carriage and attempted to take Georgiana as well."

"And who is Mr. Wickham?" Mr. Bennet slanted a narrow-eyed look at Darcy as he asked, his hard words unaffected by their rapid pace as they neared the stable.

"He is the son of my father's steward. He is a gambler, a wastrel, a spendthrift and, I am rather certain, a murderer. He is also the man who Elizabeth prevented from shooting at my carriage. The one who pushed her into that gorge." For that alone, Wickham deserved to hang.

"And he has Lydia?"

"I'm afraid he does."

222

Mr. Bennet muttered a low curse. "He also has a document from me saying he may marry her and promising eighty pounds a year if he does."

"Surely you mean a document for Mr. Wiekran," Darcy said as they reached the stable.

"Yes. I don't know how he plans to get around that, but it's likely he intends to use it if he doesn't go to Scotland."

Darcy nodded and flung open the stable door, revealing a cluster of startled grooms, drivers and footmen playing cards. "We need Bingley's fastest two mounts. Now."

Several of the grooms scrambled to obey.

They rode to the back of Longbourn's garden, pace slower than Darcy would like in the near dark. When they arrived and dismounted, Darcy found the moon bright enough for them to pick out the marks of carriage wheels in the soft earth. Back in the saddle, they followed the tracks to the main roadway. There, the trail became impossible. Darcy looked up and down the north-south running road, doubting the darkness that wrapped about them was fully to blame. With the amount of traffic that normally passed, trailing any one carriage would be a nearly impossible task.

"Do you know this Mr. Wickham well enough to guess where he may have gone?" Mr. Bennet asked, expression grim.

Darcy had been thinking of little else as they rode. "I would wager Scotland, to marry your daughter," he replied, queasy at the thought of having to call Wickham brother, which was undoubtedly the other man's intention. "Unless he plans to marry her under the name Wiekran."

Mr. Bennet exhaled gustily. "That would not be so terrible."

"Except that I suspect him of murdering a wagon driver."

Mr. Bennet studied him in the near dark. "But you haven't proof, I assume, as he's still at large."

"Correct."

"Are you looking for proof?"

Darcy nodded, suspecting where Mr. Bennet's questions might lead.

"If he marries Lydia, will you keep looking?"

"Would you wish me to stop?" Darcy asked.

Mr. Bennet shook his head. "No, but may I assume he expects you to stop?"

"Yes." Deciding he owed Elizabeth's father more than one syllable, Darcy continued, "Normally, he would be correct. In the past, I have covered for his bad behavior. Hidden the truth from my ailing father so as not to distress him. Paid Wickham's debts." Not sought retribution for what he'd done to Elizabeth and attempted to do to Georgiana, to spare his sister's name. "He has every reason to believe that marrying Miss Lydia will cause me to call off the investigation I've commissioned." Had Darcy created this monster that was George Wickham?

"But not in the case of murder?"

"No. Not in the case of murder. If I can find proof, I will see him tried."

"As you should."

Darcy didn't need Mr. Bennet's approval, yet it pleased him to have it. "I believe the bigger question, then, is if you would prefer to have a widowed daughter or a ruined one?"

"Two bad choices," Mr. Bennet said. "Is the widow of a hanged man more or less of a pariah than a woman who is ruined? Especially if she married the man after he committed the murder. My goal is to get Lydia back, in my care, safe and sound. If she bears a child, we will handle that somehow, whether or not she marries. Don't let the marriage or lack of one be the issue."

Clear on what must be done, Darcy said, "I will go north?"

"And I south, but I suggest we agree to meet at Longbourn if and when there is no reasonable trail."

To that, Darcy agreed. He couldn't search endlessly. He'd readied for a ball, not a ride to Scotland.

By the time he turned back for Longbourn in the small hours of the morning, thoroughly exhausted, Darcy felt certain that Wickham and Miss Lydia hadn't gone north. At least, not directly so. Whether that meant that he was wrong about Wickham's intentions to marry Lydia or meant that Wickham knew him well enough to guess that Darcy would go north, he simply didn't know. He could even have first veered west to avoid detection, or zig zagged across the countryside. The uncertainty over which tormented Darcy throughout his ride, giving no ground as he put his exhausted, borrowed mount in the care of a sleepy groom in Longbourn's stable. Darcy noted the horse Mr. Bennet had borrowed being brushed down and went in.

He found Elizabeth still awake, waiting with her father. They looked up in hope as he entered. He shook his head, then dropped to sit on the sofa Elizabeth occupied.

"Too much to hope for, I suppose," Mr. Bennet said. "And a scant hope it was. I found word of a carriage carrying a couple that matched their description along the road south, but I guessed wrong at the split, or they didn't stop again. I believe they made for London."

Worry carved deep lines in Mr. Bennet's face, as well it might. In London, they could disappear, the city a veritable warren of places to hide.

"What will we do?" Elizabeth asked, looking back and forth between them.

"I will go to London and begin a search," Darcy replied.

"I'm going with you," both Elizabeth and her father stated in unison.

Elizabeth cast her father a wry smile and continued, "And I believe Mr. Bingley will come as well."

"Bingley?" Darcy rubbed his temple.

Elizabeth reached to clasp his free hand. "After you left, Jane and Mr. Bingley came into the kitchen, Miss Bingley on their heels. Mr. Bingley called for a carriage to bring Georgiana and me back here."

Darcy nodded. He should have thought to call one.

"Miss Bingley said that was a splendid idea." Elizabeth smiled slightly, the expression at odds with her worried, tense features. "Then Mr. Bingley declared that he would join in the search for Lydia. Miss Bingley definitely didn't care for that idea. She told him Lydia's disappearance was none of his business."

Darcy nodded again, Miss Bingley's reaction not surprising him. "What did Bingley say?"

"He looked directly at Jane and said he would make it his business."

Were Darcy not so exhausted, that would have drawn a smile from him too.

"Miss Bingley said the news would get out and Lydia would be ruined," Elizabeth continued. "Mr. Bingley replied that if Miss Bingley said a word to anyone about it, he would get some cousin he named to keep house for him and send her to live with some other relative whose name I can't recall. Miss Bingley was not pleased. Nevertheless, she persuaded Mr. Bingley to stay until the end of the ball. I believe mainly to forestall speculation as to what was going on."

"So, no actual news got out," Darcy said.

"No news got out, but according to Jane, Miss Bingley and Mrs. Hurst said some, ah, unflattering things about Mama and Lydia, and

Mary and Kitty, which is a bit much as they haven't even met Mary and Kitty," Elizabeth said. "Mr. Bingley concurred that his sisters behaved badly."

"Bingley concurred?" Darcy asked. "When did you talk to him?"

"After the ball," Elizabeth replied. "He came here ostensibly to support me and Georgiana. Mama started having hysterics when she found out Lydia had eloped. She kept moaning about why they couldn't wait for the banns and how the family is ruined."

"I doubt that matters to Bingley," Darcy said, recalling Bingley's smitten look when they discussed Miss Bennet in Meryton.

"It didn't seem to." Elizabeth's smile grew, still at odds with the lines of tension marring her brow. "He said that it didn't matter if Lydia was ruined. He wants to marry Jane, so the only daughter left to be concerned about is Lydia."

"I assume Miss Bennet and Mr. Bingley are now engaged," Darcy asked, looking to Mr. Bennet.

"Yes."

That was a relief. At least Darcy didn't need to worry about how Wickham's scheme would impact Elizabeth's favorite sister. "We need a new plan. Riding about the countryside searching for them has done no good."

Mr. Bennet leaned forward. "As far as I am concerned, what matters the most is Lydia's safety, both short term and long term. If she marries this Mr. Wickham and he is not hanged, it seems to me that she will be a hostage and I will endlessly have to pay to keep her safe. Mrs. Bennet and I can weather whatever storm comes from her status. We cannot keep her safe from her husband."

Darcy broke the brief silence that followed that declaration, saying, "We should make ready to leave at first light. You may, of course, stay with us in Darcy House, Mr. Bennet."

In a mercurial change of mood, Mr. Bennet offered a wry smile and a shake of his head. "I believe I will stay with Kitty and Mr. Smith."

"But why?" Elizabeth asked.

Mr. Bennet turned to her. "Kitty informed me that your husband is allowing them to stay rent free in a house he owns." He turned to Darcy and added, "Thank you for that."

Neck heating at his wife's look of surprise, Darcy waved his hand in dismissal.

"No one told me," Elizabeth said.

More amusement alleviating some of the strain on his face, Mr. Bennet said, "You must take that up with your husband, my dear, because Kitty assumed you knew." He shrugged. "Regardless, I'll be staying with them. It will give me the opportunity to spend time with Kitty, to come to know Mr. Smith better, and to observe the generosity of one of my recently acquired sons."

Elizabeth gave her father a bemused look. "Well, so long as you understand that you are welcome to stay with us."

"I do and I won't forget it." A touch smug, Mr. Bennet continued, "And you should understand that I have every intention of visiting Pemberley's library."

Elizabeth shook her head indulgently at her father and rose from the sofa. "We had best make ready, then, and see if we may take any sleep. We have a long day." She twisted her hands tight together, clearly full of worry. "We'll want to start as early as we can."

Agreeing, Darcy stood as well. They bid Mr. Bennet good night even though it was nearly morning. As they parted ways, Darcy noted that Elizabeth's father went to the back of the house, in the direction of his library, rather than up the steps with them. In the hall outside her room, Elizabeth stopped and turned to him. A sudden lightness in his chest, Darcy realized she meant to kiss him goodnight.

"What about Georgiana?" she asked, brow lined with worry.

He blinked once, owlishly, his overtired mind adjusting to getting a question rather than a kiss. "We have few options. London with us, though we'll be busy searching, or here with your mother and Miss Bennet." He tried not to grimace.

"Or my mother and Jane could escort her to Pemberley."

Darcy considered that. He didn't overly like the idea of Mrs. Bennet and Miss Bennet seeing Pemberley before Elizabeth could. Yet, Georgiana would be well looked after there by Mrs. Reynolds. She could resume lessons with her old masters. Most of all, she'd be away from all the tumult and reminders of Wickham.

"And, if we ever need to say that Lydia was with them…" Elizabeth's gaze searched his face as she spoke.

"A lie?"

"Well, not as great a one as inventing a whole fictional family, but yes."

He shook his head. "She will come to London with us."

Elizabeth nodded. "As you like." She came up on her toes, kissed him and, leaving him desperately wanting more, slipped away into her room.

Chapter Twenty-Six

With the dawn, Elizabeth woke to Jane packing.

"What are you doing?" Elizabeth muttered, blinking against the rosy light coming through the open curtain.

"I heard you and Mr. Darcy talking last night in the hall."

Elizabeth tried to recall what they'd said. That Georgiana would go to London?

Jane took another gown from their wardrobe. "If you are off to London to search for Lydia, I am, too."

"And that has nothing to do with Mr. Bingley going?" Elizabeth asked archly, then stretched her mouth into a yawn.

"If it does, it has as much to do with finding Lydia," Jane said and continued packing.

"But who will stay with Mama?" Elizabeth asked.

Jane's hands stilled. Abruptly, she sat on the end of the bed. "You're right. Mama needs me."

"And Mr. Darcy, Papa and I will be looking. We'll do what we can to find her," Elizabeth said. "You're needed here. We can't leave Mama all alone in her state."

Jane let out a sigh. "You're right. I should be here. I know." She swiveled to face Elizabeth. "Promise me that if I can be of any help, you'll send for me."

"I promise," Elizabeth said and rose to make ready to leave.

Later, as footmen carried her cases down to Mr. Darcy's waiting carriages, putting the luggage atop the smaller of the two, Elizabeth sought her father in his library. "Jane wanted to accompany us to London, but I think Mama needs her more."

He glanced up from his work, last minute details he organized before his unexpected departure, but kept writing as he said, "You are right. Mrs. Bennet will require someone to manage here. In ordinary circumstances she would do well enough, but she is so upset about Lydia that she is completely irrational." He didn't look up again as he kept writing.

Elizabeth left him to his work and went to see if anything else needed doing before they could depart. As nothing did, she bid Jane farewell, didn't wake Mrs. Bennet, and joined Mr. and Miss Darcy in their carriage. Moments later, Mr. Bennet climbed in. The sun still low on the horizon, they were on their way.

By the end of their first day in London, the searchers for Lydia numbered the Smiths, the Gardiners, Colonel Fitzwilliam, several Bow Street Runners, Mr. Bingley, Elizabeth, her husband, and her father. How Lydia and Mr. Wickham could evade so many, even in a city so large, Elizabeth couldn't fathom. Anxious and worried as she was, it satisfied her to feel that they were doing all they could to find the two.

And yet, a week went by with no news of Mr. Wickham's or Lydia's whereabouts. They did receive word, through Colonel Fitzwilliam's evening progress reports, that Mr. Wickham had been handed considerable funds by the colonel of the unit into which he'd enlisted as Mr. Wiekran, and absconded with them. Or rather, spent them, as inquiries Mr. Phillips made around Meryton found that Mr. Wickham had stopped paying for what he bought and started gambling excessively after he received the contract from Mr. Bennet.

At the end of the week, Mr. Bennet and Mr. Bingley returned to Hertfordshire. The Gardiners and Smiths kept looking, but with the start of a new week the Gardiners returned to their more normal lives, not having the resources to suspend their usual duties for long. Darcy continued to pay Mr. Smith, and thus he continued looking, and Kitty along with him. Colonel Fitzwilliam's evening visits to report on his progress tapered off. Georgiana, who'd pulled the full story of how Elizabeth had met her brother from them, skulked about Darcy House like a wraith, eyes puffy from crying. Elizabeth began to despair.

Nearly two weeks after Lydia's disappearance, Elizabeth sat in a chair in the back parlor at Darcy House, trying to read a book. Her nerves were frayed beyond anything she'd experienced before. Awareness that her little sister was alone, without recourse, in the company of a murderer, rendered her to secret tears by the end of each day. She'd lost weight. Her skin had taken on a sallow undertone. She wished to be strong but, in truth, she felt little better than Georgiana appeared to be.

Mr. Darcy was at a writing desk, poring over a stack of reports, every one he'd received from the start of the investigation into the sabotaged bridges to today's short missive about the lack of progress in locating

Mr. Wickham and Lydia. He'd read them before, searching for anything he'd missed, and Elizabeth wished he would stop. They wouldn't tell him anything new.

"What if they aren't even in London?" she blurted.

Mr. Darcy looked up. "They are."

"How do you know that? Maybe they really did go to Scotland. Maybe they doubled back after letting themselves be seen at that inn."

He shook his head. "If they'd gone to Scotland, they would be married already, and I would have received a note with Wickham's demands."

She rubbed at the tension in her forehead. "I don't know if I should hope for them to be married now." She blinked, trying to hold back tears, a fear greater than a damaged reputation plaguing her. "But I do hope…"

"What?" Her husband came to his feet. "What is the matter?"

She drew in a shaky breath. "I must hope that he believes her wellbeing is important to his financial situation."

In two long strides Mr. Darcy was across the parlor. He dropped to a knee before her chair and gently took her book. Setting it aside, he clasped her cold hands in his strong, warm ones. "He won't hurt your sister."

Elizabeth shook her head. Now that she'd admitted the fear, it only grew. "How can you know he won't? He can't have any good in him."

"He does not. He is a creature of indulgence and greed, but also of self-preservation. He courted your sister for gain, and he will keep her as well and happy as he can, both to secure that gain and because having her willing in his schemes is far easier. He always does what's easier."

Elizabeth squeezed his hands, wanting to believe him. "But what if she becomes unwilling. You know how Lydia can be. He may deem it easier…easier to…" She couldn't say it.

"He won't give up on his plans to gain from us. He needs her."

Elizabeth searched Darcy's face, reading complete surety. Finally, she nodded.

He kissed her hands.

Footfalls sounded in the hall. Elizabeth looked past her husband as he released her hands and rose to his feet. Darcy House's butler appeared in the doorway with a silver tray.

"Yes, Edwards?" Mr. Darcy asked.

"A letter, sir, addressed to you from Mrs. Younge." The lady's name came out with a note of distaste.

Elizabeth sought back, trying to recall if she'd heard of a Mrs. Younge.

Mr. Darcy hurried to take the missive. "Thank you."

Edwards nodded and retreated down the hall.

Not bothering to return to his desk, Mr. Darcy opened the letter, read it, and passed it to Elizabeth, his eyes bright.

Elizabeth took in the return address, an unfashionable neighborhood halfway across town, then turned the page over.

Dear Mr. Darcy,

> *Forgive my impertinence for writing to you, but I do not want you to be my enemy. Mr. Wickham came to my lodging house today. I fed him and Miss Lydia Bennet a meal. I also refused them lodging, claiming I had no spare rooms. She chatted away. She believes they will be married soon. I have no idea what his intentions are. Since she is your wife's sister, I assume you are interested in her.*

> *I do not know where they went after they left here. I do not think they knew, either. I made it plain to Mr. Wickham that he is not welcome here and that I hope he does not return. I told him I only gave them a meal in sympathy for Miss Bennet's situation. I do not think he believes me, since he is used to people succumbing to his charm.*

> *Several times since Ramsgate, runners have called to ask me questions, as recently as this past week. I am willingly providing the above information so that you do not need to send more.*

M. Younge

Elizabeth looked up from the letter, relief making her limp. Lydia was happy, so even if Mr. Wickham was completely vile, her sister was being treated well. "M. Younge? Who is that?"

A severe frown made Mr. Darcy appear quite foreboding, but Elizabeth didn't believe the expression aimed at her question as he replied, "She is the woman in whose care I placed Georgiana. The one who permitted Wickham to court her in Ramsgate."

"Oh," Elizabeth said, startled. "I see. That makes sense, then." Both why Mr. Darcy appeared grim, and why Mr. Wickham would seek the woman's assistance. "And you hadn't thought to ask her if she'd seen them?"

"Of course, I had." He gestured to the letter. "Or rather, I sent people to do so."

"Yes. Of course." Elizabeth drew in a steadying breath. "My apologies. I'm so worried, and tired of being worried. I know you are doing all you can." She frowned slightly, considering her words. "More than I've any right to expect, actually. Why are you so diligently seeking my sister?"

She waited, worried he would speak again on how others reflected on his name. Not that he would be wrong, but she wished for a different motive. Something that spoke less to the towering pride she'd witnessed in him on past occasions.

He sank into the chair nearest her, scrubbing his hands over his face. "I feel my family created the villain George became."

"Created him?"

"Yes. He is the son of my father's steward. He was a bright, golden, lively child and I was his opposite. My father doted on him."

Sympathy for Mr. Darcy welled in her, followed by guilt. She knew what it was to be that cherished, beloved child and she'd seen firsthand how such blatant paternal preference made others feel. She suddenly wished she'd tried harder to bring her younger sisters to their father's attention. Especially Mary, who hadn't known the love of either parent. No wonder she'd been so eager to wed and never return to Longbourn.

Mr. Darcy continued, unaware of the tumult his words sparked in her, saying, "My father spoiled George soundly. Educated him alongside me. Gave him an appreciation and expectation of a lifestyle that he was not born to and would never have." He shook his head. "He was so very angry to learn that my father had left him a rector's living. Livid. George expected a great sum. His share of the Darcy fortune, as he'd always had his share of my father's love. I cannot even blame him. I expected the same."

"But, the living, may I assume it was a good one? A worthy life to hand to him?"

"It was but he didn't want it. He demanded I buy it from him, which I did, for three thousand pounds."

Elizabeth gaped at him. "Three thousand pounds? Then he already has enough to live on. Why risk so much to marry either of our sisters?"

"I don't know what he was doing, but when the living became vacant, he demanded it. I assume because he needed more money. Of course, I denied it to him."

"He wanted double inheritance?" Elizabeth asked, shocked.

"At least triple. And now he's murdered a man, though I doubt he intended to, and held a gun on me, attempted to elope with Georgiana, and nearly killed you, and still I've done nothing. Yes, I set runners to investigate him, but I've done nothing to expose him for who he is, only allocated funds to salve my guilt. I caused your sister to be abducted. He would never have been in Meryton if not for me."

Elizabeth shook her head. "No. I mean, yes, he probably would not have been in Meryton if not for you, but you did not cause Lydia to be abducted. Mr. Wickham charmed her, and she permitted him to do so." She leaned forward, clasping Mr. Darcy's hand. "You are not responsible for his evil."

He covered their joined hands with his free one, meeting her gaze. "I feel responsible. Much as I inherited my father's estate, I inherited Wickham. My father's blatant favoritism made Wickham into a man who expects everything."

"His actions are and always have been his own."

Mr. Darcy's gaze searched her face, then he drew in a long, shuddering breath.

Pulling her hand free, Elizabeth left the letter on her chair and went to him, hugging him to her where he sat. "You are not responsible," she repeated.

His arms came about her, tight, and he buried his face against her. He did not cry. Elizabeth murmured soothing sounds nonetheless, stroking his back. After a long moment he released her. She stepped away, turning to make a show of smoothing her skirt, to give him time to regain his composure.

Mr. Darcy stood. "Let us call on Mrs. Younge and see if she can tell us more."

"Her letter made it sound as if she would not welcome that."

"Do we care?"

Elizabeth offered a tight smile. "No. We do not."

He called for the carriage and they went up to secure their outerwear, London having grown colder in recent days. Elizabeth knocked on Georgiana's door, then cracked it open to find her sitting in the window, pale but composed, and let her know they were going out.

The journey began slow, it being afternoon, but once they left the more fashionable parts of London their pace quickened. Soon, Mr. Darcy's carriage, though the smaller and less fine of the two, stuck out enough to garner stares. Elizabeth was glad of Darcy's footmen, riding outside to deter too much interest. Farther into the neighborhood than she wished to go, they halted before a well-maintained townhouse and alighted.

A maid answered their knock, took in their garments, and permitted them inside to wait, then disappeared down the hall. Not long after, footfalls sounded, returning.

Elizabeth looked down the hall to see not the maid but a woman perhaps half again her age, attractive enough were it not for the wary, hardened expression she wore. She studied Elizabeth a moment, then turned to Mr. Darcy as she halted before them.

"Mr. Darcy."

He dipped his head. "Mrs. Younge." He deliberately turned to Elizabeth to say, "Mrs. Darcy, this is Mrs. Younge. Mrs. Younge, my wife."

A wry smile touched Mrs. Younge's mouth. She gestured to her left. "Join me in the parlor?"

"Will we be overheard?"

"The staff I can do nothing about except hope they will keep to their work. None of my boarders are the sort to be idle in the middle of the day. They're at their various places of employment, except an expectant mother who is on bedrest and so won't be creeping down the staircase to listen to you." Mrs. Younge turned from them and went into the indicated parlor.

Seeing her husband hesitate, Elizabeth followed, Mr. Darcy a half step behind.

The room was small but perfectly adequate to its role. The furnishings were better than Elizabeth expected. Old, but well kept. She sat on one side of the sofa opposite the one Mrs. Younge already occupied. Mr. Darcy joined her.

"I put everything in my letter," Mrs. Younge said without preamble.

Mr. Darcy glowered at her.

Elizabeth sat forward. "So you said and we are sensible that we're interrupting your day in an unwelcome manner, but you must understand that he took my sister. Please, is there nothing more? Any detail you left out?"

Mrs. Younge pursed her lips. Finally, she said, "Miss Bennet said, to Mr. Wickham's annoyance, that they had to change locations because 'they' were getting too close. 'It means starting all over again,' she said.

She also said, 'George believes your house is safe, because they must have already checked here.'" Mrs. Younge shrugged and added, "To me, that sounds as if he intends to marry her."

Elizabeth sat back, digesting that. "Our goal is to get her away from him."

"Do you know what sort of man he is?" Mrs. Younge asked.

"He attempted to shoot Mr. Darcy and he pushed me down a gully, which very easily could have killed me."

Anger sparking in her gaze, Mrs. Younge turned to Mr. Darcy. "Why do you not do something about him? With all your money and influence, how can you permit George Wickham to walk free?"

Mr. Darcy flinched, waking a surge of protective anger in Elizabeth, but his voice was even as he replied, "Because I do not bribe or coerce. I cannot see him tried without evidence and he is too cunning to leave any."

"So, you let your pride get in the way of doing what is right?" Mrs. Younge snapped.

"I let what is right keep me from doing wrong."

They glared at each other while Elizabeth sought for something to say to defuse the tension. Antagonizing Mrs. Younge wasn't getting them information, assuming she had any more than she'd already revealed. A tense silence drew out but Elizabeth, drained by weeks of worrying for Lydia, could find no words that didn't sound like pleading, reprimand, or accusation.

"You never sought to retrieve any funds that may have gone missing while I was in your employ," Mrs. Younge finally said, voice neutral. "I assume this is because you are too proud to sully yourself with such trifles?"

Mr. Darcy sat up straighter. "Would you prefer I come after you?"

"What I'd prefer is to know that if you had evidence against George Wickham, you would use it, rather than hide it away to protect Miss Darcy's reputation."

Silence echoed in response to that.

Elizabeth swiveled on the sofa to regard Mr. Darcy. He would, would he not? He'd said all along that the only reason he hadn't brought charges against Mr. Wickham was because he wouldn't damage Georgiana's reputation without the proof to make those charges stick. Had that been a convenient excuse?

"If I could make it more than my word against Wickham's that the masked gunman was in fact him, I would proceed with charges." He spoke those words firmly. Not loudly, but with unwavering conviction.

"He came here and threatened my life if I should give testimony," Mrs. Younge said quietly. "I am not noble. I will not take the stand if he has a chance to walk free afterwards."

Expression intent, Mr. Darcy leaned forward. "What do you know?"

"I know he left Ramsgate to delay you. I know that he suggested I may have suspicions about who sabotaged the bridges and caused that poor man's death and said that if I mentioned those suspicions to anyone, he would see I meet a similar fate to the wagon driver." Mrs. Younge drew in a breath. "I also have a document, signed by Mr. Wickham, promising me nine hundred pounds as compensation for giving him access to Miss Darcy, to be paid upon his marriage to her."

"Surely that, coupled with your word, is all that is required?" Elizabeth said eagerly to her husband.

"Yet, you came forward with none of this before," Mr. Darcy stated, not seeming to note Elizabeth's words.

"As I said, I have no intention of giving Mr. Wickham the desire and opportunity to do me harm."

"What changed?" Elizabeth asked. Was Mrs. Younge that sympathetic to Lydia?

"He returned with your sister, as I wrote. When he issued his threat, I told him never to come back. I even purchased a pistol and learned to use it, in case he did. He's proven that he will not leave me alone. I do not enjoy him lurking in the shadows of my life, ready to do me harm."

"So you're entirely self-serving?" Mr. Darcy said with a curl to his lips.

"I prefer calling my choices self-preservation and yes, entirely. I can't afford the luxury of doing what is right despite the risks."

"But you'll testify now?" Elizabeth cut in before the animosity shared between her husband and Mrs. Younge could change that. "Please?"

Ire softening as she studied Elizabeth, Mrs. Younge said, "I will. Once he has been arrested and you agree that testimony about Miss Darcy's near elopement will be allowed. Without the motivation, my testimony is worthless and uncorroborated."

Elizabeth looked at her husband and he nodded grimly.

"Thank you," Elizabeth breathed, relieved.

"I'll take the contract," Mr. Darcy said stiffly.

Hardness returned to Mrs. Younge's face. "No. You will not." She cocked an eyebrow. "You can employ that intimidating scowl all you like, Mr. Darcy. I know you will not harm me. Besides which, I do not have it here. That wouldn't be safe."

"You will secure it and turn it over."

Mrs. Younge's smile was cold. "Once the trial is underway, I will. Much like the pistol I bought, the contract is something I never intended to use but feel safer keeping in my possession."

"That seems wholly reasonable," Elizabeth said. Mr. Darcy turned his dour look on her but much like Mrs. Younge, Elizabeth was unintimidated. Ignoring him, she asked, "Is there anything else you can tell us? Any detail at all?"

Mrs. Younge shook her head. "I wish there were. Your sister, though obviously impetuous and full of the giddiness of youth, should not be doomed to a life as Mrs. Wickham."

Elizabeth stood. "Thank you, Mrs. Younge. We will inform you once he's taken into custody."

Mr. Darcy rose to his feet, still frowning.

"You are welcome, Mrs. Darcy and, please, do not inform him that I've spoken to you until he is no longer free to take vengeance on me."

Elizabeth nodded. Feeling some hope of freeing her sister from Mr. Wickham's evil, even if that meant seeing him hang, Elizabeth led the way from Mrs. Younge's home.

Once they were settled in the carriage and being carried away from Mrs. Younge and her less than reputable neighborhood, Elizabeth turned to her husband. "Will you be willing to let Georgiana testify at the trial, if it comes to that?"

"It won't come to that," he said. "When we returned to London, I sent men to talk to the servants Mrs. Younge hired in Ramsgate. Four of them would make good witnesses against Wickham and make Georgiana's testimony unnecessary. Their testimonies will publicize her willingness to elope, but two of them eavesdropped on Wickham and Mrs. Younge persuading Georgiana to do so a short time before I arrived. They claim Georgiana was browbeaten into going."

Elizabeth pursed her lips. Not quite the assurance for which she'd hoped. The carriage jolted over uneven cobbles. Working not to sound accusatory, she said, "You never told me that."

He blinked, appearing confused. "I didn't think to."

"Even though I am your wife, and this matter is of great import not simply to you, but to me as well?"

Lines of thought and worry cleaved into his forehead and she regretted her words. He didn't need more strain. "I apologize. I am not yet accustomed to sharing my life so fully." He studied her in that intent way of his and she realized she'd missed those looks during the weeks since Lydia's disappearance. "But I want to be. I will do better in the future."

That reassured Elizabeth somewhat but she wanted more. Rather than press him directly again, she ventured, "Your plan to have the staff testify won't fully shield Georgiana's reputation."

Mr. Darcy nodded. "I know, but I cannot let a murderer go free to protect Georgiana."

Relieved, Elizabeth permitted silence as they clattered along increasingly smooth roadways back to Darcy House.

Chapter Twenty-Seven

After Darcy sent word of Mrs. Younge's confirmation that Wickham and Lydia were in London, Bingley and Mr. Bennet both returned from Hertfordshire. Mr. Bennet took up residence at Darcy House as they recommenced the search, a welcome addition to the household as Elizabeth alone couldn't cheer Georgiana, who obviously still harbored affection where George Wickham was concerned. But by the eve of the fourth day, it was a rather dismal gathering as the three men sat to their port after dinner, Elizabeth and Georgiana having retired to the parlor.

Idly turning his glass in his hand, Darcy wrestled with how much to tell Elizabeth's father about his plans to press charges against Wickham, a quandary which had troubled him since Mr. Bennet's arrival. They'd discussed the possibility of Darcy doing so, but that had been when he had no evidence. Now, he would have Mrs. Younge's testimony to bolster what the staff in Ramsgate claimed. Charging Wickham with murder had gone from a hypothetical to a reality. A reality that Darcy would do all in his power to see come to fruition, especially if Wickham managed to marry Miss Lydia.

Wickham would be a terrible husband for many reasons but the most salient was that he would be happy to hurt Elizabeth's sister if he thought it would hurt Darcy. Which it would because it would hurt Elizabeth. Her pain was his pain, and Darcy wouldn't be able to alleviate that pain except by funneling funds to Wickham. A husband had complete control over his wife and Lydia could be beaten, imprisoned, or made to live in horrifying conditions while neither Darcy nor Mr. Bennet could legally do anything. If Wickham had married Georgiana, it would have been much the same. He would not only have obtained her dowry, he would have coerced Darcy to hand over huge sums of money for her wellbeing.

Suddenly, he thought about Richard and his wife, the former Anne de Bourgh. Richard had said he was marrying Anne partly for her good. Although many men would be happy to marry Anne for Rosings, no one else would have married Anne for Anne's benefit. Richard not only treated Anne well, he endeavored to teach her to be a better person.

"We'll return to Hertfordshire tomorrow," Mr. Bennet said into the silence that hung over the table.

Darcy looked up, surprised. He waited for an explanation, knowing that it would come without prompting.

"Mrs. Bennet is upset that the banns haven't been read for Jane and Mr. Bingley," Mr. Bennet continued. "She is predicting all sorts of problems if they don't marry as soon as possible. While I disagree with that, she is correct that if the banns are read and the marriage takes place, everyone's lives will be simpler."

"That seems reasonable," Darcy said. He glanced at Bingley. "Is there any reason to delay?"

"Mrs. Bennet has let the cat out of the bag, as it were," Mr. Bennet answered before Bingley could speak. "Everyone in Meryton knows that Lydia ran off with Mr. Weikran, as they still know him, and there is immense speculation as to why. I'm not going to explain it."

"Ah," Darcy said. Had Bingley reconsidered, then, in view of the extent of the scandal? "So you mean to delay the union?"

Bingley shook his head, expression resolute. "My sisters disapprove. Caroline says she will never marry well if she's connected to Miss Lydia, but at this point, I would rather ease Jane's mind than my sisters'."

While he respected Bingley's devotion, and appreciated it, Darcy found Miss Bingley's worry valid, echoing his fears for Georgiana's future. While Georgiana had years available to put Lydia's scandalous behavior behind her, Miss Bingley was seeking an attachment now. "If he marries her, the scandal will be less."

"That's what Caroline says." Bingley set his glass down on the table. "She wishes me to wait until we know the outcome of this, ah, troubling circumstance before I ask."

"Wouldn't that be wisest?" Mr. Bennet said with what Darcy suspected to be feigned indifference.

Once again, Bingley's expression hardened. "I don't care. I love Jane. I want to marry her. No outcome will change that. I will marry her the moment we reach Hertfordshire."

"That may be a bit extreme. Possibly you should wait until after the banns are read," Mr. Bennet said.

Bingley stared at Mr. Bennet a moment, blinked, and then chuckled. "Well, yes. I can wait that long. Reluctantly."

That moment of mirth quickly faded into dull silence once more.

Struggling with his conscience, Darcy decided he must admit, "I plan to press forward with murder charges. I have fresh evidence."

Bingley swiveled to look at him. "Murder charges? Against whom?"

Darcy grimaced. He'd forgotten his and Elizabeth's less volatile tale of how they'd met. That showed what came of lying. Confusion and hurt feelings. Though Bingley didn't appear too hurt as Darcy recounted the truth of that day, skirting only Georgiana's involvement but with the tangible feeling that Mr. Bennet guessed what was left out.

When he finished, Bingley said, "I'd no idea that your wife is so brave, or Wickham quite so vile. You are lucky Mrs. Darcy happened by. I cannot imagine how it must pain you to contemplate calling that man brother."

"Second thoughts now?" Mr. Bennet asked.

Bingley turned to him with a confused frown. "About?"

Mr. Bennet smiled slightly. "Never mind."

With a shrug for what he couldn't understand, Bingley turned back to Darcy. "So you mean to go through with it, then? Even if Wickham marries Miss Lydia?"

"I do not see that there is a choice. His actions caused a man's death."

Bingley nodded, then winced. "Caroline will not be pleased. Neither will Jane, for that matter, but I hope that as her husband I can help ease her pain. Maybe I should get a special license."

"It will be an unpleasant business all round," Darcy agreed, thinking of Georgiana. "But, as I said, I cannot see that I have any choice. Now that I have more than my impression that the masked gunman was Wickham, the accusation must come to light. Of all the things I've permitted Wickham to get away with over the years, murder cannot number among them."

"No. Certainly not," Bingley agreed.

"Yes, and before I forget," Mr. Bennet said, pulling a folded page from his coat. He passed the paper to Darcy. "Read it if you like. It empowers you to act on my behalf in regard to Lydia. It's of doubtful legality." Mr. Bennet shrugged. "But it might stave off trouble until I can be sent for."

Bingley looked back and forth between them and grimaced. "A messy business, all of it. Very unfortunate."

To that, Darcy could only agree. He accepted the page and then set down his hardly touched port. "Should we join the ladies?"

Bingley and Mr. Bennet departed the following day, sinking Darcy House into an even deeper pall than before they'd arrived. As the search continued, Darcy simmered with frustrated anger, that George Wickham should mar his family's life so. And yet, he could conceive of no solution. No amount of dedication or funds seemed to help. Time passed and still there was no sign of Wickham

Several Sundays later, he'd begun to debate an outright reward for the man. A hundred pounds to anyone who could lead him to Wickham. No, five hundred. Darcy would see a likeness of Wickham in every paper. The scandal that would cause could hardly be worse than the limbo in which they were living.

He went down to breakfast to find Elizabeth pushing food about on her plate. He didn't need to ask what troubled her. The answer could only be, 'My sister is in the care of a murderer she is about to marry, a man we must see apprehended, tried and hanged.'

Georgiana entered shortly after Darcy's arrival. She wore a forced smile which, sadly, was an improvement, and offered, "Good morning, Fitz, Elizabeth."

Elizabeth looked up. "Good morning."

Georgiana filled a plate and came to the table. "It's so quiet without Mr. Bennet. I wish he could have remained longer."

"As do I," Elizabeth said, mustering a smile. She turned to Darcy, "Is there anything of interest in today's paper?"

He looked down at the folded paper left beside his place at the table by his conscientious staff. He'd been so wrapped in his recriminations against Wickham that he hadn't even noted it. "I will see."

They ate in silence punctuated by the occasional effort for normalcy until Elizabeth stood. "If you'll excuse me, I've time before church still to read a letter or two. I'm afraid I've fallen terribly behind." She sighed. "They're all letters from my sisters and Charlotte, trying to be cheerful and asking for news I do not have."

Darcy stood while his wife left the room then sat back down to find his sister watching him.

"George truly is an awful person, isn't he?" she asked.

"I'm afraid he is."

"He might have killed you if Elizabeth hadn't stopped him, and he nearly killed Elizabeth." She swallowed. "He tried to elope with me and then he lied about his name and ran off with Lydia."

"Yes." Among other, lesser transgressions.

She pursed her lips. "Elizabeth was right when she said I shouldn't be out yet and you were right to agree with her."

Darcy raised his eyebrows.

"I…I loved George," Georgiana admitted. "Even after I didn't elope. Not loving him isn't why I didn't go. It was because I didn't want to hurt you and, well, because I knew it was wrong." She dashed at tears forming in her eyes, her firm expression that of someone who refused to cry. "I thought he would simply wait, or try again, but he didn't. He picked another way to hurt you. It was never about me, was it? It was only ever about you. How could I not see that? How could I not see that he never loved me? He just hated you." She dropped her gaze to her plate.

Darcy stared at her with no idea what to say. Why had Elizabeth gone? She would know what to say. "He is charming. He's charmed Miss Lydia as well."

"And she is silly and rash and ought not be out, either," Georgiana muttered at her half eaten breakfast.

"That is likely true." He wanted to stop there, but realized he had to tell her what might happen. Now was a good time, with Elizabeth occupied. Ultimately, taking legal action against George Wickham was his decision, and he should not lean on Elizabeth for this. "Georgiana, I have something I must tell you." He then succinctly told her about the sabotaged bridges and the death of the wagon driver. "It was murder. He probably intended the same for me. If his plan had worked, my three servants in the carriage would have died as well."

"That's…that's…" She stared at him, eyes wide and face chalky. "That's so horrible. I can see why you didn't tell me before now." She shook her head. "Why did you tell me now?"

Darcy braced himself. "For Mr. Wickham to be convicted of murder, we need to explain his motive for attempting to prevent me from reaching Ramsgate."

Georgiana cringed. She turned away, staring at nothing. After a long pause, she said, "I know you want to protect me, but I am a Darcy too. If I need to testify, I will. I cannot let a murderer go free. I will hate it. I'll probably cry and make a fool of myself, but I have my duty as well."

Pride welled in him. She may have behaved badly on recent occasions, influenced by Mrs. Younge and Wickham, but his sister was correct. She was a Darcy and a ward and little sister of whom he could be proud. "I don't believe you will need to testify. I have four members of the staff in Ramsgate already willing to do so."

"Still, I will if I must."

"That is very brave of you," Elizabeth said as she entered the room. "I didn't mean to eavesdrop, but I heard the last part and didn't want to interrupt." She turned to Georgiana. "Miss Darcy, I now believe you are mature enough to be out." She glanced at Darcy.

"Once this is over, I agree," Darcy said. "Grownups take responsibility, but your testimony would be more impressive if you are not out."

"And doing so in the midst of a scandal seems inopportune," Elizabeth added.

"I can wait." Georgiana sighed and dabbed at her eyes with her napkin. "In fact, I wish to wait." She stood up. "I'd best ready for church."

"As will I," Elizabeth said, waiting to walk with Georgiana.

Darcy called for fresh coffee and tried to lose his thoughts in the paper while he waited for Elizabeth and Georgiana to be ready to leave for church. Sometime later he was halfway through his coffee and starting to think he might have to find his relations and urge them along when footfalls raced down the hallway. Elizabeth flew into the breakfast parlor and charged up to his chair, a piece of thick paper in hand.

She thrust the page at him. "The carriage is already waiting. I'll get my cloak."

Darcy accepted the page, thoroughly bemused as his wife whirled and raced away again. He looked down, found the letter the wrong way around, turned it, and read.

Dear Mrs. Darcy,

With Richard's permission, I've used all my spending money sending servants to various churches to find if banns have been read for either Mr. Wickham or Mr. Wiekran and Lydia Bennet. Below is the address of a church where they were read.

Again, I am sorry for how I once behaved. Perhaps this news makes amends more fully than my earlier, admittedly grudging and only written at Richard's insistence, apology.

Wishing you success in your dealings with Mr. Wickham,

Your Cousin, Anne Fitzwilliam

Darcy dropped his gaze to the address. Somehow, he was already free of his chair and moving. In the entrance hall, he grabbed his greatcoat from his waiting butler. At the top of the staircase, Elizabeth and Georgiana spoke, voices slightly raised, but he'd no time to seek the reason.

"Advise Mrs. Darcy that horseback is faster," he told Edwards. He pressed the page on the man. "Send runners to this church. I'll see my horse saddled."

Not waiting for a nod, Darcy whirled and strode through the house. He burst into the kitchen and was across it and out the other side before his stunned staff could even react. Long legs carried him through the garden to his stable. In moments, three grooms scurried about, readying his mount.

And then Darcy was astride and urging his bay down the alleyway. With no clear thoughts on what he would do when he got his hands on Wickham, he took the cobbled streets as quickly as he deemed safe. Services hadn't begun yet, giving him time, but the church was across town and the streets were clogged with carriages.

The only thing Darcy knew for certain was that this would end. Whatever else happened today, George Wickham would meet his fate.

Chapter Twenty-Eight

He'd been genius in getting that signed agreement from Mr. Bennet and his poor excuse for an attorney. He now was Wickham again, and that's whose name he had on Mr. Bennet's agreement that he could marry Lydia and expect eighty pounds a year for it. The document was both legal and binding. And it had the advantage of being made out to George Wickham. A dot of ink changed the badly written e to a smudged c. The letter r easily became an h and the n simply needed another loop to be an m. He had considered becoming Viekran, but he worried that he might have trouble answering to so different a name.

That paper had allowed Wickham to take Lydia south, to London, because with it they could marry anywhere banns could be read. South not only threw Darcy off the trail, because he would expect them to go north, but also provided a better place to hide. Wickham knew London well. So what if he'd been forced to spend almost every last coin to his name to keep them hidden? That was nothing to what he would soon have from Darcy and it elated Wickham to know that his fleeting money had stacked up so well to Darcy's fortune. Even with all his wealth and his fancy Bow Street Runners, Darcy hadn't been able to ferret them out.

The easiest part had been convincing Lydia that he must be Wickham now. He'd merely had to tell the truth about how Darcy always ruined everything because he couldn't forgive Wickham for being old Mr. Darcy's favorite. He'd listed all his woes from the living he'd been promised to his inability to pay for a fine enough wardrobe after Darcy had ordered the merchants of Lambton not to extend him credit anymore. He'd left out any mention of Georgiana, but that was only polite consideration for his soon to be wife's tender feelings.

He mentally cursed the nosey landlady whose willingness to give him up to the runners required a move into another parish. It meant reading the banns again. But there's been no help for that. The marriage had to be legal.

And it would be. The banns had been read two times in this parish already, uncontested. Today was the third. The only thing that marred

Wickham's triumph was the way Lydia giggled each time the priest said 'Wickham,' which seemed to disconcert the man. Not that Wickham truly cared. He didn't require a happy priest. It wasn't as if he intended to ever attend church again.

If only the stubborn rector had agreed to marry them today, it would be done. But he refused to do a Sunday wedding, citing the need for the ceremony to be performed between eight in the morning and noon. Impossible, as the banns had to be read first and the service would not be finished until after noon. The stupid priest insisted on following the rules. And he wouldn't even consider shortening the service, although he must know most parishioners would be happy to get out early.

Fortunately, this was the last time Wickham and Lydia needed to be in a public service in this church. They were too exposed here. Once they were married, Wickham planned never to sit through another boring sermon, and this rector had the most boring sermons Wickham had ever heard. But Wickham wanted his good will, so he forced himself to listen so that he could comment favorably on them. Both were hard.

"This is the third time of asking," the priest droned. "If any of you know cause or just impediment why these two persons should not be joined together in Holy Matrimony, ye are to declare it."

Silence. Wickham grinned. Lydia beamed. The priest paused, looking about. In his mind, Wickham urged the man to move on with the service.

"I object!"

Wickham didn't need to look. It was Darcy's voice.

Lydia, however, did turn, and screeched, "Mr. Darcy. George, it's Mr. Darcy. He's come to ruin everything."

Slowly, Wickham rose and turned to face his nemesis. "He has no authority."

"My authority is here." Darcy held up a document. "Signed over to me by Mr. Bennet."

With a sardonic smile, Wickham strode forward. People made way for him as he moved into the aisle. Fortunately, that put him on the opposite side of the church from where Darcy stood. "Whatever you have there, it is useless. Mr. Bennet signed a document approving our marriage. Besides, it doesn't matter. The law says that only a parent or guardian can disapprove of the banns. You are neither." Was that the law? Wickham didn't have a clue as to whether a proxy was legal.

Darcy leveled a hard look on him. "Who I am doesn't matter. Miss Lydia should not marry a murderer."

The assemblage gasped.

Wickham held his smile. "Murderer? I should sue you for slander. Who is it I am supposed to have murdered?"

"Frank Miller."

"I've never heard of him," Wickham sneered, trying not to show a stab of worry. Darcy wasn't one for bravado.

"I don't doubt that," Darcy said. "But your sabotage of a bridge in Kent caused his death."

More murmurs from the mass of churchgoers. Was there any hope that none of them had heard about the bridges?

"What is he talking about?" Lydia asked.

"I have no idea," he said, not taking his attention off Darcy. "Calling me a murderer must mean you are deranged." He waved at the rector. "Please finish the banns."

The rector turned to Darcy. "I don't know what is going on, but he has a point. Are you Miss Lydia Bennet's guardian?"

"No. But I am acting for her father."

Wickham glanced past the rector, to where he knew a small door at the back of the church led to another room. Should he grab Lydia and run? Could Darcy really stop the ceremony? Could he cross the entire church in time to catch them? They could disappear. Start over in a new church.

"I've sent for the runners," Darcy said, his voice holding something near regret. "You could stay here and let the rest of the banns be read. You won't be married, but the banns will be read. Do you wish to stay?"

Silently, Wickham cursed how well Darcy could read him. Was Darcy bluffing about the runners? Probably not, but how much time did he have? Once he was married, he was safe.

Staying was a gamble, but Wickham was good at winning. "I'll stay, if you promise to allow the rector to marry us. It is still before noon."

The churchgoers shifted, undulating like a sea. Darcy looked about, obviously assessing his options.

Seeing a chance for help if he needed it, Wickham raised his voice, playing to the crowd. "I love this woman and I say, let us be legally married before you use your wealth to have me imprisoned on a spurious charge. I am simply the poor son of your father's steward and have nothing to counter your power. You are going to extremes to keep me from marrying your wife's sister."

The people about them rumbled, casting angry looks Darcy's way. Wickham grinned. If it came to a vote, he would win, but there wouldn't be a vote. There would be here and now, and the rector would marry them because Wickham had the congregation on his side.

He squared his shoulders, raised his chin and declared, "I'll stay. I'll stay for love." He met Darcy's gaze, smug. "You would not see your brother arrested."

"For murder, I would."

Wickham studied Darcy. Darcy meant it.

It wasn't murder, it was an accident. He hadn't intended anyone but Darcy to die.

He might not be convicted. He had been careful. He didn't have an alibi, but he was certain no one could place him there. They couldn't put him at the scene and Darcy would protect Georgiana, denying proof of a motive.

Wickham turned back to the rector. "Finish the banns and marry us."

"No."

A woman's voice, this time, and unknown to him. He whirled to find that an attractive, well-dressed woman stood at the back of the church with Georgiana. Two of Darcy's servants stood behind them.

Georgiana met his gaze, hers icy and nervous, but her voice was steady as she said, "I will testify against you. I'll tell everyone why you wanted to murder Fitz."

"And I will testify against you also," the woman who was with Georgiana said. "I stopped you from shooting him."

Whispers raced through the church. The parishioners were enjoying the show. Wickham wasn't. Was this the woman who'd thwarted his careful plan? He'd hardly seen her face. Could she identify him? How long had she watched him before she acted? He wanted to kill her, but she was too far away, and Darcy's men would surely attempt to stop him.

Wickham ran, darting around the altar to the sound of Lydia's scream. He was into the church's private rooms, the holding place for vestments and wine, in seconds. He slammed the door closed and threw the bolt, then raced to the window.

He flung the window open and climbed through. Legs pumping, Wickham ran along the back of the church and up the side. He saw

Darcy's carriage. Could he steal it? He could take the old driver, Daniels. But there was a tiger, and men arriving on horseback in the familiar garb of runners. Wickham turned and bolted.

He ran through alleys, seeking ever worse areas of London. Narrow, twisting streets in which he could hide. His heart pounded. His lungs burned. Finally, he stopped. Hands braced on his thighs, he dropped his head, gasping for breath.

What did Darcy know? How did he know? What could he prove? He wouldn't do anything on a guess. He must have evidence.

Wickham snapped upright. Mrs. Younge. That was how, who and what. She'd told Darcy something. Probably promised to testify. This was all her fault.

She owed him. She'd never come through on her promise to help him marry Georgiana and now she'd ruined his revenge on Darcy a second time. She'd taken his hundred pounds and given him nothing in return. Less than nothing. Now, she threatened to take his life as well.

Wickham could think of a few things to do about that.

Electing for a less attention garnering pace as he seemed to have evaded immediate pursuit, he sought a better section of London again. As he walked, he searched for anything he could steal that might help. A different coat. A hat or at least a scarf. He needed to hide his telltale golden mane. To play down his memorable good looks. He must reach Mrs. Younge's boarding house undetected. Everyone would be at church, but he could certainly find some money, or something to sell and then, because of what she'd done, he would set the place ablaze. Burn it down. It was the least she deserved for all she'd done.

Once he had his money and his revenge, he would leave town. He could hole up somewhere in the countryside, perhaps Wales, even, while he figured out how to free Lydia from Darcy and marry her. Now that the banns were read, more or less, he had three months.

When he reached the boarding house, he found the cook at home, which only meant that the first part of his plan proceeded with ease. She readily recalled him and was happy to trade charm for some samples of what she was preparing for Sunday dinner. He waited until her back was turned and slipped deeper into the house. She'd likely believe he'd left through the garden and might be hurt that he'd gone without a word, but what did he care? She'd be no use to him after today. Without a boarding house, she'd be out of a job.

Inside Mrs. Younge's office, he rummaged in her desk, finding neat ledgers and stacks of letters. He flung everything that wasn't money aside but still found none. He came to a locked drawer, which was promising. Breaking the lock, he found it did indeed contain money, but only three pounds. Surely, she had more. Frustrated, he used her letter opener to cut into the upholstered seat of her chair, then turned it over and did the same to the bottom. Still, nothing. He took down a small watercolor and checked the back. Shoved all the books and ledgers from her shelves. He even tossed the thin rug aside and studied the floorboards.

Finally, standing in the middle of the room, fists balled in frustration, his attention returned to the door. The house seemed quiet. He didn't know the exact location of her room, but that must be where she kept anything of value. He couldn't light the place until he got what was coming to him.

He turned back to the desk and took up the small, possibly silver, letter opener. Opener tucked against his side, to be sold later or used as a weapon, he left the office. Far from sneaking, he strode up the staircase. Charm was always his best weapon.

Upstairs, where he'd never been, a wide clean hallway met his seeking gaze, door lined in both directions. From one direction came moans of distress and murmured voices. Someone suffering. Nothing of interest to him except as a room to be avoided. Whatever it was, it must be bad to keep them from church. At the end of the hall in that direction, he sighted a second staircase, going both up and down.

He turned the other way. Spying a single door at the far end, he strode down the hall. The end room would be the nicest. She would have taken that one.

He went in to find a very tidy space and carefully closed the door behind him. A four poster bed occupied much of the room, austere under its lace trimmed canopy. A chest stood against the wall on the far side, between two narrow windows. Bypassing, for now, a dressing table and wardrobe, Wickham went to it, drawn by the lock. He dropped to his knees and, using the letter opener, worked to pry it open.

The door creaked behind him. He whirled, coming to his feet.

Mrs. Younge stood in the open doorway, eyebrows raised. "Mr. Wickham."

"Mrs. Younge," he gritted out, trying to summon his usual charm for this woman who had done him so many wrongs.

She gestured to her dressing table. "I came to get laudanum for Mrs. Farrow. She's having a very difficult delivery."

He pointed the letter opener at her. "What's in that chest?"

She shrugged, crossing to the dressing table. "Keepsakes."

"Where is my hundred pounds?"

She opened the single drawer on the table and reached deep inside. "I told you. It's in a bank. Do you really believe I would lock a hundred pounds in a chest in my room? The chest may be locked but it can be carried, though what's inside matters only to me."

"Why don't you open it and permit me to judge that?" And once he had whatever she kept locked in the chest, well then, this woman, with all her aggravations, wouldn't be worth anything to him anymore. In fact, if he silenced her, he wouldn't even need to go to Wales.

One hand braced on the tabletop and the other in the drawer, she looked sideways to ask, "Why are you here, George?"

"Darcy came to the reading of the banns. He said he's going to see me tried for murder."

"And that involves me how?"

"I know you told him. About me and the bridges."

Mrs. Younge frowned. Her gaze dropped to the letter opener he brandished. A woman's wail of pain echoed down the hall, setting Wickham's teeth on edge.

"Mr. Darcy told you that I agreed to testify against you?"

"He didn't need to. I know him, and you."

"Hm." She closed her eyes, dropping her head to her chest.

"Remorseful, are you? Do you think that will spare you my wrath?" He moved closer, menacing. Why was her hand in that drawer still? Did she actually clutch laudanum, or his money? His gaze skimmed the tabletop, taking in a small dark bottle. He'd wager anything that was the laudanum. "You'd best begin telling me how you're going to get me my money before I run out of patience with you."

"Mum, someone's been in your office and—" the cook said as she came down the hall, breaking off when she sighted Wickham with the letter opener. "Mr. Wickham? What are you doing?"

"Get back in your kitchen," he growled.

The laboring woman screamed again.

A man rushed from one of the far rooms. "Mrs. Younge, where is that—" He too broke off as he sighted Wickham in the bedroom.

The cook's eyes were wide, but her mouth went flat. "Mum, is he threatening you?"

"He is, and if someone has been in my office, I imagine it was him," Mrs. Younge said with her usual calm.

"I'll send for the watch." The cook started backing down the hall.

"No one is calling any guards," Wickham snarled. Things were getting out of hand. He glanced over his shoulder. He could get through one of those windows. Surely, he could drop to the ground safely. He inched closer to Mrs. Younge, letter opener in hand. "Mrs. Younge is going to close and lock that door and open that chest, and then I'm going out one of those windows."

The cook had backed all the way to the top of the steps. "I'm calling the watch."

"Anyone gets anyone, if I even see anyone else, I'll kill her," Wickham snapped.

Mrs. Younge turned, her hand coming out of the drawer at last. She brought the other up to meet it. Nearly close enough to lunge for her now, Wickham realized he stared down the barrel of a gun. A yowl of pain echoed down the hall, coming from the laboring woman. Wickham lunged for Mrs. Younge, aiming the knife at her heart.

A loud report rang through the room, but he didn't hear it.

Chapter Twenty-Nine

Between them, Elizabeth and Georgiana got Lydia into the carriage, though she kept up a stream of protests about how George would be back soon all through the church, into the street, and into the carriage. Even though they were only three, having left Mr. Darcy speaking to the rector and the runners, Elizabeth met Georgiana's gaze and nodded to the forward facing seat. They all crammed in there, Lydia between them, as they made their slow way back through traffic to Darcy House.

"I don't see how George will know to come here," Lydia said as they disembarked.

Elizabeth kept close to her sister, pleased Georgiana walked on Lydia's other side. She wished to get her sister inside before it could occur to Lydia to go looking for 'her George.' All three strode up the steps together. The door opened to a studiously impassive Edwards, though Elizabeth could feel the interest that radiated from him as they removed their hats and cloaks.

Meeting the butler's gaze over Lydia's head, Elizabeth said, "Lydia, would you like to tell us where you were staying so that we might have your belongings brought?"

Lydia turned to her, frowning. "Brought?"

"Well, yes. Do you not think it would be nicer to stay here?"

"I'd rather we stay with Kitty, if we must stay anywhere, but my George said he would take us somewhere special. He has everything planned."

Smile fixed, Elizabeth said, "Well, then, we can bring your things here while you wait so that you'll be ready."

"Very well, though why you should be so bossy, I don't know, except that you do so enjoy telling me what to do." Lydia rattled off an address near the church. "It would have been easier if we stopped there on our way here."

Having seen the neighborhood and suppressing a shock of worry that her young sister had been in such a place, Elizabeth nodded to the butler. "If you would please see it arranged, Edwards?"

"Right away, madam."

"And, Edwards, you may want to enlist several footmen."

"Oh, I should think two could carry all our bags," Lydia said. "I've only a valise and George a case and a trunk."

Edwards looked to Elizabeth. "I will personally ensure enough men are sent to see to everything, Mrs. Darcy."

"Thank you."

"We should have tea," Georgiana said brightly.

Relieved to have Georgiana with her in this, with her opinion of Mr. Wickham totally changed, Elizabeth nodded. "A splendid idea. Tea is always good. Let's go to the back parlor." Wrapping an arm in Lydia's, which felt too thin, Elizabeth started them walking.

Lydia craned her neck as she passed the front parlor. "But it looks very nice in there and that way I'll be waiting when my George arrives."

"That one is terribly drafty," Georgiana said. "The big front window, you know. The back parlor is much cozier."

They went to the small back parlor and Elizabeth called for tea and had a fire lit. Taking in how much thinner her little sister looked after weeks in Wickham's care, she guided Lydia closest to the blaze. Georgiana sat near the door, expression intent, and Elizabeth wondered if the other young woman planned to tackle Lydia if she attempted to leave.

"This is nice," Lydia said, snuggling into the chair.

"Would you care to borrow a shawl?" Elizabeth asked. Lydia wore one of her summer gowns. She'd embroidered tiny rosebuds all about the hem, sleeves, and neckline, which she'd lowered. It squeezed Elizabeth's heart to picture Lydia alone and hungry, toiling in some awful, dingy room, decorating her least warm gown to look pretty for the last reading of her banns, working on that dress so she might wear her warmer ones. When Elizabeth saw Wickham, if he didn't appear in need of a few good meals as well, she was going to have a thing or two to say to him.

Not that she supposed he would care about her anger when he faced a noose.

"A shawl would be nice," Lydia answered, holding her hands out to the flames. "I suppose you have a great many of them and so won't mind." She looked about. "I can see why you decided to marry Mr. Darcy even though he's quite awful."

"Awful?" Georgiana asked sharply.

"Well, yes, the way he's tormented my George all his life. So much that George went by Mr. Wiekran when we met because Mr. Darcy is always hunting him down and trying to take away anything that makes him happy, like me." A wide grin split Lydia's face. "Only, the banns have been read and we can marry whenever we like."

"But—" Georgiana began.

Elizabeth stood, saying, "Let me send for that shawl." She crossed to the door, sighted a footman and waved him over. Voice low enough that she hoped not to be overheard, she asked, "Please send a maid for my warmest shawl. Also, if you could let the staff know that my sister is not permitted to leave the premises at this time. Should the need arise to prevent her departure, any measures aside from harming her are acceptable."

Wide eyed, the young man nodded. "Yes, Mrs. Darcy."

"Thank you." She went back in and retook her seat.

Lydia peered at her. "Is it very horrible being married to him, Lizzy? You don't look as if you've been sleeping well."

"I haven't been sleeping well but it's nothing to do with Mr. Darcy. It's because I was so worried about you."

"About me?" Lydia waved that off with a flap of her hand. "Then you are silly. George takes wonderful care of me."

"But you're so thin," Georgiana said. She cast Elizabeth a worried look, probably wondering if Lydia had descended into madness.

"My George brought me food every day." Lydia pulled her lips back into something akin to a snarl. "If he couldn't afford to buy us much, that is because Mr. Darcy has taken everything from him."

"My brother does not take things from Mr. Wickham," Georgiana snapped.

"Really? Then why did he charge into the church and chase George away?"

Georgiana jutted out her chin. "For your protection."

"I don't need protection from George. He accused my George of something to do with a man dying and chased him away." Lydia swiveled to look at Elizabeth. "What does Mr. Darcy say George did? George had to leave because of whatever it was, so I couldn't ask him."

Elizabeth drew in a deep breath. Lydia would have to know eventually. "Do you recall the man who tried to shoot at Mr. Darcy on the bridge? The one who pushed me into the gully?"

Lydia nodded, eyes wide.

"That was George Wickham."

Lydia stared for a long moment, then shook her head. "Who says so? You only saw him for seconds and you hadn't met George yet."

"Mr. Darcy recognized him."

"He's only saying that to ruin George's life." Lydia's voice rose in pitch. "It's all a lie and you're going along so you can have nice things. There probably wasn't even a carriage or a bridge or anything. Mama said you looked awful, but I bet you fell sneaking out to meet Mr. Darcy at night, or something reprehensible like that, and made up the whole story about the bridge to hide the scandal."

"You mean, like how you sneaked out to meet Mr. Wickham?" Georgiana said flatly.

Lydia turned to her. "That's different. George and I are in love. Elizabeth didn't even know Mr. Darcy."

"Then why would she sneak out to meet him?" Georgiana asked.

Elizabeth cast her a quelling look. "Lydia, there was a bridge and Mr. Wickham waited at it to try to waylay or possibly even kill Mr. Darcy. You must accept that."

Lydia shook her head. "Did you recognize him?"

"Yes."

"You saw him briefly before you were knocked out. How could you recognize him?

"I mainly saw the back of his head and the set of his body, but he turned around several times. He hadn't pulled his scarf up yet to hide his face, and his hat didn't cover all his hair."

"I won't believe you. All you recognized was hair. You're lying," Lydia said mulishly.

Georgiana leaned forward in her chair. "And the reason Mr. Wickham wanted to stop Fitz was because he was trying to—"

"Is that the tea service I hear?" Elizabeth cut in, trying to glare some sense into Georgiana. The last thing Georgiana's reputation required was Lydia knowing her most scandalous secret. Yes, it would come out if she testified, but there was no reason to reveal it earlier. Testimony would only come if Wickham was caught.

The sound Elizabeth had merely hoped she'd heard in the hall coalesced into a maid coming with her shawl. Grateful for the interruption, Elizabeth directed the maid to Lydia. While her sister arranged the shawl to her satisfaction, Elizabeth continued to frown at Georgiana, hoping to quell her.

Conversation continued in an agitated and precarious manner until tea truly did arrive. Lydia then stopped talking while, with little decorum or manners, she devoured enough for three people. Georgiana watched first with surprise, then a touch of disdain but, finally, when Lydia kept eating, with sympathy.

As Lydia's eating slowed, firm footfalls sounded in the hall. Recognizing her husband's tread, Elizabeth turned to the parlor doorway. Mr. Darcy entered appearing aggrieved, tired and grim.

Lydia looked up, half of a small cake in hand. "Where is George?"

Darcy snapped his gaze to her. "I do not know. He evaded us."

Lydia smirked. "Good."

Frowning, Darcy turned back to Elizabeth. "That was good thinking with Edwards. Men are there now, in case he shows up."

"What do you mean?" Lydia put her half-eaten cake down. "Men are where? Waiting for who?"

Expression bleak, Mr. Darcy turned to her. "Men are at the room in which you recently stayed, waiting to take Mr. Wickham into custody for murder and attempted murder."

Lydia shot to her feet. "Do not say that. My George isn't a murderer. Even if he pointed a gun at you, you made him do it. You always make him do terrible things."

Elizabeth's husband eyed her sister with disgust. As much as she appreciated the sentiment, she couldn't permit him to look at Lydia that way. Standing, she went to her sister. "Shh, Lydia, sit down. Mr. Darcy is tired. You're tired. We'll sort this all out. Sit back down."

Lydia turned and threw her arms about Elizabeth, sobbing, "He isn't a murderer. My George isn't a murderer."

Elizabeth stroked her back. "You may have to accept that Mr. Wickham isn't entirely the man you want him to be."

"But he is. He is noble and smart and handsome and an officer."

"Actually, Mr. Wickham took his commission under a false name, so he was never an officer, and it's come to light that he stole a considerable sum from his unit."

Lydia let out a wail, and Elizabeth glared over her sister's shoulder at her husband.

Mr. Darcy shrugged. "She will need to know everything eventually and you should both know it too. I've sent an express to your father."

Face pressed to Elizabeth's shoulder and still crying noisily, Lydia said, "I don't need Papa. Just let me marry and all will be well. I'll be so terribly happy with my George."

Elizabeth held her sobbing sister tight. Georgiana once more regarded Lydia with pity. Mr. Darcy scowled and pivoted, about to leave. A footman rushed in. Everyone except Lydia turned surprised looks on him.

The young man halted, blinked, bowed and came upright again to extend a folded page to Mr. Darcy. "The lad who brought it said it's urgent, sir."

"Thank you. Wait a moment."

The footman nodded and looked down, waiting.

Watching Mr. Darcy open the letter, Elizabeth frowned, recognizing the paper, though she couldn't place it. Not her sister Jane's stationary, or Charlotte's. Nor Mary's or Kitty's or her father's. But paper she'd recently—

"Have the carriage made ready," Mr. Darcy ordered the footman.

"Yes, sir."

As the young man disappeared, Darcy crossed to hold the letter out for Elizabeth. She read it over her sister's shoulder.

Mr. Darcy,

This is to inform you that Mr. George Wickham is dead. He entered my home, ransacked my office, sneaked into my bedchamber and threatened me. In the presence of two witnesses, I shot him and killed him.

I am arranging for the body to be removed. If you wish to confirm the identity of the housebreaker, you should come.

M. Younge

"Oh no," Elizabeth breathed. "Should I accompany you?"

"What is it?" Georgiana asked, wide eyed. "Where are you going? What's going on?"

Lydia pulled away from Elizabeth, turning. Mr. Darcy drew the page back but Lydia, with a choking sound, snatched it from him. Gaze on Mrs. Younge's words, she let out a low keen.

Mr. Darcy grabbed the page, folded it and shoved it in his pocket. Meeting Elizabeth's gaze he said, "No. Remain here with your sister."

"I'm going," Lydia cried. "It isn't my George and I'm going."

"Mrs. Younge knew him well," Mr. Darcy said. "She would not be mistaken."

"She said you should come identify him. That means I should go. It may not be him." Desperation edged Lydia's voice. "I know it isn't him."

"Mrs. Younge?" Georgiana repeated. "Fitz, what's happened?"

"Mr. Wickham broke into Mrs. Younge's boarding house and threatened her. She shot him."

Georgiana's face went white. "Is…is he badly hurt?"

"He is dead."

Lydia began sobbing again and Elizabeth collected her in her arms. Georgiana slumped back into her chair, stunned. Elizabeth decided that she would speak to her husband about his strategy for the delivery of bad news later.

"May I go and identify him?" Georgiana asked. "If I don't, I'll always wonder if he is out there."

Mr. Darcy studied his sister a moment and then asked, "You said you were willing to testify. Why?"

"I could have written to you. I think Mrs. Younge always read my letters to you, but I could have written something when I was at one of my lessons. I even thought about it once. It is my fault that all this happened. I enjoyed his attentions, even knowing that accepting them was wrong. Because this is all my fault, I—"

"Partly your fault," Elizabeth interrupted. "A small part." She would also speak to both her sister and her husband, again, about accepting blame for the actions of another. There was such a thing as being too responsible.

"Perhaps," Georgiana continued. "But if I had acted as I should have, Frank Miller would still be alive. I want to go with you, Fitz."

Mr. Darcy looked at Elizabeth. She realized that her husband sought her advice in the matter, warmed by his trust even in the midst of such a terrible day. She nodded.

Mr. Darcy turned back to his sister. "You may come."

"If she gets to go, so do I," Lydia said. "I have more right."

This time, Elizabeth shrugged in response to her husband's look. Lydia may be right, but she'd also demonstrated that she must be considered a child still, not a grown woman. More than that, Elizabeth doubted her sister would behave reasonably.

She'd no idea if Mr. Darcy thought of any of those things, but he nodded his acceptance of Lydia's presence as well.

Chapter Thirty

Darcy knocked when they arrived, and Mrs. Younge let them in, her expression unreadable. "If you will, the body is still in my room."

"You see?" Miss Lydia said as they followed Mrs. Younge up the steps. "My George would never be in another woman's room."

Darcy had to work not to contradict that. How little she knew him.

They went up and turned to follow Mrs. Younge down the hall, to the final door, which stood open. Inside, a body lay, appearing carefully arranged under a blood-spattered quilt. A woman in an apron knelt nearby with a bucket and scrub brush, which she plied to the floorboards. Little dark droplets were everywhere. The woman glanced up at them but then went back to scrubbing.

Mrs. Younge led them in with a sigh. "I wish I hadn't shot him in here. I'll never get all the blood out. The rug and my quilt are a loss."

Elizabeth cast her a startled look, mirroring Darcy's surprise at the woman's coldness and calm.

Mrs. Younge shrugged. "I always worried it would come to this, from the moment I realized he was responsible for the bridges, though I'd hoped not at my hand."

Darcy looked back to Miss Lydia, to gauge her reaction to the body.

She stood framed in the bedroom doorway. "It…that man isn't tall enough to be my George."

"He is," Mrs. Younge said and pulled back the sheet to reveal a white face.

"It's him," Georgiana said, voice weak, and Darcy wondered if he shouldn't have let her accompany them. "It's George."

Elizabeth inched forward to study him, this man whom she'd seen but twice, but who had impacted her and her family so very much. "He must have been rather handsome," she murmured, then shuddered. She stepped back to stand beside Darcy.

He took her hand. Her fingers were like ice.

Miss Lydia stayed in the doorway, shaking her head. "That's not my George."

Darcy leveled a frown on her. "It is. That is George Wickham. I've known him my entire life."

"No," Miss Lydia said. Tears leaked from the corners of her eyes, making gleaming trails down her cheeks. "It's not my George. I won't say that it is."

"Did he have any defining marks?" Mrs. Younge asked calmly.

"He has a scar on his right shoulder," Darcy supplied.

Mrs. Younge looked to Miss Lydia. "Do you concur?"

Reluctantly, Elizabeth's sister nodded. "He does. It…it looks like an x, like on a map. He said Mr. Darcy gave it to him."

Elizabeth glanced at him in question as Mrs. Younge, apparently with no qualms about touching a dead body, knelt and pulled the quilt down farther.

Darcy shook his head. "He received it falling from a tree that I said he shouldn't climb because it had been struck by lightning and was dead inside." He looked down at the body, filled with sudden sorrow. George never listened.

"Regardless of who was at fault," Mrs. Younge said, adding a sympathetic look for him that Darcy took to mean she knew which of them had been, "I assume this is the mark?" She pulled back the blood soaked shirt to reveal a scarred x on Wickham's shoulder.

Miss Lydia inched closer to look down, then jumped back. "He said…he said it meant he was the t-t-treasure." She shook her head. "It's not him. That's not my George. You put that there."

"I could hardly place a scar I knew nothing of," Mrs. Younge said as she once more covered the body.

"It's not my George," Miss Lydia wailed.

"It's George Wickham," Georgiana said. "Why am I sad he's dead? He told me he loved me and couldn't live without me. Then he ran off with someone else. I-I should hate him. I should be happy."

"He loved me," Miss Lydia screeched with sudden volume. "He told me he never loved anyone else."

"He never loved anyone," Mrs. Younge said. "He loved himself too much."

Somewhere down the hall, a baby started crying, likely roused by Miss Lydia.

Mrs. Younge rose to her feet, grimacing. The baby's cries grew louder, as did Miss Lydia's. Loud, noisy sobs that didn't sound as if they came from a woman who believed the man she loved to be alive.

"Mrs. Darcy," Mrs. Younge said with her usual composure, that trait a large part of what had won her position as Georgiana's guardian. "I would like a word with your husband. If you could take your sister and Miss Darcy to the kitchen you'll find wine in the larder, tucked away behind the beer keg. I believe both could use a glass."

"Yes. Very well." Elizabeth slipped her hand from his.

"Sara can show you," Mrs. Younge added.

At that, the scrubbing woman looked up. She nodded and dropped her brush into the bucket. Standing, she wiped blood pinked hands on her already dirty apron as she turned to Elizabeth. "Right this way."

They collected a sobbing Miss Lydia and left, taking at least some of the noise with them. Darcy had to credit Mrs. Younge's unwavering calm. The cacophony of wails combined with the tang of blood in the air and the body on the floor had him gritting his teeth in a bid to maintain coherent thought.

Mrs. Younge stood where she was, looking down the hall, until Elizabeth, Miss Lydia, Georgiana and the maid turned down the staircase. She then walked past him to close the bedroom door, further muting the baby's cries. Darcy turned to her with raised eyebrows.

"Nothing improper, I assure you," she said as she recrossed the room.

He studied her, frowning. Much as he respected her calm and appreciated her recent assistance, he did not care for Mrs. Younge. "What, then?"

"I'm going to tell you where to find the contract I had with Mr. Wickham. I want your word that you will not retaliate against the person holding it for me. He or she had no idea of what it was. I'll send them a note telling them to give the contract to you. It is sealed, and I told them… Well, you don't need to know the lie they believed. I could burn the page myself, but I believe you will feel better if you do so, to know for a fact that it is done."

Despite his animosity for Mrs. Younge, her request seemed reasonable. "No retaliation. I promise. Considering everything that's happened, I can't be angry with someone who was deceived."

"Very well, then. It's Mrs. Flynn, your housekeeper."

Darcy started, sacking her his first thought.

Expression wry, Mrs. Younge said, "We became friends. As I said, she has no idea what she's holding for me. You promised."

He could not deny that, so he said, "I will compensate you for your trouble in this matter." He gestured, taking in the ruined rug, the body and the quilt.

Mrs. Younge peered up at him. "As much as I enjoy taking your money, Mr. Darcy, I heard what Miss Darcy said. I saw the worried look Mrs. Darcy gave her, and you. It seems to me that it is important that you acknowledge this is not your doing. Mr. Wickham's blood on my bedchamber rug is not your fault."

Darcy stared at her. "I know that."

"Do you? Because, he had an unhealthy obsession with you and, knowing him as I did, it seems to me that he also had a knack for imposing on you." An aggravating amount of sympathy in her eyes, she said, "So I thank you, but I do not need your money, Mr. Darcy. At least, not any more of it than I've already taken."

Darcy frowned. The woman would steal from him but wouldn't take his assistance when he offered? "If there are any undue expenses, alert me."

"If there are any undue expenses, I will. Will you see him buried?"

Darcy looked down at the once again shrouded form. Miss Lydia was correct. The body on the floor looked too small to be George. "No. I wouldn't know where to do so." In this, Darcy would put his sensibilities, his family's happiness, first. Even though he knew that George would desperately wish to be buried alongside generations of Darcys, Georgiana and Elizabeth did not need that unmovable reminder of a man who'd done them so much harm. Darcy didn't need it, either. He didn't wish to take Wickham back to Pemberley to be buried, a constant reminder of the failure of two generations of Darcys to curtail one man's evil.

"Is there anyone I should contact?" Mrs. Younge asked.

"He had no family. No friends."

"Merely a string of people he charmed and used," she concluded. "Very well. We will consign him to England's care, with every other vagabond."

Mrs. Younge showed Darcy to the kitchen where they found Elizabeth, Georgiana and Miss Lydia seated at a small table. The maid, at a nod from Mrs. Younge, went out, presumably to resume her grim work. Darcy glanced about the neat, ordered room.

Miss Lydia surged to her feet, arm extended to point at Mrs. Younge. "Murderer. You murdered my George."

"Only because he threatened to kill me."

"You're lying. George would never do that."

"I have two witnesses."

"They are liars too." Miss Lydia hurtled around the table, arms outstretched, hands clutching like talons.

Darcy caught her about the waist. She heaved against him, so he lifted her high enough that her feet no longer touched the ground. "Calm yourself."

Miss Lydia squirmed, trying to get free. She kicked him with her heels, eliciting a grunt of pain. "She killed my George."

At least, he supposed, she was acknowledging Wickham's death now.

"We should go," Elizabeth said, coming to his side.

Georgiana appeared on the other, expression pinched.

"She murdered my George," Miss Lydia shrieked.

Darcy grimaced, the sound driving into his skull. Elizabeth touched his arm and nodded in the direction of the doorway.

"Wait," Mrs. Younge said. "Miss Bennet, let me show you what Mr. Wickham did to my office." She had steel in her voice.

Darcy hesitated, turning back around, trying to ignore the writhing banshee in his arms.

Mrs. Younge met his gaze and said, "Please." She walked past him and turned left, gesturing.

As he must go that way to leave anyhow, Darcy carried Miss Lydia over. She stopped struggling when she saw the chaos. Mrs. Younge slipped away and returned quickly with a man and a woman.

"Miss Bennet," Mrs. Younge said. "You don't believe me, but I was not the only one there. I don't want you to live in doubt." She stepped aside, gesturing to the two she'd brought.

The woman stepped forward first, then the man. Both witnesses described what had happened. Miss Lydia began to cry again, quieter now, and claimed they were lying. Seeing the fight had left her, Darcy set her down. Georgiana stood to one side beside Elizabeth, studying the floor.

When her witnesses finished speaking, Mrs. Younge looked from face to face. She shrugged and said, "That's all I can do."

Miss Lydia allowed Elizabeth and Georgiana to lead her to the carriage, where she, blessedly, fell into nearly silent sobbing, wrapped once more in Elizabeth's arms. Seated across from the two women with

Georgiana next to him, Darcy let his lids close as Daniels navigated the streets of London. He could picture nothing but Wickham's prone, sheet draped form, Mrs. Younge's words echoing in his mind.

Had Wickham imposed on him? Recently, yes, but surely not always. Once, they'd been friends.

Growing up, it had been the other way around. Wickham had always been there for him. For a great many years, he'd been Darcy's only friend as there'd been no other boys his age nearby that met with his family's approval. Richard, Darcy's nearest male relation in age, hadn't lived close and, though only a few years separated them, those years had meant a great deal more in their youth.

No, an older cousin with whom he'd spent a few weeks a year couldn't compete with the daily presence of George Wickham, pleasant and charming even as a child, and Darcy was too studious, too awkward, and too shy, to form friendships at school.

Yet, looking back on their relationship, Mrs. Younge's words in his mind, he wondered now if Wickham had tried to isolate him. When Richard's family sent him for visits, Wickham had always been there, making certain they played the games they always played, at which Wickham excelled, or new ones of his invention, at which he also excelled. Wickham's favorite had always been one where they would hide together and Richard, who knew Pemberley not half as well, must find them. Richard hadn't cared for the game and would often ask if he could take a turn hiding, but somehow Wickham's way always prevailed.

On the occasions when Darcy had visited Richard, he'd received frequent letters which required prompt responses. He recalled penning them with great aggravation, because Wickham knew how slowly he wrote and how many hours composing replies would take. At the time, he'd interpreted the letters as Wickham needing him. Now, he wondered if the goal had been to keep him close, so he never went long without devoting time to Wickham. To keep Darcy accustomed to, possibly needing, Wickham's presence in his life.

He opened his eyes, looking down. He felt a strange, guilt-inducing relief at Wickham's passing. He felt free. No more debates about how to fix Wickham's evils, or if he even should. No more of that nagging, familiar worry, wondering what terrible crime Wickham would perpetuate next. Darcy, Georgiana, Elizabeth…they were free.

And it hurt.

Darcy rubbed at his chest, feeling hollow. He regretted…not Wickham's death, exactly, but the realization that the boy he'd spent his childhood with hadn't simply failed to grow into the man Darcy and his father had both hoped he would. No, Wickham hadn't gone wrong somewhere. Hadn't failed to meet his potential.

Because the truth was, that boy Darcy remembered, the golden haired, charming child his father had loved, Darcy's dearest friend in his youth, that boy had never existed. George had never been who Darcy had believed him to be.

They were a silent procession, even Miss Lydia quiet now, when they finally arrived and reentered Darcy House. Darcy let Elizabeth and Georgiana settle Miss Lydia in a guest room while he retrieved Mrs. Younge's contract from Mrs. Flynn. His housekeeper seemed a touch confused but Mrs. Younge must have dispatched her letter and a lad quickly, because Mrs. Flynn was ready with the sealed contract.

Leaving his housekeeper with no explanation, Darcy went to find his wife, who sat with his sister in one of the small parlors. After confirming the contents of the page, he showed it to Georgiana and Elizabeth, saying, "I can burn this now or show it to Miss Lydia before I burn it. If she sees it, she may reveal it to others."

"Show her," Georgiana said. "She needs to know what kind of man Wickham is…was, rather. I'm glad you showed it to me. I feel both more and less a fool. More, because I was blind to their plot, and less, because, well, there was a plot. Does that make sense?"

"Yes," Elizabeth said. She went over to Georgiana and gave her a hug.

Later that afternoon when Miss Lydia emerged from her room and they showed her the contract, she asserted that someone had forged Wickham's handwriting, and started crying again.

Chapter Thirty-One

Elizabeth's father arrived the following afternoon to take Lydia home, which suited them well as Mr. Darcy had declared that morning, rather abruptly, that they would go to Pemberley the next day. Elizabeth went with Mr. Bennet to the room they'd given Lydia, where they found her puffy faced and groggy from too much crying and too much wine the night before. Elizabeth crossed to open the curtains, to let in the afternoon light while their father endured Lydia's sobbing and rather skewed tale of how Mrs. Younge had murdered her husband.

When Lydia began the story for the third time, Mr. Bennet broke in with, "We're leaving within the hour. Make ready." He gestured to Elizabeth, who'd perched on the foot of the bed.

Ignoring Lydia's sobs, they left the room. Elizabeth closed the door firmly behind them. "I'll send a maid to help her."

Mr. Bennet nodded, starting down the hall. "Mr. Darcy's letter said only that you had Lydia, that she is not married, and that Mr. Wickham fled the church."

Elizabeth scrubbed fingers over her forehead. She'd forgotten that news of Mr. Wickham's death had come after her husband sent word to her father. "I'm sorry. I should have told you before we entered her room."

Mr. Bennet paused in his steps, then resumed. "So he is dead?"

"He is." Elizabeth sighed. "Would you care for tea?"

"It hardly seems the time and yet, I've been hours on the road and expect hours more."

She nodded and led the way to the small back parlor, found it empty, and went in. She called for a maid, sending for tea and requesting assistance for her sister, adding, "She will require someone possessed of forbearance and calm."

Nodding, the maid who'd come left the room.

"Now," Elizabeth's father said, turning to her. "What happened?"

"Mr. Wickham broke into the home of an acquaintance and threatened her, before witnesses. She shot him." After a moment, Elizabeth thought to add, "Dead," and shuddered.

"I see." Mr. Bennet sat quietly for a moment, then asked, "And Lydia is not married?"

"No."

"Well, we'll cope. It's going to be hard on Mrs. Bennet, especially if Lydia is with child. The neighbors won't be kind."

"I know. It's all so awful." Elizabeth swallowed back tears. She didn't know who the tears would be for, exactly, and they wouldn't help.

"What will you do now?"

"Mr. Darcy wishes to go to Pemberley, as we'd planned to do before…before all of this. I believe it will do Mr. Darcy and Georgiana good to go home. They require peace and the familiar."

Sympathy in his gaze, her father asked, "And what about you? What do you require?"

Elizabeth smiled at her father's care. "It will do me good to see my husband and new sister happy, and to visit my new home."

"The banns have already been read twice for Jane and Mr. Bingley. You could return to Longbourn with me and Lydia and remain until after the wedding."

Elizabeth shook her head. "Thank you but I wish to stay with Mr. and Miss Darcy." Her husband, who was out meeting with his man of business, seemed oddly quiet since leaving Mrs. Younge's. Elizabeth imagined that even if they had grown estranged over recent years, losing such a large part of his life as Mr. Wickham hurt Darcy. Georgiana as well.

"Will you attend Jane's wedding?"

Elizabeth shook her head. "I would like to say yes but I don't know." No official period of mourning existed for losing a man who'd been nearly a brother to them, but surely Mr. Darcy and Georgiana required time to grieve.

Her father kindly turned conversation to other things while they had tea, then collected Lydia, left regards for Mr. Darcy, and departed. Alone, Elizabeth asked for the smaller carriage to be brought round and then went to check on Georgiana, knocking lightly on her door.

"Come in."

Elizabeth opened the door to find her sister by marriage sitting in her bedroom window seat. She stepped in and lightly closed the door. "How are you?"

Georgiana let out a long, slow breath, not quite a sigh. "I…well enough, I suppose. It's odd, is all. George is dead and it's very sad." Her voice choked but she cleared her throat. "And not sad, because he wasn't really who I thought. Not if he did all those terrible things." She shrugged. "I don't know."

Elizabeth crossed to her. "Perhaps because he's gone there is no point in worrying over what sort of man he was. You can simply be sad for the George Wickham you lost."

"Yes," Georgiana said, swallowing. "I can be sad for that."

Elizabeth wrapped Georgiana in her arms, holding her close, a touch awkward because Georgiana was in the window seat and Elizabeth stood, but with all the hope for comfort she could offer. For a moment, the younger woman clung to her but then she pulled back, wiping her eyes.

"It was very brave of you to offer to testify," Elizabeth said.

Georgiana gave a trembling smile. "I had to. It may not have been all my mess, but since I was partly responsible, I had to help clean it up."

Elizabeth realized Georgiana had grown up a great deal since she first met her.

Georgiana cleared her throat again. "Well, I had better pack. Fitz said he wants to leave for Pemberley in the morning."

Elizabeth nodded. "Yes, and although I haven't known your brother for long, I've already learned that when he says morning, he means as much."

"He does," Georgiana said and stood.

Elizabeth went back across the room. "I'm off to make a call. I won't be long."

She let herself out of Georgiana's room and continued down the hall to her own to gather her outerwear. As she donned her bonnet, her gaze went to the door that adjoined her room to Mr. Darcy's. In her fear at having her little sister in the care of a murderer, she'd forgotten her vow to become Mr. Darcy's wife in more than name. They'd been progressing nicely down that path, and she'd felt certain that once they left Longbourn for Pemberley, the matter would be resolved.

But they hadn't gone to Pemberley. They'd rushed back to London and Elizabeth had been awash in her fears for her sister, her worry for

Georgiana's happiness and even Jane's, ever since. Now, Mr. Darcy was plunged into mourning. Was he the sort to rail against death by embracing life, or to sink for a time into quiet sorrow? She wished she knew him well enough to know. All she could say for certain was that he would recover. Evidence of that faced her every day, for he'd lost both parents already.

With a sigh, she finished tying her bonnet, then donned her cloak. She went down to the entrance hall with great reluctance. She knew Mr. Darcy wished to leave for Pemberley as early tomorrow as possible and there was one call Elizabeth must make before departing London. Whether she wanted to or not, she must visit Mrs. Fitzwilliam and thank her for sending word about Lydia. A note wouldn't be adequate.

On the way over, Elizabeth rehearsed the words she would say to the former Miss de Bourgh. She wished to sound appropriately grateful without giving any hint that she felt Mrs. Fitzwilliam's actions were to atone for her past behavior. To imply that would be to make accusations that Elizabeth felt too careworn to argue.

When she arrived at the townhome Colonel Fitzwilliam's marriage had made his, she was welcomed in. In a rather gaudy parlor that Elizabeth suspected still bore Lady Catherine's mark, she and her hostess exchanged polite greetings. They both sat and Mrs. Fitzwilliam sent for refreshments.

Encouraged and determined to have swift, smooth discourse Elizabeth said, "My family and I are very grateful to you for informing us of where we could locate my youngest sister. You have not only my thanks but that of both the Darcys and Bennets."

"And?" Anne said after a long moment of silence.

Elizabeth shook her head. What had she left out? "And we've taken matters in hand, thanks to you."

Mrs. Fitzwilliam waved that off. "I didn't mean, what happened to your sister and Mr. Wickham, though I heard he's dead. I meant, do you not want an apology from me for my past behavior?"

"You sent a letter."

Mrs. Fitzwilliam pursed thin lips. "My husband was right, then. He said you would not mention that I have wronged you."

On guard for recriminations or possibly shouting, Elizabeth remained silent. She should have risked insulting Mrs. Fitzwilliam with a note. She didn't know if she had the wherewithal to endure another bout of anger and recrimination.

After a second awkward silence, during which Elizabeth resolved to leave if her hostess began screeching, Mrs. Fitzwilliam said, "I asked Richard if I could begin anew with you. You see, he is very good friends with Mr. Darcy, and I would not want either of them to give up that friendship, which will surely suffer if you and I cannot get along. I thought perhaps my assistance in the matter of locating your sister would permit us to pretend my earlier behavior never took place."

"What did he say?" Elizabeth asked, encouraged by Mrs. Fitzwilliam's reasonable tone.

"He said no. He said you can never start anew, which is why you must endeavor to start well. He also said that one wrong and one favor do not cancel each other out. That the past is always with us. It's part of who we are."

"True," Elizabeth said. "But your assistance was an act of kindness. It does not balance the past, but it does put the past farther into the past. Now, our last interaction can be counted as good." For now, at least.

Mrs. Fitzwilliam nodded. "Yes. Rather than not good. I only wish I had received the information earlier." She pursed her lips again. "I am not asking you to forget what I did or even to forgive me for it. All I'm asking is that you allow my husband and your husband to maintain their friendship. I do not have any idea how much that friendship means to Mr. Darcy, but it means a great deal to Colonel Fitzwilliam."

"That is a reasonable request," Elizabeth said. "I'm not certain it was necessary for you to make it. I would not attempt to interfere with my husband's relationship with his cousin."

Mrs. Fitzwilliam appeared thoughtful. "That is good to know. I will remember it."

"Remember it?" Did the other woman mean to behave monstrously again, testing Elizabeth's dedication to her professed lack of desire to interfere between the two men?

"Yes." Mrs. Fitzwilliam looked down. "I will keep your words and actions in mind as an example of appropriate behavior. Richard tells me that you are a good person to mimic in this."

"Oh." Elizabeth didn't know if that should flatter her or cause alarm. Perhaps both, for it was flattering but she didn't wish to be scrutinized and copied. That seemed like a great deal of obligation to put on her. "Who else's behavior did he recommend?"

"No one's." Mrs. Fitzwilliam smoothed her skirt, downturned face evincing a pink blush. "There isn't anyone else. Richard is my only friend, and he says I am not yet ready to visit any of our other relations."

"Well, I'm certain that will change." At least, Elizabeth hoped, for Mrs. Fitzwilliam's sake, that it would.

A bustle sounded in the hall and maids came in with the tea service, to what Elizabeth suspected was mutual relief. Mrs. Fitzwilliam served with concentration and care, and they chatted about the weather and the Darcys upcoming removal to Pemberley, without any fresh mention of why they were leaving. Elizabeth wasn't certain that was tact on Mrs. Fitzwilliam's part. She imagined the other woman simply didn't realize that Mr. Darcy might wish quiet after losing a man who'd grown up alongside him.

Overall, Elizabeth counted the visit as a success but as the carriage carried her back to Darcy House, she couldn't shake Mrs. Fitzwilliam's declaration about lacking friends from her mind.

Edwards opened the door for her on her return. Accepting her cloak, he said, "Mr. Darcy is in his office. I informed him that he missed Mr. Bennet."

"Is he displeased?" Elizabeth asked, removing her bonnet.

"I do not believe so, madam, but he asked for you, if you have time."

"Of course." Adopting a cheerful expression that she hoped was warranted, Elizabeth went to find her husband.

She found him in the middle of his office shelving ledgers, his coat draped over the back of the chair behind his desk again. The sight of his broad shoulders and chest constrained merely by his shirt and waistcoat brought her instantly back to thoughts about the single door that separated their bedchambers. Pressing such thoughts aside, she knocked lightly on the frame of the open office door.

Darcy looked at her and the lines of strain on his face eased. "Elizabeth. Come in. You went to visit Anne?"

She entered and closed the door behind her, though the staff at Darcy House didn't seem prone to eavesdropping. The click of the latch seemed over loud. "I did. I deemed her contribution to locating Lydia too great for a simple note of thanks."

He nodded and shelved the last ledger he held. "That was good of you. I would understand if you'd only written."

"I'm happy I went." Elizabeth moved deeper into the room, her slippers soundless on the thick carpet. "She worked very hard to behave well. She says that she doesn't wish us to be enemies, or to harm your friendship with Colonel Fitzwilliam."

Darcy turned fully to her with a slightly surprised look. "That is considerate of her."

"She also said that he is her only friend." Elizabeth looked up at her husband, shaking her head. "That's sad."

"I don't think her mother allowed her to have friends, with the possible exception of Mrs. Jenkinson."

"Mrs. Jenkinson was her companion, I believe? She was visiting family when we…the one time we visited, but I've heard Georgiana mention her."

"Yes. She's about Aunt Catherine's age. I was never certain who she was really there to keep company more, Anne or her mother."

"Regardless, she was being paid to do it. That isn't the same as having friends."

Mr. Darcy nodded. "I suppose not. Friendship is voluntary."

"Which means Mrs. Fitzwilliam hasn't had any practice in making friends." Elizabeth considered that for a moment and added, "Still, she can learn."

"It's late in life for her to learn, but Richard will be a good teacher. He has friends everywhere."

Elizabeth heard the unspoken, 'unlike me,' at the end of that statement. She studied the tension in her husband's jaw. The downward pull to his mouth. The sorrow that lingered in his dark eyes. "Perhaps he does have many friends, but I don't think Mrs. Fitzwilliam was either lying or mistaken when she indicated that he values your friendship."

"He values all his friends."

"If so, that's why he has so many of them, but Mrs. Fitzwilliam described her husband's friendship with you as being important. I don't believe she thinks you are one of many."

"Perhaps." Mr. Darcy shrugged. "You must realize it isn't a topic men generally discuss."

Elizabeth smiled. "I suppose not." She reached to take his hand, feeling that he needed a physical connection. He seemed…sad.

"Speaking of forming friendships, I'm sorry to have missed your father. Did you offer that he might stay the night and return to Hertfordshire tomorrow? He's always welcome."

279

Elizabeth shook her head. "No. If he wishes to remain in London tonight, he has other relations on whom he may call." She squeezed the hand she held. "I think you need quiet."

"I will have quiet at Pemberley," he said, returning the gentle pressure.

"Yes, but that does not mean that you and Georgiana should endure another evening of Lydia sobbing loudly enough to be heard throughout the entire house."

"On that, we can agree." The slight smile he added to those words didn't ease the sorrow in his eyes.

Elizabeth tugged on his hand. "Put your arms around me."

Darcy's eyebrows lifted. "Put my arms about you?"

"Yes. I want to hold you. It pains me to see you so sad."

"I don't need coddling. I'm a grown man."

"I didn't say you need codling, Fitzwilliam. I said that I want to hold you because it hurts me to see you suffering. It would be purely for my benefit."

His smile a touch more real this time, he nodded and wrapped his arms about her. She brought hers up to hold him and, after a long moment, he lowered his head to her shoulder. Elizabeth wished she were taller but as she comforted her husband, despite the tumult of the past weeks, a feeling of deep contentment stole through her.

Chapter Thirty-Two

Darcy had never felt so worn thin. Wickham dying didn't feel at all the same as the loss of his parents. There was no sharp pain. No engulfing despair to claw free of. Not a single tear.

Only a sort of poignant sorrow. A feeling of being too calm. The sensation seemed far more like waking from a long, deep illness than of losing someone. Too much relief, and guilt over feeling that relief, colored Wickham's passing for his death to be like the other losses Darcy had experienced.

Never before had he been so thankful to return to Pemberley. To the solitude, the quiet, and the familiar. Darcy loved his home.

And yet, as he introduced Elizabeth to the staff and showed her about, he had to work to banish memories of his childhood, running and playing alongside Wickham. Georgiana could feel it, too, he knew. He saw it in the way her gaze lingered on Wickham's usual chair at the table where luncheon was served. In her slight smile as she glanced at a single vase, the twin broken while playing a game of hide and seek that had turned into tag.

When they reached the room with the pianoforte, where a young Georgiana had insisted on performing many recitals for him and George, she turned to them and said, "I believe I will go to my room and rest. I'm certain you can finish showing Elizabeth around without me."

"Rest well," Elizabeth said.

Georgiana nodded and went back the way they'd come.

"The library is this way," Darcy said. A hand on the small of Elizabeth's back, he turned her.

"Do you know, I believe I will actually become lost at first, living here," she said as they walked. "I'd no idea Pemberley was so vast."

Darcy smiled fondly. "It's a grand home."

"Very." Elizabeth looked up at him askance. "I can see why you love it."

"I do."

Her hand fitted into his. "I didn't mean to make you sad. It was a compliment."

"I know. You did not." She didn't answer and he realized she wouldn't pry, but he wanted her to know. He wanted someone to understand. "I can remember running through these halls as a child, laughing and shouting with George. I was never so free with anyone as with him."

"Well, you were young. Children are often less restrained than adults."

Darcy squeezed her hand lightly in acknowledgment of that, but he knew that wasn't why. "I believe I was even more inhibited as a child than as an adult. I knew a great fear of putting a foot wrong. Of failure. Or being noticed for the wrong reasons. George had a way of making me forget all of that, until..."

Elizabeth halted and turned to face him, likely unaware that they stood outside the library. "Until?"

"Until we were punished. Somehow, something always ended wrong."

She raised an eyebrow. "Were you punished equally?"

He shook his head. "George was always sent back to his father. I have no idea how he was punished."

"And you?"

"It depended on the severity of the crime. My father once made me stand in the corner, facing the walls, with a vase balanced on my head for an hour. He said that if it fell, he would take a crop to me."

"Would he have?" Elizabeth asked, eyes wide.

"I don't believe so. He never once did, despite years of threats."

"What had you done?"

"We'd used the table that held the vase as a ladder, to climb onto one of the mantelpieces in the ballroom. In the process we damaged the table and broke the head off one of the swans carved into the mantelpiece."

"That...well, that is rather terrible of you, isn't it? Why did you want to climb onto the mantelpiece?"

"We'd taken all the cushions from the chairs that line the ballroom and piled them in front of the fireplace, and we wanted to jump into them."

A smile curved her mouth. "Let me guess, that wasn't your idea?"

"They rarely were. Not the ideas that landed us in trouble. I don't believe I had the creativity."

"Well, then, hopefully our sons won't, either."

His hand tightened on hers. "Our sons?"

"Well, yes. I daresay we can hope to have some. Not that there's anything wrong with daughters. Not from my perspective, at least, being one."

He caught her other hand, twining their fingers. "I do hope to have sons, and daughters. I believe we're missing an important step in that, though."

Her cheeks pinked but she didn't look away from his gaze. "A very important step."

"One we could easily see to?" He tugged slightly to draw her closer.

"Very easily," she whispered, coming up on her toes.

Darcy released her hands to crush her to him. Everything fell away, until his world was only Elizabeth. Her full lips. Her soft skin. Her hands in his hair.

Now that he'd started, he couldn't stop. He wanted to find a room, any room for privacy.

"Show me your bedroom," she said, reading his mind.

He scooped her into his arms and carried her up a flight of stairs, kicking the door closed behind them.

After that, Darcy found he felt considerably less melancholy. He couldn't even feel guilty about that because every time he saw his wife, touched so much as a lock of her hair, even thought about her, a giddy joy filled him. He considered that maybe he should be embarrassed by that and did try not to grin like a fool in the presence of others, but he could hardly be bothered to care.

Still, he did have one complaint. From the day after they arrived at Pemberley, they had a surprising number of callers. He thought of himself as a man newly married and wished for the privacy that would afford, but their neighbors had read the date of the wedding in the newspaper months ago.

Finally, after over a week with very little time alone, he complained to Elizabeth as they read in the parlor after dinner, Georgiana having gone to bed a half hour prior.

Looking up from the novel she held, Elizabeth met his annoyance with a chuckle. "But it would be insulting if they didn't call."

"I wouldn't mind the insult," he muttered.

She cast him a quick smile. "Would you really be happy if people didn't accept me? Because if they didn't call, that is what they would be saying."

"Then I wouldn't call on them and I wouldn't miss them."

"But your neighbors are pleasant people," she protested. "And from various conversations, I gather that you've known most of them since childhood."

"I have." Darcy grimaced in defeat. "And you are correct, of course. I am glad they call and that you return their calls, but I only associate with the people who live nearby because they are nearby. I wouldn't make any effort to spend time with them if they lived far away."

"I daresay most acquaintances begin that way and while I agree that only some become fast friendships, how else are friendships to begin?"

He frowned at that. She made a fair point. "You are right. I shouldn't neglect them." He couldn't help but add, as a slight rebuke, "But they aren't my first choice of friends."

Elizabeth smiled in a too sweet way he didn't trust and said, "Is there anyone you would like to spend time with? We could invite someone here."

To that, he had a firm answer. "Richard or Bingley."

"Colonel Fitzwilliam seems very nice, but he is married to Anne." Elizabeth marked her place in the book and closed it, expression thoughtful. "She did try very hard to be polite when I went to see her, and she does need to learn. I would like to include Georgiana in any decision to invite her here, however."

Darcy had a fair idea what his sister, who hadn't seen Anne since the evening they'd so abruptly departed Rosings, would say to that. "And Bingley is about to marry."

"Yes." Elizabeth met his gaze. "And you have yet to decide if we will attend."

He knew they should. Their attendance was important to Elizabeth, and her family, and Bingley. Darcy was simply loath to give up even the oft-interrupted peace they'd found at Pemberley.

"You will need to decide, or let your lack of decision be one," Elizabeth said a touch tartly and reopened her book.

Frowning, his contentment effectively shattered, Darcy contemplated attending Bingley's wedding and his very short list of friends he would like to invite to Pemberley. Richard and Bingley both had many friends, but Darcy had only them. There were other men with whom he was on good terms, of course, but no others he would describe as a very good friend.

Now Richard was married to a woman who, while quite well known to Darcy, was not one he considered a desirable guest and one he had only a slim hope of his wife coming to like. Nor could they invite Richard without Anne. He was too good of a man to be an absent husband, especially with how much Anne needed him. Darcy wouldn't ask that of him, regardless.

Bingley, fortunately, was about to marry a woman who Elizabeth would always wish to see. That did not, of course, mean that they would be together all that often. Bingley had many obligations on his time and a wife and family would only add more.

Who, then, did that leave Darcy?

His gaze went to Elizabeth. For her, they would attend Bingley and Miss Bennet's wedding, but also for him. Darcy didn't wish to be like Anne, with only his spouse as his friend. He wasn't gregarious. He didn't require a great deal of socializing or conversation. He didn't need many close acquaintances.

But he had friends. He valued them. He'd missed Richard's wedding and now regretted that, despite the circumstances. Attending such an important event in someone's life created shared memories. It showed care and respect. Darcy knew he wasn't good at telling people how he felt about them, so he should endeavor to do better with his actions, to show them.

Sitting in his favorite parlor in Pemberley, Elizabeth reading nearby, he vowed that he would show those he cared for most that he did care. Especially his sister, his friends, and his wife.

Epilogue

Elizabeth watched in the mirror as her husband fastened the heavy sapphire and diamond necklace about her neck, then rested his hands on her shoulders, studying her. Much as she loved the extravagant piece, she dropped her gaze to her jewelry case, smiling as she sighted the little filigree necklace he'd bought her in Meryton. She still wore it often, but tonight was an occasion for glamor. Tonight, Pemberley was resplendent and full. They'd invited their neighbors, their friends, and their families to celebrate Georgiana's engagement.

Elizabeth reached to touch the filigreed necklace, then met Darcy's gaze in the mirror. "It will always be my favorite."

"It isn't the first I bought for you. This set is." He nodded to the sparkle of diamonds and sapphires that adorned her decolletage, wrists, fingers, and hair.

She turned to wrap her arms about his neck. "And I love them, but the necklace from Meryton is the first you actually presented to me, and it means more to me than all the diamonds in England." She came up on her toes to lightly kiss him, keeping enough distance between them not to flatten his cravat.

Darcy tightened his arms about her, wanting more. Even after six years, he always took full advantage of any opportunity to kiss her. Not that she minded.

She laughed against his lips and tipped her head back to meet his eyes. "Stevens will never forgive me if you walk into that ballroom mussed."

"Stevens be damned," Darcy growled and tugged Elizabeth back for another kiss.

"Ah hem," Darcy's valet coughed. "I have your sapphire cufflinks, sir." Stevens let out a beleaguered sigh and added, "And I will fetch a fresh cravat."

Elizabeth waited until Darcy's valet retreated before laughing again, then wriggled free of his arms. "I am going down in case Mrs. Reynolds requires me. Not that she ever does. We are so very lucky to have her."

As she descended into the already bustling house, many of the guests having arrived days ago, Georgiana's engagement the perfect excuse for a house party, Elizabeth recalled her first glimpses of Pemberley. She'd been rather daunted, as she recalled. Helping Mrs. Flynn manage Darcy House in London had given her a false sense of capableness that Pemberley had quickly proved unearned. The vast mansion required far more skill than Elizabeth then had. More than that, she truly had become lost several times, trying to find various rooms. She smiled at the recollection, checked in with Mrs. Reynolds, who did indeed have all in hand, and then went to their largest parlor.

The room, with a full grand piano in the center, bustled with people. Elizabeth paused in the leftmost of the three large doorways, taking in the clamor before her. All her sisters were there, as well as her parents, the Gardiners, and many relations on Darcy's side. Mrs. Fitzwilliam, surprisingly plump now and smiling, stood in conversation with Jane, who was round for a different reason. Again. Mary, Kitty and Elizabeth herself had two children each, and hoped for more, but Jane seemed set to outpace them all, with three already and another on the way.

"Elizabeth," Caroline called, sighting her. She turned, hands outstretched to clasp Elizabeth's. Beside her, Charlotte smiled.

Immediately beyond the two women, their husbands chatted, Charlotte's soberly dressed as the rector in Kympton ought to be, and Caroline's flashy as befit the second son of an earl. Elizabeth went forward to greet the two women, clasping Caroline's hands warmly before turning to offer a similar welcome to Charlotte. She counted herself very lucky on both fronts; that Charlotte had wedded so near to her, and that Caroline had become an easy, amiable friend after marrying Lord Arthur. Sadly, her sister, Mrs. Hurst, had only grown more pinched, stuffy and aloof. Elizabeth had already sighted her beside Mrs. Bennet, the two studying the gathering with critical gazes.

"How are you both this evening?" Elizabeth asked.

"I am well and looking forward to the dancing," Charlotte said. "It's difficult to find an occasion for it as a rector's wife." She said this without rancor, casting her husband a fond look.

Caroline laughed. "I daresay I have the opposite trouble. Lord Arthur is still as enamored with London life as when we met. I'm going to have to have another baby simply so I may beg off for some quiet in the country."

"Are you now?" Elizabeth looked Caroline up and down, trying to decide if she spoke figuratively or imparted news.

"Someone must try to keep up with Jane," Charlotte said. "It won't be me. We've the one and that is enough, but then you are both younger than I am."

Too-loud laughter sounded across the room and Elizabeth grimaced, not needing to look to know the source. Lydia. She hadn't wished to invite her youngest sister, especially without her husband Mr. Mullens, but had seen no polite way to exclude her. If her husband had been with her, her laughter wouldn't be so loud.

When it became known that Lydia carried Wickham's child, Darcy had arranged a marriage for her to an elderly, childless clergyman who wanted to have a comfortable old age. Darcy had justified the expense to Elizabeth by saying that his family had not done the right things for Wickham but should do better by his child. Elizabeth hadn't been fooled. Darcy had done it to make her happy.

Lydia was now Mrs. Mullens, and her husband, though not caring for travel, was living longer than anyone had expected. To everyone's surprise, Lydia became quite fond of Mr. Mullens, who spent his limited energy arranging for the upbringing of George Mullens and teaching him his letters. Elizabeth and Darcy both hoped that Mr. Mullens would live a long time, since he somewhat restrained Lydia's behavior.

Fresh laughter sounded, this time Mrs. Fitzwilliam's giggle. As one, Elizabeth, Caroline, and Charlotte looked to where she and Jane still spoke, now joined by Brigadier Fitzwilliam and Mr. Bingley.

"Oh look," Caroline cried. "Here come Georgiana and Mr. Carter."

Elizabeth turned to see her sister by marriage entering the parlor on the arm of her betrothed, Mr. Carter. Both looked sublimely happy, heads high and smiles wide. Georgiana had grown into a lovely woman, graceful where once she'd been gawky. Sure now, rather than timid. She'd been right to wait even longer when, at seventeen, Elizabeth had suggested she should be out. Georgiana had the good sense, hard earned, not to seek a husband until she knew herself.

"Let us go give our well wishes," Caroline said.

She started across the room into the growing crowd forming about the tall, elegant couple. Charlotte cast Elizabeth a parting smile, then followed Caroline. Sighting them, their husbands moved to join them.

Elizabeth hung back, stepping off to the side near the lefthand parlor door, watching with a smile. It pleased her to see so many of those she loved and cared for in one place. Her smile broadened as she recalled the previous day in the garden, with all the children gathered. Now consigned to the care of maids and nannies, yesterday they'd all run free in the neatly trimmed grass. There'd been squeals and laughter. The occasional great big shimmering tears for a toy purloined or a skinned knee. Little George, the oldest of the lot at five, had very seriously attempted to organize a game of tag. Elizabeth and Darcy's two boys had done their best, despite the younger having very little idea yet how games worked, and looked on their tall blond cousin with adoration. Mr. Bennet had even joined in, so much easier as a grandfather than he'd been as a father when Elizabeth was young.

Arms stole about her waist, the warm, familiar presence of her husband tall and solid behind her. Elizabeth leaned back into his strength and comfort, even as she observed, "Mr. Darcy. Embracing your wife in a parlor full of guests is hardly appropriate behavior."

"No one is looking," he murmured against her ear.

"But they could look."

"Let them."

Elizabeth wrapped her arms over her husband's, clasping his hands in hers. "Mama and Mrs. Hurst have turned this way. Now I'll have to endure a lecture about propriety."

"Then your only course is to enjoy our impropriety and, when the time comes, you will have to be brave and endure their wrath."

Elizabeth's smile grew. "Brave? Yes, well, I can be brave."

His arms tightened about her. "I know. Your bravery is how we met. Without it, my life would be empty."

Elizabeth turned in his arms to look up at him. "Oh, I don't know. I like to think we would have found one another. Some way."

"I'm certain you're right," he replied and there, without a care for decorum or his cravat, he kissed her.

~ The End ~

About the Authors

Renata McMann

Renata McMann is the pen name of Teresa McCullough, someone who likes to rewrite public domain works. She is fond of thinking, "What if?" To learn more about Renata's work and collaborations, visit **www.renatamcmann.com**.

Summer Hanford

Starting in 2014, Summer was offered the privilege of partnering with fan fiction author Renata McMann on her well-loved *Pride and Prejudice* variations. More information on these works is available at **www.renatamcmann.com**.

Summer is currently partnering with McMann as well as writing solo works in Regency Romance and Fantasy. She lives in New York with her husband and compulsory, deliberately spoiled, cats. The newest addition to their household is an energetic setter-shepherd mix...not yet appreciated by either of the cats. For more about Summer, visit **www.summerhanford.com**.

Get Your Thank You Gifts! Sign Up for Our Mailing List Today!

Visit: **www.renatamcmann.com/news/**

Made in the USA
Las Vegas, NV
17 June 2022

50384714R00164